Praise for *The Haven*

'Another mesmerising, gripping and evocative read from the Queen of Cornish Noir'
Lisa Jewell, bestselling author of *The Family Upstairs*

'An engrossing, immersive novel that swept me into the twisted utopia of Winterfall Farm. A dark delight that lingers long after the last page, I absolutely loved it'
Eve Chase, bestselling author of *The Glass House*

'I loved this book, a masterly unravelling of a utopian dream that gradually becomes a nightmare. Lyrical descriptions and utterly believable characters'
Elly Griffiths, bestselling author of *The Locked Room*

'Engrossing, tense, psychologically astute. A gripping, emotionally taut exploration of idealism turned sour'
Tammy Cohen, author of *The Wedding Party*

'A deliciously dark and tense exploration of human nature. There's trouble brewing in paradise'
Emma Haughton, author of *The Dark*

'A beautifully written story with vividly drawn, believable characters I really cared about'
Sarah Stovell, author of *Other Parents*

'Captivating and totally absorbing – this is the kind of pure escapism we need right now'
Susi Holliday, author of *The Last Resort*

'A compelling, brilliant story of the dark things we all bring to our visions of utopia. Beautifully written, and full of emotional punch . . . I loved it!'
Gytha Lodge, author of *She Lies in Wait*

Amanda Jennings has written six novels, and numerous short stories for anthologies and magazines, and is published both in the UK and abroad. She is a regular contributor to BBC Radio Berkshire and a long-standing judge for the Henley Youth Festival literary competition, has taught writing workshops, and enjoys appearing at literary festivals. Before becoming an author, Amanda worked at the BBC as a researcher, and studied History of Art at Cambridge University. She lives in a cottage in the middle of the woods in Oxfordshire with her family and a varied assortment of animals.

Also by Amanda Jennings

The Storm
The Cliff House
In Her Wake
The Judas Tree
Sworn Secret

The Haven

Amanda Jennings

ONE PLACE. MANY STORIES

HQ
An imprint of HarperCollins*Publishers* Ltd
1 London Bridge Street
London SE1 9GF

www.harpercollins.co.uk

HarperCollins*Publishers*
Macken House, 39/40 Mayor Street Upper
Dublin 1, D01 C9W8, Ireland

This paperback edition 2023

1
First published in Great Britain by
HQ, an imprint of HarperCollins*Publishers* Ltd 2022

Copyright © Amanda Jennings 2022

Amanda Jennings asserts the moral right to be
identified as the author of this work.
A catalogue record for this book is
available from the British Library.

ISBN: 9780008410346

MIX
Paper from
responsible sources
FSC™ C007454

This book is produced from independently certified FSC™ paper
to ensure responsible forest management.

For more information visit: www.harpercollins.co.uk/green

Printed and Bound in the UK using 100% Renewable
Electricity at CPI Group (UK) Ltd

Dedicated to all those working in our NHS who have done
an incredible job caring for so many during the pandemic,
including our youngest daughter who required surgery
in the first lockdown. Thank you for everything.
You are the very best of us.

'There is nothing like a dream to create the future.
Utopia today, flesh and blood tomorrow.'

VICTOR HUGO

Present Day

I open the windows wide and the noises from the square below flood the room. Voices greeting each other. A cockerel crowing. Dogs barking in reply. Young girls laughing in harmony on their way to school. The smell of oranges and almonds mixed with fresh-from-the-oven pastries from the bakery next door. The sun pushes through the window and tiny particles of dust glitter in the shaft of light.

I cut up an apple then pour my coffee. Short and black in a small white china cup with a chip on the rim. Then I reach for her letter and slide my finger along the seal of the envelope to open it. The familiar writing warms me and I smile as I anticipate her news. Inside the letter is a page torn from a magazine.

I unfold it and my heart stops. The coffee cup slips from my fingers and smashes on the tiled floor. My breathing quickens. I stare at the photograph which accompanies the article and a cold sweat inches over my skin in spite of the heat. The features staring back at me have haunted me for years. Though marked by time they are as recognisable as my own.

Alive?

I grip the table to steady myself.

CHAPTER ONE

Tara,
February 1995

'Maybe it would be better coming from you?'

'Me? Really? I mean, if that's what you want. But, well ...' He hesitated. 'I haven't even met them yet.'

We walked through the extravagant wooden door of St John's College and stepped onto the rain-slicked pavement. The world outside hummed with cars and buses as they drove along the wet road, headlights illuminating the midday gloom, windscreen wipers swiping arcs through the drizzle. We joined the swarm of weekend shoppers on Magdalen Street who scurried this way and that, heads lowered, coats buttoned up against the miserable cold. As I watched them, an unexpected stab of jealousy struck me in the gut. Jealous of their uncomplicated lives. Jealous of them having nothing more pressing on their minds than which shop they were hurrying to, which café they'd refuel in, or how long they had left until their parking ran out. Jealous they were free from the uncertainty and fear which gnawed like a couple of ravenous rats.

'You look like you're about to face a firing squad.' Kit's voice cut through my thoughts. He lifted my hand to his lips and kissed it, then pulled me to a standstill, ignoring the grumble of a woman forced to move around us. 'It'll be OK,' he said. 'I promise.'

I gave a weak, unconvincing smile. Kit was wrong. And not just about lunch. None of it was going to be OK. How could it be OK when the unknown loomed so large and threatening, a wall around me, trapping me inside it. When I was younger I'd imagined myself as a chess piece. Being moved from square to square by my parents. Inexplicably I allowed them. Perhaps it was easier to let them make my decisions than muster the energy to fight them.

'We only want what's best for you,' my mother would say. 'Don't you want that too?'

What was best for me was conventional achievement. Money. A successful career. A sensible car with comprehensively researched insurance. A well-showered husband and two polite children who won prizes at school and practised the piano without being asked. She could hardly contain herself when my university acceptance dropped onto the mat. She droned on and on about the potential husbands I'd meet. A smorgasbord of cultured intellectuals who played tennis and skied and wore shoes with 'real leather uppers'. An army of fictional Sebastians and Ruperts who'd walk me through cloistered courtyards reciting Wordsworth and Tennyson and Yeats.

'My very own daughter at Oxford University.'

I'd discarded the letter on the table. 'I'm not sure I'll go.'

Her face drained of colour as she clutched her imaginary pearls. 'Not go?'

'I might take a year off.'

'A year off?' she breathed. 'Doing *what*?'

'I don't know,' I'd said breezily. 'Travelling probably.'

'*Travelling?*'

In the end I didn't go travelling. The thought of weathering my parents' devastation was exhausting. I also didn't fancy backpacking alone. So in October, desperate to escape and gain some sort of independence, I loaded suitcases into the boot of my father's car and tuned out my mother's relentless excitement. My stomach tumbled with nerves on the journey. I was convinced I wouldn't fit in. Convinced I'd make no friends. That I'd be alone, skulking in the corner of a dusty library, struggling with the work, and being ignored by the braying, entitled hordes basking in the glow of their privilege.

But on day four I met Kit.

'It'll be all right. Remember I love you.' He ran the tips of his fingers over my cheek.

I chewed my lip. 'Did Jay say how late he'll be?'

Kit shook his head. 'Time is a concept which he's apparently rejected.' He took my hand and we started walking again. 'He'll be there though. He won't go back on a promise.'

Kit and Jeremy were in their third year and had been friends since the first day of freshers' week. The friendship was intense, close as brothers, the kind I'd found elusive. I wasn't unpopular at school, I'd had nice friends – friends I no longer kept in touch with – but never anybody I'd formed a bond with.

On the fourth day I forced myself to brave the college bar. Jeremy was the first person I noticed. He was sitting in the corner of the airless basement holding court with a group of fuck-me-eyed girls who hung on his every word. But my gaze drifted quickly off him. Jeremy wasn't my type. It was the guy beside him who grabbed my attention. Unruly blond hair. Grungy, with understated good looks, wearing a faded black T-shirt, jeans, and battered trainers. He turned and caught me staring, held my gaze for a moment, then smiled and looked away, glancing back to smile again. I watched him for a while, serene in that rowdy, hormonal room, the space he occupied tranquil. I wanted to crawl in with him. We kissed outside the bar in the shadows, the music and drunken shrieks from inside fading as we melted into each other. We held hands when we walked to his room. Our fingers entwined. His thumb stroking the side of my hand. Each touch electric. The sex was incredible and we were inseparable from that moment on. As we lay together afterwards, he talked about Jeremy. It was clear how much the friendship meant. So when, a few days later, he took me to meet him, I was riddled with nerves. Would he like me? Was I good enough? Would he take one look at me and turn down his thumb like a displeased emperor? But Jeremy welcomed me with open arms and the two of them drew me into their friendship. We became a three.

In Kit and Jeremy, I found my tribe: impassioned, unconventional, free-spirited.

Three dreamers.

'Maybe we should live on a ranch in Wyoming or a hammock on a beach in Guatemala?' I'd say as we passed a spliff around.

'Or a croft in the Highlands. Breed some hairy cattle and look for kestrels.'

'I've always wanted to live on a farm somewhere. As part of a community. Grow our own food. Break our chains and create a better life.'

Our conversations made me tingle. It was as if no dream was too big. I yearned for adventure. There was so much out there. I wanted to drown in it. From the deserts of Africa, to the jungles of Costa Rica, to the souks of Morocco; I wanted it all. If Kit had suggested packing rucksacks and heading off to travel the world for the rest of our lives, I'd have said yes, yes, *yes* without hesitation.

But fate had something different in mind.

'Hang on,' Jeremy said, when I asked him to join us for lunch. 'As some sort of chaperone?'

'Please?' I pressed my hands together in prayer. 'You can use your magic powers on them.'

'Magic powers?' He laughed and lit up.

'Hypnotise them or whatever it is you do to people.'

He laughed again.

'They've had my life planned since conception and this is about as far away from their plan as you can get.'

'It's karma then.' Jeremy pushed open the window and let out an exhalation of smoke in its vague direction as a winter chill flooded the room.

I smiled as I imagined my parents grappling with the concept of karma. 'Please, Jay? For us? Free food and drink?' A fresh tide of anxiety surged inside me. I turned to Kit. 'Maybe we should run away? Pack clothes and a toothbrush and disappear.'

Kit laughed but I wasn't joking.

'Run away without me?' Jeremy looked theatrically shocked.

'You can come too. But only if you come to lunch.'

'Of course I'm coming. I like the idea of being your mediator.'

I'd booked a table for five at the brasserie on Turl Street. It was loud and busy, not too expensive but not too cheap, with a menu written in French to satisfy my aspirational parents. My father would order 'Steak frites. Blue. Leave the garnish in the kitchen.' My mother would have something which sounded more sophisticated than it was, *coq au vin* or *confit de canard,* 'a green salad instead of potatoes. No dressing.'

My nerves thrummed as we neared the restaurant. I hesitated before pushing open the door and looked at Kit. 'They aren't ...' I searched for the best word of many I could have selected. 'Easy.'

'It's fine. I'm used to difficult parents.'

The restaurant was a barrage of hubbub, heat, and smells. I scanned the room for my parents. They were sitting at a table in the corner in starched silence. A bottle of red in front of my father. My mother's eyes fixed straight ahead. The restaurant manager hurried over to us, his distaste obvious, readying himself, I imagined, to throw us out. I informed him we were joining my parents for lunch and he looked us up and down, nose wrinkled, mouth stretched in revulsion. A wave of nausea swept through me, triggered by the smell of charred meat and overwhelming dread. For a horrible moment I thought I was going to throw up on the shoes of the sneering manager.

I grabbed Kit's arm. 'I'll phone them instead—'

But then my mother caught sight of us. I watched her expression change as she took in the sight of me, her initial pleasure melting away with her smile, replaced by undisguised horror which only deepened as we approached. What was it that bothered her most? The ribbons woven into my head full of plaits? The ring through my nose? My tie-dyed cotton trousers? Or was it the boy holding my hand? Scruffy-haired, Greenpeace and Amnesty badges pinned to his moth-eaten charity shop sweater, rips across both knees of his jeans.

'Hi Mum.' I bent to kiss her cheek and tried not to let her obvious instinct to recoil get to me. 'Dad.' I smiled at my father, who reached for the already half-empty wine bottle. 'This is Kit.'

My mother shoehorned an uncomfortable smile onto her face. My father stood and begrudgingly held out a hand.

'Nice to meet you both.' Kit shook my father's hand without any sign of nerves. I envied his ability to remain unfazed in any situation. It didn't matter who he was talking to, or where they came from, he never showed any hint of intimidation. 'I've heard lots about you.'

My mother threw me a hard stare. 'Sadly we can't say the same.'

I glanced at Kit, who smiled.

'You said someone else is coming?' my mother said to my nose ring.

'Yes, our friend Jeremy. Is that still OK?' I willed Jeremy to walk through the door. I should have reminded him not to be late.

My father asked what we wanted to drink – an orange juice for me, a pint for Kit – then clicked his fingers aggressively for the waitress. I gave her an apologetic smile, but she didn't seem to care.

My mother's stony expression was hardening by the second and, as my father ordered a second bottle of red, I fought another urge to bolt. Kit reached for my hand beneath the table and gave it a squeeze. My skin felt clammy. This was worse than I'd imagined. What on earth had I been thinking?

'The steak looks all right,' my father said to Kit as a waiter passed with a tray of food for a neighbouring table.

'Actually, I don't eat meat.'

'Don't eat *meat*?' My mother stared at him, open-mouthed, as if he'd slapped her.

'I'm vegetarian.'

'No meat at all? Not even chicken?'

Kit shook his head genially.

She exchanged an unsubtle look with my father. 'A *vegetarian*?' she mouthed.

My father appeared amused. 'Your loss, that. Not much better than a thick, juicy steak.'

Jeremy chose this moment to walk through the door and I could have kissed him. I stood and waved, and he strolled over, casually dressed in a creased but clean white shirt and jeans. His confidence lit up the room. People watched him as he passed, drawn by his rockstar good looks, shaggy dark hair which curled at his collar, sculpted cheekbones and unparalleled self-confidence.

'Hello, hello!' He flashed us his brilliant smile. His energy was a tornado whipping around us. 'I have to say I'm starving. Gagging for a drink, too.'

My mother gawped as if he were speaking a foreign language.

My father's brow furrowed. 'I'm sorry. Who are you again?'

My stomach churned. Jeremy was supposed to calm everything down, not make things a hundred times worse.

'Jay. Kit's best friend.' Jeremy pulled out a chair and sat down, then reached for the bottle of wine and poured himself a glass. My father's jaw hit the floor. 'Lovely. So, Mrs ...?' He turned to me, tilting his head quizzically. 'You know something? I don't know your surname.'

'Wakefield.' I cleared my throat. 'These are my parents, Jane and Keith Wakefield.'

Jeremy winked at my mother. 'Well, Jane, I can see where Tara gets her looks.'

Despite a welling panic, I let out a burst of nervous laughter, but then I noticed my mother blushing, her fingers reaching for a tendril of hair, a smile twitching, tickled by the hackneyed cliché.

When it came to sniffing out weak spots in people, Jeremy was a truffle pig, and he had the measure of my parents within moments.

'Jane,' he said, over a pint in the college bar later. 'Is a woman obsessed with acquiring *more*. She wants more than a husband soaked in red wine and mediocrity. More than a semi-detached house on a suburban street in Hertfordshire. Disappointment oozes from her pores. If she wasn't so bitter, I'd pity her.' He drained his glass and pointed at me. 'Your parents are a cautionary tale.'

And he was right. I was terrified of ending up like them. Unsatisfied, unfulfilled, and stuck in a greyscale, insular life.

'So what do you want to do after university?' my father asked Kit as he poured another glass of wine.

'I've not given it much thought. I'll probably see where things take me.'

My father stared at him for a moment or two, perhaps waiting for Kit to laugh and tell him, no, he was joking, of course he was planning to go into accountancy or finance. But Kit held his stare and offered nothing more.

My father turned to Jeremy. 'And you? Thoughts on a career? Or do you also lack ambition and drive?'

Jeremy scoffed. 'A career? You mean truss myself up in a suit to slave for some arsehole with a trophy wife and a country club membership?'

'Maybe not now, Jay?' Kit raised his eyebrows and shook his head imperceptibly.

But Jeremy pressed on. 'No, Keith. I've no intention of working myself to death to line the pockets of greedy fat cats.'

My father put his glass down. 'Sounds as if you're scared of hard work.'

Jeremy smiled. 'I'm not scared of anything. But the system bleeds us dry. I watched what it did to my dad. Took everything from him then left him for dead. But think about it, Keith. Why do we need a job anyway?'

'To pay for things?' Irritation inched in around the edges of my father's words.

Kit stiffened as Jeremy leant forward, eyes alight. 'Things?'

'Yes. *Things*. A house, car, clothes.' He gestured around him. 'A meal in a restaurant. A nice big television?'

'A television! Christ. Television rots your brain, Keith. Give that rubbish up immediately. So why do we want these things? If we didn't desire them we'd be free. No more need to work day in day out, hour after hour, for years and years, fuelled by a rabid desire for *things* we don't need. And when we get whatever it is we've desired? Satisfaction? No. The void is filled by desire for something else.' Jeremy smiled at my father. 'The fat cats don't even have to get their hands dirty. The marketing men to do the grubby work for them. It's their job to convince the rest of us that without these *things* we can never be happy. That way we keep turning the wheel. Grinding away so we can buy things we didn't even know we wanted until they told us we did.' He leant back and crossed his arms. 'Just imagine, Keith. No alarm clocks. No mortgage. No suffocating debt. All you need to do is step off the wheel.'

My father didn't speak for a moment or two, but then he reached for his drink. 'There's nothing honourable in being unemployed.'

'There's nothing honourable in working so hard you lose sight of what really matters. Believe you me, I know that first-hand. I know the damage it does.' Jeremy picked up his glass and drank, his thoughts distant for a moment or two.

My father's cheeks were now a deep shade of plum. Jeremy smiled and pushed his glass towards him for a top-up. Kit's face had paled and he shifted in his seat awkwardly while staring at the menu. The stilted silence was unbearable. This was all a horrendous mistake. I needed it to be over.

'I'm pregnant.'

Everybody stared at me. I felt faint. Kit reached for my hand.

'What did you say?' My mother wrinkled her forehead as if she hadn't heard me properly.

I took a deep breath. 'I'm pregnant. Kit and I. We're ... I'm pregnant ...' My words faded beneath the weight of my parents' mushrooming horror.

'Don't be silly. Of course you're not.' The words came out in a strangled squeak. 'You've just gone to Oxford.'

The table was pin-drop quiet amid the restaurant clamour.

'I don't understand,' she whispered. 'How did this happen?'

Kit and I exchanged looks and Jeremy lifted his hand to conceal a snigger.

'Don't get fresh with me. I know *how* it happened. I'm asking how the hell you could *let* this happen? I thought you were supposed to be clever? We give you everything then you ruin your life with this ...' She hesitated, nose wrinkled as if she'd smelt something bad. 'This *person*.'

'Don't, Mum. Jesus—'

'I love your daughter, Mrs Wakefield.' Kit smiled at me. 'And I'm going to look after her and the baby.'

'Christ almighty. You're *having* it?' My mother's hand flew to her mouth in shock.

I bit back the all too familiar rage.

The truth was, up until that precise moment, I wasn't sure I did want the baby. I'd done the test on my own in the loo in the pub. The instructions said it would take up to two minutes, but those two blue lines switched on in seconds like Christmas lights on Regent Street. I'd slipped out of the pub and walked down to the river and sat in the freezing cold. As I stared at the moon bouncing off the water, people laughing and revelling in a bar nearby, I decided to end the pregnancy. I wouldn't tell anybody. Not even Kit. I'd give a false name at the clinic. Do it quickly. Get it over with. But I wasn't able to keep it from Kit. I went to him, tears streaking my cheeks, trembling. His face fell.

'What's wrong? What's happened?'

When I told him he burst into joyful laughter.

'Are you serious? A baby?' His grin broke his face in half.

Rather than feeling relieved by his reaction, I felt trapped. I should have told him that. Should have told him how scared and unsure I was. But I didn't. I lied and said I was happy too. Despite being plagued by uncertainty as we'd walked into the restaurant, facing my mother's displeasure and my father's disgust switched something on inside me. How dare they judge me? How dare they judge Kit? What gave them the right to be horrified?

'Yes,' I said, my voice steely. 'We're having the baby.'

'But what about your degree?'

'I'm giving up my degree. I never wanted to go to university anyway—'

My father swore loudly and slammed his fist down. People on nearby tables started to mutter and stare. 'I cannot believe what I'm hearing!'

'You stupid, *stupid* girl.' My mother's eyes had narrowed to slits. 'You're going to throw your life away for a vegetarian layabout?'

'Come now, Jane. There's no need for this.' Jeremy rested a hand on hers. 'I'm sure this is a shock, but I'm telling you, there isn't a couple alive who love each other more than these two.'

The bombshell had rendered my mother immune to Jeremy. She shook away his hand. 'I don't care if they are Romeo and bloody Juliet, this is a *disaster*.' She turned her burning eyes on me. 'You've hurt me more than I can say and you should be ashamed of yourself. What are you thinking? I mean, look at you both. You can't even take care of yourselves, let alone a child.'

'That's not—'

She rounded on Kit. 'You've destroyed my daughter's life. Don't you dare talk to me. Don't. You. *Dare*.' She looked back at me, tears glazing her eyes. 'I was too soft on you. I should have been tougher when you started being difficult. I should have taken you to a psychologist. My bloody mother told me not to. Said rebelling was part and parcel of growing up. What did *she* know?' My mother shook her head then took a deep breath, and a blanket of stoic calm settled over her. 'You know what? Have the baby. You want to ruin your life? *Fine*. Ruin it.' Then she stood and grabbed her coat from the back of the chair, put it on and buttoned it angrily. 'Keith, we're leaving.'

My father glanced at the bottle of wine.

'*Now*, Keith!' she shouted.

The restaurant quietened with shock. My mother stared straight ahead, handbag clutched to her chest, as the silence gave way to a ripple of whispers which rumbled around the room.

She refocused her anger on me. 'After everything I've done for you. Everything I gave up.'

My father opened his wallet and cast two twenty-pound notes disdainfully on to the table. Then they were gone.

Kit and I stared at each other, eyes wide, hands gripped.

'I think that went well?' Jeremy reached for the wine and poured what was left into three glasses. He lifted his towards us. 'To you, your very lucky child, and true love. Screw the rest of them.'

CHAPTER TWO

Kit,
March 1995

They wend their way along familiar country lanes flanked by unruly hedgerows and fields of languid cattle. It rained yesterday and the vegetation is fresh and vibrant. Despite the beauty around him, the thought of driving through the gates of his childhood home fills him with uneasy apprehension.

Tara stares out of the window at the passing Gloucestershire countryside. 'Do you miss it?'

'No.'

No hesitation. No dithering. He misses nothing about it.

Regret wriggles through him. He thinks of his child cocooned in Tara's womb. He never wants his child to feel as he does now. He wants his child to be excited to come home, to miss home, to burst with halcyon memories. Tara glances at him, perhaps expecting him to elaborate. She's asked about his childhood and family many times, but he always fobs her off with the scantest detail or a change of subject. Since the train-wreck lunch with her parents, she'd been more determined to meet his, a terrier with a bone.

'I don't understand. Are you embarrassed by me? Ashamed of the baby?'

'Ashamed of you? God, no. It's the other way round. I'm ashamed of *them*. Seriously, Tara, you'd loathe them.'

'Maybe I can make up my own mind?' She'd reached for his hand and stroked it. 'You need to tell them about the baby.'

'Why?'

She laughed. 'I don't know. Because it's what you do?'

He eventually agreed and now they are close to where he grew up and a ball of dread is hardening in the pit of his stomach. The thought of them contaminating what he and Tara have makes him lightheaded. He reminds himself this is what Tara wants. So he'll do it for her. He'll smile. He'll be civil. He will tell them the news and brace himself for their poison.

They drive through the village with its sandy-coloured cottages and bountiful hanging baskets holding scarlet geraniums and shocking pink fuchsias. Past the church and picturesque pub decorated year-round with patriotic bunting. Past the village shop which sells homemade jams and farm-fresh eggs and the local rag, filled, as it always has been, with strongly worded letters, estate agent adverts, and ludicrous articles about the minutiae of little England.

Tara knows he comes from privilege – he'd confessed with genuine disgust that he was educated at Eton – but as they drive through the huge wrought-iron gates of Ashbarton Coombe her face registers unchecked shock as the extent of his family's wealth becomes clear. He wants her to say something, anything, that will let him know what she's thinking, but she doesn't breathe a word as they follow the mile-long driveway through lush parkland dotted with shiny thoroughbred horses and past the lake with its polished wooden rowing boat tied to the jetty he used to jump off as a child. Ancient oak trees and sprawling cedars stand majestic. Beyond the fields, hidden from sight, is the stream which runs through the woods and the decaying remains of the camps he'd built during endless summer holidays when he escaped the house.

She finally opens her mouth to speak. 'I should have worn a dress.'

He pulls up in front of the house and stills the engine. 'You look perfect.'

'My mother would faint if she saw this place.'

He stares through the grubby windscreen at the house. An ostentatious country pile with three stone steps leading up to an oak-panelled entrance, leaded windows and turreted chimney breasts, manicured yew balls and wisteria and ivy cloaking the yellowy stone. Inside is a ballroom, a library with over ten thousand books, eleven bedrooms, two kitchens, a basement filled with dusty bottles of wine which cost more than his car, and two decades of unhappy memories.

Tara's mouth is open a fraction as she absorbs it. Her hand rests on her stomach as if shielding the baby's eyes. Kit climbs out of his battered 2CV, the car he bought when he sold the vintage MG he was given on his twenty-first birthday. The remainder of the money he donated to a homeless charity, which had pissed his father off. *Good*, he'd thought at the time. *Good*.

Tara takes his hand and they crunch over the immaculate gravel carpet towards the entrance. The door opens before they reach it and Patsy appears. Her face crinkles with joy as she outstretches her arms in welcome. She is unchanged, frizzy grey hair pinned back with a multitude of hairpins, black trousers perfectly ironed, a crisp white shirt, an apron tied around her waist.

'Hello! Dear, *dear* Kit!' Patsy bustles down the steps and throws her arms around his waist. The familiar smell of talc and furniture polish envelops him. 'And this must be Tara?' Patsy clutches her hands beneath her chin in delight.

'It's lovely to meet you, Mrs Balfour.' Tara holds out her hand. 'Thank you for inviting me.'

Kit realises too late to stop her making the mistake and kicks himself for not preparing her.

Patsy lets out a soft laugh of tinkling bells. 'Oh, no, no, dear. I'm not the lady of the house. I'm just the housekeeper.'

Kit's skin itches as his allergy to Ashbarton sets in.

Tara flushes red and looks at Kit helplessly. 'I'm sorry. I didn't ...' Her voice fades with embarrassment.

Kit takes her hand. 'This is Patsy. She's an angel.'

Patsy giggles. 'I've missed you, lovey.' She smiles at Tara. 'And it's a pleasure to meet you. Kit's told me all about you on the phone. And, forgive me, but oh *look* at you!' She gazes at Tara's stomach lovingly. 'When Kit told me I nearly burst! Nothing as magical as a baby and, looking at the mama, this one's going to be a beauty.'

Tara smiles and her hand moves instinctively to her stomach.

'My parents don't know, do they?' He isn't sure why he's asking this. Of course Patsy hasn't told them. She's been in his life as long as he can remember and is more of a mother to him than his own.

'Gosh, no. No. Of course not. *No*. It's your news. I'm just over the moon you told me!' Then she rubs his shoulders. 'You're going to be the best daddy. Lucky little mite.'

Patsy steps away from him and her bubbling excitement is replaced with earnest professionalism. 'Lady Balfour asked you to show Tara to the Blue Room ...' She hesitates, but seems to gird herself for what is coming. 'She also said to tell you they won't be joining you for dinner.'

Kit's hands clench and he sucks air through his teeth. The words sting. He'd specifically said it was important, that he had news, that he wanted to introduce Tara.

Of course they'd do this.

'Did they say why?' Well-practised at hiding his emotions, he delivers the question without any hint of the anger and disappointment he's feeling.

Patsy hesitates again. 'No. They left for London about an hour ago. Your mother said there's a chance they'll be back for lunch tomorrow. Depending ...' She pauses, sympathy softening her features into the gentle pity he's seen countless times before. 'On whether your father wants to visit his club.'

Kit doesn't miss a beat. He clears his throat and gives a tight nod. 'Thank you, Patsy.' Then he smiles at Tara and takes her hand. 'I'll show you up. Patsy, Tara will be sleeping in my room.'

'Maybe they forgot we were coming?' Tara follows him. The ornately carved staircase is flanked with sombre portraits of hateful ancestors looking down their unfeasibly long noses at anybody passing.

'They didn't.' Anger has rendered him almost monosyllabic. He is experiencing a visceral reaction to the snub. This rejection of Tara – of what's important to him – hurts.

They walk along the corridor and pass what his mother calls the Blue Room. Tara stops abruptly. Her intake of breath is audible. 'Oh my God.'

He walks on, but she isn't following. He turns and sees her take two steps inside. He returns to the door and leans against the doorframe. She walks in, turning in wonder, eyes drinking in the room.

'It's straight out of a Disney film or Buckingham Palace.'

The room holds a four-poster bed, plush velvet curtains held back with gold-tasselled tiebacks, a huge velvet sofa and a highly polished table on which is an extravagant vase of hydrangeas in pale blue and white.

'It's the same size as the entire downstairs of my house.'

Kit slumps onto the bed. 'Welcome to my family.' He kicks his boot against the Persian rug. 'Wealthy. Vacuous. Total fucking arseholes.'

She sits on the edge of the bed next to him, her gaze still scanning the room, brow furrowed unable to comprehend it. 'How come you didn't tell me you were Little Lord Fauntleroy?'

He drops his head into his hands.

She laughs softly. 'I'm joking.'

'Sorry. I know. It's just … I hate it. All of it. Them. The house. The fact they have all this money while people struggle to make ends meet. I hate that they care about things that don't matter. Parties. What school people went to. How they dress. Who their bloody parents are. I hate that they look down on people and I hate that we are born into this wealth and did nothing to deserve it. And—' His voice cracks with emotion he isn't expecting. He takes a deep breath and lifts his head to look at this beautiful girl who has stolen his heart and carries a baby he already loves more than anything in the world. 'I hate that they don't want to meet you and I hate that now you have every right to hate me as much as I hate them.'

Tara pulls him close and whispers, punctuating her words with featherlight kisses. 'Hate you? Are you kidding? Listen, crazy man. I don't care about *any* of this. It means nothing. And you know what? If they can't hang around an extra half hour to see their son when they haven't seen him in months, then sod them.'

Kit's insides cave in with relief. 'My mother's favourite mantra when we were young? "Children should be seen and not heard and preferably not seen."'

'She sounds vile. I hate her. Both of them. And I've changed my mind. I don't want to meet them. And who cares if they never see their grandchild? We don't need their poisonous crap. We don't need any of them. We have each other.' She pushes him back on the bed and straddles him. When she leans forward to kiss him, her braided hair falls in a beaded curtain around their faces. 'Your parents, this house, the fancy schools. The fact you need to catch a bus from your gate to the front door. None of this is *you*. You know that, right?'

After they have sex they dress, then Tara smooths the blue silk throw and smiles at him. 'I love you,' she says. 'Now let's get the hell out of here.'

Energy surges through Kit as they go back down the staircase.

With every step he grows stronger. This moment is big. Walking out of his old life and starting afresh.

'What should I tell them?' Patsy asks.

'To go fuck themselves.'

Patsy smothers a laugh. 'Maybe not those exact words, but I'll make sure they get the gist.'

Kit kisses her. 'Thank you, Patsy. For everything. For your kindness. And for looking out for me all these years.'

Her eyes glisten with tears. 'You've grown into a fine young man. I'm proud of you.'

The words skewer him. He clears his throat and smiles, holding back his own tears. 'We'll let you know when the baby arrives.'

'Oh, do! I'd love that. I think it's a little girl.' She smiles at Tara. 'I can tell by the glow on your skin, lovey.'

Kit laughs.

Patsy dabs her eyes dry then kisses Tara on both cheeks. Then she nods once. 'Good luck to you both. You'll be grand.'

As he walks out of Ashbarton Coombe for the last time, he wonders why he didn't do it sooner. There was nothing here for him. There never had been. He wasn't close to his older brothers. They had nothing in common but their genes. The whole family viewed him as if he were a curiosity in a Victorian freak show. The Wild Boy. Feral and unkempt. Running barefoot through the grounds of the estate. Shinning up trees. Poking fires. Choosing to spend time with the housekeeper or gardener over them. Will they miss him? They won't even notice.

They get into the car and close the doors. He puts his hands on the steering wheel and grips it.

'How are you feeling?'

He smiles at her. 'I'm feeling fine. Better than fine. You and our baby are all that matter now.'

CHAPTER THREE

Dani,
April 2002

Home. A word you don't really think about. You just say it. Go home. Stay at home. Nice home. Warm home. But it was a word I never used. It never sat right. I'd lived in a few places. Moved around a bit. None were *home*. Home is where you're meant to feel safe, right? But where I lived, on the sixth floor of a block on the Nelson Estate in Leyton with my mum and cretin Eddie, felt the opposite of safe. The place was a shit-hole. Mouldy walls. Stairwells which stank of piss where lads younger than me bought drugs from each other with money they got from nicking bikes off primary school kids. Pretty much every night the cretin would roll in from the pub off his tits to smack Mum from one end of the flat to the other. Nobody gave a shit. The neighbours knew what he did. The walls were thin as cigarette papers and I could tell by the way they hurried past, avoiding my eyes, *not my business* scrawled across their faces. Did they hear it all? Each thump against her doughy flesh? The names he threw like rice at a wedding? Did they bury their heads in a pillow too?

On my fourteenth birthday he didn't go to the pub as usual. Weird, I thought. Maybe he's staying in to celebrate my birthday? Maybe he's got me a present? Maybe tonight he won't hit my mum? Stupid me.

Stupid me.

While Mum fetched our tea in we watched telly. Cretin Eddie was a scrawny rat of a man but that night he filled the room like a giant. There was something not quite right about him. It was creeping me out. Not what he was doing – he was doing what he always did when he was in the flat, sitting in his chair, knocking back beers as if he were dying of thirst – but the way he looked at me. Staring right at me. Not even blinking.

Mum arrived back with battered sausage and chips. 'Birthday treat!' she said, as she dumped the bag on the side.

Eddie ate his chips and sausage in his chair, fingers slick with grease and ketchup, jaw churning round and round like a washing machine. Mum opened a Battenberg and stuck last year's birthday candle through the marzipan, then lit it with Eddie's plastic lighter. Then she sang *Happy Birthday*. Sang probably isn't the right word. Mum is the world's worst singer. Eddie glared all the way through as she squeaked and stumbled her way to the end. When she finally finished it was hard to know who was more thankful: her, me, or the cretin.

I kissed her anyway.

'Thanks, Mum.'

'You've haven't had your present yet.'

She handed me a box wrapped in tatty newspaper and I pretended to be surprised when I opened it. It was always Milk Tray. Not a bad present to be fair.

'I tried to get the man in black to bring it.' She laughed.

She made this joke every year. I still didn't get it, but laughed anyway so she wouldn't feel bad. Cretin Eddie's eyes were still crawling all over me. When I looked at him he licked his lips.

'I'm done in.' I didn't want to be near him a second longer. 'Think I'll go to bed.'

'Goodnight, love. Happy birthday.'

Eddie said nothing. Just stared. It gave me the shivers. 'Goodnight,' I muttered.

As I left the room I noticed Mum watching him. Nervous. Chewing her lip. Fingers playing with the plastic lighter.

The shouting started as soon as I closed my bedroom door and in no time Mum was doing the snotty-kid crying she did when she knew what was coming to her. She'd been with the cretin for years, but still hadn't worked out a way to calm him down when he was a five-foot gorilla banging about. My stomach turned over and over as I lay in the dark and waited for the smacking to start. But it never did. Instead footsteps thudded towards my door and stopped outside. Mum screamed so loud and panicky it made my heart judder.

'Leave her alone!'

Next thing I knew, my door was flung open and the black shape of him loomed in the doorway. Mum was grabbing at his clothes, a mad woman, screeching and hitting and pulling.

'No, Eddie. Please! Keep away from her! Keep *away*!'

'Fuck off, you bitch.'

Then he smacked her so hard she fell. She got up. Screamed. Ran at him. Jumped on to his arm and hung there as I watched, frozen, blanket pulled up to my chin, heart pounding my ribs.

'Please.' Her voice was soft now. Begging. But I could hear the fear and the hairs on my neck prickled. '*Please* don't do this.'

Then the cretin laughed. 'Oh *shit*, Becky. Are you *jealous?*'

Even in the dim light I could see Mum trembling as if someone was shaking her. 'God help me,' she whispered. 'If you lay a finger on her I'll call the police.'

His body stiffened, fists balling into tight rocks at his sides. 'You'll do what now?'

'Please don't touch her.'

The ratty cretin snarled then followed my mum as she ran into the sitting room.

I held my breath and lay statue-still as he hit and she whimpered. It was years until the front door finally slammed. I hovered at my door, listening carefully to make sure he was gone, then crept out on legs made of jelly.

Mum was huddled in the corner of the sitting room, and – oh my *God* – she was in a state. The worst I'd ever seen. Blood ran from a gash on her forehead. The bone running to her shoulder was bent in the middle. Her lip was split in half, one eye was swollen shut, and her face was turning the colour of plums.

'Mum?' I knelt beside her. 'Can I get you something? A headache pill?'

She coughed and blood sprayed my hand.

'Purse,' she mumbled. Her teeth were coated in blood like a vampire. She jabbed the air weakly in the direction of her handbag on the back of the chair. 'My purse.'

I rummaged in her bag for her purse and tried not to cry. When I passed it to her she could hardly open it her hands were shaking so hard. She managed to pull out the only note she had. Twenty pounds. Then she tipped the purse upside down and shook out a few coins. Scrunching the note around them, she thrust her hand out towards me.

'Pack a bag.' She paused with the effort of forcing the words out. 'Clothes. Toothbrush. Then go.' She touched the cut on her forehead and winced as she inspected the blood on her fingertips. 'Before the pub shuts.' A few tears escaped and rolled down her cheeks.

'No, Mum. I can't—'

'You have to.'

'Not without you. What if he goes for you again?' We both knew it wasn't an *if* but a *when*.

She shook her head, inhaling with pain. 'He'll find us. You have to go.'

'How long for?'

She stared at me, good eye blinking, tears gathering. 'Don't come back.'

'What? No!' I shook my head back and forth. There was no way I was going without her. Out there alone? No way. 'I'm not going. You can't make me.'

'You can't stay here!' Tears fell down her bruised cheeks. 'I can't keep him away from you forever.'

Her words kicked the air from me. She was serious.

'You're throwing me out?'

She turned her head so she didn't have to look at me. 'No drugs. Don't sell your body. And do whatever it takes to keep safe. You hear?'

Icy fingers of fear scratched my skin.

'But it's raining. And dark.' I dropped my head. I was too old to be scared of the dark, but I was. Always had been. 'Can I go in the morning?'

'Take my coat. If you stay dry you won't get sick.'

I glanced at the door expecting that shrunken monster to burst in at any moment. 'But he'll go crazy and hurt you again.'

'Just go. If you don't then only God can help you.' Her good eye drifted closed and she rested her head against the wall. 'And He stopped giving a shit a long time ago.'

CHAPTER FOUR

Tara,
New Year's Eve 1999

Jeremy walked into the bedsit holding a six-pack of lager and a bottle of cheap vodka. He'd dumped his latest girlfriend that morning after two short weeks. Kit and I hadn't even met her.

'So what happened?' I asked as I picked up scattered Lego and listened to the gathering crowds on the street and music blaring from next-door's open window.

He shrugged and cracked open a can as he slumped on the sofa. 'Not on the same page.'

Jeremy was never 'on the same page' as any of his girlfriends, an array of symmetrically-featured, oddly anodyne girls, who moved in and out of his life on a conveyor belt, never lasting longer than a month. He wasn't interested in them. They appeared no more than a dull accessory. There was part of me which suspected Jeremy was in love with Kit, though Kit dismissed this with a laugh when I mentioned it once.

'You sure you want to spend tonight with us?' I said, shoving a couple of Skye's books on the shelf. 'Millennium Eve with a two-year-old isn't going to be much of a party.' Every cell in my body wept with exhaustion. Skye was useless at sleeping, much preferring to be up and chattering away, dancing, giggling, being busy.

'Who else would I spend it with?' He smiled and stretched his legs out. 'Anyway, I don't want to party. I want to watch the world collapse. Right here in this bedsit with my favourite people.' He reached for the remote and turned the television on.

'And if it doesn't collapse?' Kit was standing at the hob whisking eggs in a mug, butter spitting in the saucepan, the smell of toast filling the cramped room.

'It will and it's going to be beautiful.'

Kit rolled his eyes and tipped the eggs into the pan.

Our bedsit was up two flights of stairs lined with a patchwork of damp spots. Junk mail and flyers were piled up in the dank hallway where an old bike with one wheel was discarded at the foot of the stairs. Getting a pram up and down was a nightmare so we never bothered; instead we carried Skye everywhere in a wraparound sling my mother informed me would bend her spine and cripple her. We moved in a few months before Skye was born. I left university at the same time. We decided Kit should finish his degree, so needed somewhere close to Oxford, and this place, just outside Cowley, was the cheapest we could find. We told ourselves it wasn't for long. Soon we'd move to somewhere bigger with less mould and functional heating, but two and a half years later we were still there. Kit jacked in university when Skye arrived. It felt wrong, he'd said, to sit in a stuffy lecture hall listening to tutors drone on about Homer and Ulysses and not be supporting us. There was money of course – the trust fund – but he didn't want anything to do with it.

'I want to provide for my family myself. I don't want their dirty money.'

Kit got a job in a timber merchant and worked extra hours stacking supermarket shelves on Saturday and Sunday nights. Yes, things were tight and the bedsit small and damp, but there was no doubting the love within its grotty walls. When Kit wasn't working he spent every moment with Skye. He was a doting father and as soon as he was home would scoop her up and cradle her in his arms, singing softly, telling her stories, marvelling at her perfect features.

'We made her,' he'd say with wonder in his voice as we watched her sleeping. 'You and me. Can you believe it?'

Kit had an instant connection to Skye the moment I told him I was pregnant. For me it was as if an alien had invaded my body. I tried to picture the baby floating safe and protected inside my womb, but all I managed to manifest was an amorphous, featureless mass. I spent my entire pregnancy convinced there was something wrong with me. Why wasn't I wired properly? Where was my maternal empathy? Even when she started turning somersaults and kicking, instead of joy I battled a niggling resentment. I'd finally escaped home and fallen in love, but rather than freedom and adventure, I faced a mountain of nappies and responsibility and the nagging fear I was going to be the world's worst mother. I knew nothing about parenting and I was terrified of screwing this tiny life up. Kit said it was normal. Nerves were expected. He had every confidence in me. I tried to be as excited as him. Every day I hoped my doubts would dissolve, but they didn't. When she was born, the midwife wrapped her up in a rough white blanket and passed her to me.

'Isn't she beautiful?' Kit breathed, his eyes shining.

I stared at her and wondered when somebody better qualified to care for a baby was going to appear and take over.

Then, on the second day, I was lying in bed on the ward. Kit had gone back to pack a bag with a few bits and pieces I needed and Skye was sleeping in the plastic cot beside me. I was hungry and the ward was claustrophobic. I got out of bed, put slippers and a dressing gown on, and walked slowly, body battered, out of the ward and into the lift, and down to the kiosk near the main entrance. I stared blindly at the shelves. No idea what I wanted. I went for a cheese and onion slice and a carton of blackcurrant juice then joined the queue behind a woman paying for a pile of glossy magazines and a man with a portable drip holding a bottle of Coke. Then it hit me.

My baby.

Every maternal cell in my body ignited. Panic coursed through my veins as I realised she was up there vulnerable and unprotected. I threw the food and drink on the counter and moved as fast as my postpartum body would allow. I jabbed frantically at the lift buttons, my mind full of horrendous thoughts. I tore back the cubicle curtain and ran to the crib. When I saw her lying there, safe and cooing softly, blinking back at me, I burst into tears of relief. I held her tightly. Rocked her. Breathed in her intoxicating smell and stroked her soft sheen of golden hair.

'I will never, *ever* leave you again,' I'd whispered.

And that was that.

As Kit and I turned our attention inwards on Skye, Jeremy became increasingly political. He joined activist groups and spent time demonstrating and planning minor acts of anti-social rebellion – defacing statues, letting the tyres down on police cars, organising busloads of people to attend rallies – and became a prominent voice in student socialism, often called on to talk at gatherings held in dingy pub back rooms. It wasn't long before he dropped out of university, a few weeks before finals, and moved to a squat in North Oxford, swapping artsy prints of Che Guevara and Trotsky for shouty posters advocating anarchy and piles of books written by free-thinkers and libertarians. If there was a cause that undermined the foundations of society then Jeremy was signed up.

As the clock crept towards midnight and the turn of the millennium, I held Skye in my arms and watched the crowds on the streets below. There was music. Dancing. Laughing and cheering. Early fireworks decorated the sky. There was a carnival atmosphere.

'Shall we go down?' I asked Kit and Jeremy.

Jeremy, eyes locked on the television, didn't respond.

Kit kicked his foot. 'Come on, Jay. Turn it off and come down with us. Television rots your brain, remember?'

'And miss the show?'

Kit and I exchanged a look. Jeremy had explained the millennium bug a couple of times, but I didn't really understand it, perhaps too sleep-deprived to grapple with the complexities of the digital Armageddon he was so obsessed with.

Kit glanced at me with a smile, then stepped between Jeremy and the television so he was forced to look at him. 'Sure?'

Jeremy pushed Kit aside, eyes finding the screen again, lifting his can to his lips and drinking. 'Yes, I'm sure. I can't believe you're not going to stay and watch.'

Kit laughed. 'You really think the world's going to explode?'

Jeremy shrugged. 'Who knows? Without any code fixes in place, when that time change happens, nine nine to zero zero, everything will collapse. The power stations will go dark. Plane controls will scramble. Communication lines will fail. Over the next few months there'll be food and fuel shortages and society as we know it will disintegrate.' As he talked his body twitched with excitement. 'Burn the monster down and we'll be free to build something beautiful. A phoenix from the ashes.'

'But before that people have to starve?'

Jeremy glanced at me. 'Humans adapt quickly. They'll set up farms and smallholdings. Communes. They won't have to rely on the state. People won't starve. They'll become self-sufficient. Grow food. Catch it and fish it. They'll be healthier, no longer stuffing sun-starved bodies full of chemicals. No more slaving so the morally bankrupt can buy jet planes.'

Something about Jeremy's words wriggled beneath my skin. Was it fear? Kit and I had a child to take care of. The last thing I wanted was an apocalypse. I never argued with Jeremy. His crazy opinions and rants amused me usually, but his apparent lack of empathy was galling.

'You know there are people out there profiting from this hysteria, don't you? Fearmongers making money off a paranoia *they* are fuelling. Books, survival kits, water purifiers, weaponry, domestic protection. Vultures getting rich off worst-case scenarios.'

Jeremy smiled. 'Better than being a sheep and following the herd without thinking.'

'You can be a smug arsehole sometimes.'

He winked. 'You still love me though.'

I smiled and shook my head with mock exasperation. 'Come on,' I said to Kit. 'If the end of the world is twenty-three minutes away, I want a last dance.'

Jeremy refixed his gaze on the television.

Kit reached for a blanket from behind the sofa, picked Skye up and wrapped it around her. 'You want to watch Mama dancing on the street?'

The three of us stood on the pavement amid the revellers. The smell of sulphur and marijuana hovered in the cold air. Skye was nestled in Kit's arms, warm in her blanket, her eyes closing with sleep. I reached out and stroked her hair.

'The stuff Jay was saying,' I said. 'It's got me worrying.'

'Because the end of the world is nigh?'

I smiled. 'No, not that. But don't you ever get scared by all the things that could go wrong? Being responsible for her feels over-whelming. Keeping her safe, giving her a good life. Money. How will we ever afford to move to somewhere with more space? We can't sleep on a sofa bed next to our daughter forever.' I hesitated. 'Sometimes I think he's right. I mean, you working all hours for a pittance. And what for?'

'Listen,' Kit said softly. 'All that matters is we have each other and we have Skye. I'm working these jobs temporarily. Until we get sorted. I'm going to get a job which pays decent money ...'

The crowd began to shout out the countdown to New Year in unison.

Ten. Nine.

'... we'll get a bigger place ...'

Eight. Seven.

'... everything will work out. I promise ...'

Six. Five. Four.

'... I'll look after you.'

Three. Two.

'I love you.'

One.

'I love you too.'

As the crowd erupted into cheers and chants, he kissed me.

We stood there, our family of three, cocooned amid the jubilant clamouring and excitement and fireworks which decorated the chill night sky. It took a moment or two for me to realise there was no sign of the catastrophe Jeremy had prophesied. Music played. Lights shone from the houses and flats around us. No planes had fallen out of the sky. From nowhere I was filled with an overwhelming sense of hope. The future might be unknown, but it was ours to grasp hold of and it was going to be OK. I slipped my hand into Kit's and squeezed it.

Back in our bedsit, Jeremy was still staring at the television but now it was muted. On screen a reporter was being buffeted by the celebrating crowd in Trafalgar Square. Jeremy didn't look up when we came in. His face was dark and cloudy as he watched the flickering celebrations.

'Happy New Year!' Kit cried, slapping him on the back.

But Jeremy didn't smile. 'Is it?' He looked at us. 'Another year, decade, another millennium of people suckling at the rancid tit of capitalism. Ask them why they're so happy.' He gestured at the on-screen revellers. 'They won't have a clue.'

There was a tangible anger in his words. Kit laid a hand on his friend's shoulder.

It was a moment or two before Jeremy seemed to shake himself free of whatever was dogging him. 'Sorry. Look, I'm fine,' he said, forcing a smile. 'Ignore me. I hate New Year's Eve. I shouldn't be around people really.' He stood and let out a sigh. 'I think I'll leave you to it. Get some air and clear my head.' He rubbed his face. 'Guess I was hoping for change, you know? A reset button.' He smiled and, though his anger had dissolved, a hint of sadness lingered in his eyes. 'Guess I'll have to tear the place down myself.'

CHAPTER FIVE

Kit,
July 2001

Kit checks his watch and leans back against the bonnet of his car. It's baking hot and though he's parked beneath one of the lime trees which line the street like policemen at a parade, the heat bearing down through the leaves is intense. He scuffs his toe against one of the many cigarette ends which litter the pavement, no doubt smoked by other bored clock-watchers waiting for sons, husbands, or friends. The entrance to Wormwood Scrubs with its huge arched doorway between castellated towers is more Norman castle than category B prison. Jeremy has served two months of a four-month sentence following his assault of a uniformed officer. Of course, he swore blind he only ever intended to march peacefully, but Kit had his doubts. During the trial he'd shown no sign of remorse.

'One of those things,' he'd said. 'Wrong time, wrong place.'

The wrong place on this occasion was outside a branch of Barclays Bank in central London during the May Day riots. Someone had hurled a brick. Others joined in. A window was smashed. The police charged in, kitted out in full riot gear, and when an officer attempted to detain Jeremy he'd received a punch in the face for his troubles. Tara had inhaled with shock when he'd told them. But Jeremy, if anything, seemed proud. As the judge read the verdict, he'd stood in the dock, chin lifted, a single fist clamped across his chest in defiance.

Kit wonders if the people wandering past in the sunshine, chatting, listening to music, eating ice creams, are as happy and relaxed as they appear. Though he wouldn't swap Skye and Tara for anything, he is starting to feel hemmed in. Life has become routine and insular. A couple of months ago he was promoted at the timber merchant, and while this meant a few more pounds per hour, it had moved him out of the yard and behind the counter. He yearns for fresh air and space. Tara can tell something is wrong, but he won't tell her the truth, the dissatisfaction brewing inside him; it's not fair to put that on her. Instead he smiles and says everything is fine.

The small door to the left of the turrets opens and Jeremy appears. Kit pushes himself off the car and waves. Jeremy waves back. Kit half-jogs to meet him and when he gets near, Jeremy drops his bag and they embrace, patting each other on the back, and Kit realises how much he's missed his company.

He takes Jeremy's bag and slings it on the back seat and they climb into the car.

'Let's get out of here.' Jeremy flicks two fingers up at the prison as Kit pulls away from the kerb.

'So how was it?' Kit notes how tired Jeremy looks. How much weight he's lost.

Jeremy stares out of the window, fingers tapping a rhythm. 'Well, there was a lot of time to think,' he says finally. Then he balls his jacket and places it against the window and lays his head on it. 'It's good to be out.' His eyes close. 'And it's good to see you.'

Jeremy shifts his weight to get comfortable and within minutes his features relax as sleep takes hold. Kit glances at him and notices a scar bisecting his eyebrow and feels suddenly protective of his friend.

The journey back to Cowley is a little over an hour. Jeremy sleeps the whole way. Kit stares straight ahead at the motorway stretching out in front of him, a thick grey slice through the countryside, linking conurbation to conurbation, carrying hundreds of thousands of exhausted people from work to home to work again. Is that living? Is Jeremy right? Is it all a pointless waste of time? A grind with no purpose.

As soon as Jeremy opens the door to the bedsit, Tara squeals and runs to hug him. 'So how's our jailbird? We've missed you!'

Jeremy laughs. 'Pleased to be out and I've missed you too.'

Skye appears behind Tara and her face breaks into a smile. She pushes past Jeremy and jumps into Kit's arms. 'Daddy! Daddy! Mama and me made biscuits.'

'For Jeremy?'

Her face drops and she eyes Jeremy, mouth a cartoon frown, and shakes her head. 'For me.'

'Hello Skye.' Jeremy's words are starched. It still surprises Kit how awkward he is around children. 'How are you?'

Skye hides her face in Kit's neck and whispers words he doesn't catch.

'I can't wait to see these biscuits,' he says.

'You can have one. But not him.' She gives Jeremy a suspicious glare.

Jeremy smiles at Tara. 'Whatever's cooking smells incredible.'

'Baked potatoes and veggie chilli.' She smiles. 'I thought you'd appreciate a bit of home-cooked food.'

Kit opens three bottles of beer as Jeremy eats ravenously. When he's done, he pushes his plate away and falls back against his chair, hands resting on his stomach. Skye is still mashing butter into her potato, a spoonful of butter for every spoonful of potato, each mouthful glistening gold on her plastic spoon.

Jeremy reaches for a beer and lifts it, a pendulum between finger and thumb. 'You know something? Every man in that place was lost. Society doesn't care about them. They've been written off.

Wedged in a vicious cycle. Break the law, do time, get out. Break the law again. The system is to blame.' He lifted the beer to his lips and drank. 'It's broken.'

Tara and Kit don't comment. Tara takes the spoon from Skye, whose interest in her golden potato has waned, and offers a mouthful which Skye takes absently before sliding off the chair in search of something more fun.

'These people have no choice but we do. I've been angry for too long, since my dad died, lashing out at anything and everything. But my anger was shackling me. Anger, resentment, and dissatis-faction are boulders we lug around. It's time to cast them off. The establishment holds us in contempt. It imposes rules and we obey like sheep. When we don't they lock us up. Well, not anymore. I've had enough of talking and marching. Writing slogans on homemade placards and being ignored. It's time to start *doing*. I want to make a difference. Be the change I seek.' Jeremy leans forward and gently bangs the table with his fist. 'Let's *do* something. Build something. Start living properly.'

His words ignite something dormant within Kit, each syllable electric. He wants to yell, 'Yes, yes, *yes*!'

Tara's head is lowered so he can't see her face as she pushes the remnants of Skye's potato around the plate with the spoon. What is she thinking?

'So?' Jeremy says then. 'Are you up for it?'

'What?'

'Moving somewhere. Together. Some land with like-minded people. Setting up a community. Grow our own food. Become self-sufficient. Off-grid. Break free of this shit.' He gestures around the room in a sweeping movement.

'Even if we wanted to, we can't.' Tara lifts her head to watch Skye, who has pulled a book off the shelf and is sitting with her legs outstretched, turning the pages.

'Of course you can.'

'You're serious?' Kit studies Jeremy's face, watching for signs of hesitation. There are none.

'I've never been more serious about anything. We should do it. There's nothing stopping us.'

'We have Skye. We can't just take her off-grid. She's not a pot plant you can pick up and place down.'

Tara's words pile up in Kit's brain. 'She's right, Jeremy. We have to put Skye first.'

'You would be putting her first. You'd be giving her a unique, idyllic life people dream of.'

'But that's what it is. A dream, not reality.'

'We can make it happen. We can build a simple, beautiful life. "I went to the woods because I wished to live deliberately. To see if I could not learn what it had to teach, and not, when I came to die, discover I hadn't lived." Not my words. Thoreau's.' He bangs his fist on the table again. This time more firmly. 'We can make it happen.'

Kit has a flash of Skye running through meadow grass. Barefoot. Golden curls glinting in the sunlight.

'It sounds perfect. It does,' Tara says. 'But utopias never work. People set out with a common goal, a shared dream, but someone always goes nuts and eats everybody else.'

Jeremy shakes his head vehemently. 'You're wrong. I've met people who've done it. Remember that trip I took to Wales last year? I stayed on a commune for a few weeks. The couple who run it were inspirational. When off-grid communities work, the results are beautiful. Don't you want that?'

Tara clears the plates and walks them to the kitchenette. She leans back against the worktop and looks again at Skye.

'We're ready. Deep down you both know it.' Jeremy pauses for a beat, then looks at Kit. 'All we have to do is buy some land.'

Kit's cheeks redden as his chest constricts. 'You mean me?' He glances at Tara, who is chewing her lower lip.

'You have the money.'

The thought of the money makes Kit feel sick. 'It's not mine.'

'It's a trust fund in your name.'

'I don't have access to it—'

'Until your birthday at the end of the month.'

Kit looks at both of them in turn as unspoken words thicken the air and Skye talks animatedly to the teddy she is reading to.

'Tara, you know I don't want anything to do with the estate.' Kit turns on Jeremy. 'You know it too. I don't want to even think about it. Inherited wealth goes against everything I believe in. I thought you felt the same?'

'I do. Individuals hoarding vast wealth is wrong. *If* it perpetuates the system. But if you do good with—'

'Nothing *good* will ever come of that money.'

'What if you use it to build your family a better life? Help others. Give those who are lost stability and purpose? An opportunity to reach their potential. Surely that's using it for good?'

Panic grabs Kit. He thinks of his parents. Pictures them sitting either end of their colossal dining table. His father reading the *Financial Times*. His mother flicking blindly through a magazine, sipping black coffee as Patsy delivers poached eggs and a silver rack of perfectly cooked toast. He watches his mother wave her away without uttering a word and Patsy returning to the kitchen to scrape the uneaten eggs into the bin.

'Tara?' he whispers.

Her features soften. She walks over and wraps her arms around him. 'I understand.' Her breath is warm against his skin. 'We both do.' She leans back from him and strokes his face.

'I loathe what it stands for.'

'I know.'

Kit looks at Jeremy, who nods and gives a tight smile, then reaches for his beer.

'I'm sorry,' Kit says then.

Jeremy raises his head. 'Don't be. I get it. It's fine. It's—' But he stops himself and nods again. 'As you say, it's just a pipe dream. I got overexcited, that's all. It's been a tough few months and I haven't slept much. I shouldn't have put it on you.'

Later that night, as Tara eases herself back beneath the blankets having resettled Skye on the mattress beside them, Kit turns on his side to face her. Her skin is bathed in soft orange from the street lights and below their window drunks bellow at each other as they fall out of the pub.

'Should we use the money to buy somewhere to live?' he whispers.

She reaches for his hand which she tucks beneath her cheek. The weight and warmth of her head is reassuring.

'Truthfully?' she whispers back. 'I don't think you should do anything you don't want to do.'

Her hesitation is clear and the reply deflects responsibility back to him. But what had he been expecting? That she demand he buy them a place? Perhaps he wants her to. It would absolve him of guilt. He could have held his hands up and said, 'I did it for you.'

Was it insanity not to use the money to move his family out of this cramped bedsit and provide them with a space to thrive in? Green fields and fresh air. Freedom to run. Birdsong instead of police sirens and blaring horns. The things from his own childhood he'd taken for granted.

'I want what's best for you and Skye.'

'But not at the expense of your principles. I believe in you. We can do it without that money. I'll get a job too. We'll work hard and save, and when we can afford it we'll move and it will taste sweeter.'

CHAPTER SIX

Dani,
April 2002

I sat on the steps of the Gielgud Theatre beneath a poster of a play about a cuckoo's nest starring the hot American guy from that film about the kids who kill the bitches at their school. People flooded by, so excited and chattery they didn't see me in the doorway even though they had to step around me to get past. I felt safer there than anywhere else. It was brightly lit and whatever time it was there were hundreds of people crawling around Leicester Square. With Mum's warning about staying dry ringing in my ears, I'd tucked myself as far under the overhang above the door as possible and managed to avoid getting drenched. The only sleep I'd had since she threw me out was a few uncomfortable hours on the bench outside the flats. I prayed she'd change her mind and come and get me. By six in the morning it was clear she wasn't going to so I caught the tube into central London with no clue where I was going. I got off at Holborn because of the weirdo who got on at Chancery Lane and sat right next to me stinking of booze and puke and asking where was 'that cow Marie'.

I spent the day wandering, watching buskers, window shopping. I bought the world's most expensive pizza and a bottle of Coke, then treated myself to a box of fancy chocolates which were pretty but tasted gross. I pretended I was the type of fancy lady who could walk into those shiny shops and spend a gazillion pounds on a pair of flip-flops and I tried not to think about Mum. If I did I started crying. By mid-morning I only had thirty-seven pence left and nowhere sold anything to eat for that. As the hours went by I got hungrier and hungrier until I found myself in the bright buzz of Leicester Square that evening with a growling stomach. I didn't know a person could be that hungry. And I wasn't the only one. I started seeing starving people everywhere. From my spot on the theatre steps I watched a raggedy bag of bones mumbling and muttering as he searched the bin like a lucky dip at a school fair. When he pulled his filthy arm out I had to use every scrap of willpower to stop myself running over and yanking whatever he'd found right out of his skeleton-hand.

When the cuckoo play finished, the glittery people flowed back out of the doors, even more excited and chattery than when they went in. They buttoned their coats and hurried into the rain, heads bent, collars up, rushing past me and my grumbling tummy. I sat up straight like the keen girls in school, hoping to catch their attention, but they looked straight through me as if I were a ghost. I was too shy to hold out my hand and beg for change like some of the others did. I wasn't ready for that.

When the theatre had emptied a bitch in a brown and orange bow tie came out and shooed me away like a stray dog. 'Loiter somewhere else,' she said with a nasty sneer.

'But it's raining.'

'It's April in England. It rains. Now clear off, you're making the theatre look messy.' She exchanged looks with another bitch in a matching bow tie then both of them glared at me. I glared right back which made them roll their eyes and shake their heads, and I heard the first bitch mutter, 'Kids these days.'

I found another doorway. It was near an air vent which blew out warm air that smelt of chicken chow mein. It wasn't far from the theatre, but I still got soaked to the skin on the way. Mum's coat wasn't waterproof and now it was wet it smelt bad. I drew my knees in to my chest and rested my chin on them and wondered if it was nearly time to find a bin.

'Hello there.' A man was standing in front of me. He was quite old, maybe forty, and looked like my maths teacher with round glasses, bald head, a crumpled grey suit with a wonky tie. He smiled. 'Do you need money?'

My stomach wailed in reply. 'Yeah, maybe,' I muttered. 'A few pounds? For food.'

He took his wallet out and peeled a ten-pound note from a thick wad. He held it out towards me, still smiling. I reached for it.

He bent down and whispered in my ear. 'Suck it first.' He drew back from me and waved the note in the air.

'Sorry?'

'You have to suck it properly, mind.' He gestured to an alleyway opposite filled with wheelie bins and piles of soggy cardboard boxes. 'Down there. It won't take long.'

A fireball of sick rose up and burnt my throat.

The pervert moved in closer. I leant back as far as the door behind me would allow. 'Look, you whore, suck my fucking dick and I'll give you the money. If you don't I'll find a policeman and tell them I caught you pickpocketing.'

A bubble of spit had collected in the corner of his flubbery mouth and I couldn't look at anything else.

'Leave her alone.'

I turned my head and saw the most beautiful man I'd ever seen in my life. Even with hunger and sick bubbling inside me I could still see how fit he was. Surely a model or an actor? Or maybe a rock star with his dark shaggy hair and chiselled cheekbones and eyelashes the girls at school would kill for.

'Piss off and mind your own business,' growled the pervert.

The man ignored him and crouched down in front of me. 'How old are you?' His voice was soft around the edges.

I didn't answer right away. If I told the truth he could call social services and I'd end up in some manky care home. David from school lived in a care home and he told me pretty much all the kids got fiddled with every night. Even the ugly ones. Everybody called him a big fat liar, but I was pretty sure he was telling the truth and there was no way I was risking it.

'Sixteen.'

'Really?'

His eyes dug into me and I knew I wouldn't be able to lie again. I dropped my head and as I did the pervert swore under his breath. I looked up in time to see him running across the road and melting to nothing in the rainy shadows.

'Arsehole,' the other man said.

The man's soft voice and film-star looks meant I literally couldn't talk.

'You hungry?'

The pervert slithered into my thoughts. Then I heard Mum telling me to keep safe, her voice muffled after cretin Eddie's beating. Was this man the same as all the others? Like cretin Eddie and that pervert with his grubby tenner and the rapists prowling the corridors of David's care home. Maybe they were all bad? Even the film-star ones.

'I won't hurt you,' he said, reading my mind. 'My name's Jeremy and I don't think it's safe for you out here alone. Let me buy you some food and we can talk about getting you home.'

Home? No way.

'I'm fine,' I mumbled. 'I'm going back in a bit. I needed a sit-down, that's all.'

He didn't move. 'Come on. Let's get you something to eat. Somewhere you can dry off. You'll be safe. I promise. We'll go where there are lots of people.' He smiled. 'Burger and fries? Pizza? Whatever you want.'

Burger and fries? My stomach jumped up and down and begged me to say yes. 'What do I have to do for it?'

He laughed.

'I'm not joking.'

'You don't have to do anything. I can see you're hungry, that's all.'

'Mum says there's no such thing as a free lunch.'

'It's eleven o'clock at night so this isn't lunch.'

I didn't reply.

His smile faded and he leant forward, hands clasped in front of him, elbows resting on his knees, close enough for me to notice how flawless his skin was. 'No strings, OK?'

The burger, fries, and milkshake were – no word of a lie – the best thing I'd tasted in my whole entire life. My belly sighed with joy as I stuffed the food into me. He drank coffee and we talked and it was as if we'd known each other forever. He was so easy to talk to and when I spoke he listened, *really* listened. His words were made of syrup, buttery and sweet, and when he laughed his eyes crinkled up. If I'd had a magic lamp right then, my first wish would be that Susi Court and Amy Holliday would strut in, thinking they owned the place as usual, and see us together, chatting and laughing, and assume he was my boyfriend. The thought of their pretty bitch-faces crumpling up with jealousy made me tingle all over.

As I pushed the last few chips into my mouth, he took a heavy breath, which made me look up and stop chewing. 'What?'

'You know you shouldn't be on the streets alone.' His tone was serious. 'It's time I took you home to your parents.'

My stomach somersaulted. 'Why?' I wiped my mouth with the back of my hand. 'I mean, you don't have to take me. I'm fine getting back. It's straight on the Central Line. I take the tube all the time. It's no big deal.'

'I don't think you're telling me the truth.'

I started to protest, but he talked over me.

'Listen to me, Dani. Your parents will be concerned.'

I thought about trying to lie again. Pretending I had a family like the one he was imagining. Parents who'd be killing themselves with worry. A mother sobbing in a large shiny kitchen. A father out on the streets, calling my name, frantically banging on doors.

'Dani?'

I didn't reply.

'Your mum will want you home.'

I laughed then, a quick snort of bitter laughter which, to my horror, set me off crying. I swiped at the tears with my sleeve. 'Mum doesn't give a shit.' I held his gaze like schoolkids in a stare-off.

'Whatever happened, I'm sure they want the chance to sort it out.'

'Mum doesn't care and my dad is dead.' This wasn't true. Dad wasn't dead. He lived in Worthing with a woman with dyed red hair. But I hadn't seen him in years so he might as well be dead. I couldn't be bothered to go into the whole cretin Eddie thing. 'She threw me out anyway. So ...'

Jeremy didn't say anything and an awkward silence grew like mould.

'She gave me twenty quid and her coat,' I said to fill the gap with something. 'I'm fine.'

Still he didn't speak or move. He'd frozen into a beautiful waxwork with marbles for eyes.

There was a yell outside. Lads pissing about. He glanced out of the window in the direction of the noise. 'What about school?'

'Don't go anymore.' Not a lie because I realised right then I couldn't go, could I? I didn't have my uniform or PE kit or pencil case. They'd send me home before I'd even got to registration.

'You've nowhere to go?'

I shook my head.

'And nobody's missing you?'

My stomach flipped over and I shrugged, which was pretty much saying *no*, but without the risk of crying. I looked at my fingers and picked at some grime which was wedged beneath my nail. I'd only been on the streets for twenty-four hours and already I'd spent my money, got soaked to the skin, had a pervert offering me money to suck him off, and got so hungry I considered fighting a homeless skeleton for bin-food.

'I can help you.'

'How?' I whispered without looking up. 'If you give me money someone will take it.'

'I'm not talking about money. I can offer you somewhere to stay. Somewhere with food, your own room, and other people. Somewhere you'll be safe.'

CHAPTER SEVEN

Tara,
August 2001

My mother used to describe herself as a 'professional mother' when I was younger. She took the job of me very seriously. I went to the dentist every six months and was never late for ballet. She made sure I got enough sleep and sent me to school every day with a well-balanced lunchbox covering all the main food groups. Routine. Boundaries. Micro-management. These were the markers of good mothering as far as Jane Wakefield was concerned. When things unravelled in my teens, she consulted a library of books in an effort to work out how to cope with her opinionated, rebellious daughter, and concluded hormones to be the culprit, thereby absolving her of responsibility. In my mother's eyes nobody was as good at mothering as she was, so it came as no surprise that from the moment Skye was born she disapproved of the way we parented. It took no time at all for her restrained incredulity that our newborn didn't have what she called 'a bedtime routine' to evolve into full-blown horror when she discovered Skye slept cradled in the crook of my arm.

'A baby in *bed* with you? Who on earth told you this was acceptable practice?'

'Nobody. We're going by our instincts.'

'Your *instincts*?'

'Yes, we do what feels right. Comfort her if she cries. Feed her if she's hungry. We let her take the lead.'

'I'm sorry? You let an eight-week-old baby *take the lead*?'

Soon after this, childcare books and photocopies of 'helpful' articles written by joyless Victorian-style nannies arrived in the post. She made daily phone calls asking after *Baby*. Was the room pitch black for nap time? Were we using nappy rash cream? Had we started weaning? Kit and I used every excuse we could think of to decline invitations to visit them. Deflecting the continuous judgemental advice was exhausting; it was easier to keep away. But as Skye's fourth birthday approached we were faced with a barrage of phone calls begging us to visit. Kit convinced me it was good for Skye to have a decent relationship with at least one set of grandparents, so reluctantly I agreed we would go for lunch and stay the night. My mother was over the moon.

'It's not going to be that bad,' Kit said.

'Are you sure? It's going to be thirty-six hours of *what that child needs*.'

He laughed. 'It's going to be fine. They'll see how happy she is and, who knows, they might even admit there is more than one way to raise a child.'

Kit's optimism was misplaced. Skye was up and down from the lunch table like a Jack-in-a-box. She'd take a mouthful then slip off her chair and run over to the window or the cat or the colouring laid out on the coffee table. My neck burned as my parents sipped their wine and cut their meat in turbid silence.

'Perhaps she has that condition,' my mother said, lips pursed. 'The one that affects their attention. Does she throw things at school?'

'She's not at school. She's four today, Mum. Children don't start school until the year they turn five.'

My mother rolled her eyes. 'Nursery then. Does she throw things at nursery?'

'Why are you obsessed with her throwing things?'

'That's what they do. The ones with the attention thing. Throw things.'

I glanced at Kit who mouthed, 'Don't rise.'

But I couldn't help myself. 'Actually, we're thinking of home-schooling her.'

'For God's sake,' my mother breathed, shaking her head and exchanging a look with my father.

Skye skipped up to the table and took a roast potato from Kit's plate, which she ate like an apple as she skipped back to her colouring.

'Skye? Will you sit with Daddy while you eat that?' The note of pleading in my voice annoyed me.

'Why?'

My parents bristled as if her voice sent an electric charge through them.

'Because that potato looks delicious,' Kit said. 'Maybe we could share it?'

Her face lit up. 'Of course!' She clambered on to his lap and held out the potato. He took a bite then kissed her.

'You know, this horrendous lack of structure will wreak havoc on her development. Do you really want to handicap her academically?'

Kit beat me to it with a response far more controlled than mine would have been. 'There is nothing wrong with Skye. She's bright and engaged and has been cooped up in the car for nearly two hours in the heat to get here. She's full of beans and it's her birthday. There's plenty of time for her to learn to sit at a table, but right now she's enjoying being here and that's more important than forcing her to sit still.'

The rest of the lunch was an uncomfortable mixture of stilted conversation and loaded silence. I zoned out, gazing through the security-locked, double-glazed, net-curtained window at the stripes mowed into the small rectangular lawn. As I stared at those parallel paths leading nowhere a paralysing dread filled me.

Was this where we were heading?

I shook myself free of the stripes and refocused on the conversation and was horrified to hear my father grilling Kit about money.

'... life isn't like that. You can't swan about ignoring your responsibilities.'

'That's not quite fair—'

'Kit takes his responsibilities extremely seriously.' I reached for Kit's hand. 'Nobody loves Skye and me more than he does.' Kit squeezed my hand. 'We're very happy.'

My father tutted loudly. 'Happy? Will you be *happy* when you're freezing to death in your hovel because you can't afford the bills? Are you *happy* sponging off the state? *Happy* with the constant threat of eviction?'

'We're doing fine,' Kit said calmly.

'And that's what you're aiming for, is it?' my mother shrilled. 'Don't you want more for Skye than *fine*?'

My anger mushroomed. How was I related to these awful people? My grandmother strode into my thoughts. A magnificent woman who dressed like Katharine Hepburn, swore and drank whisky and chain-smoked. Who divorced my philandering grandfather without a backward glance, then set up a company making canvas for bags and tents during the war. Who gave me mugs of cider when I stayed over and regaled me with tales of the dashing American soldiers she'd taken dancing and rolled her eyes when talking about my mother. 'Don't make the same mistakes as she did, darling. Take risks. Don't let a day pass without giving it a jolly good kick in the balls.' No older than twelve, giddy on cider and the thrill of the word *balls*, I'd laughed until my tummy ached.

'Skye has everything she needs.' I fought to keep my voice calm. 'She has Kit and she has me and we love her in a way you never loved me.'

'You think we didn't love you?' My mother's eyes widened in bafflement.

'You loved my achievements. Top grades. Poetry prizes. A place

on the hockey team. Winning a schools maths medal. You loved
going to parents' evening and hearing teachers tell you how hard-
working I was. You love that I got into Oxford. But do you love
me? Unconditionally? No matter what I do or who I become or
what choices I make? No. Neither of you are capable of that sort
of love.'

A thick fog hung over us as my mother gathered herself. When
she spoke the edges of her words were sharp, her voice solid with
contempt. 'Who do you think you are? You think you know
everything, don't you? I gave up my life for you. Your father worked
all the hours to provide for you. You wanted for nothing. We didn't
force you to do those things. You did them yourself. You were a
brilliant child with the world at your feet and we were proud of
you. Is that so awful? To be proud of one's child?'

My eyes burned with furious tears. 'It was never about me, it
was always about *you*. Perfect child. Perfect genes. Perfect bloody
parents.' None of this could ever be unsaid. As I spat the words
out I knew any relationship we had left was crumbling to nothing.
'I pity you both. You're drowning in disappointment. But if you've
taught me one thing it's that I want my life to be the polar opposite of yours.'

'Why are you so cruel, Tara?' my mother stage-whispered.

I laughed bitterly.

My mother gestured at my father, indicating she expected him
to speak.

My father seemed momentarily surprised, but then gamely
grabbed the baton. 'Your mother's right. We sacrificed everything
for your education and you repay us by getting pregnant and
dropping out of university? And look at the state of you. Ridiculous
hair? Metal in your face? We don't recognise you, Tara. You've
been a catastrophic disappointment over the last four years, but
did we abandon you like his parents?' He flicked his fingers dismiss-
ively in Kit's direction. 'No. We put our shame aside and stood by

you.' He paused and cleared his throat. Then he reached for his glass while avoiding my eyes. 'Your mother and I, well, we believe you're not up to the job of parenting Skye—'

'Keith.' There was a warning note to my mother's strangled whisper. 'Now isn't the time—'

'I think now is the perfect time.' Kit's patience had run dry. My stomach churned. 'Go ahead, Keith. What is it you want to say?'

My father squared his shoulders and took a deep breath, puffing his chest out like a bullfrog. 'Your mother and I believe Skye would be better off living with us.'

Kit exploded with a burst of incredulous laughter.

'We feel it's in our granddaughter's best interests she be raised by us.'

The smile fell away from Kit's face and his stunned disbelief mirrored mine.

'She needs to go to school.' My mother lifted her chin.

'She's *four*!'

'Pre-school. She needs to learn to read and count. Did you see how quickly she did the puzzle with me, Tara? How excited she was? A light switched on—'

'Yes, she loves puzzles! We do them all—'

'We've consulted a lawyer about applying for custody. He says—'

'A *lawyer*?'

It was a horror film. My vision swirled as I looked in rapid succession from one parent to the other.

'You both need to stop now.' Kit's voice was eerily calm. 'Neither Tara or I would let Skye spend one hour away from us, let alone whatever fresh hell you're suggesting. You're insane. On what grounds would a court take Skye from us?'

My father levelled his eyes on Kit. His fingers tightened around his wine glass. 'Incompetence. Neglect and …' He hesitated for a beat. 'Drug abuse.'

'Drug abuse? What are you talking—'

'We've smelt it on you.' My father narrowed his eyes. 'You think we don't know what marijuana smells like? You might think growing up in a one-room crack den is the right environment for a child, but we don't, and we have no intention of standing by as our only grandchild gets hooked on heroin before her fifth birthday.'

'Kit's right.' I stood, my entire body shaking, my knees weak. 'You're insane.'

Kit stood too. 'Tara didn't want to come today, but I told her we should. I said it was right Skye spends time with her grandparents and that despite your faults you deserved a relationship with her. I was wrong. The last thing either of you deserve is one moment with our precious girl and I hope you regret this day for the rest of your miserable lives.'

Then he walked over to me and rested his hands on my shoulders. 'Don't listen to a word they've said. You are a brilliant mother and Skye is a beautiful, *happy* child.'

He went over to where Skye was colouring, apparently oblivious to what was raging around her, and bent to pick her up. 'It's time to go home now, angel.'

'But the cake?'

'We're going to have it at home. A chocolate one.'

'Oh, good. I like that better than the one here.' She leant close to Kit's ear. 'It's got fruit in not icing.' Then she made a face.

As I walked from the table to join my family, my father tried to grab my wrist. I snatched my arm away. 'Don't touch me.'

'You're going to take her back to that dead-end life?' My mother's voice crackled with tears.

'That's exactly what we're going to do. We're going to take her home and get on with our lives. Without you.'

'Jesus. That was intense,' Kit said, once we were safely in the car and driving away.

I wasn't able to reply. I squeezed my eyes shut and tried to

59

control my shuddering body; I didn't want Skye to see me crying. We drove the rest of the way back in stunned silence.

Kit ran into the Co-op in Cowley for a chocolate cake and candles and back in our home we sang, ate cake, then curled into a knot of three and watched *Shrek*. I stared at the screen and made a conscious effort not to look at the patches of damp on the ceiling, Skye's mattress on the floor, the tiny window which was the only source of natural light we had, as my parents' voices rang in my ears.

As soon as Skye fell asleep, we made up the sofa bed and I collapsed, emotionally battered. Despite a strained relationship with my parents I never imagined us becoming estranged. Kit didn't get into bed with me. Instead, he came round to my side and sat on the edge, then leant over and switched on the small reading light clipped to the side of the sofa. He was holding some folded paper. 'Jeremy gave me this a few weeks ago.'

They were estate agent particulars.

'I didn't show you before because I was determined to make this work but after today ...' His voice faded and he dropped his head. 'I think there could be so much more for us. Not comforts or luxuries, but a lifestyle that suits us better. Something more enriching. At the moment we're round pegs jammed into square holes. Maybe it's time we found a life that fits?'

I glanced at Skye, who was peacefully sleeping. Her golden curls fanned out on the pillow. Her features relaxed as she breathed softly.

Then I reached for the details.

On the front page was an imposing granite farmhouse set against a bright blue sky.

Winterfall Farm, Nr Launceston, Cornwall.

'Cornwall?'

'Bodmin Moor.'

I opened the particulars and scanned the details. Stone

outbuildings. Drystone walls enclosing grassland. A ruined cottage. Views overlooking the wide expanse of moor. Thirty-four acres. Its own water supply from a well. The inside of the house hadn't been touched in decades. There was an Aga, light blue and stained with rust. A flagstone floor. Everything was tired and decorated in a way that suggested its owners were elderly and earthy.

'He's found others,' Kit said. 'The couple he met in Wales. A friend of theirs who knows plants and medicines. A couple of his own friends.'

'And he's asked you to buy this place for him?'

'I'd be buying it for us, Tara, But I'm happy to share it.'

'You think we could live with people we don't know?'

'We'd have to meet them first. If we don't get on with them, we won't do it.'

I looked at the particulars again. The farm was beautiful. It was easy to picture Skye there, the Cornish air pushing the pollutants out of her lungs, her face dusted with freckles from the sunshine. 'But we don't know the first thing about growing food?'

'We'd have to learn and it will be hard work, but we'll be together. Doing something brilliant.'

I thought about my parents and the nuggets of painful truth hidden in their hateful words. This life wasn't doing anything for us and we were stuck. A farm offered so much. An idyllic childhood for Skye, filled with fresh air and space, part of a supportive group of people who'd enhance her life.

'And the money? I know how much it means to you to leave it alone.'

'Jeremy's right, if we do good with it that's all that matters.' He rested his hand on mine. 'What do we have to lose? This bedsit, a thousand like it, will always be here. We can come back if things don't work out. But if we don't try, won't we always wonder what might have been? Maybe that's worse than trying and failing?'

'But it might work out,' I whispered.

Kit smiled. 'And if it does we can hold our heads high and know we did something magical for our family. For you, me, and Skye.'

I thought of my grandmother. The glint in her eye as she told me to take risks and kick life in the balls. 'Let's do it. Oh, Kit. Let's try.'

CHAPTER EIGHT

Kit,
March 2002

Kit closes the rear door of the Land Rover he'd found in the classifieds in *Farmer's Weekly* and gives it a pat. Every nerve in his body thrums with static electricity. It feels surreal, as if they are living in the words of an adventure book. Since the offer on the farm was accepted, he's read everything he could find in the library on subsistence living, smallholdings, off-grid communities, and wildlife indigenous to Bodmin Moor.

Tara is crackling with happiness. Her energy and excitement are palpable. Over the last few days, as they packed their belongings into boxes, some for the farm, others for the second-hand shop, she didn't stop grinning. It's an exhilarating new chapter and any niggling doubts Kit might have harboured have evaporated. The move feels powerful, perhaps even spiritual, as they join like-minded people with a common purpose. Kit recognises the strength in being an intrinsic part of a small community. For too long, people – himself and Tara included – have gathered in towns and cities not by design but by accident. Geographical decisions governed by housing prices, school league tables, and commuter routes. Disconnected communities. They'd lived in Cowley for four years and Kit would struggle to recognise any of their neighbours in a crowd.

Before they set off, Tara holds up the disposable camera she bought at the chemist. 'Photo to mark the occasion?'

Kit smiles and picks Skye up. A man is approaching with a dog on a lead and Tara catches his attention. His eyes dart between them nervously. 'Would you mind taking a photo for us?'

For a moment Kit thinks he might say no, but then he reluctantly reaches out for the camera. They stand together, the three of them, and smile. The man hands the camera back to Tara. She thanks him but he's already scurrying away.

'I won't miss Cowley,' she says, watching him go.

When they are finally in the car Kit turns in his seat to smile at Skye, who is strapped in her booster, clutching a small bag of toys and books. 'Ready?'

She nods and grins so hard she might burst.

'I can't believe we're really doing this,' Tara says.

He kisses her then takes a breath and starts the engine.

Tara and Kit are making a detour to the Severn View services to pick up Anne and Bruce, who have no car but managed to cadge a lift for their caravan from Lampeter. When they stop, Skye cranes her head and strains against the car straps to see where they are. 'I can't see any ponies,' she says.

They use the service station toilets and Kit buys a chocolate doughnut for Skye. She sits on the kerb and licks the frosting off while the four adults hitch up the caravan. Bruce is an ox of a man, approaching six and a half feet, barrel-chested and solid, with a shaved head and bushy beard. Tara sits in the back with Skye and Anne, and he squeezes his bulk into the passenger seat, knees to his chin.

'Do you have enough space?' Tara asks.

'I'm grand,' he says, attempting to manoeuvre himself to smile at her.

'Is he a grizzly bear, Mama?' Skye whispers.

'Shush.' Tara puts her fingers to her lips, then glances at Anne, who smiles.

Skye is growing fractious, fidgeting and whining, asking if they can go home. The word *home* jars with Kit. He's amazed at how quickly he has disengaged from the life they've left behind. It's already a shapeless memory. The bedsit feels no more a home than Ashbarton Coombe. He wonders if he will ever call anywhere home. The word is an anathema. If it wasn't for Tara and Skye, he suspects he'd spend his life wandering from place to place, nomadic and solitary, sleeping beneath the stars and moving on with the dawn. Is he imagining, then, the magnetic pull of Cornwall? Is it possible Winterfall Farm will be somewhere he belongs?

'What do you think of my bracelet?' Anne's voice shakes Kit from his thoughts.

Skye is struggling in her seat, her voice tight and high-pitched as she begs to get out. Kit glances in the rearview mirror and sees Anne shaking her wrist so the charms on her bracelet jangle.

Skye stops straining against her straps and nods. 'I like the hearts. One. Two. Two hearts.'

'It used to belong to a friend. But I was scared one day and she gave it to me. She said it would keep me safe.'

Skye fiddles with the bracelet. 'From monsters?'

Kit smiles at Anne in the mirror.

'Yes,' she says. 'It was monsters.'

'Can I have it?'

'Are you scared?'

Skye considers this for a moment then shakes her head.

Anne tickles her tummy. 'Then you don't need it!' Skye laughs and pushes Anne's hand away.

Tara and Kit had liked Anne immediately. They'd all met at a pub in King's Cross on a balmy September afternoon. Kit had been nervous. What if they didn't get on with these people Jeremy had gathered? Or they were freeloaders wanting a rent-free farm to live in? Would they dismiss him as a spoilt little rich boy? Everything was riding on that meeting. But he'd had nothing to worry about. It was clear from the off that they had much in common with the colourful group of bohemian strangers. As well as Anne and Bruce, there was Dean, a construction site labourer Jeremy met when at an anti-fox-hunting rally. Then Dean's brother, Ash, who scratched a living busking with his guitar on the pavements of Brighton. Ash had a sparse goatee and long, unkempt hair tied back loosely. Mary was a gentle woman with long white hair and a childlike, melodic voice who, according to Jeremy, knew everything there was to know about natural remedies and healing. Mary was exactly how Kit would have imagined a herbalist in her mid-fifties with a working knowledge of Wiccan practices. Dressed in an over-sized white smock, decorated with silver bangles, beads, and a large amber pendant which hung on a leather cord around her neck. They were all easy-going and optimistic. Peaceful not anarchic. Hopeful not angry. All of them yearning for a more harmonious way of life.

Tara and Anne talked as if they were old friends that night. Anne was one of those people it was impossible not to warm to. She had a wide, generous smile and kind eyes fanned with laughter lines. She was a natural with children, letting Skye prattle on and on, patiently answering a barrage of random questions. Not only that but she and Bruce were experienced off-gridders with a multitude of valuable skills. Bruce had been something of an eco-warrior in his youth – chaining himself to condemned trees, picketing animal testing centres, protesting Trident – but in his own words he'd mellowed.

'It's an exhausting business,' he'd said with a shy smile. 'Being angry all the time.'

Bruce and Anne, an ex-Jehovah's Witness, fell in love in their early twenties when he worked in a pub kitchen near the farm where she had a seasonal job picking fruit. Not long after, he used his modest savings to buy a caravan and they found a few acres in Wales for a peppercorn rent and learnt how to live self-sufficiently.

'The reed-bed sewage system he made worked perfectly,' Anne told them while gazing at Bruce with obvious love and pride.

'The work got harder as we got older and we'd been cut off from the world for a long time. We missed people.' He'd reached for Anne's hand across the pub table. 'So we welcomed volunteers. People who came to stay for a few weeks. Helped out in exchange for food.'

'That's how we met Jeremy,' Anne said.

Jeremy smiled.

'Most people were lovely,' she went on, 'but then a man arrived and brought this atmosphere with him. A black cloud followed him. He became verbally aggressive so Bruce asked him to leave.' Her face fell. 'We woke up the next day and he'd gone. But he'd trashed the place first. Put holes in the water storage. Slashed the polytunnels. Let the animals go. Killed one of our hens. Broke her neck.' She winced.

'God,' breathed Tara. 'That's awful. Why did he do it?'

Bruce shrugged. 'Wasn't at peace with himself. Something went off in his head.'

'We didn't have the energy to rebuild. We were lost.' She took a breath. 'Luckily for us, a day or two later, fate gave us Jeremy, who made contact and asked if we'd be interested in joining a commune.' Anne smiled at Jeremy. 'And now here we are, with you all, feeling hopeful again.'

The following day Kit called the estate agent and arranged to visit the farm with Jeremy. They put in an asking price offer on the spot. Kit was surprised to find that spending the trust fund was cathartic. It was as if he were draining the poison. Once he'd started he was happy to continue. As well as the farm and Land Rover, they used the money to stock up on various supplies, following a discussion on what they should and shouldn't be buying. Yes to decent tools. Yes to well-made kitchen equipment. Yes to basic foods such as flour, rice, pasta, and cooking oil. Yes to tarpaulins, rope, oil lamps, and a substantial delivery of wood. Yes to salt, sugar, matches and candles, and, though there'd been debate, a decent amount of beer and cider.

'Not quite self-sufficiency, is it?' Kit had said with a laugh as he and Jeremy loaded the van.

'It's a buffer. We need to ease into it, keep spirits up. It'll take time to grow our own food and make things we barter with. This isn't an exercise in survival. It's a long-term project.'

While it was a yes to many things, it was a no to others. Soaps, shampoos, bleach, washing-up liquid, toothpaste, hot water, and heating were vetoed.

'Mary has recipes for soaps and toothpaste,' Jeremy said. 'And we don't need any medicines.'

'What?' Tara furrowed her brow.

'Mary is amazing and without relying on doctors we'll be a step closer to independence.'

'What about a few basics? Antiseptic, painkillers, maybe some antibiotics if we can get hold of them?'

'We don't need them. Honestly, what Mary doesn't know about herbs and plants isn't worth knowing. She has a remedy for everything.'

Tara and Kit bought a basic first aid kit anyway – Calpol, antiseptic cream, plasters and the like – in case Skye cut herself or ran a temperature.

'It makes sense to have it,' Tara said. 'I don't know why he's so adamant.'

'He's got carried away, that's all,' Kit had replied.

They stop at the estate agent in Launceston to collect the keys. The woman in the office eyes them suspiciously and is reluctant to part with the key. Kit isn't surprised. They are a motley crew, Tara with her ribboned plaits and nose ring, with a grubby-faced, barefoot child on her hip. Kit wearing ripped jeans and Jeremy in flip-flops, his flowery shirt unbuttoned to the waist. The battered Land Rover outside attached to an ancient caravan decorated with colourful hand prints and crudely drawn flowers. Then the beaten-up royal blue and rust minivan Jeremy bought from a retiring window cleaner for a couple of hundred pounds.

'I'll need to see identification.'

'Why?' Jeremy counters. 'It's our house. Just give us the keys.'

'It's standard practice.' She reddens beneath the weight of Jeremy's stare.

'You assume because we aren't wearing suits we can't afford a house?'

The woman's mouth forms an oh-shape in surprise. 'I didn't … I meant … I—'

A man in a pinstriped suit and thin red tie emerges from a back room to stand beside her. 'Everything all right, Cynthia?'

'I was just explaining we need to see identification before we hand over keys.'

The man looks them up and down without any attempt to conceal his disdain. 'Standard practice. One doesn't—'

'And I was just explaining that—'

'Driving licence?' Kit reaches into his pocket to retrieve his wallet.

Cynthia smiles with relief as the man studies the licence, eyes narrowed, searching, Kit presumes, for signs of forgery to confirm his prejudice. He returns it without a word then opens the cupboard on the wall behind him which holds an array of keys. He places a set on the desk then melts back into his office.

Cynthia hands the keys to Kit with an air of apology and he thanks her.

Jeremy leans forward on the desk. 'You should be ashamed of yourself, Cynthia.'

Her eyes widen and Jeremy laughs. 'I'm teasing you, Cynthia. I wouldn't have given us the keys either.' Then he winks and turns away. 'Pricks,' he says, as they reach the door.

Kit glances at Cynthia, worried she might have heard, but she's too engrossed in whispering with her pinstriped colleague.

They reach the outskirts of the moor and the land either side of them falls away in a khaki carpet and Kit's heart starts to beat faster. Charcoal-coloured rocks and the occasional standing stone puncture the moorland, standing sentry on the land as they have done for thousands of years and will do for thousands more. The empty vastness is a drug in his veins. He can't wait to feel the grass beneath his feet, breathe in the peaty rawness, rest his palms against those ancient stones. They leave the A30 and trundle through farmland and the occasional postcard-perfect hamlet before turning onto a narrow track and juddering over the cattle grid and potholes which come thick and fast, the caravan pitching as it follows obediently.

'Nearly there,' Kit says.

When Winterfall Farm comes into view Anne gasps.

'Well, I never,' breathes Bruce.

The farmhouse is grey and more imposing than Kit remembers. Large windows gaze over the moor. The yard in front of the house is bordered on one side by a range of ramshackle stone outbuildings, part-paved with a few original cobbles, the rest aged concrete with mighty weeds pushing through cracks, moss coating it like spilled paint. There's a ruined greenhouse behind the house and on the other side of the yard is an open-sided barn with a rusted corrugated roof, shot through with holes, housing a long-dead tractor and a large rotten straw bale wearing a cloak of mould and mushrooms. Behind the outbuildings are the two meadows enclosed with drystone walls in need of repair, and a stile leading on to the moor. To the right of the fields is a large copse of trees and a stream that feeds the well which they hope will one day provide their water. Behind the greenhouse lies an orchard reclaimed by nature and time with fruit trees battling to keep from drowning in a sea of brambles and weeds.

The views of the moor are breathtaking. Wild and expansive in a palette of bright spring greens and greys, dotted with ferns and splashes of yellow gorse. The March sun shines on the house and lights the tiny quartz sparkles. The sky unfurls for miles, streaked with white cloud, and dotted with birds circling on thermals miles above.

Anne climbs out of the Land Rover, hands on hips, a smile on her face. 'Beautiful. Just beautiful.'

Over the next few hours they familiarise themselves with the house and grounds. Bruce can hardly contain his excitement as he walks through the overgrown orchard, rubbing his beard, identifying the fruit trees, which include apples, plums and pears. 'There are wild strawberries here as well. Look, see?' He drops to his knees and clears the knotted weeds from the base of a spindly leafless bush. 'And this is a raspberry. This place,' he says, his eyes filmed with tears. 'It's incredible. Truly. It's ...' His words fade as he is overcome by a naive and joyful wonder.

They are interrupted by the gentle purr of an engine approaching. 'That'll be the van,' Kit says, as Jeremy shouts a greeting from the yard.

As they leave the buried orchard, Bruce pauses to give it a final nod of appreciation.

Dean waves brightly as he parks the van. Ash jumps out of the passenger seat and stretches his arms. The high-top van is borrowed from a friend of Dean's to bring the items of furniture and household equipment they'd scavenged from skips, pavements, and fly-tipping spots, or bought from charity sales or already owned. When Dean jumps out of the van he's followed by a large black and tan dog who bounds after him, sniffing and wagging as she explores the yard.

'You didn't tell me you had a dog.' It's clear from Jeremy's body language and wary eyes he isn't keen on dogs.

'A bloke in the pub was selling her and the twat trying to buy her wanted her for fighting. I couldn't let that happen. It's fucked up. I've called her Sasha. Here, girl! Here, Sasha!'

The dog trots over and sits at his feet and Dean reaches down to scratch her head. Tara and Skye walk over, and Tara holds out her hand for Sasha to sniff. When the dog wags her tail, Tara bends to ruffle her neck. Sasha licks Tara's cheek and Skye giggles.

'Stroke her here,' Tara says. 'On her shoulder. She likes that. Never put your face too close to hers, understand?'

Skye reaches out and tentatively strokes the dog. 'Can she be mine too?' Skye looks up at Dean.

'Definitely! She belongs to all of us. Me, your mum, you. Everybody.'

Skye beams and whispers something excitedly in Tara's ear.

The air hums with optimism. Happy exclamations echo around the courtyard as they unload the vehicles. Plastic water butts are rolled over to the barn. Tools are deposited inside the only stone shed with a lock. Rucksacks containing whatever possessions they'd brought with them taken into the house.

The group naturally gravitates to Jeremy with questions and it isn't long before he's standing in the centre of the yard, a traffic officer directing where everything should go. Kit's relieved he's taken control. He'd been fearful that, because the deeds had his name on, people would assume he'd make the decisions, and that's the very last thing he wants. Kit has enough self-awareness to know he's a great foot soldier but not a leader. Jeremy on the other hand is born for it.

Bruce carries the sacks of food and cooking equipment into the kitchen, while Mary sets up her apothecary in the pantry, squealing with delight as she does so.

'All these shelves!' she says when Kit carries in another box of brown glass bottles and places it on the flagstone floor.

Outside Kit finds Jeremy dragging a large tarpaulin to the barn. Kit jogs to help him and they haul it next to the old tractor. Jeremy smiles and wipes his forehead. 'Isn't this great?'

'I can't believe we're actually here.'

'I promise we'll make this work. All of us. We'll create something incredible. You'll see. This place, Winterfall, will be a blueprint for a new way of living.'

Kit smiles and nods. 'It feels good. Really good.'

A little while later, Kit takes their bags up to their bedroom. Assigning rooms went without a hitch when the group met up a few weeks earlier and Jeremy went through the floor plan. There was an obvious choice for Kit and Tara, a large double room in the main house, with a small room adjoining it which had most likely been used as a dressing room, with space for Skye's mattress and enough room beside it for Tara and Kit to sit with her. They wedge the door open so she doesn't feel shut away, then help her unpack, smiling as she natters to her toys and tells them all about their new home.

Bruce and Anne's caravan is parked in the corner of one of the fields near the animal sheds. The caravan has a double bed at one end with storage beneath. The kitchen area has been stripped out and in its place is a table and a bench, on which are a number of candles, two packs of cards, a large container holding boxes of matches and lighters, and a pile of well-thumbed yellowed paperbacks.

'You're sure you don't want a room in the farmhouse?' Kit had asked them.

'That's kind, but we love the caravan. It's our home.' Then Anne had smiled. 'And it gives us a bit of privacy.'

Privacy was something Tara and he had already sacrificed when Skye arrived, but in the house there is even less, and there is something about seeing the caravan's seclusion, its door opening away from the farmhouse so, if you were looking from the inside out, you'd never know anybody else was nearby, which sends a shiver of jealousy through him.

Jeremy's room, another large double, is opposite Kit and Tara's. Mary is in a small double at the back which overlooks the orchard, and opposite her are Ash and Dean. There's a damp, run-down bathroom on the same floor for everybody to use, and next to that a steep, narrow staircase leading up to two attic rooms with sloping ceilings and dormer windows.

When the sun goes down, Jeremy finds the box of oil lamps and candles and hands them out. 'Not having electricity will be the hardest thing to get used to,' he says, as he passes around boxes of matches. 'As well as no lights or boiler, it means we can't charge our mobile phones.'

'There's a landline, though?'

'There's no phone line.'

'How do we get help if there's a problem?'

'There won't be any problems we can't deal with ourselves.'

The furrows in Tara's brow deepen.

'I mean in an emergency?'

Jeremy stares at her for a moment as if he might try and tell her there won't be any emergencies. But then he nods. 'Yes, of course, we need to think about things like that. In an emergency there's a phone box. It's only a couple of hundred yards down the lane. We passed it on the corner before the cattle grid.'

Later, Kit and Tara are lying on their mattress, the smell of their washing powder on the sheets seeming to be the only thing remaining from their old world.

'Are you happy?' Kit whispers, kissing her.

'Yes. Very. Though I keep thinking somebody is going to appear and take it all away.' She looks at him and strokes his cheek. 'Is she asleep?' she whispers.

Skye is out of sight, tucked into the room they have christened her 'nook'. He holds his breath and listens, then nods.

They make love silently, then lie together, limbs entwined, her body warm against his, his arms looped around her, their breathing synchronised. Somewhere outside an owl hoots. The dog responds with a half-hearted bark then the house stills. The silence is so loud it rings in his ears. He didn't realise how much he'd missed this quiet until now. When he was a child he'd often creep out of the house at night. He'd lie in the rowing boat moored on the lake or hide in the soft grass in the fields, and stare up at the stars, a billion balls of fire a billion miles away, and imagine he lived on one. This place, this farm, is one of those stars. A new world. Somewhere they can be free. Somewhere he can build a home for his family.

CHAPTER NINE

Dani,
April 2002

Then he told me about the farm.

The way he talked about it made it sound like a magical world. Narnia or Neverland. Where happy people spent their time sitting in the sun and eating bread still warm from the oven. Where there were no rules and no school and everybody looked after each other and had something he called a *common goal*.

'They are good people. A family, but better. There's no fighting. We laugh together and work together. It's a safe place. Nobody's hungry or cold or scared.'

'Sounds nice.'

'We grow our own food. We have animals. There's so much space, Dani. You wouldn't believe it.'

I thought of Mum then. With her bust lip. Waiting in the flat for the cretin to get in and beat her up again. Would Jeremy let her come too? But as I was about to ask him, I realised there was no way she'd come. I couldn't even get her to leave Leyton, let alone move to a farm with a bunch of hippies.

'Have you ever heard of a *utopia*?'

I shook my head.

'Utopia is a place where everything is perfect. Where everyone is happy. A haven. We've created a haven at Winterfall Farm and I want to share it.'

'Oh, shit.' I sat back in my seat and crossed my arms. 'Is it a *cult*? Are you a religious crackpot?'

Jeremy looked surprised for a split second. 'A cult? No, definitely not. We oppose organised religion, which uses fear and the promise of immortality to control us. Am I spiritual? I'd say yes. Human beings are naturally spiritual. Connected to the world we inhabit and each other. But, no, Winterfall Farm has no links with religion.'

I didn't understand what he meant. I thought spiritual was religious. Was he trying to confuse me on purpose?

'Don't look so worried.' He held up his hands as if I'd pointed a gun at him. 'Honestly, no pressure. It's up to you. But if you want somewhere safe to get back on your feet, work out what you want to do, then you're welcome. The food is really good. Bruce, the man who does the cooking, makes the best flapjacks you've tasted. You can stay as long as you need. Everybody's free to come and go. Say the word and I'll put you on the next train back to London. But you'll be safe, Dani. Safe, warm, and fed.'

His words made me lightheaded. The more he said the more tempted I was. What did I have to lose? If I stayed where I was, I faced another night on the streets, starving, cold and wet, trying to keep away from child molesters.

'Where is it? This utopia.'

'Cornwall. Bodmin Moor.'

'*Cornwall?* Jesus. That's *miles* away, isn't it?'

He laughed. 'The place is incredible. The moor is breathtaking. There are wild ponies living on it and sometimes they come so close we can feed them apples from our hands.'

I tried to picture myself feeding apples to ponies a million miles away, but it was too hard and doubts flickered like a faulty light-bulb. 'But I don't even know you. I mean, yeah, you seem nice.' I hesitated. '*Really* nice. But what if you're trying to – I don't know – murder me or something?'

'You're right not to trust me.'

'It's not—'

'You don't know me. Of course, you need to be wary.'

He reached into his jacket pocket and pulled out a photograph, which he slid across the table. I picked it up. It showed a group of people, smiling, squinting into the sunlight. I stared at it, trying to take in every detail. Soft white clouds streaked the pale blue sky. A big dog with a red scarf around its neck lay on the grass at their feet. One of the women was laughing, her eyes crinkled, a chicken held in her arms. Next to her was a man with a little girl on his shoulders. His hands gripped her ankles and her fingers knotted into his hair. She had golden curls which shone in the sun. Everyone was dressed in the type of clothes cretin Eddie would hate.

Fucking hippies. Soap-dodging scroungers. Look at the bloody state of them.

But I pushed his sneering away. To me, with their nose rings and hair wraps, colourful prints, shaggy hair, bare feet and beaming smiles, they looked spectacular, like jungle birds.

'I can't see you.'

He smiled. 'I'm taking the photo.'

I put the photograph back on the table and he tucked it into his jacket pocket. 'This is my family and they will welcome you with open arms.'

The way he spoke about them rammed home how unwanted I was. I glanced out of the window at the rain which hammered the darkness. I thought of Mum's mangled face. The pervert with his bubble of spit. The skeleton searching the bin. I didn't want any of it. I didn't want to be scared or hungry or cold. I didn't want to be alone. I wanted to be part of that photograph.

'And if I don't like it I can leave?'

'You have my word.'

What other option did I have?

'I'll come, but if it's shit, or you do anything weird, I'm gone, OK?'

He smiled as if he'd won a prize in a competition. I ignored the voice in my head telling me he was a crazy serial killer who lured idiot girls to his lair using syrupy words and a photo of some hippies he'd never even met, and reached for my milkshake. I finished it, slurping up every last bit, then nodded.

CHAPTER TEN

Tara,
April 2002

Those first few weeks unfurled like a glorious holiday. Our spirits soared as we settled into our new way of life. I loved to watch Skye playing outdoors. Making daisy chains. Paddling in the stream. Throwing sticks for Sasha – who never tired of the game – then giggling as she deposited them at her feet and barked for more. Skye bloomed before our eyes. The sun dusted her skin with freckles and colour. Her hair became a wind-tangled knot of curls. Earth ingrained the soles of her feet. She was thriving, just as we'd hoped she would.

We'd gathered on day two to discuss the schedule of works and assign roles. Everybody looked towards Jeremy once we were assembled in the meadow not far from Bruce and Anne's caravan. Without discussing it, the entire group elected him leader. With his enthusiasm, vision, and infectious optimism, he was the natural choice. Nobody questioned it.

We sat in a ring on the grass with mugs of cider and cheese sandwiches. Butterflies flitted from wild flower to wild flower and the air rang with birdsong and the distant babble of the stream.

'Bruce will talk us through our list of jobs in a minute,' Jeremy said. 'We'll be looking to prioritise our food supply. Long term we'll install a reed bed to deal with the waste, but for the time being we'll stay on mains water. We need to make sure the water supply from the well is sufficient to handle the needs of the farm with water for animals, for us, for irrigation. There's no electricity, which means no heating or hot water. Bruce and I have been looking into the use of methane which a number of communities have success with. This would give us the luxury of hot water, but not this year.'

'Don't panic,' Anne chipped in. 'You get used to the cold water. Some of you will prefer it. I do.' She smiled. 'Washing-up is fine and, I promise you, before long you'll wonder why you ever needed a dishwasher or television or a power shower.'

I'd be a liar if I said I wasn't concerned about the hot water. It was the biggest problem for me. I'd always started every day with a steaming shower and I knew I was going to find this the hardest thing to get used to.

Jeremy must have read the concern on my face. 'Nobody is saying this will be easy. But the sacrifices will be worth it. We've got used to creature comforts at the flick of a switch. It's what we know and now we have to *un*know the things we take for granted and in doing so we'll unlock our potential.' He looked at us all. 'Now, when it comes to food and labour, Winterfall Farm will operate as a collective. Everything we produce will be shared and we'll embrace the principle from each according to their ability, to each according to their need.' He smiled. 'Now I'll hand over to Bruce who'll give an overview of what needs doing over the next few weeks and months.'

Jeremy gave Bruce an encouraging smile, and the huge man blushed, before clearing his throat and running a hand through his beard a couple of times as if for reassurance. 'Growing enough food for what we need, well, it isn't going to happen overnight. It'll be eighteen months before things get going.'

Eighteen months? I glanced at Kit, but his face showed no reaction. The group had discussed our plan to make things – jewellery, willow baskets, jams, pickled vegetables – to use for bartering with locals for items we needed, but until then we were resigned to using Kit's trust money, a dirty secret the group didn't discuss. Kit didn't mind. He was happy to see it dwindle.

'The sooner it's gone the better,' he said.

'We won't be self-sufficient for a while, but it won't be long until we start to produce. We'll get some fast-growing crops potted up in the next few days then, all things being well, we'll harvest our first vegetables towards the end of April, beginning of May. Lettuces, spinach, carrots. Radishes are fast. Beets, too. By mid-May we'll have early peas and as the year goes on we'll be digging potatoes and parsnips, picking beans, and cutting cabbages and winter greens. Leeks grow well and once courgettes take hold you can't stop them.' He smiled. 'We'll need some manure to improve the soil, but the local farmer should be happy to give us some or sell it.'

Bruce's warmth radiated outwards. His gentle voice, so at odds with his hulking presence, was accompanied by a frequent easy smile, and as he told us in his calm, measured manner how we'd prepare the land and plant out the seedlings, an overwhelming sense of surety took hold of me. Bruce knew what he was talking about. It might have been Jeremy's enthusiasm fuelling our engine, but this man, with his kind eyes, weathered hands, and doll-like wife who gazed at him with undisguised adoration, was going to navigate our journey.

'As well as getting the beds ready for the germinated seeds, we'll need to get the animal enclosures secure. The orchard cleared and cut back if we want fruit this season.' Bruce looked at Jeremy. 'Think that's it for now.' Then his face broke into a broad smile and he chuckled. 'It's nice to be part of a group.' He reached for Anne's hand and smiled at her. 'Anne and I have missed it. Thank you for having us here.'

We wasted no time. As soon as we'd finished our lunch we set to work. Bruce had staked out a corner of the bottom field to be divided into separate beds. The grass needed turning over, compost dug in, and the polytunnel frames set up. Mary, Anne and I sat in the sunshine and chatted happily as we pushed seeds into planting trays, sprinkling each bedded seed with enough water to set them on their way. Once we'd planted the trays we carried them into the house. The sitting room had been designated as the germination room and before long the entire room was given over to the trays of seeds, too precious to risk weathering a cold snap.

I was surprised how protective I was of them, checking them regularly, lightly pressing the soil to make sure they weren't too dry, watering when needed. A week or so later, when I noticed the tips of tiny green shoots I cried out in excitement. Mary rushed in and was so overwhelmed she shrieked and grabbed me and we spun a circle in shared joy.

Ash and I volunteered to drive to the neighbouring farm to buy the manure we needed for the seedlings. We were bubbling with excitement as we set off. The old world, the world of concrete and damp walls, grey skies, lack of hope, was a hazy memory now. The yardsticks by which we measured our lives had shifted and the prospect of getting our precious seedlings into the ground gave us all a natural high. We rattled over the cattle grid and drove until we reached the track which led to the next farm. Ash slowed the car to drive through the gate and into the yard. There was a huge black barn on our left holding all manner of farmyard equipment. Up ahead was a bright yellow tractor and a variety of stone sheds and a large open-sided cattle barn.

Ash stilled the engine and a man appeared dressed in a navy boiler suit, flat cap, and heavy rubber boots. As we climbed out of the Land Rover his face fell as if he'd set eyes on aliens. Of course we knew we were a novelty. We'd often notice people paused at our gate, craning their necks to catch a glimpse of these peculiar creatures they'd heard rumours of. I'd always smile and give a cheery wave, but they mostly hurried away.

'Once they know we aren't thieving or causing damage they'll relax,' Bruce said genially. 'People never trust strangers. It's instinct. But soon as they know there's no threat, things'll change.'

'I hope so,' I replied. 'I don't want them to hate us.'

Bruce smiled. 'They don't hate us. It'll take a bit of time to get used to those beautiful ribbons of yours, that's all.'

The farmer said nothing as we approached, but I could see the cogs in his brain whirring as he took in our nose rings, kaleidoscopic clothes and flip-flops, and put two and two together.

'Hi there.' Ash held out his hand. 'I'm Ash. This is Tara. We—'

'The folk that moved into Winterfall.' He nodded in the vague direction of our farm.

'Yes, that's us!' Ash smiled. 'We're planting some vegetables and were hoping to buy a few sacks of manure?'

The man said nothing.

'Do you have some for sale?'

Heat rose up my neck as the farmer stared at me. 'Ash, maybe we should—'

'You know farming?' The man interrupted.

Ash grabbed the question and beamed. 'Some of us do. The rest are learning. We planted some seeds. They grew. Now we need to put them outside because they can't stay in the sitting room forever …' His voice faded as the farmer's hostility revived.

'All sleep together up there do you?'

'What?'

'Orgies?'

Ash lifted his hand to smother a laugh.

'Orgies?' I tried not to catch Ash's eye. 'No, no. Nothing like that. We just wanted to get out of the city, that's all.'

The farmer didn't look convinced.

'Maybe you should come up and have a look at what we're doing? We could show you round.' I'd hoped this might melt him, but if anything his expression grew colder. My heart sank. Was this what they all thought of us? That we were untrustworthy strangers with metal in our faces, walking around barefoot and having group sex? Part of me wanted to tell the old bigot where to stick his manure, but it wouldn't help. We were going to be neighbours for the foreseeable future and the aim was to forge a relationship with the goal of trading. Making friends was vital. 'You should come for tea. Bruce makes great cakes. He's the one who knows about farming. You'd have lots to talk about.'

'No thank you.' Then he turned and gestured with a dismissive hand to the towering pile of muck on the other side of the yard. 'Take what you need and don't be causing any trouble.'

'Trouble?'

'Rubbish. Drugs. Stealing. Ruining this place with your ways.'

'Our ways?'

'It's two pound a sack. Cash. Leave it on the wheel of the tractor.'

We filled some sacks with the foul-smelling muck then loaded them into the boot of the Land Rover. The stony-faced farmer didn't take his eyes off us for a moment.

'Thank you,' we called as we got into the car.

It was only when we were safely away from the farm that we finally gave in and laughed until tears rolled down our cheeks.

'Bruce is going to have to bake a serious cake for that one,' Ash said. 'Jesus. That stuff stinks!' He rolled his window all the way down. 'Orgies,' he said with a chuckle.

'I bet if we walked into the pub they'd all stop talking and stare at us, like they did in that pub in *American Werewolf*.'

I laughed. 'It was exactly like that, wasn't it? When he said the word *orgies* I nearly lost it.'

The only person who didn't find it funny was Jeremy.

'Idiots.' His contempt was clear. 'That kind of societal bullshit is what we're trying to escape.'

'To be fair, it must be a shock to find yourself living next to a group of hippies who—'

'What?' Jeremy's face clouded over. 'He called us a group of hippies?'

'No, but I guess that's what he's thinking—'

'That we're a bunch of lazy hippies lounging about smoking weed and singing Kumbay-fucking-*ya*?'

'Look, Jay, the old man was probably born on the farm and has never been out of Cornwall. It was funny, honestly. Nothing more than that. And why do you care what he thinks anyway? It's not the first time somebody's made a snap judgement. People stare at me wherever I go. Screw them.'

Ash nodded. 'The guy's a nut roast, if you ask me.'

'He'll come round,' Anne said. 'They nearly all do.'

'Forget about it.' Kit touched Jeremy's arm. 'Let's get the manure turned into the beds so they're ready for our seedlings.'

Jeremy pursed his lips, hands on hips, and finally forced a smile. 'Sure. Sorry. I'm not happy them thinking the worst of us.'

'I know.' I smiled at him. 'But don't let it get to you.'

The others had drifted towards the Land Rover and began hoisting the sacks of manure onto their shoulders and walking them over to the vegetable beds.

'You're right and I overreacted,' Jeremy said then. 'I feel protective of you all. Of this place and the importance of what we're doing here. I didn't realise how much until now.'

Everybody worked hard to get the vegetables planted. Trays of precious seedlings were carried out in a procession and Bruce showed us how and where to plant them. When the seedlings were tucked into their beds, we moved on to preparing for the animals. One of the stone sheds opened on to the field. This was allocated to the goats. Ash and Dean erected post and wire fencing to create a grass enclosure the goats would have access to during the day. Kit made a door for the shed out of an old sheet of ply he found in the barn, which we could raise and lower using a rope pulley, and secure with a cleat drilled into the wall. We repaired the drystone walls and Anne helped us construct an area in one of the other sheds for milking. Water troughs were filled and straw shaken out for beds and used to line the nesting boxes for the hens.

Anne and Kit were collecting the chickens and when we heard the Land Rover engine approaching, we all crowded around the gate like paparazzi.

'They're beautiful girls.' Anne beamed as she jumped out of the Land Rover. 'Just you wait.'

The hens were 'point of lay' Anne told us, which meant it wouldn't take long before we had eggs. There were ten in total: seven red, two white, one black. Anne opened the lid to one of the boxes they were transported in to show Skye, who peered in and cooed with wonder.

'I *love* them,' she whispered, eyes gleaming.

Kit and Dean had constructed a wire run and a coop out of pallets clad with old floorboards they'd grabbed out of a skip and a broom handle for a perch. The nesting boxes were made from apple crates they'd discovered in the ruined greenhouse. We released them into their new home and watched as they shook the journey from the other side of Launceston out of their feathers and settled down to scratch and peck.

A few days later I woke to find Kit's side of the bed empty. Morning sun poured in through the window. It was a perfect day. A corn-flower sky. Bright sunshine. Every colour almost neon. I noticed two figures sitting in the field. Jeremy and Mary. They were sitting cross-legged, hands resting on their knees, palms upwards, faces tipped towards the sun. Were they meditating? Jeremy was the last person I would have expected to meditate. He was a bundle of energy, always fidgeting, always on the move. His inability to sit still for any protracted length of time was comical. It was surreal to see him poised there, motionless, a statue in the grass.

Skye's pattering feet made me turn. She smiled and ran into my arms. I picked her up and kissed her. 'Did you sleep well, baby?'

She nodded then wriggled out of my grip and ran to the bathroom. When she reappeared we walked downstairs; the smell of fresh bread was a magnet. Anne and Bruce greeted us in the kitchen with excited smiles.

'Good morning, my lovelies!' Anne put down the mixing bowl she was holding and wiped her hands on a cloth, then crouched in front of Skye. 'I've a surprise for you.'

Skye's eyes grew round as saucers. 'What?'

'I'll show you.'

They walked out of the kitchen hand in hand and I poured a coffee from the pan on the Aga. 'Surprise?' I asked Bruce.

Bruce grinned as he tipped oats from a large Kilner jar into a bowl. 'You'll see.'

'Is Kit around?'

Bruce reached for the syrup and poured a generous amount into the oats. 'He was down early. Said he wanted to get on with stacking the logs he split yesterday.'

Kit had taken on the role of house woodsman and fire-builder. He was obsessed with fire. There was nothing he loved more than standing in front of a blistering bonfire. He'd set up a wood chopping area at the back of the house beside the orchard wall and built a covered store to stack the prepared wood ready to be used on the wood burners and fires in the house.

'Has he had a coffee?'

Bruce shook his head. 'It was still brewing. I said I'd run it up to him.'

'I'll take it.' I poured some into another mug and added a splash of cold water to dilute Bruce's brew, so strong it made the rest of us wince.

But as I was walking towards the back door, there was a thunder of feet and excitable squeals as Skye barrelled in. She was holding two perfect eggs aloft, one in each victorious hand.

'Mama! Mama! Blackie and Snowy had *babies*!'

Anne laughed. 'Told you it was a good surprise!'

Skye held them out to show me, cradling them in her palms as if they were made of glass. 'Mama,' she whispered, eyes shining with wonderment as she raised her left hand a little. 'This one is *warm*.'

'Well, I never.' Bruce folded his giant frame to crouch in front of my daughter. 'That's real treasure. Tell you what,' he whispered conspiratorially. 'Would you like one? You can be the first to have a boiled egg and soldiers.'

I left Skye chattering away to Bruce and Anne while they boiled her egg and toasted bread and took Kit his coffee. He was bent over, wearing a T-shirt, his lean and muscular arms glistening in the morning sun, stacking logs beneath the shelter. When I called to him he turned and smiled, put down the log he was holding and wiped his brow.

'You're up early.' I said, handing him the mug of coffee.

He thanked me as he took the mug. 'I was awake so thought I'd watch the sunrise on the moor. I walked up onto the tor. The view is incredible up there. You should come with me one day. You'd love it. How's Skye this morning?'

I smiled. 'Beside herself with excitement. The hens laid their first eggs. Anne took her to collect them and now dear Bruce is boiling one for her. He's even making her soldiers.'

'Lucky girl! I quite fancy that myself.'

'I saw Jeremy meditating earlier.'

'Meditating?'

I raised my eyebrows and nodded. 'With Mary.'

'A first for everything, I suppose.'

'I wouldn't have thought that was his thing at all.'

Kit shook the dregs of his coffee on to the grass. 'Maybe all anarchists mellow eventually.'

'Just don't call him a hippie …'

Kit laughed and looped his arm around my shoulder as we strolled back down to the house. He smelt good. Sweat and earth and contentment. I heard an echo of my mother's voice telling me when I was fourteen or fifteen that a lawyer or a doctor, preferably a surgeon, and at a push an accountant would make the best choice of husband, and smiled to myself.

As we neared the back door Skye ran out. 'Bruce cooked Blackie's egg. Come see! Come see!'

I watched Kit show Skye how to slice the top from a boiled egg as Bruce and Anne looked on with fondness, smiles on their faces, and a warm glow spread over my skin. Was it really this easy?

Had we done it?

Had we somehow stumbled on the perfect life?

CHAPTER ELEVEN

Kit,
April 2002

Kit wakes early. His body clock has reset and more often than not he's now up before the sun. Tara didn't have a good night, restless and wakeful, so he's careful not to disturb her as he climbs out of bed. The rain patters against the window, tapping out a rhythm, the heavier drops from the gutter onto the porch providing a base beat. He grabs his jeans and T-shirt off the floor. Bends for his boots with yesterday's socks tucked into them, then pauses at the door of the nook and sees Skye sleeping deeply, arms thrown up in surrender, covers awry, pyjama top ridden up to expose her soft tummy. She looks so vulnerable his heart skips.

The house is still. Sasha raises her head with mild interest as he walks past her in the hallway where she sleeps on a folded blanket.

'Want to come?' he whispers, as he opens the door. She takes one look outside, at the heavy, rain-laden sky, and lays her head back down in answer.

There's no movement from Bruce and Anne's caravan. They'll be awake soon though. Bruce likes to get the bread on in good time so it's ready for breakfast. The rain hammers the corrugated barn and the wind pushes through the copse. The weather stings his face. It feels good. He feels alive. He climbs the stile and is welcomed by the now familiar shapes of the moor – the pillows of grass, rocks, dense parcels of vegetation – otherworldly, today, in their shrouds of grey.

Each day he pinches himself. He can't believe he lives here. The moor has burrowed inside him, knotting its fingers around his innards, claiming him as a part of itself, like the buzzards and wildness and changeable skies. This is the closest he's felt to belonging. He cannot imagine ever leaving.

As a child he spent all his time outside, building dens, wading in the river, lying belly-down in the long grass watching rabbits scamper in and out of their warrens. He finds solace in nature. Proximity to wildlife grounds him. His father – whose only interest in animals was served on a plate or viewed through a gunsight – never understood this side of his son. He thought him soft, abnormal, his love of animals something to be dealt with. When Kit was twelve, his father decided to take him on a hunting trip. Kit thrummed with anticipation on the journey up to Scotland in his father's beloved Bentley. Spending time with his distant father seemed exotic and he basked in the glow of unfamiliar attention. They stayed in an ostentatious, chintzy hotel and woke at the crack of dawn. His father's hunting friends greeted Kit with enthusiastic claps on the back and promises in stereo that this would 'make a man of you, young Balfour'.

'See him?' Kit's father handed him the binoculars as they lay side by side in the undergrowth.

Framed in the lens was a stag. Kit's heart raced; he'd never seen anything more spectacular. The men around them whispered. Guns were raised. The stag turned its majestic head. Its eyes locked on to him. For a moment they were connected. A split second later two shots ripped the morning stillness apart and the stag crumpled.

Kit screamed. 'No! What did you do? No!'

'For God's sake, child,' his father hissed. 'Stop whining like a pathetic girl.'

They'd trekked over the tufted grass to where the stag had fallen. The animal lay still, glazed eyes fixed on the sky, mouth open in a noiseless cry, a ragged bloody hole torn into his side.

Kit shook with the effort of controlling his emotions, which would do nothing but anger his volatile father.

'Pull yourself together.' His father's words were heavy with disgust. 'You're humiliating me.' He thrust his hand deep into the gaping wound of the stag. 'It's time to grow up, boy. You'll be blooded, a rite of passage, boy to man. Christ knows you need it.' Then he dragged his hand, warm and sticky with the felled deer's blood, down the length of Kit's face.

They drove back to the hotel in stony silence.

'You useless *shit*!' his father shouted, when Kit climbed out of the Bentley. 'You've got blood on my ruddy upholstery. Clean the damn car!'

Kit cleaned every inch of it, crying and scrubbing and saying sorry to the magnificent stag over and over and over, while vowing never to kill another animal again.

Back at Ashbarton Coombe, Kit lit a fire in the corner of the garage next to the Bentley, then climbed his tree house to watch it burn. To his disappointment, Patsy noticed the smoke and the fire brigade were called. But not before the Bentley was destroyed. Kit had been unable to contain his glee as he watched his father weeping on his knees beside the blackened car, wheels melted, windows shattered, his face smeared with black.

The rain has eased to a drizzle by the time Kit arrives back at the farm, though the sky remains dark and threatening. Bruce is sitting on the steps of his caravan, a mug gripped in his hands, jacket on, hood up. When he sees Kit he raises a hand in greeting.

'You're up early,' he says, as Kit nears. 'Peaceful out there?'

'Beautiful.'

'Not many places better in the world than this spot.' He blows across the top of the mug then sips.

Skye yells a greeting from the front door and runs into his arms. She makes a face when she realises how wet he is, but in her excitement it's quickly passed over. 'The goats are coming, Daddy! It's *today*!'

'Are they?' He feigns surprise. 'I'd forgotten.'

'Yes they *are*! It's the best day!'

Kit carries Skye into the kitchen and finds the others eating toast and drinking coffee.

'He's not back,' Tara says, as Kit kisses her. 'I can't believe he'd miss the animals arriving.'

Jeremy left for London a few days ago, though none of them know why. Kit hasn't given it much thought, but Tara is more curious and hasn't been able to let it go. 'I don't understand why he slipped away without saying anything,' she'd said. 'It's so odd. Are you sure he didn't tell you why he was going?'

Kit had shrugged. 'Just that he wouldn't be long. I know Mary needs a few bits from Baldwins. Distilling equipment and some oils. Maybe he's picking that up?'

'Seems a long way to go for supplies. I'm sure they'd have posted them.'

Kit had smiled. 'Remember it's Jeremy we're talking about. Since when did he do anything the normal way? He's probably got something else he needs to do at the same time. You know, kidnap the Prime Minister or burn Parliament down.'

'I still don't get why he'd miss such a big day.' As Tara sips her coffee, he can see her thoughts turning over.

'I wouldn't think too hard about it. To be honest, he's not that fond of animals. Welcoming goats probably isn't on his list of priorities.' Skye taps him and he turns to see her offering him a bite of her bread and jam. He grins and takes a bite. 'Mmm, that's good.'

She skips away to offer a bite to Bruce.

'When do you want to leave?' Anne asks him.

'Wouldn't mind changing out of these clothes and having a quick wash. Say twenty minutes?'

When they get there, Anne insists the two goats are fine to travel in the back of the Land Rover, but they aren't as convinced, and as the farmer looks on with undisguised amusement, the two of them coax the animals towards the vehicle and, with considerable effort, sweat, a lot of swearing and the odd head-butt, finally manage to heave them in one at a time. Once safely loaded the goats seem to accept their fate and travel with their heads between Kit and Anne, gazing out of the rain-spattered windscreen, mesmerised by the wipers and Kit's jumper, which they tug at periodically.

They park up in the yard and Kit grins as he opens the rear door. Skye is ready to explode with excitement. Sasha starts to bark maniacally as soon as she sets eyes on the goats and Dean grabs her collar and holds tightly as she pulls and strains against his grip, deaf to his attempts to calm her.

'Guess I won't be letting her off around them until they've made friends.' Dean clips her lead to the collar and hauls her over to the sheds where he attaches her to one of the metal tie rings. He ruffles her neck, but she's too focused on the goats to notice. The goats don't seem bothered by her as they gaze around the yard and assess their new surroundings. The snow-white goat with a pink muzzle and blue eyes is the bravest and hops out onto the cobbles as if she's been travelling in the back of a Land Rover for years. The second, black and brown with dark brown eyes, follows hesitantly. Anne talks softly to them while shaking a bucket of feed and walking backwards towards their enclosure. The goats need no encouragement and follow the bucket as the rest of the group move behind them, arms outstretched, encouraging noises coming in unison, until the newest residents of Winterfall are safely shut in their paddock.

'So,' Anne says, smiling at Tara and Skye. 'We all had a chat last night, and we decided Skye should choose their names.'

'Me?' Skye looks overwhelmed, as if she might cry. Kit smiles at her and lifts her onto the wall. He wraps his arms around her waist so she can't fall and they watch the goats explore their new home oblivious of the rain which has started up again. They gambol around, every now and then stopping to snatch a mouthful of grass, then giving a joyful hop and skip.

'That one is Snowy.' Skye jabs the air in the direction of the white goat then looks at the other. 'We already have Blackie the hen.' Skye thinks hard, her brow crinkled with the effort. 'Rosie?' She looks at Kit for affirmation.

He nods. 'Good names.'

Skye looks at Anne, who smiles. 'Snowy and Rosie. Perfect.' Skye claps excitedly and laughs as Snowy spins a circle and bumps into Rosie.

'They're pretty settled,' Anne says, after they've watched them a while. 'Let's get out of this rain. In the morning we'll get some milk off them.'

Bruce lights up with the promise of milk, and while they're warming up with cups of sweet tea, he talks them through what the new arrivals will bring to the table. Each of the girls should yield between four and eight pints a day.' He grins. 'We can make custard and yoghurt, delicious with stewed fruit when the berries appear, and until you've eaten homemade goat's cheese sprinkled with salt and pepper with slices of fresh-picked cucumber you've not lived.'

Everybody slopes off for a rest after lunch before afternoon jobs. Kit loves this time of day. The household is peaceful, with full bellies and pleasantly weary from the morning's work. It's been six weeks and they've settled into a comfortable routine. Though Skye's never been one for naps, she looks forward to this quiet time, happily curled up on her bed, looking at a book or chattering away to her soft toys.

Kit sits in the battered armchair in their room, sanding the knife handle he's making. It's a labour of love. The wood taken from the first tree he felled at the farm. He is hoping to have it finished for Skye's birthday. Tara is staring out of the window, rivulets of rain streaking the glass, the wind rattling as if knocking gently to come in.

'He's back.' Her fingers absently graze the window.

Kit doesn't look up from his sanding. The handle isn't the right shape yet and he's finding it frustrating. He sands away at a bump and blows away the dust.

'There's somebody in the car with him.'

Kit looks up at her. 'Who?'

Tara squints and leans nearer the pane. Her breath blooms on the glass and she wipes it away with her sleeve. 'It's hard to see with the rain. They're still in the car. A woman, I think?'

Kit places the wood and sandpaper on the floor and joins her at the window. He looks down at the van. His view is distorted by the rain, which makes it hard to distinguish the figures inside. But, yes, Tara's right. There's a woman in the car.

'I don't recognise her.'

Jeremy gets out and walks to the back of the van and opens the door. He reaches in for a small holdall. Then moves to the passenger door and opens it. They watch him talking to whoever is in the front seat, hand outstretched.

Then the woman emerges from the van. Except it isn't a woman.

'Oh my God,' Tara whispers. 'She's a child.'

The girl is petite, dressed in jeans and battered trainers, white with a green stripe, and a grey overcoat, which swamps her frame. She stares at the house, her body language hesitant, then glances over her shoulder as if looking for an escape.

Kit runs from the room. What the hell is going on? Why has Jeremy shown up with a stranger? A child?

By the time he reaches the front door Jeremy is walking in. But the girl isn't following. She is frozen to the spot. Eyes fixed on the upstairs windows.

'Who is she?' Kit mouths.

'I'll explain.' Jeremy looks at him briefly then turns back to the child. 'It's OK, Dani. Come in out of the rain.' He gestures at the girl, beckoning her as if coaxing a timid animal.

Kit steps nearer to Jeremy and leans close to his ear. 'What's going on?'

Jeremy smiles at the girl, a blanket of calm draped over him. 'Dani needs somewhere to stay. I said she'd be welcome here with us at Winterfall. I said we'd look after her.'

CHAPTER TWELVE

Dani,
April 2002

One thing Jeremy didn't tell me was how in the middle of nowhere the place was. I followed him off the train. The station was tiny, just two platforms, a brick hut for a waiting room, and a covered wooden footbridge over the railway line. There was a family making a racket screeching and hugging and jumping around a woman with two huge red suitcases and a bright green umbrella. They scurried out of the rain in a bustle and the station fell quiet, just us and two seagulls fighting over a crust of bread. Did seagulls mean we were close to the seaside? He hadn't mentioned that.

We half-ran through the car park in the rain and stopped at a battered old van with some shadowy letters on the side spelling out the name of a window cleaning company. I don't know what I was expecting him to drive, but it wasn't that. He didn't look like a window cleaner. He grabbed my bag and threw it into the back and I wondered if next week the newspapers would be plastered with some grainy last-seen-alive picture of the shadowy shape of me climbing into this shitty van being watched by the shadowy shape of a does-anybody-know-this-man? I got into the van anyway because I had no clue where I'd go if I didn't, then we drove for what felt like hours, and turned up a bumpy lane which had no painted lines, no street lamps, and not a single person in sight. Everything was grey. Even the greens. It was nothing like the photograph. Where were the bright colours and sunbeams? It was muddy and grim and there was nobody to hear me scream. My heart was thumping fists against my ribcage. I glanced at Jeremy, who was whistling happily while tapping the steering wheel with his fingers, which only made my heart thump harder.

I was going to die.

'Are we nearly there?' My voice was weak and scratched against my parched throat.

He smiled and slowed the van then turned the wheel. 'We are.'

Seeing the house did nothing to calm my heart down. It was huge and old and without doubt riddled with ghosts. The rain had got even heavier. There were puddles all over the cracked yard which was a sea of weeds. There was a sad, wet dog – the one from the photograph I guessed – huddled in a doorway of a stone shed, attached to a rope which was tied to the wall.

I'm not going to lie, if Jeremy had shown me a photograph of this gloomy spook-house, I'd have stayed on the streets in London and taken my chances with the perverts and bins.

'I think I made a mistake.'

'You're bound to feel nervous.'

I dropped my head and stared at my hands as I pulled at my fingers aggressively.

'It doesn't look its best in the rain. That's all. Let's get inside. Find you some food. You must be hungry.'

He was right. I was starving and dog-tired. He'd told me to get some sleep on the plastic seats at Paddington, but I hadn't even managed five minutes, then by the time we sat down in the more comfortable seats on the train, I was way too wired. I'd had no sleep for two days and my body was screaming.

Jeremy got out of the van, opened the back for my bag, then came round and opened my door.

'Come on,' he said. 'It's OK.'

It was the opposite of OK. I wanted to cry. This was the worst mistake of my life. As I climbed out, something caught my eye above me. I looked up and saw a woman watching me from one of the windows. I stopped dead in my tracks. A flash of fear skated over me. Was it a ghost?

'That's Tara,' Jeremy said. 'The woman with the ribbons in the photograph?'

The woman turned away and melted into the shadows.

Jeremy opened the door to the house. A man with scruffy blond hair and clothes that needed a wash was in the hallway. He stared at me, then looked at Jeremy, confusion all over his face.

Jeremy turned and smiled. 'It's OK, Dani.' He flicked his fingers a couple of times to encourage me in. 'Come in out of the rain.'

The man fell back into the darkness as if he'd been swallowed whole. I closed my eyes as a tumbling fear curdled my stomach like old milk. I tried to make my brain work. Tried to work out what else I could do. If I ran away, where the hell would I go? I didn't even know the name of the station we came into. I had no choice. I had to follow him. But as I stepped forward my knees buckled. Oh God. What was I doing?

'This is the main house,' he said, as I hovered beside him.

This was insane and the opposite of what Mum meant when she told me to keep safe.

'Most of us sleep here. Anne and Bruce, who you'll meet in a bit, have a caravan in the field.'

He disappeared down the dim hallway, pointing at a door on the right as we passed. 'The dining room. We eat dinner together every day. It's nice to gather to discuss what we've got done and plan the following day. When the evenings are warmer we'll eat outdoors.'

My stomach cramped as the woman from the window appeared on the stairs. She smiled as she came down. I tried to return it, but my face was paralysed.

'Dani, this is Tara.' Jeremy smiled at us both.

All I could do was stare at her. She was amazing. A hippie queen with hundreds of long, thin braids gathered loosely in a bright purple ribbon, a rainbow of other colours woven into the plaits and beads threaded through the ends. There was a silver ring through the middle of her nose. She wore red and orange billowy trousers and a white vest top with no bra. She had no shoes on and her toes sparkled with silver rings.

'Hello, Dani.' Her voice was warm and soft. It reminded me of Mum.

He took me into a large kitchen. Pots and pans and boxes of vegetables all over the place. There was a sack of flour in one corner and a pile of wood near an ancient-looking cooker. Despite the chaos, the smell was warm and sweet and made my stomach growl. The scruffy blond man was busy cutting a slice of bread. He put the bread on a plate then reached for a large jar.

'Jam?'

I managed to nod and he spooned a large dollop of jam the colour of Mum's wine on to the bread and used the back of the spoon to spread it. He pushed the plate across the table towards me. I took my coat off and searched for somewhere to put it.

Tara held out her hand. 'Here,' she said. 'I'll take it.'

My cheeks flushed hot and I dropped my head feeling the sting of tears. I reached for the bread and took a bite. The bread was soft and fluffy, and the jam had whole strawberries in which tasted like sweets. My stomach cried out with joy as I swallowed.

Two people walked into the kitchen then. A giant man with a crazy beard and brown leather skin, and a slim woman with shoulder-length mousy hair, wearing a grey raincoat, jeans, and black rubber boots. She carried a bowl of different coloured eggs which she put on the table.

'Hello.' A beautiful smile cut her face in half. 'A guest. What a treat!' Then she put her arms around me, too quick for me to back away. 'I'm Anne.' She gestured at the hairy man with her, dressed in a thick green sweater with patches on the elbows. 'This is my husband, Bruce.'

'You do the cooking.' The words fell out of my mouth before I could stop them.

Bruce laughed and his eyes crinkled. 'How did you guess?'

I glanced at Jeremy. I felt as if I'd been caught spying and shame warmed my cheeks.

'Did he tell you about my flapjacks?' Bruce's smile widened. 'I took some out of the oven an hour ago. Want one?'

I hesitated then nodded. The thought of a flapjack popped the bubble of tension in my body and allowed a little to leak away.

'You're honoured.' Jeremy laughed. 'Bruce usually guards his flapjacks with his life until teatime.'

Bruce put a square of flapjack on the plate next to the bread and jam and winked at me.

'So, Jeremy, how do you know Dani?' Tara was smiling, but I could hear the real question which hid behind her fake one: *Who the fuck is Dani?*

'It's a long story, but the short version is Dani needs a place to stay.'

'Just for a few days,' I mumbled.

'You can stay as long as you want. Isn't that right?' Jeremy cast his eyes around the others, who didn't immediately reply. I could see they had questions. I broke off a corner of flapjack. It was sweet, sticky, and delicious, but as I chewed, eyes fixed on the plate, I was aware of them mouthing things at each other, gesturing, trying to talk without me hearing. My skin burned.

'Tara,' Jeremy said at a normal volume. 'Can you show Dani where the bathroom is, then up to the attic rooms. Dani, you probably need a rest? You must be shattered after a tough few days. There's time to meet the others later on.'

I was glad I didn't have to deal with anybody else right then.

My head was jumbled and achy, stuffed full of names and emotions already. It would burst if I tried to fit anything more inside. I picked up the flapjack and followed Tara out of the kitchen and up the staircase. There were no lights and it was all very dark. The stairs and banister had thousands of tiny holes spattering them and there were patches on the walls where the plaster had fallen away. Halfway up the staircase was a dusty window, which let in a smear of murky, grey light.

At the top of the stairs, Tara pointed out a door on the right up ahead. 'Kit and I sleep in there. With our daughter, Skye. She's having a rest at the moment, but I'll introduce you later.' Then she pointed to a door opposite. 'Jeremy's in there. And this is the bathroom.' She pushed open the door nearest her and tutted under her breath. 'It needs a clean. Sorry. It's Ash's job this week. I'll remind him.'

The bathroom smelt damp and was littered with towels. The old blue basin was streaked with toothpaste and the mirror was crying out for a polish.

I walked in and closed the door and gripped the sides of the basin with both hands.

'At least you haven't been murdered yet,' I told my reflection.

My reflection wasn't convinced, which was fair enough. It was early days and there was still the possibility this house a million miles away from anywhere was filled with smiling psychopaths who wanted to cut me up and bake me into a pie. I lifted the seat of the toilet and drew back at the sight of the bowl. It needed a good bleach. I thought of Mum in her Marigolds, loo brush in hand, and felt the thud of homesickness. I wished she was with me. I pictured her singing along to the radio, using her bottle of bleach as a microphone, wiggling her hips as she scrubbed at the bowl.

I washed my hands and looked for a clean towel, but in the end I wiped them on my jeans then gingerly opened the door.

Tara smiled. 'The rooms upstairs are pretty basic. There's a sleeping bag and pillow. They're clean. We picked up a load of things like that from charity shops.' I followed her up a narrow staircase which was even darker than everywhere else. My heart started up again. I tried to make myself feel better by reminding myself attics weren't half as terrifying as basements.

'Bad things happen in attics as well as basements, *idiot*,' said the unhelpful voice in my head.

Tara filled the silence with words as we walked. 'In the mornings we grab breakfast from the kitchen. Bruce wakes up early to bake the bread and cake, so he can show you what there is. At lunchtime he puts a few bits and pieces – bread, cheese and salad, some apples, that kind of thing – out around midday. Again, help yourself. Supper is at six.'

She pushed open a door on the right at the top of the stairs. The room was small with a sloping ceiling and a window set into an alcove. There was a mattress on the floor on which was a flat pillow on top of a folded green sleeping bag. There was no carpet, only bare, unpolished floorboards and no curtain at the window. It smelt damp and the air was stuffy.

'It's not usually this gloomy.' She tried to smile but didn't find the energy. I would have bet everything I had – which wasn't much – that she wanted to race back down to fire questions at Jeremy. 'The window looks over the moor. When the sun is out it's brighter in here.' She hesitated. There was a look on her face as if something was hurting her. 'I can see you're tired, but are you … OK? Is there someone we should call? Your mum? Dad? Anybody else?'

Tears sprang to my eyes and I shook my head, chewing frantically on my lower lip to stop from crying.

'Oh, Dani.' She reached out to touch my arm. 'Look, I'll leave you alone for now. Maybe we can talk later?' She stepped closer to me. 'You're safe here. And if you want to get back home, we'll help you. Try not to worry.' She walked towards the door then paused, hand resting on the doorframe. 'Shout if you need me. I'll hear you from our room.'

I was sick with tiredness and the jitters but, as Mum told me all the time, crying wouldn't help anybody. I stood in the centre of the room, listening to her feet on the stairs, then inhaled deeply and let my breath out slowly as I took in the room. There was nowhere to put my clothes, so I put my bag beside the mattress and lay down. My brain was whirring. Despite everybody telling me I was safe, I didn't feel it. I stared at the door. Half-expecting it to open any minute. I got up to lock it but there was no key, so I moved my bag in front of the door. I knew it wouldn't stop anybody getting in, but it was something and, to be honest, I was past caring. I was shattered. If I didn't sleep soon I'd probably die of tiredness and do the psychos' job for them. I climbed into the musty-smelling sleeping bag and zipped it up to my chin.

The next thing I knew I was being shaken awake. My head was groggy, stuffed with sleep; it took ages to work out where I was, and that it was the woman called Anne who was trying to wake me.

'Sorry. I didn't mean to startle you. But you've been asleep all afternoon and we're about to eat. Do you want some dinner?'

I blinked slowly, trying to drag myself from sleep, and she waited while I crawled out of the sleeping bag. I didn't want to leave the room. The thought of having to see people gave me the fear, but I was hungry. The flapjack hadn't even touched the sides. So I followed her downstairs, mute and churning with nerves, the noise from the dining room building like thunder.

We stopped outside the door. 'It's like the first day of school, isn't it? But you've nothing to fear. Everybody's lovely.' Then she smiled.

The dining room was large and painted a powdery blue with black beams and a fireplace with a fire crackling in the grate. The table was the longest I'd ever seen and made of very dark wood. The room flickered with candles and old-fashioned oil lamps which sent shadows dancing around the walls.

Everyone stopped talking when I appeared in the doorway. I hovered there, not brave enough to follow Anne in, knees trembling. This was nothing like the first day at school. It was a billion times worse. One by one, the faces grew smiles. Seconds later, the room erupted. People stood. Chairs scraped against the stone floor. The air filled with hellos and welcomes and so-nice-to-meet yous. The smiles grew wider and toothier. The only person who didn't jump up was Tara who sat and chewed anxiously on the side of her thumb. There was a child on her lap. The little girl from the photo with her golden curls and button nose. She whispered something in her mother's ear. Tara smiled and stroked her forehead, sweeping the mass of unruly curls off her cute-as-a-puppy face.

'This is Dani.' Jeremy's voice yanked me away from Tara and her daughter.

The grinning people formed a semicircle around me. The muttering stopped and the room was still, the volume turned all the way down so my own breathing became deafening.

'Dani will be staying for a while and I hope you will all go out of your way to make her feel welcome. Dani,' Jeremy swept his arm around the circle. 'This is our Winterfall family.'

I wanted the floor to swallow me in one greedy bite. This was worse than reading from *Jane Eyre* in class. Worse than waiting to be picked last in PE. Something began to tighten around my chest.

'Anne and Bruce you've met already.'

Their smiles grew bigger. Then their faces blurred until all I could see were the smiles. I tore my eyes from them, but then realised it was the same with the others. Blurry faces with enormous smiles. I wanted to run, but I was nailed to the spot. They introduced themselves one at a time in a nauseating Mexican wave. The names flying in and out of my head too fast for me to grab hold of.

A man with shoulder-length brown hair and a grey T-shirt. 'Hi Dani. I'm Dean. Welcome to Winterfall Farm.'

Then the scruffy blond man. 'I'm Kit. Hello again.'

Then another. Long hair, tied back. Wispy hair on his chin. *I'm Ash. Welcome...*

The room was an oven. Baking hot. No air. My head spun as I tried to breathe in. The cords around my chest tightened, squeezing my lungs so they couldn't inflate.

I'm Mary...

The faces mushed together. The smiles merged as if made of Plasticine and invisible hands were squashing them into a big mess.

I was going to throw up.

I whipped around and pushed past Jeremy. Acid puke burned my throat. I wrenched open the front door and tore across the pitch-black yard, stumbling through puddles I couldn't see, tripping over stones. I reached a wall and grasped it with both hands. My head swirled as I pulled as much cold air into me as I could.

I wanted Mum. Was she looking for me? Had she thrown Eddie out? Why had I come here? Because a handsome man bought me a milkshake and showed me a photo?

What was wrong with me?

A hand on my lower back startled me. It was Tara. She was holding one of the old-fashioned oil lamps like Florence Nightingale, her face glowing in the soft orange light. She smiled, not in a manic way, but gently, reminding me of the nurse at school who gave out cough sweets no matter what you went to her for.

'Maybe you should sit down?'

I did as she said and slid down on to the damp grass and dropped my head between my knees. When the faintness eased a bit, I looked up and nodded.

She was crouched in front of me, the lamp on the ground. Even in the half-dark I could see the worry on her face. She held a mug out towards me. 'Water?'

'I don't know what happened,' I whispered, taking the mug. 'It was hot in there. I'm sorry. I—'

'You have *nothing* to apologise for.'

I looked back towards the house. 'The others aren't coming are they?'

'I said I'd check on you. Told them you needed space.'

'I shouldn't have come here.'

'That's OK. You can go back, but best to leave in the morning. It's late. If you leave now you'll arrive in London after midnight. Rest here tonight. I know you must be scared, but you're safe, I promise. We'll get you on a train tomorrow.' Her tone was motherly and her words soothing. 'I'm concerned you haven't eaten. Are you hungry?'

I nodded.

'I'll get you some food.'

'I don't want to go back in that room.'

'You don't have to. Eat in our room if you want? Or the attic. I can leave you alone or sit with you. Whatever you want.'

It was then the little girl appeared, skipping through the darkness to stand beside her mother. She leant against Tara and absently took hold of one of her plaits and fiddled with the beads while she watched us.

Tara smiled at me. 'This is Skye.'

'Is the girl sad?' Skye whispered.

'A bit.'

Skye made a sad face and reached out to rest her hand on my cheek. 'I'm four,' she said, holding out her other hand, five fingers splayed.

Tara laughed and took her daughter's hand in hers. 'That's five fingers. Four is this many ...' She carefully folded Skye's thumb down, then leant forward and kissed it. 'Four.'

Skye held her hand out again, managing to keep her thumb tucked. 'I'm this many. How old are you?'

'Me?' I glanced at Tara. She was staring at me. Eyes asking questions again. My stomach clenched. 'I don't have enough fingers to show you.'

Thankfully, a bark from the shadows interrupted us before Tara had a chance to push me on an answer.

'Shit. Dean's left Sasha out. Hang on, I'll check the animals are locked away then untie her. Skye, will you look after Dani?'

Tara disappeared into the darkness and the dog started barking excitedly.

'Do you like stories?' Skye asked. She was a perfect doll with huge eyes and smooth skin, dressed in dungarees and adorable red wellies.

I nodded and her eyes lit up. 'You can hear the story my daddy reads. My bedtime one.'

Tara came back with the dog bouncing at her heels.

'Poor love,' Tara said. 'We got goats today and she isn't used to them yet, so Dean tied her up but obviously forgot her.'

'I'm a bit scared of dogs,' I said, as Sasha pushed her nose into me.

'Sorry.' Tara pulled on her collar and heaved the dog away from me. 'She's a big softie.'

'Mama,' said Skye. 'Dani's going to hear my story with me.'

'We'll have to choose a good one then.'

Skye slipped her hand into mine and we walked back to the farmhouse with Sasha bounding ahead. As we passed the dining room, I dropped my head and hurried on. I sat with Skye in her small sleeping area and she introduced me to her soft toys while Tara went to find me a plate of food. She brought up a cheese sandwich, an apple, another square of flapjack, and two mugs of sweet milk, one for me and one for Skye. She didn't ask any difficult questions, just sat there with no expression while Skye chattered and I stuffed the food down.

When Kit appeared I tensed. It was hard to look him in the eyes. I wished I was somewhere with Tara and Skye and nobody else. He sat on Skye's mattress, his back against the wall, and began to read. Skye nestled into the side of him, her thumb in her mouth, staring at the pictures in the book. His voice seemed to relax me, and it wasn't long before I was pulled into the underwater world of *The Water-Babies*. I felt a jab of disappointment when he finally closed the book. I'd never had a bedtime story before.

'Do you want me to come upstairs with you?' Tara asked as I stood up.

I shook my head but nerves jangled in my stomach. I felt safe in this cosy space and would have liked to sleep there instead of alone in the attic with its weird smell and rattling window, but I wasn't brave enough to ask.

Someone, Anne I guessed, had placed two oil lamps and a little jar of flowers on the window ledge. But it didn't make me feel at home. If anything it made me lonelier. I lay on the mattress and wriggled all the way into the sleeping bag, until my head was covered. My breath heated up the dark space and, like I used to do when I was little and Eddie was banging about the place, I imagined I was a rabbit in a hole, hiding from a bloodthirsty fox.

Don't make a sound.

Don't move a muscle.

Don't even breathe.

My stomach didn't get the memo and rumbled angrily. Despite the cheese sandwich I was still hungry. I thought of the skeleton man rifling through the bins in London. Was he still there? Had he moved to a new bin? Had he starved to death? I shuddered.

Then I heard footsteps on the stairs.

The footsteps – Tara's, I assumed – walked up to my bed.

'Dani?'

My heart skipped a beat. It was Jeremy. I emerged from my cocoon and sat up.

'I wanted to have a quick word.'

He held a plate in one hand and an oil lamp in the other. He sat on the floor beside the mattress and crossed his legs.

I nodded.

'Tara says you want to leave in the morning.'

My skin flushed. I was unable to look him in the eye.

'We overwhelmed you downstairs. That was my fault. I'd asked them to give you a proper welcome, but I can see how daunting it must have been.' His hand reached out and rested on mine. 'I want you to be happy here. Do you understand?'

I could only nod. My voice had dried up.

'Give us a chance, Dani. This place is different to everything else you know. Of course you're unsettled. It's to be expected. Especially after the difficult time you've had. I can see bad things have happened to you. That you've been let down. Abandoned. But this farm can become your home.'

His words settled in my head like a layer of snowflakes making everything clean and still.

'You can leave whenever you want, but maybe give it a few days?' He smiled then reached into his pocket. He held a train ticket out towards me. 'This is the return part of your ticket. It's valid for a year on any train back to London. You keep hold of it. You can leave any time.'

I stared at the ticket, then at him. Then I reached for it before he could change his mind.

'Treat being here like a holiday? Sleep, eat, rest. Then you can work out what you want to do.'

His eyes dug into me. I'd never had a holiday before. I recalled how he'd rescued me from the pervert and how good that milkshake tasted. He was right. Everybody else had turned their backs on me. But not him. He'd taken care of me.

'No need to decide now. But at least think about it?'

After he left, I slipped the ticket into the inside pocket of my bag with my last thirty-seven pence, and crawled back inside the sleeping bag. 'Yeah,' I whispered. 'A holiday sounds nice.'

CHAPTER THIRTEEN

Tara,
April 2002

Jeremy rubbed his face, weary of the conversation. It was obvious he wanted to be elsewhere. 'I hear what you're saying, but I don't think putting her back on a train to London is the right thing to do. There was no way I could have left her. She was cold, starving hungry, and being preyed on by a middle-aged creep trying to pick her up for money.'

Anne, Bruce, and Kit were sitting with Jeremy and me around the dining table. Mary, Dean and Ash had gone up to their rooms. Sasha was asleep on the floor in front of the fire. I wasn't comfortable with the situation. Jeremy shouldn't have brought somebody into the group without consulting us, but the fact that the person was a vulnerable and obviously disturbed child? It was unacceptable. Jeremy, however, didn't seem to see he'd done anything questionable at all.

'I'm exhausted,' he said. 'I got no sleep last night. Can it wait until the morning?'

'I'm sorry but I don't think it can. She's a child. You can't just bring a child here.'

He hesitated. 'She said she's sixteen.'

I shook my head. 'There's no way she's sixteen.' I leant forward and put my hand on his. 'Her parents will be beside themselves.'

'Not from what she said. She told me her mum threw her out. A drug addict. Said her dad's dead.'

'She could be lying.'

'Why would she lie?'

I sighed and leant back in my chair. 'Then we need to call the authorities.'

'And have her taken into care? How is that better? The state won't help. She'll be shoved into an institution and forgotten about. Surely it's our moral duty to look after her? Dani needs us. She's had a tough time, but we can look after her and nurture her. We can make a real difference.'

'This isn't about us. We have to do what's best for her. You shouldn't have brought her here.'

'I didn't have a choice.'

'We're going round in circles. You *did* have a choice. Of course you did. You shouldn't have brought anybody here – let alone a *child* – without discussing it with us first.' The others wore blank, non-committal expressions. Even Kit. 'Am I the only one who thinks this is wrong?'

Anne was fingering the charms on her silver bracelet. 'I can see what you're saying.' There was a tremble in her voice. 'But Jeremy's right. She's safer here than where she was. And maybe that's the most important thing for the time being?'

I chewed my lip. 'I think it's more complicated,' I said.

Jeremy murmured something then tipped his head back as if looking for answers in the cracked plaster above.

'I'm sorry. Honestly, I'm not trying to be difficult. I know you wanted to do the right thing and God knows she needs somewhere to go. Poor kid looks as if she hasn't eaten or slept in weeks. But we can't take a child off the street and bring her here without telling anybody.' I scanned their faces, searching for signs they understood what I was saying. 'I mean, couldn't it be seen as kidnapping? If her parents have reported her missing and the police find her here, could we be prosecuted for abduction? Kit?'

Kit hesitated. 'Look, we can't do anything more tonight. We'll talk to her in the morning. Get a clearer picture of what's going on. Maybe she had a fight with her parents and, yes, now they just want her home. But maybe it's more sinister.' Kit smiled at me and took my hand. 'You're asking the right questions, but let's get the facts first. If she wants to go home, one of us can take her back on the train or take her home or call her family and talk to them.'

Anne cleared her throat and pursed her lips, her face betraying uncertainty. Whatever she was about to say clearly wasn't easy for her. 'I was about the same age when I got out,' she said quietly. 'Not long turned sixteen.'

Bruce closed his eyes, his face contorted as if he was feeling himself the pain she was reliving.

'Back then every part of my life was controlled. I wasn't allowed friends outside of the group. *Bad associates*, they called them. Wasn't allowed to stay for after-school clubs. I made the athletics team but wasn't given permission to train.' She smiled. 'I was a good runner, too. One of the fastest in my year. My teacher even wrote to them, but they wouldn't hear of it. My father was a powerful and violent man. He'd beat us with a belt for any transgression, however small. Whatever we did wrong we got the belt. One strike for knocking a drink over. Ten for talking back. I'd spend hours dreaming of escape. I packed a bag with clothes, a bit of money, and a toothbrush, and hid it under my bed. It would have been the belt if they'd found it, but the comfort of knowing that bag was there would help me sleep anyway.' She paused and smiled again, but then some distant memory surfaced in her mind and diluted the smile to nothing. 'I began to hate my mum. Surely, I thought, if she loved me, *really* loved me, she'd speak up against my father? But she believed he was right. That our way of life was the only way and if we didn't follow the rules we were sinners. Well, I rebelled. If I was going to be a sinner then I was going to jolly well sin. Smoking. Drinking. Sex with boys in the toilets at school. I did it all. My father heard about it from one of the others who told on me. When I got home from school he hit me with his belt so hard he tore the ligaments in his shoulder. While he was crying out in pain, I grabbed that bag of mine and I ran.' For a moment she was lost in the recollection, then she smiled at Bruce. 'I was lucky. The parents of my best friend let me stay with them. They protected me when my father came for me. They fed me and put me in touch with people who could give me advice. Helped me find my wings. Then I met Bruce.' She smiled again. 'And he showed me what love was.' She cast her eyes around the table. 'If I hadn't been brave enough to run, if those people hadn't taken me in, who knows how many more scars I'd have.' Anne's story echoed around the dining room and I dropped my head. She leant forward and put her hand on my knee. 'You're right to worry. You are. But maybe this child needs us. Sometimes children are failed. Failed by their parents. Failed by the state. Kit's right, we should talk to her tomorrow, but if she needs refuge then I think we need to do what we can to help.'

I couldn't sleep that night. This wasn't unusual. I'd been living with insomnia since my late teens. My brain would start racing and once it was off there was little I could do to rein it back. That night it was jammed full of haunting pictures of Skye. As I listened to Kit's steady breathing, the owl hooting outside, the wind rattling the window in its frame, I tried to push the black thoughts away. But it was impossible. Every time I closed my eyes I saw her huddled on the streets, scared, alone and hungry. The image was unbearable and my heart went out to Dani's mum. Whatever had happened, the poor woman would be mad with fear. *I'll look after her*, I promised the woman in my head. *I'll make sure she's safe.*

Then I heard Dani's door. Her feet on the stairs. I presumed she was going to the bathroom, but her footsteps descended the main staircase. I jumped out of bed and followed, my immediate thought that she was running again, but as I came down the stairs I heard a noise in the kitchen.

'Are you OK?' I whispered, as I walked in.

She jumped and turned. Her shocked face was lit by the moonlight which came in through the window.

'Sorry,' I said. 'I didn't mean to startle you.' She was dressed, but I couldn't see her bag anywhere. 'Are you leaving?'

She seemed surprised by the question. She shook her head. 'I'm hungry,' she whispered. 'You said help myself. I'm sorry if—'

'Sit down and I'll make you something.' I smiled and gestured at one of the stools.

As she moved past me to take a seat I caught the smell of her. Unwashed hair. Deodorant covering faint body odour. The hint of cigarettes.

I lit the oil lamp and the soft light filled the centre of the room and sent the rest into shadow. I opened the door to the stove burner and added two logs, and the glowing embers crackled as they leapt up to lick the wood. 'Are you cold?' I said. 'If you are, it's warmer over here.'

'I'm fine.'

'What do you feel like?'

She shrugged and picked at a splinter of wood on the table.

'Beans on toast?'

Dani's face lit up. 'You have beans?'

I laughed. 'For special occasions.'

I went to the store cupboard and rifled through the tins of soup and corn and tomatoes and found a can of beans, then tipped them into a pan, and lifted the lid on the stove. 'It takes a bit longer to heat up on this.'

'That's OK. I can't sleep.'

'Me neither.'

She wrinkled her nose and made a face of shared commiseration. I cut a slice of bread and took a toasting fork off the hook on the wall behind the oven. Bruce had fashioned a few from lengths of stiff wire held together with twine to form a handle, the end splayed like the tongue of a snake. 'Want to toast it? We've no electricity, so no toaster. You have to do it on the fire.'

Dani furrowed her brow in confusion, then pushed herself off the stool and came over. I pressed the prongs into the soft centre of the bread and handed her the fork.

'If you pull that chair over – careful, not to burn yourself on the door – then hold the bread near the fire. Don't put the bread right into the flames. Not unless you want beans on charcoal. You need to watch it like a hawk. Once it's started to turn it can burn in moments. When one side's done, take the bread off, turn it and do the other.'

'Cool,' Dani whispered.

I smiled.

'I thought I heard voices.' Kit was standing in the doorway in his T-shirt and tracksuit bottoms, hair stuck up in random directions, rubbing sleepy eyes.

'Sorry if I woke you.'

He shook his head. 'Making toast?'

Dani nodded but didn't take her eyes off the bread.

Kit and I watched her tuck into the beans on toast. She shovelled the food in as if she'd never had a meal in her life. My heart ached for her. I couldn't stop thinking about her poor mother. I imagined her consumed with fear, a myriad of horrific scenarios battering her sleep-deprived mind.

'This is good,' she said with her mouth full as she chased the last few beans around the plate with her fork, leaving orange snail trails in the flickering lamplight.

When every last bit had gone, she pushed the plate away and sat back.

'Better?'

She nodded.

'Still hungry?'

She hesitated. 'Maybe? What else is there?'

'Cake?' Kit said.

Her eyes lit up. 'Will Bruce mind?'

'No,' Kit said gently. 'He won't mind a bit.'

I was hit by an overwhelming love for Kit then. How different he was from my own father, a man who valued propriety over kindness, who believed children were *women's work*.

Kit retrieved the cake tin from the cupboard. Inside was the unfinished carrot cake from the day before, rich and moist, peppered with swollen sultanas, Christmas spices, and flecks of carrot, wrapped in brown paper and tied with string to keep it fresh. Kit unwrapped the cake and cut three slices.

Kit smiled and took a bite. Dani hesitated then tucked in greedily. I picked at the last slice, my eyes fixed on Dani, unable to ignore the foreboding which churned in the pit of my stomach.

CHAPTER FOURTEEN

Kit,
April 2002

Dani is monosyllabic when she finally comes out of her room. The more relaxed child wolfing down beans and carrot cake last night has withdrawn into her sullen teenage shell. Tara and Jeremy sit at the table with her. Kit leans against the stove while Mary potters in her cupboard, mixing oils and filling the kitchen with the heady scent of rosemary.

Dani is adamant she wants to stay. Stiff nods. Grunted yeses and nos. Eyes locked on the bread and jam she's eating for breakfast.

'Can we call someone?'

A shake of her head.

'We'd feel happier if we did. Are you sure you don't want to call your mum? Just to tell her you're safe?'

Tara's desperation tugs at his heart. To the outside world she's a rebel, but the unconventional clothes and hairstyle tell a lie. Tara isn't a rule-breaker. She likes to do the right thing. She is responsible. Every decision she makes is governed by the potential ramifications.

'No.'

'A grandparent or a teacher you trust?'

Another shake of her head.

'Can you tell us why you ran away from home?' Tara winces

as the question leaves her mouth. Kit can tell how frustrated she is by trying to get Dani to open up and failing. He gives a reassuring smile, but she doesn't smile back.

Jeremy whispers something in Anne's ear. Anne glances at Dani then nods.

'Dani, love?' she says. 'Would you like a cup of tea?'

Dani nods and Jeremy gestures to the rest of them to follow him. They leave Anne bustling about cheerily, filling the kitchen with singsong chatter, and follow him into the dining room. Jeremy closes the door behind them.

'I think we should leave this for now.'

'But—'

'When she's ready to talk, she'll talk.'

Tara's face is pale with anguish.

Kit rubs her shoulder. 'Honestly, nobody is going to say we've done the wrong thing by giving her somewhere safe to sort herself out. Give her some space and time and she'll open up, and when she does we can help her decide what to do.'

Tara is chewing on the edge of her thumb. 'What if it was Skye who'd run away and we didn't know where she was?'

'Then we'd be grateful that people took her in and took care of her until she felt ready to come home.'

Tara's eyes flicker as she takes in his words.

'Give it a few days.'

Tara sighs then nods. 'Fine,' she says. 'We'll try again in a day or two. But if I could get a message to her mum, I'd feel happier.'

Mary nods. 'I think that's right. In the meantime, I'll give her a few drops of lemon balm tincture. It's wonderful for anxiety.'

Jeremy walks over and puts his arms around Tara. 'We're doing a good thing. If we can help Dani we are making a real difference.'

Tara nods and pulls away. She smiles but Kit sees the doubts still bubbling away beneath it.

'Will you join Mary and me for a meditation?'

Tara laughs and shakes her head. 'No, I'm good. I'm going to take Skye for a walk. I promised her we'd look for tadpoles in the stream.

'Maybe tomorrow then.' Jeremy smiles. 'I think you'd find it beneficial.'

Kit is splitting logs up at the wood store and listening to Tara and Skye, who are on the other side of the wall in the orchard. They are spraying the gooseberry plants with a concoction of garlic, vegetable oil, and washing-up liquid which Mary swears will keep back the army of tiny creatures intent on destruction. Tara is teaching Skye how plants use sunlight and water and the colour green to grow. As usual Skye asks a ream of questions and Tara patiently answers them all, engaged and interested, dropping in information hidden in did-you-knows and you'll-never-guesses where she can. Watching Skye absorb the world around her is Tara's passion. She isn't driven by self-sufficiency or trading with locals or communal living; for her it's the opportunity to educate Skye in a creative, enriching environment. Out beyond the walls of Winterfall, Skye would be starting school in September. While Kit has battled doubts about home-schooling, Tara is adamant. For her school was dry and dull, a chore rather than enjoyable, made unbearable with her parents breathing down her neck. Micromanaging her time. Writing weekly emails to school for 'clarification'. Dissecting every comment at parents' evenings, analysing her reports, demanding she explain the lost ten per cent rather than congratulating her on the ninety she achieved.

'I don't want that for Skye,' she'd said to Kit. 'My imagination was squashed. My stories were an exercise in semi-colons not colours. I want her to be driven by creativity and curiosity. What good is learning by rote? By constant comparisons to others, to the class average, the national average, and league tables? Children should be free to learn at their own pace, to explore what fascinates and moves them. And no child needs bloody exams. Forcing individuals to sit standardised tests and using the results to pigeon-hole them. I love her company. Why would I want her to spend most of the day away from me? Having her home from a full day exhausted and crabby. And if she's here she gets to learn skills: cooking, looking after animals, learning about the world by experiencing it.'

When Kit finishes stacking the freshly split logs, he walks into the orchard. Dani is sitting near them, knees drawn up to her chest, her heavy grey coat swamping her. Mary is tying the sprawling French beans to bamboo canes with green twine. Skye has given up on the spraying and is holding a large stone, watching a snail crawl slowly over it.

'Daddy, can you see his shiny path?' She tilts the stone and points at the snail as Kit draws near.

He crouches down and stares at the snail with its bright yellow shell decorated with a perfect geometric spiral.

'And look,' she whispers. She holds her finger gently in front of the snail's horn then touches it lightly. The horn retracts like a spring and she squeals with joy.

'How about a walk before lunch?' Kit calls over to Tara.

'Lovely. Fancy that, Skye? Dani?'

Dani looks at Tara and shakes her head.

'Why don't you stay and help me wash the sheets if you don't want a walk?' Mary says, smiling at her.

It's obvious from the mild horror which spreads over Dani's face that the idea of doing laundry with Mary is even less palatable than the thought of a walk.

'We won't go for long.' Tara gives the gooseberry bushes one last spray, then walks over to them. 'Maybe we'll find the ponies?'

Dani shrugs and gets to her feet, kicking the soil with the toe of her trainer.

Tara tries hard to make conversation as they walk, but Dani is unresponsive. It's as if the more Tara talks the more Dani shuts down. Kit wants to tell Tara to relax. Dani reminds him of himself at the same age. Adults were the enemy. But Tara is trying so hard and he doesn't want to interfere, so instead he walks up ahead with Skye. His daughter's patter is in direct contrast to Dani's monosyllables, each utterance unconnected to her last, a tumbling cascade of childish consciousness. They cross a narrow bridge of half-rotten timber planks which straddle a small stream. Skye stops to throw a few stones into the water, then skips over the bridge and grabs Kit's hand again.

Though yesterday's rain has moved on, the sky remains overcast and a mantle of mist hovers over the moor. As they walk out from the shelter of the lee of the hill the wind picks up and whips at their skin. Dani pulls her coat tight around her body and scans the moor, her eyes darting left and right in staccato. 'It all looks the same.' Her voice wavers with uncertainty. 'What if we get lost?'

'We won't get lost.' It's only been six weeks, but already he knows this part of the moor. He's even become familiar with the more unusual tufts of grass or clumps of vegetation, using them as markers, along with standing stones and stacks, even the undulations of the ground, to guide his way to the various views which steal his breath.

Dani tightens her arms around her body and glances back in the direction they've come.

A little further on Kit hears the distinctive *kee-yaa* of a buzzard. A pair of them are circling above, their outlines shadowy through the gauzy mist. As Dani and Tara stop beside him he points upwards. 'See the buzzards?'

'Where, Daddy?' He scoops Skye up, leans his head against hers and points.

Dani squints and searches the sky.

'They're birds of prey.' Kit suspects Dani hadn't come across many buzzards in the concrete jungle of London. 'Until not long ago they were endangered.'

'How come?' Her eyes are now bolted to the circling birds.

'Years ago they were shot on sight by gamekeepers to stop them getting the pheasants and grouse. There were fewer than a thousand breeding pairs in the whole country. There's plenty now. I think those two have spotted something to eat.'

Kit scours the moor beneath the buzzards and catches a flash of white nestled in the muted green, resembling an item of discarded clothing. He squints through the flat light trying to identify it. It's only when he gets near he sees it's a lamb, unmoving. He crouches to study the pitiful creature, the remains of the membrane covering half its face in a sweep of grey muslin, blood and yellow mucus slicking its body.

'Ugh,' breathes Dani, as she draws up beside him, her face twisted in disgust. 'What is it?'

'A lamb.' Tara speaks with soft reverence.

Kit rests the flat of his hand on the lamb's body. The whorls of wool are sticky and damp. Still warm. No more than a few hours old. Kit scours the moor for signs of its mother, but there are no sheep to be seen. He drops his head and allows the sadness to wash through him.

'Poor thing,' Tara says.

'What's the gunk on it?'

'The birth sac. Where it—' Then Kit feels a stirring in the feeble body.

'Its eyes moved,' Skye says as she runs forward two steps and drops to the ground. She puts her small hand on the lamb's head. 'Hello?' she says. 'Can you hear me?' Then she turns to Kit, eyes round as saucers, smiling. 'It's not dead, Daddy!'

'It will be soon, angel.' Kit strokes the hair from the side of her face and tucks it behind her ear.

'But it moved.'

Kit gives the lamb's body a rub but there's no response. He stands and takes Skye's hand and moves backwards, his eyes on the motionless creature.

'Are you leaving it?' Dani's voice is riven with horror.

'There's nothing we can do for it. The farmer will find it.'

'No!' Skye's eyes fill with tears and she tugs on his hand. 'Daddy!'

'It's as good as dead already.' He picks Skye up and kisses her cheek, but she pushes him away. 'It's too weak,' he says. 'It won't make it.'

'Can we give it milk or something?' Dani asks. 'They eat milk, right?'

He looks back at the lamb, limp and fragile, a matter of minutes – if that – from death. 'It hasn't a chance,' he says, taking his sweater off. 'It's too far gone.' But despite his conviction he bends down and lays the sweater on the grass and carefully lifts the lamb onto it.

The lamb twitches.

'I knew you'd save it, Daddy.'

Kit glances over his shoulder at Tara, who gives him a what-can-you-do shrug and smiles. He shakes his head as he swaddles the lamb, wrapping it snugly, then cradling it close to his chest.

'Don't get your hopes up.'

As they walk back towards the farm, Kit rubs the lamb to get some warmth into it, glancing down every so often to check for signs of life or death. Though there's no movement, he can detect faint, rasping breaths.

'Why did the mother leave it?' Dani asks.

'Can't say for sure. Maybe a first-time mum with no maternal instinct. Didn't understand what she was supposed to do. Or maybe she knew the lamb was too weak to survive after a difficult birth.'

Dani walks close to Kit, her gaze fixed on the lamb. If nothing else it has distracted her thoughts from whatever she's run from.

'Do you want to hold it?'

Dani steps sideways away from him with comedic panic. 'Hold it? What if I hurt it?'

'What are you going to do? Drop-kick it?'

Dani stares at the lamb warily.

'Can I, Daddy?'

'Dani first?'

Skye's mouth turns upside down, but Tara ruffles her hair and bends to whisper something and Skye nods. Kit gently places the lamb against Dani's chest. 'Cross your arms, one underneath it. Like this ... The other holding it against you.'

Though unsure, Dani does as Kit instructs and folds her arms around the lamb as if it might crumble to dust.

'OK?'

Dani nods, not drawing a breath, never taking her eyes off the near-dead lamb nestled against her chest.

When they get back, Anne springs into action.

'We'll try and get some colostrum replacement into him.' Anne strokes the lamb's nose with the edge of her thumb as Dani holds it. 'Getting him warm and something in his belly is pretty much his only hope.'

'What about some Recuse Remedy?' Mary says. 'We can put a couple of drops on his tongue. Ginger and honey won't go amiss, either.'

'Well, it can't hurt, but first we need a warming box,' Anne says, acknowledging Mary with a smile. 'Someone will have to watch him. We don't want him getting too hot either.'

'I will,' Dani says.

There is a glimmer in the girl's eyes. Kit knows Anne is as doubtful as he is about the lamb's chances, but it's unspoken between them that there's no harm in trying, if only to keep Dani engaged.

'What about one of the apple crates from the barn?' Ash says. 'Any good for a warming box?'

'Perfect. If you can line it with straw, lovey, that would be great. A nice thick layer.'

'Sure.' Ash wanders out, taking a roll-up cigarette from behind his ear and pulling his lighter from his pocket.

Kit stokes the fire while Tara pulls up a chair for Dani and Skye leans over the lamb, stroking its forehead and muttering encouragement.

'Is it still alive?' Dani asks quietly.

Kit crouches beside the chair and places his palm on the lamb's chest. 'He's hanging in there. But I don't—' He stops himself. 'Let's keep our fingers crossed, shall we? He's a fighter.'

As he watches Anne make the colostrum replacement, Kit envies her knowledge and experience. She pours some long life milk into a pan she sets on the stovetop, then puts two teaspoons of sugar into a mug.

'Skye, sweetheart. Can you pass me two eggs?'

Skye runs to the larder and appears moments later with eggs which she hands over very carefully. Anne separates them into two bowls and put the whites to one side. 'Bruce will make some lovely meringues with that.' She winks at Skye, who claps gleefully, then tips the yolks into the mug and mixes them with the sugar. Then she dips her finger into the pan of milk. 'Needs to be a shade warmer than body temperature.' She pours the warm milk into the mug and stirs vigorously. 'I doubt the lamb got any colostrum from its mother, which they need as soon as possible,' she says to Dani as she crouches beside her. 'This isn't the same, but there's goodness in it.' Anne smiles at Dani. 'First I need to give him a good rub. Skye, will you hold the mug?'

It moves Kit to see how intently the children watch every move Anne makes. He is struck once again by what a privilege this life is for Skye.

Anne talks under her breath and peels back the folds of the sweater. She rubs the lamb vigorously.

'Isn't that too rough?' Dani asks.

Kit wonders the same.

'It won't hurt him,' says Anne as she rubs. 'Mum should've licked him clean to get his heart pumping.'

The lamb responds to the rubbing by opening his eyes a fraction. It's not much but enough to make Dani gasp.

'Now the milk,' Anne says softly.

She holds the lamb's head vertical, palm supporting his throat so she can deliver spoonfuls of the sweet mixture into its mouth. As she pinches open its jaw, the lamb struggles weakly.

'That's good, right?' Dani asks. 'That he's fighting?'

'That's good.'

On the first couple of attempts, the milk dribbles out and runs over the lamb's velvet muzzle, but on the third he seems to understand and his lips make tiny instinctive suckling movements.

'That's it,' whispers Anne. 'Good lad.'

She feeds it another spoon of the butter-coloured liquid and this time the lamb swallows and as it does its eyes flicker again.

'He's drinking it.' Skye's whispered words are threaded with wonder.

'I hear we've found an orphan,' says Bruce, as he walks in through the kitchen door.

It might have been Bruce's voice or perhaps the sugary milk has hit the animal's bloodstream, but the lamb replies with a feeble bleat.

'Mama, he talked!'

'Does that mean he's going make it?' Dani asks Anne.

'It means he's a step closer than when you found him. I'd say you two are his guardian angels.'

Dani and Skye smile at each other and Kit's stomach pitches.

'He needs a mum,' Anne says, as she gives him another spoonful. 'He won't last on long-life cow's milk.'

Dani strokes his head, softly, as if caressing the finest glass. 'Come on, little one,' she whispers. 'You can do it.'

'I'll take him back to the farmer.'

'But he's ours!' Skye cries. 'We love him!'

'He needs a sheep mummy,' Tara says, stroking Skye's hair.

'I'll take him now. Does one of you want to come with me? I need someone to hold the lamb in the Land Rover.'

Skye throws her hand up excitedly.

'I think we someone a bit bigger. In case he wriggles.'

'What about you help me milk the goats?' Anne says quickly.

Skye's eyes light up.

'Maybe you could go with Kit?' Tara says to Dani.

Dani looks uncertain but then glances at the lamb and gives a nod.

The farmer is in the large open-sided barn on the main yard shaking feed from a dirty yellow bucket along the metal trough for the heifers who have their heads thrust through the railings and are greedily eating. When he hears the Land Rover he looks up.

Kit cuts the engine and raises a hand in greeting.

'Bring the lamb,' he says to Dani as he steps out of the car and on to the mud. The stench of cows and silage is heavy in the air.

A scowl blooms on the farmer's face and Kit knows he's made the link between these two new faces and the 'Winterfall hippies'.

Kit straightens his shoulders and strides confidently towards him, offering his hand. The farmer hesitates, palpable distrust in his rheumy eyes, then gruffly shakes it, squeezing harder than he needs to, a warning rather than a greeting. He's in his sixties at least, tall and well-built with deep lines folded into his rugged skin displaying years at the mercy of the moorland weather like the rings of an oak.

'Found a lamb on the moor.' Kit nods back towards Dani. 'One of yours, I think. Mum nowhere to be seen. Looked dead but, well, seems he's not ready to go just yet.'

The farmer walks over to Dani and reaches out a calloused hand and roughly grasps the lamb's face, turning it left to right. 'It's a dead one.'

'No. No, he's alive!' There's a lightness in her voice, as if she expects this revelation to surprise and delight the farmer. 'He moved so we gave him special milk and he drank it.'

'Shouldn't have bothered. Won't make it. I've no time to be nursing a sick one. Let it down there.' The farmer gestures to a corner of the slurry-slicked yard. 'I'll see to it after I've fed the cows.'

'You mean kill him?' Dani's eyes widen and she turns her shoulder away to shield the lamb from the farmer's murderous intentions.

'It's nearly gone.' The farmer's voice has softened a fraction. He holds out his hand, beckoning for the lamb.

Dani shakes her head.

'Give him the lamb.' Kit curses inside. Of course this would happen. He never should have brought Dani with him. He should have come here alone. Given over the lamb to its inevitable fate. Then lied to the girls. Told them the farmer was overjoyed they'd saved it and that it was already frolicking in the fields with the other lambs.

'No.' Dani glowers at the farmer, the belligerent teen act back in force.

'Give the farmer his lamb, Dani.' His voice is harsher than intended and Dani turns her glare on him, before spinning around and marching away from them, past the Land Rover and down the track.

Kit swears under his breath.

'She's taken to it?'

'She's not had it easy. Difficulties at home.'

The farmer takes his cap off and smoothes his yellow-tinged snowy hair before repositioning it. 'I haven't the time to care for a dead lamb.'

'I know.'

'Should've left it where it were.'

'I know that too. Like I said, she's had a tough time, and up on the moor, when we found it, I didn't want to upset her, that's all. I should have been stronger.'

The farmer watches the retreating figure of Dani in her grubby jeans and trainers, drowned in her heavy coat, feet stomping. 'Wait a sec,' he says to Kit and walks off in the direction of the barn.

Kit hesitates, wondering if he should be following Dani, but then the farmer reappears carrying a large bottle fixed with a grubby rubber teat in one hand, and in his other an old carrier bag. He holds both out towards Kit. 'Bring the bottle back when you're done. The powdered milk you can keep hold of or ditch.'

Kit stares at the gifts as if it is some sort of test.

'I can see what it means to the lass. If it survives the night, bring it back and we'll try and find it a ewe. I've got some girls I'm keeping an eye on in the barn. Due to drop in the next day or two. Might be I can persuade one to take the little one on. I've a couple expecting singles.' He pauses. 'If it dies, tell her she did nothing wrong. Just what God intended.'

The two men hold each other's gaze and an understanding passes between them.

Kit takes the bottle and carrier bag, and nods. 'Thank you.'

'And, well, it's ...' The farmer's eyes wander, skin visibly pinking at the collar, as he shifts awkwardly. 'My wife said I should've given your friends a better welcome when they came by. She says I'm too harsh with my words. Expect she's right.' He looks Kit briefly in the eye and gives a tight smile. 'Think we should start afresh.'

Kit smiles. 'We'd like that.'

One of the heifers bangs the rails. The farmer glances back at it before returning to Kit. 'If the lamb sees morning bring it back.'

Kit slows the Land Rover as he draws alongside Dani. She refuses to look at him. Instead she walks faster, eyes fixed stubbornly ahead, cradling the lamb beneath her chin.

'Get in the car.'

'No. You're going to let that man kill him,' she says angrily.

'I'm not.'

She slows a little and casts him a brief glance.

'He gave us some milk and a bottle. He said if it's alive in the morning he'll find it a mum.'

Dani stops, but seems to hesitate, regarding Kit warily. He wonders how many times in her life she's been let down or lied to by adults.

'I promise you. We're going to try and save him, but we need to get some milk inside him quickly. So jump in and let's get back and get a bottle made up.'

Dani keeps hold of her glower as she relents and walks round to the passenger side. As Kit drives back to Winterfall she huddles over the lamb, whispering to it, too quiet for him to make out what she's saying. He thinks again of the look on her face. Distrustful. Guarded. The sadness which clings to her tugs at his heartstrings. What has she run from? His heart aches for her.

He will never let anything bad happen to Skye.

Never.

CHAPTER FIFTEEN

Dani,
April 2002

'You know what will help?' said Mary, as Anne made up the bottle of milk. 'Some ginger and peppermint oils rubbed onto the little poppet's chest and tummy.'

Mary, I'd decided, was mad as a box of mental frogs. I also was pretty sure, though nobody had actually said, that she was a witch. Maybe not an evil witch but a witch. It was the long white hair and the way she sung everything she said and all the potions and jars of God-knows-what.

'Really?' Tara's face made it clear she didn't think oils would help the lamb at all.

'Ginger is marvellous for introducing heat, and mint, well, *mint,*' Mary said, in her creepy singsong voice, 'is just about the most wonderful thing in my cabinet and will help focus his energy on getting better, as well as being *excellent* for reviving the spirit. Mint tea is delicious, but I'm not sure it mixes well with milk. Oils are best here.'

Mary disappeared and a few moments later there was a clinking and jangling then she reappeared with two glass bottles with cork stoppers. Both had a yellow oil inside, one straw-coloured, the other dark gold. When she pulled the cork from the darker one the smell hit my nose in seconds. Warm and spicy as Christmas. Mum bustled into my head. The two of us walking down the High

Street to buy crackers, mince pies, and port. Her humming out of tune to the festive music pumping out of the shops.

Mary rubbed some oil onto the lamb's chest leaving a bright smudge on his wool. She did the same with the other oil, but she put that on his throat and between his front legs, and the smell of toothpaste overwhelmed Christmas.

Anne tested the temperature of the milk on her inner arm, same as a real baby, then sat in a chair and held the lamb tight. She lifted his head up again and then opened his mouth by shoving a finger into the corner. 'We have his head up, the bottle too, because we don't want air bubbles.'

The lamb struggled weakly and I had to bite my tongue to stop myself telling her to stop. Anne knew what she was doing and I didn't fancy her turning around and snapping at me to do it myself if I knew so much. The lamb didn't drink at first. It turned its head away and kept its eyes closed, as if all it wanted to do was sleep like cretin Eddie after a night on the booze. My stomach clenched with fear. Were we too late? Had the lamb given up and checked out already?

Anne moved the teat around the lamb's mouth and then, a proper miracle, he opened and gave it a suck.

'That's it,' said Kit, who was standing behind me.

Anne pushed the teat gently in and out and just as I thought he was about to spit it out and give up, he began to suckle. As we watched he got more into it, as if he'd finally remembered how to do it, his little nose puckering up with each suck.

'Come on, lamb,' I whispered. 'You can do it.'

'He's drinking his dinner,' Skye whispered loudly.

I glanced at her and grinned, and she clapped.

'Well done, love.' Bruce bent to kiss the top of Anne's head. The tender way he touched her sent a jealous taste creeping over my tongue as I thought of poor Mum's busted lip and cretin Eddie calling her a fat, lazy bitch. I pushed the miserable cretin from my head. I didn't want him there.

Mary boiled water for a hot-water bottle, which she then wrapped in a woollen scarf. 'If we put it in the box with him' she sang, 'he might think it's his mum.' Then she sprinkled the straw with dried mint as if she were about to cook him.

Kit stoked the fire so it was toasty and warm and within moments the lamb was fast asleep, smelling of Christmas and toothpaste, its belly full of milk. Everybody crowded around, staring down at him. It could have been a scene from a school nativity. All of them smiling, lit up from inside, as if the lamb drinking milk had switched them all on. Eddie would think they were nuts.

Soon they moved away to get on with making dinner. I sat with the lamb and stroked his sleepy face, listening to them as they talked and joked. Nothing they were saying made any sense. They might as well have been speaking a foreign language. They were so different to me. Different to the people I knew from Leyton. A million miles away from Mum and cretin Eddie.

Jeremy and Kit were talking about when they met. Everybody was listening.

'I knew I wanted to be friends with him when I found him building a bonfire in the middle of the night in the rose garden. He'd stapled a photocopy of Thatcher's face to a dummy and was trying to balance her on a pile of furniture.'

'He asked whose furniture it was. And I said it was mine.'

'Then I asked why he was burning his furniture and he said, "I don't need furniture."'

'And you nodded and said "Nothing as good as a massive bonfire" and asked if I wanted any help finding more things to burn.'

'Which,' Kit said. 'He did.'

'Did you get caught?' Mary asked.

'No. But the idiot here handed himself in.' Kit laughed. 'He thought they'd kick him out which he thought would be cool. Finishing university was far too pedestrian for a rebel of such calibre.'

Jeremy laughed and gave a nod of agreement as he raised his beer bottle in Kit's direction. 'As it turned out, the Dean was a raving leftie who loathed Maggie and when I told him it was me, he gave me a pat on the back and said, "Nice work, Ballard. Of course, the university want you to face some sort of punishment, so you'll be serving drinks and canapés at the Young Conservatives meetings for the rest of the year in lieu of prosecution and a hefty fine."'

Everybody laughed, but I didn't know why. I didn't think burning a picture of Margaret Thatcher was that funny, but maybe I missed the punchline. The only thing I knew was I was a red ball in a box of blue fish. Out of place. They all knew each other. Shared jokes I didn't get. They were relaxed in each other's company. Jeremy was right. This *was* a family, but I didn't belong.

Suddenly, and overwhelmingly, I wanted my mum.

As the thought wriggled into me and took hold, I pictured Eddie finding out I'd gone. I saw his white-knuckled fists. I saw Mum huddled in the corner as he stood over her. I saw that lip of hers splitting open again and again and again like scratched vinyl. What would he do to her? Who was going to give her headache pills when he beat the crap out of her? How could I have left her there? I should have tried harder to take her with me. She should be here with me. Away from that arsehole. There was room in the attic for her, and though she hated animals and the only gardening she'd done was a pot plant once which she killed by overwatering, she was very good at cleaning. There was no way that toilet would stay stained.

The panic that made me faint when I arrived snuck back in. I tried to remind myself why I was here. How hungry I'd been. The sound of Eddie punching Mum in the face. The smell of hot, moist alcohol fumes when he breathed on me. The care home stuffed full of rapists. But it didn't work. Thinking about the bad stuff, the reasons I'd said yes to Jeremy and got on the train to Cornwall, didn't stop me missing my mum.

I crept over to Tara and bent close to her ear. 'Can I talk to you a second?' I whispered, my voice shaky.

She said something to Kit and he took hold of Skye, who scrambled happily off her mother's lap on to his, then she led me out of the kitchen.

'What's up?'

'I miss my mum.' I dug my fingernails into my palms to stop myself crying which usually worked, but when she put her arms around me I couldn't help it and burst into tears like a baby.

'It's OK, Dani. Shush. It's OK.' Her voice was honey. 'Shall we call her? There's a payphone down the lane.'

I wiped my eyes and dropped my head. 'I'm ... not sure ...'

'I think you should. You don't need to tell her where you are, not if you don't want to, but if you hear her voice you might feel better. Maybe she'll tell you to come back? Or she might want to come and get you?'

I pressed my sleeve against my eyes to blot the tears which kept on coming, and nodded.

Tara walked down the lane with me. We didn't talk, but I let her put her arm around my shoulder. When we reached the phone box, she pulled open the door and handed me fifty pence. Then she smiled and nodded with encouragement. 'Go on, you'll feel better.'

My heart raced as I dialled. 'Hello?' My knees buckled when I heard her voice. 'Mum. It's me.'

'Dani? For God's sake, why are you calling?'

Hearing how cross she was shocked me. There wasn't one bit of joy in her at all. It was a punch to my stomach.

'I told you not to call,' she growled through gritted teeth.

I glanced at Tara who smiled and gave me a thumbs up through the glass door. I turned my back on her to shield my face. 'I miss you,' I whispered.

Then she made a weird squeaking sound. A split second

afterwards I heard Eddie in the background. Though I could hear his voice, I couldn't make out what he was saying.

'Of course it's not her,' Mum said. 'It's a wrong numb—'

Then smack. She cried out. The phone clattered on the floor. I didn't need to be there to know what was happening. I could see it all vividly. The backhander he'd given her. Her head twisting with the impact. Her skin blooming purple. Another split lip.

'Danielle? Is that you? You ungrateful bitch.' All his words were mushed into a drunken mess.

I knew I should put the phone down, but I couldn't. Horror turned the blood in my veins to ice and froze me rigid.

'It's you, isn't it? You little cunt. You think you can run away from *me*? That's what you think? Steal money, piss off, then come begging when you've had enough? That's not happening. We're done with you and your whiny bitching.'

Mum was sobbing in the background. He swore. Then another thud. A smack or a kick? Hard to tell. She stopped crying.

'Listen here. If I so much as see your ugly face anywhere near here I will *kill* you. You hear me? I will kill you both. First you. Then your bitch mother. I'll fucking kill you both. I swear to—'

I hung up.

My heart banged in my chest. Insects crawled over my skin. I closed my eyes and breathed deeply as I took in what had just happened. Mum didn't want me back and Eddie said he'd kill me if I showed up. If it was a choice between being killed by Eddie and having to eat Bruce's fresh bread for every meal and bottle-feed lambs I knew what I was choosing.

I pushed open the phone box. 'Can we go back now?'

'What did she say?' Tara walked beside me, jogging to keep up with my marching. She was desperate for me to talk to her, but I didn't want to. I kept my eyes down and my mouth shut, and focused on blocking out the sound of cretin Eddie's slurring threats.

'Dani?' Tara grabbed my arm and pulled me to a halt. 'What happened?'

'Nothing. It's fine ...' But I couldn't finish my sentence as snotty tears bulldozed my words away. I turned my head upwards, towards the sky, and tried to stop but they kept coming. She took hold of my hand and shook it gently. I lowered my eyes and stared at her.

'What happened?' she asked again, her voice soft.

'I can't go home,' I whispered.

She paused. 'How old are you, Dani?'

My stomach flipped over.

'Why does it matter?'

I dropped my head and kicked at the road, wiping my nose with my sleeve.

'Jeremy said you're sixteen. You're not though, are you? Sixteen is young enough. But if you're younger? It matters.'

Heat spread up from my chest to my cheeks.

'I'm not going to be cross or anything, but I need to know how old you are.'

I wiped more tears with my hand and looked back down the lane towards the payphone. 'Fourteen.'

She didn't answer immediately. I crossed my arms and stared at her. 'What?'

She sighed and shook her head. 'Look, I don't know what your mum said. I don't know what you're fighting about, but you're too young to be here.' She reached out and touched my arm, and I recoiled from her tenderness. 'You need to be at home with your parents. You need to sort it out, whatever it is. You need to go home.'

The word *home* was a poison dart. It hurt. I shook my head. Pursed my lip and made my eyes hard. 'I hate her. I don't know why I said I missed her. She's a screw-up. I'm not going back. You can't make me. I'll run away again if I have to.'

As I stared at Tara, with her doubtful face and her candy-floss eyes and creamy skin, her pretty features and cool, edgy hair, I realised she wasn't going to let this go. She was going to carry on trying to make things better until she made things a thousand times worse. I could see it in her eyes. She was the helping type. A know-it-all do-gooder, cretin Eddie would call her. She had the same soft smile as the volunteers at the community centre and the mums who came in to read with us in primary school, all kind and patient as I struggled with Biff and Chip while their own child powered through all the *Harry Potter*s. She wasn't going to let this lie and as much as her heart was in the right place it was going to do my head in. She didn't know the first thing about me or my life or who was missing me or who would kill me if I went back. It was time she heard a few truths. Maybe then she'd back off.

'Mum doesn't want me back because it was Mum who threw me out.'

Tara's face fell.

'She gave me twenty quid and her winter coat and told me to leave.'

'Because you had an argument?' She frowned softly. 'Look, parents and teenagers argue all the time. I was always fighting with my mum. But whatever happened, whatever you said to each other, I'm sure she wants you home.'

'We didn't have an argument.'

'I don't think—'

'Please *stop*!' My hands flew to block my ears. I squeezed my eyes shut as anger boiled over inside me. 'My stepdad was going to *rape* me. OK?' Nausea rumbled inside me as I said the words aloud. I kept my eyes rammed shut so I didn't have to see her horror or, worse, pity. 'Mum managed to stop him but then he went for her. Beat her up. Bust her jaw. Broke the bone near her shoulder. Split her lip in half. Then he stormed out and went to the pub and she told me to leave before he got back.' I slowly dropped my hands and opened my eyes. I couldn't face looking at her so I fixed my gaze on the fields behind her. 'That phone call just now? It was him. He screamed. Called me names. And … he said … if I go back—' I stopped talking to try and keep fresh tears from coming. 'He said if I go back he'll kill me and then he'll kill her. And he's not lying. I know him and he's not lying. He's *mental*. A mental psycho *cretin*. Do you get it now? I *can't* go back because if I do, I'll be *dead*.'

I almost felt sorry for her as I watched her trying to get her head around it.

'Oh my God,' she said under her breath. 'I'm so sorry.' She reached out and put her arms around me again. I resisted at first but then gave in. She smelt of earth and lavender and was warm and it felt good to be wrapped up in her. 'But it doesn't change the fact that you're a child and we aren't your guardians.'

She whispered the words but they stung anyway. Why was she still going on? Why wasn't my story enough to shut her up?

'If your mum reports you missing and the police find you here, they could say we abducted you.'

'I'll tell them I came because I wanted to. I'll say I lied about my age. Tell them about that pervert Jeremy saved me from.'

'A lawyer will say Jeremy took advantage of your situation.' She paused. 'I get that you don't want to go home, but there are people, social workers, who'll take care of you. There are places you can stay that—'

'You mean a care home? No *way*! Some kid at my school lives in one and he told us what they do to the kids. No way am I going into care. And anyway, Eddie, my stepdad, he'll find me there. If you ring the social he'll come for me.' My words tumbled out in a mess as my tummy knotted itself tighter and tighter. 'Because they will, won't they? The police or whoever. The social workers. They'll talk to him and he'll lie. He'll be all butter wouldn't melt. Because that's what he does. Then he'll threaten Mum and she'll do and say what he tells her, say everything's fine, that he's never hit her, that he wouldn't lay a finger on me. Then he'll kill us. *Please*, Tara. Please let me stay. With you and Jeremy and Skye. Here at the farm.'

She shook her head sadly. 'But you're not happy here,' she whispered.

I tried to smile at her. 'I don't think I'll ever be happy anywhere.'

I lay on my mattress and listened to the sounds of them all busying about. Using the bathroom. Chatting on the stairs. Laughing. Footsteps running up and down. Sasha's joyful barking. I figured it must be getting close to dinner time again and my tummy started bubbling with nerves. I decided I wouldn't go down. The thought of it made my chest tighten. Hopefully someone would bring food up. If not I would creep down later and search for another can of beans.

Someone, I assumed Tara, knocked and I got ready to tell her I wasn't feeling well enough to come down, but when the door opened, it was Mary's mad white-haired head which poked into the room.

'Can I come in?' she sang, as she walked through the door. She was an array of white, with a floaty top and bottoms, her amber necklace a ball of fire on her chest. She waved something at me. It was a short fat scroll of greeny-grey papery stuff tied up with string.

'Tara told us you've run away from bad people. That you were upset.'

'Oh,' I muttered. 'I didn't think she'd tell anybody.' Knowing Tara had been talking about me behind my back made me even more nervy and I kicked myself for telling her so much.

'I've got some dried sage here. I thought I'd do a cleanse to dispel the negative energy?'

'A what?'

'It's a ritual.'

'Like a spell?' My suspicions about mad Mary being a witch seemed to be right.

Before I had the chance to say no she'd pulled out a lighter and was lighting the end of the bundle. The flames took hold for a second or two then she blew on it. Sparks of fire shot out, then turned to glowing embers, and a snake of smoke rose up into the room. She waved the smoking sage around, walking it along the edges of the room, muttering, lifting it up and down and around. The smoke was thick and white and quickly filled the room, making my eyes water and my throat sting. I coughed, and she smiled at me and nodded, as if I'd done something good. Had I coughed up a fur ball of had aura or something?

'The sage will rid the negativity while you eat. When you come back up later you'll feel the weight has lifted.'

When I heard Anne calling us for dinner, I didn't hesitate to escape. Mary was still mumbling and dancing around the room with her smoke stick. I muttered something and ducked out of the room as quickly as I could. I didn't go straight into the dining room. Instead I went to check on the lamb. The kitchen was empty, thank God, and when I peered into the box, I saw the lamb sleeping peacefully. I smiled as I watched him sleeping. He looked different. Fatter. His coat shinier.

'He's done well today.' I hadn't heard Bruce come in and I jumped. 'Sorry,' he said. 'Didn't mean to scare you. I was in the larder getting the salad.'

I stared down at the lamb and watched his chest rising and falling. His nose twitched every now and then.

'The trouble with lambs is they die so easily.' Bruce smiled kindly. 'There's hundreds of things that can get the blighters. It's a miracle sheep aren't extinct. This one's doing brilliant.' He picked up a large bowl of bowtie-shaped pasta. 'Can you give me a hand? Take the salad, maybe?'

My stomach tangled with nerves again.

'Things that seem scary are never as bad as you imagine.'

I picked up the wooden bowl of salad and followed Bruce into the dining room. I paused at the doorway and peered through the gap between the hinges and frame. They were all around the table. Faces lit by flickering light from a thousand candles.

Skye waved when I was finally brave enough come out from hiding. I walked straight over to her, put the salad on the table, then sat down. I caught Tara's eye and she mouthed, 'OK?' I nodded, my whole body trembling.

'Do you want to try Dean's beer?' Mary's singsong voice danced across the table. She was holding out a bottle with some cloudy brown liquid in it. 'It's an acquired taste, but I'm sure you'll enjoy it. He makes it in his shed.'

Dean grinned. 'Most important job on the farm.' The rest of them laughed.

Mary grabbed a mug, chipped and grey with tea stains on the inside, and poured some for me. The beer smelt strong and earthy, but when I sipped it I was surprised to find it didn't taste as bad as I expected.

'It's alcoholic, so don't go crazy,' she said, topping up her mug.

After dinner, Ash picked up his guitar and started playing, and it wasn't long before everybody was joining in with clapping and singing. Except Tara who sat and stared at the candle in front of her, Skye resting on her lap, head against her mother's shoulder, windmilling a small plastic doll around her fingers.

Jeremy stood and walked over to Tara. He rested a hand on hers and at first she didn't look at him, but then he whispered something and smiled. He looked as if he was saying sorry for something. Tara stared at him for a moment then nodded her head, eyes downcast, accepting whatever he'd said with a weak smile. Jeremy patted her shoulder, then returned to his chair, clapping along in time to the guitar.

The beer seemed to have rubbed away the edges of my worry and I felt my body relax. I watched them all, trying to learn how to act like them. How affectionate they were. The way they paid attention to each other. Especially Jeremy, who sat in the corner watching us like a father and his children.

'Dani?'

Anne was at my shoulder. She smiled then crouched beside me. 'Tara told me a little about what you've been through.'

I dropped my head and chewed hard on my lip as my cheeks burst into flame. 'I wish she hadn't.'

'I think she needed to talk. She was concerned. She's a good person, Dani. Here. I have something for you.' Anne held out her hand and in the centre of her palm was a silver chain with two tiny hearts nestled in its coil. 'A friend gave me this when I wasn't in a good place. It sounds as if you and I had similar experiences.'

'It's pretty.' I didn't know what else to say.

'It'll keep you safe and help stop you being scared.'

I thought about mad Mary and the sage, the burning smell still stuck in the back of my throat. Maybe I should tell them I didn't really believe in smoky sage and magic bracelets but, before I could stop her, she was fastening it around my wrist.

'But it's yours,' I said, as she attached the clasp.

She patted my hand. 'I want you to have it.'

The bracelet was beautiful. The silver caught the candlelight and I loved how it hung on my wrist. 'To keep?'

'Until you find someone who needs it more. Then you can pass it on. But for now, it's yours.'

I tipped my wrist one way, then the other, admiring the bracelet. It was a long time since I'd had a present that wasn't a box of Milk Tray wrapped in newspaper delivered with a joke I didn't get.

'Thank you,' I said. 'I love it.'

CHAPTER SIXTEEN

Tara,
April 2002

'And you know where I am if you need anything in the night? A chat or you're scared. Beans on toast?' I smiled.

She managed a smile back. I noticed her fingers were playing with Anne's bracelet, flicking at the tiny hearts like worry-beads. I wanted to sit with her. Stroke her hair. I wanted to fill the void left by the mother she was desperately missing. The strength of maternal instinct for a child who wasn't mine, whom I'd barely spoken to, surprised me.

I think she guessed what I was feeling, maybe anticipated affection, and said goodnight then turned her back to me.

'Goodnight.' I closed the door on the smoke-scented room and went down to join the others in the dining room. Anne had given the lamb a bottle of milk and she and Bruce had gone over to their caravan. I had to admit I envied their privacy.

The others sat around the fire. Ash was strumming his guitar quietly. Dean stared at the flames, legs crossed with Sasha beside him, her chin on his knee. Jeremy was reading in the light of an oil lamp.

'All happy up there?' Mary asked as I walked in.

Happy? *No,* I wanted to say, *no, it isn't all happy up there.* 'She's fine, I think. It's hard to tell.' I hadn't been able to put Dani's phone call and what she told me afterwards out of my mind.

'She'll settle.' Jeremy didn't look up from his book.

'This isn't about her settling.' I sat down at the dining table and stared at the flickering flame of the candle nearest me. 'I still think we're making a mistake.'

'And that's your prerogative. But you said it yourself, it's not safe for her to go home. She's adamant she doesn't want to be handed over to the state and I have promised her I won't let that happen.'

I crossed my arms and sat back in my chair. He turned the page of his book, without looking up. My irritation spiked and, when I spoke, I had to work hard to keep my voice level. 'This is a community, Jay. Not your kingdom. You don't get to make any more decisions like this without us.'

'Kingdom?' He placed his book down and stared at me, dark eyes boring through me. 'When have I behaved as if it's my kingdom?'

Clearly I'd hit a nerve. That was fine; he'd hit one too.

'When you found a runaway in the city and brought her here without discussing it first?'

Jeremy held my stare and leant forward into the candlelight, which danced on his chin. 'So what do you suggest we do? Dump her back on the streets? Give her another twenty quid and wish her luck?'

'No!' Mary's eyes grew round. 'Goodness. We can't do that!'

I rubbed my face with both hands, beaten by the situation. We were damned if we did and damned if we didn't. Legally there was no leg to stand on, but morally? What choice did we have?

'No, of course we can't do that,' I said. 'I know she's missing her mum so taking her home would be the only option, but she's terrified of going anywhere near the place. God knows what kind of monster that man is.'

I reached out and pressed my nail into the top of the candle. Liquid wax flowed from the tiny gulley and burned my skin. I was aware of Kit standing and coming over, sitting on the chair beside me, putting his arm around me. I took my finger from the candle and rubbed the solidified wax away.

'Remember this is temporary,' Kit said. 'Somewhere she can rest until she works out what she wants to do.'

'And if she wants to stay,' Jeremy said. 'We'll welcome her.'

'Ash would have died on the streets if he'd stayed,' Dean said then, his hand absently caressing Sasha's fur. 'It's no place for a kid. Especially not a girl.'

They sat with their thoughts for a while, a blanket of quiet draped over them in the dimness.

'You know what we need?' Jeremy's voice was loud and bright and exploded the stillness as he slammed his book down and grinned at us all. 'Something to mark being here together. Let's throw a party!'

'I'm in!' Dean said, thoughts of Dani and Ash on the streets forgotten.

'What a marvellous idea. What about doing it on the solstice? Up at the stone circle?' Mary's eyes twinkled.

'Our first Winterfall Festival!' Jeremy's Cheshire Cat grin shone out of the darkness. 'We'll have our first crops harvested. We can prepare a feast. A celebration of everything we've achieved so far.'

Kit grinned. 'Great idea!'

As I listened to them getting excited about the thought of a party, I bit back tears. Nobody understood the unease which plagued me. I felt invisible. My voice drowned out by group consensus and the robotic repetition of Jeremy's mantra, 'She's safe so what's the problem?'

'I need some air.'

'Tara?' Kit reached for my hand.

'I'm fine. Tired, that's all. I'm not sleeping well at the moment.'

'Have I upset you?' Confusion knitted Jeremy's eyebrows together. 'We don't have to have a party.'

I laughed with disbelief and shook my head. 'It sounds great. What's not to love about a party?' Then I escaped before the tears spilled over.

I hovered at the front door and breathed in the air. It was pure and fresh like filtered water. Would I be able to smell the dirt in the air if I ever went back to a town or city? I pressed the heels of my hands into my eyes and waited for the frustration I was feeling to subside.

'Tara?' It was Kit. He drew up beside me and we stood shoulder to shoulder. 'What's up? Is there more you're worrying about?'

I looked at him incredulously. 'More than the responsibility of another child to look after? Somebody else's child? A child who's clearly suffering?'

Jeremy cleared his throat from behind us. I turned and saw him and Mary standing in the hallway. He was looking at me but she wasn't. She was gazing at him, watching him as if waiting for him to speak. It unnerved me.

'Tara, I think—'

'There's nothing more to say. I get it. Honestly, I don't want to talk about this anymore.' Then I ran out into the darkness and across the yard, and through the gate into the fields. As I jogged past the caravan I heard Anne's peal of laughter and imagined them in there, cocooned away, the two of them in their private space.

'Tara! *Tara*!' Kit called. 'Stop, will you?'

There was a weariness in his voice which dug into me. I didn't want him to be irritated or exasperated by me. I wanted him to put his arms around me and say he understood. That it was Jeremy who wasn't thinking straight. That he loved me for caring and everything would be all right.

'I'm fine,' I said, when he reached me. 'I meant it back there. There's nothing more to say.'

The sky was clear that night, the navy blue pricked with stars, the moon three-quarters full. His face was softly lit and I could see his deep concern. He reached out for me and I relented, sighing as I allowed him to pull me into him. As he stroked the back of my head and kissed the curve of my neck, the rigidity in my muscles began to melt away.

'You should have heard her talking about home,' I whispered. 'How can anybody threaten a child when she calls to say she's missing her mum?' I stepped back and looked up at him. 'Taking her in is a massive responsibility. It's not as simple as rescuing a dog from a guy in a pub or sticking a half-dead lamb in a box by the fire. I wish it were. But it's not.'

'I know that. And Jeremy knows it too.'

'Does he? Because it seems to me he isn't seeing the bigger picture. That he's only focused on being the Good Samaritan.'

Kit sighed. 'Maybe. But he told me what was going on when he found her, and I know I'd have done the same thing. You would too. He promised her somewhere safe to stay and doesn't want to go back on that promise.' A pained expression clouded his eyes. 'He reckoned the guy was going to rape her.'

I wrapped my arms around him tighter. 'Why are people such monsters?'

'Most aren't.'

But I wasn't sure. With Dani's story ringing in my ears, it felt like the good people were few and far between. The world was harsh with sharp edges and veins of cruelty which, if you tapped into them, poisoned everything with badness.

He wiped my tears away with the side of his thumb. 'You aren't. You have the biggest heart and I love you. The most important thing – something we all agree on – is that Dani is safe.' He smiled and cleared his throat. 'Will you come for a walk with me? It's a beautiful night. Skye is asleep.'

'What if she wakes?'

'Then Mary will go to her. She was the one who suggested we

get some fresh air. Said it would do us good to have a bit of time to ourselves. I think she's right.'

I nodded.

'Good.' He smiled. 'I've got something I want to show you. It's not far.'

The moon threw a dim blue light on the moor. The sounds around us were magnified. The air crisp and clear. We walked along the stream for a while, then turned up a hill, passing a looming stack of stones, then picked our way along a sheep track flanked with thick fern.

'Right,' he said. 'Jump on my back and close your eyes.'

'Jump on your back?'

'Yep!'

I laughed and clambered ungracefully onto his back. 'Don't blame me if you collapse from exhaustion.'

'Now close your eyes.'

I did as he said, resting my chin on his shoulder, his hands linked beneath me, my arms wrapped around his neck. He was warm and solid, and I'd have stayed there forever if I could, free from responsibility and the need to make decisions, happy to let him take me wherever he was going.

'Open your eyes.'

He released his hands and I jumped down. It took a while for my eyes to focus, but when they did I saw we were standing in front of a stone cottage. Well, what used to be a cottage, now more of a ruin. Even in the muted light I could see how ramshackle and run-down it was, the roof punctured with missing tiles, gaping holes instead of glass in the windows, and beneath a small porch the front door clung on for dear life by one hinge, more hollow blackness beyond. To one side of the cottage were two granite gateposts, flecked with glinting silver, a rotten gate fallen from its fastenings ensnared by vegetation.

'It's beautiful,' I said. 'Who owns it?'

'We do.'

'What?'

'It's part of the farm estate. One of the outbuildings referred to in passing in the particulars. Jeremy and I didn't see it the day we viewed. In fact, I didn't even know it was part of the farm until I went back to the sales deeds a few days ago to check.'

'Does Jeremy know about it?'

'No. At least, I don't think so. He's never mentioned it. His focus was always the farm. I'm not sure he's even walked out on the moor. Not this far anyway. It's useless, really. You can't live in it.'

'Could we renovate it?'

'Not sure when we'd find the time with so much to do on the farm.' His voice drifted, as if he were mulling the idea over. 'I mean, it would take years. I'm not sure it would even be possible without a team of builders. How would they get up here?' He smiled. 'Sadly, I think it's destined to be reclaimed by the earth. It's got a good energy though. I think the people who've lived here were happy.' He walked over then, as if being pulled by an invisible rope, and placed the flats of his hands on the wall. 'It feels at peace.'

I laughed. 'You sound like Mary!'

Kit pushed away from the cottage and smiled.

'You're right though. It's lovely.' He took my hand and we turned to go. I resisted and pulled back on his hand. 'Can we keep it to ourselves? Not tell anybody. Not tell Jeremy.'

'Sure? But why?'

I gave a half-shrug and smiled. 'I don't know. Nice to have a secret place. Somewhere we can escape to if we need some space. Does that sound weird?'

He leant forward and kissed me. 'It doesn't sound weird at all.'

CHAPTER SEVENTEEN

Kit,
April 2002

Kit is doing the night shift with the lamb. He volunteered. There's something about the stillness in the dead of night, the way the silence hums, that Kit adores. And he'll have the fire for company. He's always loved fire. As a child he would spend time with Derek, the gardener, a softly spoken man who smelt of tobacco and compost and whose hands, Kit recalls fondly, were ingrained with a road map of earth. Derek taught him how to light a fire. He let Kit poke at the flames with a stick and get so close the hairs on his skin singed. He showed him what happens when you put paraffin on a fire and how to use a tinder box to light dry leaf matter. Once, after he'd helped rake the autumn leaves, Derek wrapped two huge potatoes in foil, then buried them in the hot ashes. As Kit carefully peeled back the charred foil his tummy churned with the thrill of it. Derek gave him a dirty plastic fork and they ate the fluffy pota-toes in contented silence, watching the flames as the sky grew darker until Patsy called him in for bed. These are the happy moments in his childhood. Diamonds shining in the mud.

Kit lifts the lamb from the straw and settles himself on the chair, legs outstretched, the lamb cradled in the crook of his arm. He whispers encouragement to take the bottle. The lamb takes the teat and Kit passes his fingers over its silken black muzzle. Responding to his touch, the lamb finds a burst of energy, his eyes flicking open and settling on Kit, sucking as if he's finally worked out what he has to do to stay alive, drawing the milk into him with such vigour it bubbles out of the corners of his mouth.

Kit smiles. 'Clever lad.'

The lamb responds with a grave expression, as if aware of the enormity of what's being asked of him. He manages three-quarters of the bottle then his eyelids grow heavy and he collapses against Kit, spent, chest rising and falling rapidly as sleep takes hold. Kit sets the bottle on the floor and, careful not to squash the sleeping lamb as he bends, leans forward to put more logs on the fire. He leaves the door to the stove open so he can watch the waltzing flames, his fingers absently stroking the lamb. Is it his imagination or does the lamb feel sturdier? As if, breath by breath, the animal is inflating and filling with life.

His mind drifts to the cottage and the way Tara had responded to it. He adores this quality in her. The way she loves and feels so passionately. The way she shows indifference to those things which don't move her. He doesn't see what she sees until she points it out. Through her lens he is able to reframe what he's missed or taken for granted. Until this evening, the cottage was no more than a pile of stones with history. A crumbling relic from the past. But she saw past the decay and ruin. She saw a home. With glass in the windows, a watertight roof, a freshly painted front door. He lacks her imagination. When they first met, before Skye, she would lie in bed with him and trail her fingers over his chest and say, 'Imagine if we were on a beach in Goa or a hut in Tanzania right now.' But he couldn't imagine it. Logic kept him prisoner. Perhaps it was a need to manage his own expectations. If he constructed an ideal world wouldn't that render reality devastatingly inferior? Tara laughed at him when he said things like this.

'There's nothing wrong with dreaming,' she'd say. 'Dreams are how you work out what you want from life.'

As he stares at the fire and strokes the soft whorls of wool, swaddled in peaceful stillness, he allows himself to dream. In the flames he pictures the cottage. The walls are rebuilt. The roof repaired. Laughter fills every whitewashed cranny and crevice. He sees them at the kitchen table. It heaves with home-grown food, bowls of apples, a stoneware jug of goat's milk. There's a collie stretched out on the floor at their feet. He is resting his hand against Tara's stomach which is growing with another child. But then he sees Jeremy. Standing in their empty bedroom. Head bowed. Heartbroken. How could Kit turn his back on his friend? Winterfall Farm is his vision and it's turning out to be more of a success than any of them had hoped. With Jeremy's ideas and passion it will only grow more. No. He's committed to this. He owes his friend loyalty. Jeremy has given him unwavering friendship since the day they met. When Kit told him about the pregnancy, Jeremy grinned and threw his arms around Kit. He deflected Kit's self-doubt.

'Nobody – and I mean *nobody* – could be a better father than you.'

Kit's stomach churned. 'But what if I'm like them?'

Jeremy rested his forehead against Kit's. 'You? Never. You're going to be a great father. You will always put your family first. Always have your priorities right.' Jeremy paused and was pensive for a moment, his eyes displaying a flash of sadness. 'You would never make a selfish decision. You are kind and loyal and you love Tara deeply. And, miracle of miracles, she loves you right back. I'm torn up with envy this kid gets to have you two for parents. Lucky little git.'

Kit embraced Jeremy. 'You're a good friend.'

Jeremy smiled. 'And I will always be here for you. You and Tara and the baby. Always.'

Like clockwork the lamb wakes for another bottle a little before five. A gauzy dawn dilutes the darkness and paints the kitchen in muted greys. The lamb is bright and vocal, demanding his food with impatient snuffles. When Kit presents the bottle, he latches on and drinks in deep, desperate glugs. He doesn't stop until he's finished every last drop.

'Guess I was wrong about you, little man,' he says.

At five-thirty he hears Bruce come in.

'Morning,' he says, in a low whisper. 'Good night?'

Kit lies the dozing lamb back in the warming box then stretches his back which has stiffened from his night in the chair. Bruce bends his enormous body over the box. 'Still alive then?'

'Still alive.'

'That's grand. Those girls are going to be over the moon. You and Anne have done brilliant.'

Bruce lifts the tea towel from the mixing bowl to reveal the soft, swollen dough, and gives a nod. He flours the worktop and tips it out with a satisfying thud. He tears it into three and, with hands which move at lightning speed, shapes the loaves and drops them into tins he lined with greaseproof paper before he went to bed. As he works he hums a tune. Since they've been at Winterfall, Kit's admiration of this man has grown. Contentment seeps from his pores. Kit has never come across any person so comfortable in their skin, every bit his own man, master and slave to none and with a limitless capacity for love, not only for Anne, but the rest of them too.

Bruce is the beating heart of Winterfall.

When Kit hears the clatter of feet on the stairs, he smiles and waits for Skye to burst into the kitchen. 'Did he drink the milk, Daddy?'

'Morning, sweetheart.' She leaps into his arms and squeezes him tightly, and he walks her over to the warming box. They crouch and watch the sleeping lamb. 'He drank lots. Can you see his chest going up and down? That's him breathing.'

She beams at him. 'Now the farmer can find him a brand-new mummy.' Then she wriggles out of his arms and skips over to Bruce, who lifts her up and sits her on the worktop.

'So you're milking today?'

'Anne said I can do it by my*self*,' she says, eyes shining, fists pumping with excitement.

'Well, when you've done the milking, you bring it to me, and I'll show you how to make cheese.'

'Cheese is from *milk*?'

'Cheese is from milk.' Bruce winks and pats her knee.

CHAPTER EIGHTEEN

Dani,
April 2002

A different man, younger, maybe even a boy, in stained blue overalls tells us that Alec, who I guessed was the scary farmer, was in his office. Office? Dump more like. A filthy Portakabin with a grubby bit of card fixed to the door by a rusty nail which someone with bad handwriting had scrawled *Office* on.

The door was open and we could hear moving inside. Kit knocked. The man's gruff voice told us to come in. It was chaos, as if a giant and taken hold of the cabin, turned it upside down and shaken it like a ketchup bottle. There was crap everywhere. A bin that had never been emptied puked its contents all over the muddy floor. Balls of orange string filled a blue plastic sack. Straw scattered the floor and it looked as if somebody had walked in with a fireman's hose and sprayed mud from ceiling to floor.

The farmer was rifling through a pile of papers. He glanced at us, but didn't smile. 'Alive?'

'He is.'

I tightened my arms around the lamb. I didn't trust this man as far as I could throw him, which wouldn't have been very far at all, as he was nearly as big as Bruce. The farmer straightened his cap, then zipped up his overalls and grabbed a plastic sack from behind the door. 'Come'n then.' His voice had that same hard edge as cretin Eddie. I didn't like him.

We followed him across the filthy yard to a barn on the left of the cow shed. The farmer heaved back a huge sliding metal door, which creaked and groaned like an old woman as it moved. Inside was a long run of straw pens. In each was a sheep with a different number painted onto its back.

'These ewes are first timers or ones who've had problems. Stillborns or complications. They're in here in case they need help.'

The air in the barn was warm and the smell was thick and stuck in the back of my throat. The farmer walked along the line of pens until he reached a ewe painted with the number forty-three. She was turning circles in her pen, panting, and making noises, as if talking to herself. For a moment I worried she wasn't very well.

'She's been close for a while now. Scanned her and she's with one. She's milk in both teats. I checked this morning in case you'd be back. If your lamb has any chance then it's with her.'

The farmer looked right at me then with a wicked, but not unkind, glint. 'Had your breakfast yet?'

'Bread and jam.'

The farmer grinned. 'Better make sure you hold on to it. I know how delicate you city folk are and I doubt you've seen a birth before.' He looked back at Forty-Three. 'We have to wait, but I doubt for long. Sit yourselves over there.' He gestured to a bale of straw on the other side of the passage. 'Keep an eye on her. When you see the sac showing with the front feet pushing through, shout. I'll not be far away.'

Kit and I sat side by side on the bale of straw. It reminded me of waiting for a bus but smellier and noisier, the sheep bleating and gossiping about rams and hay and babies.

'How long will it take?'

Kit shrugged. 'No idea, but she looks pretty restless so hopefully not long.' He stood and wandered down to the end of the barn where there was a big whiteboard, like at school, with a mess of numbers, words, and scribbles. I stared at the panting ewe, who was pawing the ground as if digging for treasure, her tail flicking left and right. It wasn't long until I caught sight of something beneath her tail. Something gross, dark red, appearing out of her back end. Oh my *God*. It was worse than gross. My eyes were bolted to it. Horror and the heat of the barn made my head swim.

'Kit?' My voice stuck in my throat and he didn't hear me. '*Kit!*'

He whipped around and jogged back to me. I pointed at Forty-Three. 'Something's happening.'

As we watched, what could have been a purple alien pod pushed out of her. 'Oh my God, that's *nasty*,' I breathed.

'I'm going to get him.' Kit started off at a half-run down the barn.

Panic took hold of me. I didn't want to be in there alone. What if something went wrong? Or the lamb came? I had no clue what to do.

'Don't panic, Forty-Three,' I said. 'The farmer will be here any minute. You need to keep your baby in you a bit longer.'

I could have screamed with joy when the farmer appeared and marched the length of the barn to Forty-Three's pen. He went in and felt her stomach, lifted her tail, then patted her rump. He grabbed the plastic sack from the corner and pulled a length of orange twine from his pocket, then gestured at me to come into the pen.

'Right, lass. Hold your lamb out. Legs to me.'

I looked at Kit. 'You?'

Kit shook his head. 'You'll be fine.'

I hesitated, but then gave myself a talking-to. I had to be brave. If Mum could take Eddie's fists then I could do this. Whatever *this* was. I held the lamb out as the farmer had said and he began to roughly tie its legs together.

'What are you doing?' Suddenly I was filled with fear that this was all a trick and the farmer was going to kill the lamb just like he'd wanted to from the start.

'Don't want him wandering off. A newborn won't walk for a bit and we want the ewe to think he's fresh out of her.'

I manoeuvred the lamb to make it easier for the farmer to tie. This was the maddest thing I'd ever done. I'd never even been to the zoo before, let alone stood in a barn full of sheep all ready to give birth. With the lamb tied up like a turkey, the farmer turned Forty-Three to face the wall. Then he put the plastic sacking on the straw behind her. 'This'll catch the fluids. It's not pretty, but it works. Not always, mind. We need Lady Luck on our side.' The farmer looked at me then. His eyes were soft. When he spoke his voice was low and all the hard edges had gone. 'Now you need to prepare yourself in case she doesn't take to him. If she doesn't, well, there's nothing for it. You'll leave him with me and walk away with no fuss.'

'What will happen to him?'

'No need to concern yourself with that.'

I glanced at Kit, who smiled. I could tell by the look in his eyes that if the lamb didn't make it he'd be as sad as me. I lifted the lamb up close to my face and whispered into his velvety ear, 'Good luck, Lamb. Smile at your new mum, yeah? And be good.' Then I handed him over to the farmer and as I did I had a flash of my own mum, sitting in the flat on her own, looking out of the window with an unsmoked cigarette burning in her hand. Then I thought of Tara. Of the others at Winterfall. Bruce and Skye and Anne. I realised then that the lamb and I were the same. Abandoned by our real mums and needing new ones. I dropped my eyes to the ground and took a breath. 'Come on, Lamb,' I whispered.

'Try not to worry.' Kit rested a hand on my shoulder. 'Whatever happens, we've done all we can for him.'

I came out of the pen and Kit and I leant on the railings. We watched the farmer place the lamb on the plastic sacking. I don't think either of us took a breath. The lamb struggled for a bit, but then gave up and settled, head collapsing on the plastic as if he'd passed out with drink. The farmer put on a long plastic glove which went all the way up to his elbow, then knelt behind the ewe, the other hand on her rear. Then he rummaged around as if searching for something inside her. When he pulled his arm out I gasped. Blood and gunk slicked the plastic and his hand was gripping what I guessed was a leg inside a grey bulging balloon. He leant back and tugged hard and something gave way. The balloon tore and God-knows-what gushed out of the sheep and on to the plastic. It could have been right out of a horror film. The farmer got right in there, sticking his hands in the gunk, rubbing it over our lamb, who bleated at the grimness of it all.

Within moments the new lamb started to appear. The birth was quick and Forty-Three's baby slithered out and landed with a thump on the sack, and the barn erupted with bleating as the other mums sent excited congratulations to Forty-Three. Then the farmer grabbed the new one with both hands and rubbed it against ours, transferring all the pink-streaked grossness from one to the other until both lambs shone like sticky slugs.

'The more your lamb smells like the new one, the more chance she'll think he's hers. This new one's a girl, so your lad, fingers crossed, will have a sister to boss him about.'

The newborn was still. Not even twitching. It reminded me of how we found our lamb on the moor and I glanced at Kit, chewing the edge of my nail. He looked as jittery as I was and my stomach flipped right over. The farmer picked both lambs up by the back legs and chucked them on the straw in front of the ewe. She wasted no time in licking her own lamb clean, which made my stomach heave. I held my breath and willed her to look after ours too. I nearly cried when she gave him a lick. He bleated angrily, but she didn't care. She licked him again. And again.

'She's doing it!' I whispered. 'She's cleaning both. Has it worked? Is she adopting him?'

The farmer chuckled. 'Too soon to be sure. When the new one gets to its feet and starts to root for milk, I'll cut the twine on yours and, well, hopefully instinct will kick in.'

'And if it doesn't?'

'Your lamb should've died on the moor. He's got spirit. If he wants to live then he'll do his best.'

The farmer lets himself out of the pen. 'Come on then. She's best left in peace.'

I didn't want to leave but reluctantly followed them out of the barn, then turned to watch Forty-Three and her gunky twins until the heavy door slid closed and blocked my view.

'Can we come back later?'

'I don't think so,' said Kit. 'Alec's a busy man. Especially this time of year.'

'I've thirty head of sheep still to lamb and three horses to foal as well,' he said. 'But give me your number and I'll call later. Give an update, eh?'

'We don't have a phone at the farm,' Kit said quickly.

'No phone?'

'No electricity either,' I said, but dropped my eyes. It crossed my mind Kit might not want me discussing the farm.

'There's a payphone down the lane,' Kit said. 'We could call you? Maybe tomorrow?'

I nodded enthusiastically, and immediately felt silly and childish, so gave a single, more adult, nod.

We waited outside the cabin while he wrote his number in illegible writing on a grubby torn-off corner of paper.

'Thank you,' said Kit. 'We appreciate you doing this.'

'Should be me thanking you. Ewe must've been left on the moor at gathering. If it wasn't for you the lamb would have died.' He chuckled. 'I imagine you didn't get much sleep last night. Needy little blighters, lambs.' The farmer smiled again and as he was turning, said, 'If you need a phone or help in an emergency. We're always here.'

'He's actually really nice,' I said, as we got into the Land Rover.

'Yes. He's a good man. Anne was right. People aren't comfortable with stuff they don't know.' He paused. 'You did a good thing, Dani. You fought for that lamb. I didn't think he had a snowball's chance in hell of making it and, well, if it wasn't for you, I'd have left him for dead.'

My cheeks flushed red. I never knew what to say when people were nice.

'Fingers crossed it works out, but if it doesn't? Better to pass away in a warm barn full of sheep than alone and cold on the moor.'

Kit started the engine, but as he began to pull away there was a shout. I swivelled in my seat to look out of the back window. The farmer was trotting after us, a limp I didn't notice before making him lurch to one side, waving his arms madly.

'He wants us to stop.'

Kit put the brakes on then wound down the window as the farmer reached us. 'Something to show you.' He was panting a little, his cheeks flushed. He beckoned with his finger. 'Come with me.'

The sight which met us in the barn was as good as Christmases, birthdays, and weekends all rolled into one. In Forty-Three's pen one lamb, the newborn girl, was standing upright, wobbly, her head nuzzling her mother's neck. The other lamb, our orphaned boy, had his head shoved under Forty-Three's belly, suckling feverishly, his tiny tail flicking round and round like a helicopter blade.

'So that's it? She'll take care of him?'

'Looking that way.' The farmer beamed and removed his cap

and smoothed his hair. 'Anyway, I'm thinking this lamb has earned himself a name? Wondering what yours is?'

'My name? It's Dani. Short for Danielle.'

The farmer grinned. 'Well, that's easy, isn't it? This little man will be Danny. Short for Daniel.'

I stared the farmer and then at the lamb. I couldn't believe it. Nothing like this had ever happened to me before. My chest was close to bursting. 'Really? He's called Danny?'

'A strong name and it'll bring him luck. Want to paint his number?'

Then he showed me how to use the blue spray paint and, though my hand was trembling a little, I managed to mark Danny the Lamb's licked-clean fleece with the number forty-three.

'You're a natural,' the farmer said. 'Looks like you've been marking lambs all your life.'

I didn't tell him it was basically the same as doing graffiti but on a lamb instead of walls.

Skye, who must have been waiting for the sound of the Land Rover, clambered onto the gatepost as we drove up the lane and waved madly.

'Dani!' she cried, beaming and flapping her hands. 'Rosie and Snowy made milk!'

I got out of the Land Rover as she climbed down from the gatepost and ran to me. She grabbed my hand and tried to run. I laughed, and pulled back against her, refusing to move. She leant forward like an explorer in a gale and I let her pull me.

'In that!' she cried as we ran into the kitchen and over to a large metal urn on the side. 'There's real milk in it!'

I lifted the lid and peered in. It was full to the brim with thick, creamy milk. 'Is that all from the two of them?' I asked Mary, who was grinding some sharp-smelling spice in her stone bowl.

She stared at me then placed her trowel on the ground and wiped her earthy hands on her rainbow trousers. Then she reached out to hug me and I let her. 'Of course it is. You can stay as long as you need.'

CHAPTER NINETEEN

Tara,
June 2002

When Jeremy suggested the party I'd thought it was tone-deaf. A cynical trick to deflect the spotlight away from Dani's arrival. But I had to admit he was right. Having a solstice celebration to plan for was exactly what we needed. Not only something to prepare for, but something to get excited about. It came at the perfect time, too. The atmosphere on the farm as we began to harvest the first vegetables was electric. The place thrummed with energy. Everybody was working all the hours of the day and the field and orchard rang with laughter and animated chatter.

Jeremy was a ball of fire at our centre. The way we turned towards him reminded me of the sunflowers I'd seen on a family holiday to Burgundy. Fields of yellow flower heads tracking the sun as it moved across the sky, faces towards the warmth. The anger that dogged him before we moved to Cornwall had dissolved. In its place was a seemingly permanent aura of peace. He had an answer to any question and apart from when he was reading or meditating – which he did every morning before breakfast with Anne, Mary and Dean – was always on hand and willing to talk things through. His enthusiasm for the farm was seductive.

'Isn't it beautiful?' he said to me and Kit. 'This haven we've created?'

And it was. A perfect slice of heaven. I couldn't help myself wondering if, perhaps, it was too good to be true.

Our early harvest was bountiful. Bruce boiled over with joy as we marched victoriously into the kitchen with our overflowing baskets. Beetroots, carrots, peas, spinach, radishes and lettuce. Seeing the fruits of our labour spurred us on to work harder with the crops still growing. It fuelled the constant weeding, watering, and nurturing.

Under Bruce's patient tutelage we learnt how to preserve what we didn't eat immediately and soon the larder began to fill with jar upon jar of sliced vegetables floating in brightly coloured pickling liquids.

'Like BFG dreams, Mama,' Skye said, as she gazed up at the array of sparkling treasure.

The orchard was equally abundant. Apple and pear blossom decorated the trees with spring snowflakes and June saw our first baskets of raspberries and gooseberries. Breakfast became home-made goat's yoghurt with scattered berry jewels, a drizzle of golden honey, and a sprinkling of cinnamon. The table heaved at our evening meals. Though we still relied on our occasional supermarket trips for the staples, we started to believe that soon, maybe even the following year, we'd be producing all the food we needed and more. Winterfall Farm had delivered on its promise and, with a party on the horizon, a time to celebrate the success of our thriving community, our mood was jubilant.

The morning of the party, Skye, Dani, and I were cutting Swiss chard and sorrel in the field. The sun shone and candy-floss clouds hung in the sky. The thermals lifted the buzzards so high they'd shrunk to no more than specks on the blue. Sasha lay with us, chewing an old sheep bone she'd dug up a few days before which had become her prized possession. Dean was working hard to socialise her with the goats and chickens, and though her body was stretched elastic when they were nearby, she'd finally stopped straining at the collar to get at them. He and Dani had also taught her lots of tricks. On command, she'd give her paw, turn a circle left or right, and, if she was in the right frame of mind, when Dani clapped twice she would stand up on her hind legs, her front legs pawing the air, then come down and wait expectantly for her biscuit reward.

'There's a slug, Mama,' Skye said, reaching through the ruby leaves of chard for an enormous slimy slug with pincer-fingers.

'You're so good at spotting them.' Dani was brilliant with Skye. She had endless patience and would listen to Skye's patter for hours on end. In just over two months they'd grown close as sisters.

When we had enough chard and sorrel, we moved on to the broad beans, snapping them off the vines, and dropping them into wicker baskets. The sound of Ash's guitar floated through the air. I turned and saw him leaning back against a tree in the copse, cigarette in his mouth, strumming his guitar. I tried not to let it irritate me. If anybody was prone to skiving it was Ash. A few weeks ago I'd grumbled to Anne, but she smiled. 'Don't let it bother you. He works hard when he puts his mind to it. Some people need some space to float. Give him that space and he'll give more when he's working.'

The girls and I carried the full baskets back to the farmhouse. We passed Dean, who was hefting a barrowload of goat manure up from the muck heap to the vegetable field.

'Look!' Skye held her basket of broad beans up.

He high-fived her and she laughed, then skipped into the house.

The kitchen was a hive of activity. Mary hummed a tune as she cut squash into bright orange cubes and tossed them into an earthenware dish. Bruce was mixing some sort of batter in a huge bowl, his forehead beaded with pearls of perspiration. From outside I could hear the rhythmic thud of woodchopping. I went to the back door and leant against the frame to watch Kit as he wielded his axe, shirtless, baked brown skin glistening with sweat. He was so relaxed, so untroubled. I hadn't realised how tense he'd been back in Cowley. This life suited him and knowing this gave me a contented glow.

I walked up towards him and when he saw me he smiled and set down the axe. Then he wiped his hands on his jeans and leant in for a kiss.

'No way.' I laughed and pushed him away. 'You're a sweaty mess.'

He grinned and walked over to where his shirt lay on the floor and bent to pick up a flask. He unscrewed the lid then poured some into his cupped hand, wetted his neck and armpits, then tipped some over his face, shaking away the excess like a river-wet Labrador.

Then he smiled again. 'Better?'

'Not much.' But I walked over and kissed him anyway.

The girls and I picked grasses and ivy from the side of the barn and sat in the late afternoon sunshine and twisted them into crowns, then threaded meadow flowers through the woven green to decorate them. I wore a summer dress made of yellow cheesecloth with small white daisies embroidered around the hem. Skye wore a bridesmaid dress I'd found for a few pounds in a second-hand shop, and I lent Dani a floaty skirt to try on. It was too long for her and trailed on the floor.

'I don't mind,' she breathed, twirling from side to side as she looked at herself in the mirror. 'I feel like a princess.'

'You both look beautiful,' I said to them, and they held hands and curtsied then collapsed in fits of giggles.

We joined the others in the yard. Skye ran to Kit and spun a circle in front of him. 'Do I look pretty?'

'The prettiest girl I've ever seen.'

Everybody was decorated in leaves and flowers and colourful clothing. Ash had covered the bowler hat he used for busking with ivy and Anne had woven flowers into Bruce's beard. Mary wore a long white dress tied at her waist with a leather plaited cord.

She carried a tambourine which hung with strands of colourful ribbons. Kit and Jeremy had painted their hair green and decorated their chests with Celtic symbols using charcoal.

'Twins?' I said.

They bowed in tandem and laughed.

The stones, which were half an hour's walk away, formed a circle around thirty metres across, with ten granite monoliths, nine still standing. It was a magical place, the stone circle perfectly round, the energy within it electrifying.

'It dates from the Bronze Age,' Mary told me and Dani as we walked. 'Legend says the stones are local girls who'd danced on the Sabbath, which was forbidden. They were discovered and turned to stone mid-dance.'

'Who turned them to stone?' Dani asked.

'Some angry gods. Horrible bullies. *Men*, of course.' Mary rolled her eyes and Dani nodded solemnly and I wondered if she was thinking of her monster stepfather.

We spread out blankets to sit on inside the circle and used the fallen stone, its surface weathered smooth, as a table on which we laid out the food. Cakes and savoury pastries. A rainbow of fresh vegetables, sliced and put into the wooden bowls we'd carried up with the bottles of beer and cider. When Ash picked up his guitar, we danced. As the sun darkened to a burnt orange and sank slowly in the sky, Kit and I sat together against one of the stones, still warm from the heat it had absorbed during the day, and watched Skye dancing with Anne, shaking Mary's tambourine, her golden hair catching the setting sun and her dress setting sail as she spun.

Skye caught us watching and ran to us. She tugged on my hand and begged me to dance.

I laughed. 'No, I'm sitting with Daddy.'

'*Yes*, Mama.'

And I let her drag me to my feet.

The party went on long into the night. Kit had lit a small fire earlier in the evening with logs he'd packed into two rucksacks, which he and Dean lugged up, and we sat around it and watched the flames. Skye slept in Kit's arms. She looked so peaceful. I shifted my body so I could lie on his lap beside her, my forehead against hers, my fingers lightly stroking her hair.

Jeremy sat down beside Kit. I didn't move or open my eyes. There was a part of me that wanted him to leave us alone to enjoy this moment together. Perhaps if he thought I was sleeping he'd move away.

'Isn't this great?' His voice was light and breathless. 'I feel so alive. This group of people are beautiful. And the three of you. The family within our family. Maybe,' he continued, 'you should think about another baby?'

Kit laughed.

'I'm serious.'

'One day, I'm sure. Right now we're happy as we are.'

'But, think about it, a Winterfall baby! The first of many. *Jesus.*' He gave a sharp exclamation of excitement. 'The thought sends shivers through me.'

'So, what, you're trying to colonise Bodmin Moor?' Kit laughed again.

'Why not? Look at it. At them. How happy they are.'

'Everybody loves a party.'

'But it's not just tonight, is it? Think how different life is here to what we escaped. God. That existence drained the energy out of us, but here we create it.'

Kit didn't reply.

'Is it too much to want what we've started to last? To grow our community. To get to a stage where people from outside use us as a blueprint for living properly? We can aim so much higher, Kit. Not only reject society, but build a new one.' I imagined Jeremy smiling to himself. 'But, of course, we need more women.'

'What?'

'You can't grow a society if you can't reproduce.'

'Please tell me you're joking.'

Jeremy laughed. 'Your face! Jesus. Yes. Of course, I'm bloody joking.' But there was something in his tone which told me he wasn't.

'Jokes aside, though, are you cool with not having a girlfriend? I know Ash is finding it hard.'

'Yes, I had a chat with him about it as well. That's kind of what got me thinking about expanding the group. But for me? No. I don't need that anymore.'

'You mean sex?'

'Sex, yes. And relationships of that kind. I've been reading about celibacy—'

'*Celibacy*? Holy shit. Why?'

I was expecting Jeremy to laugh but he didn't. 'There's much written on how abstaining from sex and thoughts of sex can concentrate the mind. It frees up your thoughts for important things. There's even anecdotal evidence it provides the mind with clarity.'

'It's pretty extreme.'

'No, for me, it's the right thing. I've got more important things to think about. I want to be present. I want my mind sharp. I've got work to do here and I need to be focused.'

CHAPTER TWENTY

Kit,
June 2002

Skye is exhausted the following morning. They'd stayed up at the stones until well past midnight and she's woken in a fractious, bad-tempered mood. It's not only her. Everybody is shattered and suffering the aftereffects of the party. Ash wears sunglasses and a woollen hat pulled low over his head, and grunts as he pours himself a third coffee. Of course Bruce was still up early to make the bread, and the fresh loaves waiting on the side are a welcome sight as they stagger into the kitchen in dribs and drabs to make toast or bowls of yoghurt and mugs of coffee which they take outside into the sunshine.

Jeremy is dressed in the clothes he wore last night. He is subdued and there are dark smudges beneath his eyes. He and Mary stayed at the stones to watch the sunrise and he's obviously had no sleep.

'Daddy, can I have Coco Pops?'

'Coco Pops? When have you ever had those?'

'Dani told me about them. They're small and crunchy and turn the milk to *milkshake*.'

Kit smiles. 'We don't have any here, angel. Maybe one day, though?' He glances at Jeremy, who doesn't react, his face expressionless as he watches his bread carefully while it toasts.

'I want some.'

'How about a flapjack? Bruce won't mind,' Kit adds, when

Jeremy turns his head to look at him. Jeremy prefers they save the teatime cakes until the afternoon jobs have been done. He says it's nice for people to have something to look forward to after a hard day's work, which, everybody agrees, is an excellent idea.

'No. Coco Pops.' Her mouth turns upside down and she crosses her arms, her brow knotted in a childish scowl.

Kit picks her up and holds her, facing him, bending his head into her eye-line. 'Why don't we go to the larder and you can choose something?'

'Coco Pops.' Her voice is loud and sharpened with tiredness.

'Skye? Listen to me. I'd love to give you some but we don't have—'

'I want some!' This time she yells.

'*Enough* Skye!' Jeremy slams the toasting fork down on the side and stands. He rubs his temples as if he's in pain. 'Didn't you hear your father?'

'It's fine,' Kit says. 'I can deal with this.'

'Your father said there aren't any Coco Pops.' Jeremy's voice is unyielding. 'So you need to stop shouting and listen to him.'

Skye's eyes slowly well with tears and she buries her head in Kit's shoulder, uncrossing her arms and tying them tightly round his neck.

'Jesus, Jeremy. What are you doing? You don't need to discipline my child.'

Jeremy picks up the toasting fork and sits back down. 'She wasn't listening to you. She needs to be told.'

'Not by *you*. Christ. Tara and I are her parents and we are perfectly able to handle her without you wading in.' He puts his hand up to the back of his daughter's head and strokes her gently. 'Don't cry,' he soothes. 'Jeremy's tired, that's all. He didn't mean to shout.'

'No. We live as a group and we all take responsibility for the welfare of the children. That principle is at the heart of communal living.'

An uncommon anger wells up from the pit of Kit's stomach. 'No, that's not what's at the heart of communal living. What's at the heart of communal living is empathy and tolerance. Skye is a child and she was up late last night because we were having fun. Now she's tired and grouchy, and a bit of understanding from the adults around her wouldn't go amiss.'

'Nor would a few boundaries.'

Something snaps inside Kit. He kisses Skye, whose crying has ebbed then puts her down. He walks her over to the door and crouches in front of her. 'Will you run upstairs and tell Mama to come down and make some of her amazing pancakes?'

'Pancakes?' Skye's face lights up and she tears out of the kitchen, her feet thumping the stairs, calling excitedly for Tara.

Kit waits until she is out of earshot then walks over to Jeremy. He stands close to him, and, though he keeps his volume down, makes no effort to conceal his anger. It's the first time he's ever been angry with Jeremy. 'Don't you *ever* step in like that with my daughter again, you hear me? If she's doing something unsafe, then – and only *then* – you can take it upon yourself to get involved, but for things like that? For everyday stuff? You leave that to me and to Tara. She's a child and sometimes children are rude and spoilt. It's up to us to show them how to behave. You might think how I do that is wrong. That's fine. But you keep it to yourself and don't you ever take your mood or your tiredness or your hangover out on Skye again. Understood?'

They hold each other's stare for a moment or two before Jeremy raises a hand and steps back. 'Sure. Understood—'

Before Jeremy has a chance to follow with a *but* Kit adds, 'She's *my* child. Not yours.'

Jeremy turns away from him and takes the slice of bread, which isn't properly toasted yet, off the fork and puts it on a plate.

'I hear I'm cooking pancakes?' Tara says as she and Skye walk into the kitchen. It's clear from Tara's sleepy smile that Skye hasn't mentioned Jeremy shouting, and he decides not to tell her. It will only make her furious, and as far as Kit is concerned it's dealt with.

'There's no Coco Pops so Daddy said you'd do *pancakes*!'

Tara stretches and yawns then smiles. 'I don't know if I can even remember how to make them, but we'll give it a go.'

Skye grins and the tears and Coco Pops and Jeremy's shouting are forgotten. 'Can I help make them, Mama?'

Kit is too riled to eat breakfast with them. Every part of him is tingling. He needs to cool off. He needs space and solitude.

He heads out on to the moor and tries to process what's occurred. Jeremy doesn't seem remotely remorseful. There's an air of blame about his glowering, as if he believes Kit is wrong for telling him to back off. The incident has left Kit feeling not only defensive of his daughter, but violated by Jeremy's judgement. He reminds himself they are living on top of each other, and there are bound to be moments of strain. Add alcohol and lack of sleep, and it's a recipe for conflict. But Jeremy punched where it hurts and Kit loathes confrontation. It makes him flighty and having words with his best friend has unsettled him. Their relationship is too important to hold a grudge, so he has no option but to put it behind him and hope that next time Jeremy keeps his opinions to himself.

He rounds the bend and the dilapidated cottage comes into view. He walks up to the front door and pulls away handfuls of the long weeds which creep around the crumbling porch. He steps inside. It's musty and dank. Neglected. A mess of debris and dirt. A thick layer of dust and spiderweb quilts everything. He allows his eyes to grow accustomed to the dimness then walks further in. He peers up the staircase. The treads are rotten. The banister broken and leaning perilously. A small fireplace holds a rusted wood burner. He tries the handle. At first it refuses to budge, but with persuasion gives in. Inside the stove is a single log. Charred at the edges. A soft bed of ash beneath. How long ago did this fire burn? He pulls out the ash pan and empties it in the undergrowth outside. He gathers some small pieces of wood and a handful of sticks and bone-dry grass. Back inside the cottage he takes the log out of the stove and builds a teepee of kindling then arranges the pieces of wood around it. He moves reverently. Slowly. Building the fire calms him. His muscles relax as his anxiety eases. He reaches into his pocket for the lighter he always keeps with him. He likes to feel it in his pocket. The reassuring hardness of it. The knowledge he is never far from a flame. It's a habit he's had since childhood. Some children had comfort blankets. For him a box of matches. He lit his first fire when he was nine. It was Christmas Day. Patsy had bought the presents his teenage brothers would give to his parents with money his father had provided her. For their mother, Patsy chose a cashmere scarf from Kit's eldest brother and a selection of her favourite Elizabeth Arden products from his second brother. But Kit wanted to make her something. Derek the gardener showed him how to make a simple wooden box which he spent hours sanding and decorating with drawings then varnishing. It wasn't perfect. The edges didn't quite seal properly and the felt-tip pens he'd used had bled into the wood so it was hard to tell what some of the drawings were.

'She'll love it,' Patsy said.

But his mother didn't love it.

'What's it for?'

'Anything you want? You could use it to keep necklaces in it.'

'I have a jewellery box. An antique one.' Then she discarded it and opened the cashmere scarf which she wrapped around her neck and remarked a hundred times on how soft it was.

His brothers laughed and told him his box was a pile of shit and was only good for the fire. So while the rest of the family were watching the Queen's speech, he went down to the lake and using newspaper and twigs and matches he stole from the drawer in the kitchen built a fire. He put the wooden box on it and watched it burn. As the flames consumed it he experienced an overwhelming sense of calm as the fire burnt away the anger and hurt. He stayed by the fire until it had burnt down to nothing, then slipped the matches into his pocket, and went back up to the house.

The kindling crackles and fizzes and the flames grab hungrily at the dry grass in the stove. He leans forward and blows on the fire and, when it takes hold, he closes the stove. He waits for smoke to billow back down, meaning the flue is blocked. But the fire draws and he watches through the grubby glass as the flames weave and twist. He sits for a while and turns the incident with Jeremy over and over in his head. He has to let it go. However much it's got to him, he has to cut this loose. There's no place for enduring anger in a community like Winterfall.

He breathes deeply and stares at the fire, waiting for his rage to fade.

CHAPTER TWENTY-ONE

Dani,
August 2002

Skye burst through my door and jumped on my mattress. 'It's my birthday! It's my *birthday*!' she cried, a Mexican jumping bean bouncing up and down. 'Dani! Wake *up*!'

I groaned and rubbed my eyes and smiled through my sleep. The attic room was an oven. Even with the tiny window open it was sweltering and every morning over the last week or so I'd woken up feeling as if my head was full of glue and my body soaked in sweat.

'Mama says we're going to get *ice cream*!' Skye's eyes were cartoonishly big and round.

'You're going off the farm?' I sat up. 'Did Tara say I was going too?'

Skye nodded, hands clapping together excitedly. 'You, me, Mama and Daddy.'

It might as well have been my birthday too. The thought of a trip off the farm made my stomach buzz.

I dressed quickly and went to find Tara to check Skye's story. Anne and Mary were doing the laundry in the back yard, kneeling either side of the large plastic tub which they'd filled from the hosepipe, sweating with the effort. Laundry was the worst job on the whole farm. Even worse than mucking out the goat shed. I hated it. My arms always ached like crazy afterwards. You had to soak the washing in the cold water, then rub soap from a bar Mary made by grating a normal bar of soap then mixing it with powders and lavender oil. Even with the oil it dried out my hands. Anne said rubber gloves would stop that happening, but the thought of wearing stinky rubber gloves everybody else had sweated in grossed me out.

'Morning,' Anne said, looking up from the scrubbing. 'Sleep well?'

'It's quite hot up there,' I said. 'Did Tara say I was going with them to get ice cream?'

'If you want to. Or you can stay here and help prepare a birthday lunch for her.'

'It'll be a lovely surprise for Skye,' Mary sang, wringing out a T-shirt.

Anne didn't seem to mind that I chose ice cream over helping with lunch. But it turned out Jeremy didn't know and when he found out later that morning he wasn't keen on the idea.

'You're doing what?'

'Taking the girls for an ice cream,' Tara said. 'We won't be too long.'

His face was cloudy. 'We are trying to cut ties with the outside world. You really want Skye to witness the chaos and greed?'

My stomach flooded with panic. Surely he wasn't going to stop us going?

'It's an ice cream, Jeremy. Nothing more sinister than that.'

'It's how they hook us. The children don't need ice cream. Look how happy they are without the need for tricks and bribes.'

'What's everybody looking so serious about?' Kit appeared with Skye on his shoulders.

'Jeremy would prefer we don't take Skye for ice cream.'

Skye was about to kick off but Kit spoke quickly, his eyes bolted to Jeremy. 'Well, that's what we're doing because we promised her.'

'You want to expose her to the toxicity of capitalism?'

'No, I want to buy her an ice cream.' Kit smiled and put Skye on the ground. 'In the car, sweetheart.' Then he came over to Jeremy. 'It's nothing more than an ice cream. Anne and Mary wanted to have some time to do her a birthday lunch.'

'Why not go for a walk?'

'Because we thought an ice cream would be a treat. Relax. It's a couple of hours. We aren't going to run back to our old lives. Not even for a scoop of ice cream.'

My mouth salivated and I swear I could already taste the vanilla.

Jeremy and Kit stared at each other for a moment or two then Jeremy smiled and nodded. It was a weird smile but I didn't care. All I cared about was ice cream.

I decided to get into the Land Rover before Jeremy had a chance to say anything else. It was a proper adventure. I loved the farm but I couldn't wait to get out for a bit and see different faces and scenery. It wasn't as if life on the farm was boring exactly, but it was definitely repetitive. Breakfast. Chores. Lunch. Chores. Afternoon rest. Dinner. Then sitting around telling ghost stories or reading or talking about vegetables or listening to dull conversations about the state and capitalism and society which were, as far as I could tell, the enemy.

The fan in the Land Rover was broken and the skin on the back of my arms stuck to the seat and sweat ran down my back. I wound down the window and stuck my head out, enjoying the rush of air against my face. We turned off the main road and on to a lane which ran through a forest of enormous pine trees. When we drove into the car park we might as well have crash-landed on an alien planet. It was a glittering sea of metal, the shiny reds, blues, and silvers were harsh after the moorland colours I'd got used to. Then there were the other people. The noises. Smells. A thousand things grabbing at me from every direction. Seeing people suddenly gave me the fear. I hadn't thought it through. What if Eddie had reported me missing? What if the police were out looking for me? What if they had my photo, recognised me, and handed me back to him? Maybe Eddie had traced the phone call like people did on television? Maybe he was lurking behind one of the shiny cars?

I kept my head down and hurried along behind Tara and Kit, who were swinging Skye between them as she giggled. There was a café and a concrete seating area, picnic tables beside a huge lake. The water shimmered and families splashed and swam and ate picnics and played on boats and inflatables, their happy screams filling the dry air.

We walked down to the water's edge and found a patch of grass to sit on. People stared at Tara as we passed. I didn't know if it was because she was so pretty or because she was a walking rainbow with her ribbons and billowing trousers and jewellery jangling on her wrists and ankles. She didn't seem to care and walked with her chin held high, a strutting peacock.

'God,' she said as she looked around us. 'It's another world, isn't it?'

'Where's the ice cream, Mama?'

'I'll get them now,' Kit said. 'You paddle in the water and I'll be back before you know it. What does everybody want?'

'Can I come too?' I asked. I'd brought my thirty-seven pence and wanted to buy something for Skye's birthday.

I followed Kit into the café and stared at the sign with the pictures of the ice lollies and ice creams. It almost blew my mind wide open. I wanted everything. Two of everything.

'What do you fancy?' Kit asked.

'Are you sure?'

He laughed. 'Very sure.'

'Can I have a ninety-nine with a flake and strawberry sauce and a can of Coke, please?'

As Kit paid for the drinks and ice creams, I looked around the shop. There was nothing I could buy for thirty-seven pence.

I thought about asking Kit if I could borrow some money, but I didn't feel brave enough. When I looked up I noticed the woman behind the counter was staring at me like she thought I was going to nick something. Oh my God. That pissed me off. How dare she? I was so annoyed that when she turned her back, I reached out and grabbed a packet of Fruit Pastilles and shoved them into my pocket. Silly cow. Should have kept her suspicions to herself.

As the woman handed Kit the ice creams she glared at me with narrow eyes. I smiled at her and then took the ice creams from Kit so he could carry the drinks. I couldn't wait, and leant in for a lick. I nearly died. It was heaven on my tongue.

Skye jiggled from one foot to the other as we returned with the ice creams. I handed hers to her then licked the river of melted vanilla which had dribbled down my hand. I honestly couldn't remember ice cream tasting that good and I settled on the grass to make the most of every lick. When I bit into the flake I groaned with pleasure. Tara laughed.

'What do you think, Skye?' I asked.

'Are Coco Pops like this?' Her mouth was ringed in creamy white, a dab of melted chocolate on the end of her button nose.

'Crunchy not silky,' I said. 'But just as good.'

Tara sat on the bank of the lake and dangled her legs in the water and sipped the Fanta she'd asked for. As I finished the ice cream I watched everything around me. People drinking tea out of plastic cups. Tucking into scones piled high with thick yellow cream and chemical-red jam. A family in life jackets wobbling as they climbed into a rowing boat. A group of boys running and whooping as they launched themselves into the lake forming crooked star shapes in the air.

'Do you miss it?' Tara asked Kit quietly. I'm not sure if she meant me to hear or not.

'Miss what?'

'This. Real life. Ice creams and strangers. Electric lights. Food that comes ready-made not covered in sweat and soil. Hot water.'

I glanced at Kit, who was staring at the people as they bustled about.

'No,' he said. 'I don't miss it at all. Do you?'

Tara was interrupted by Skye, who'd run over, her cone held out with glee, ice cream all over her, thrusting the remains towards Tara's face.

'For me?' Tara said, with pretend excitement.

Skye nodded enthusiastically and Tara leant forward, mouth wide, eyes on her daughter, until Skye squealed with delight and snatched it away, collapsing into a belly laugh which set me and Kit off. As Skye skipped back down to the water, Tara's smile slipped away.

When we arrived back at the farm I saw Mary was watching for us. Kit lifted a hand and she waved then disappeared back inside.

'Now keep your eyes closed,' Kit said to Skye as he piggy-backed her into the farmhouse.

'Why?'

'You'll see.'

As we walked out of the back door we were met with the most incredible sight. The yard was transformed. They'd gone to so much effort. The table was decorated with ribbons and flowers, and piled high with platters of mouth-watering food. Cakes and biscuits. Sandwiches. A huge trifle covered in a carpet of raspberries. There was bunting made from triangles of brightly coloured fabric which looped overhead, strung from the house to the wood shed, and from tree to tree. At the end of the table was a pile of presents. While everybody crowded around Skye and was asking her about the lake and her ice cream, I ran into the house and searched for something to wrap the Fruit Pastilles in. There was a pile of old newspapers in the corner of the kitchen. Perfect. I tore off a piece and rolled the sweets up then tied it with some string from Mary's pantry. I felt a kick of sadness as I thought about my birthday chocolates wrapped up the same way.

We tucked into the mountains of food and watched Skye open her presents. She was so excited she couldn't sit still, dancing around on the spot, staring gleefully at the pile of gifts. I was ashamed how jealous I was. I wondered if they'd go to all this trouble when it was my birthday.

'I love it!' Skye said, as she opened the lip balm Mary gave her. It was in a small jar and dyed dark pink with beetroot. She dipped her finger into the gloopy gel and wiped it on her lips. It stained them red. Mary was prepared with a hand mirror and Skye looked at her reflection, pouting and turning her head this way and that as everybody laughed.

'I'm a fancy lady.'

'You are! Happy birthday, sweet girl.'

The next present was a crown of twisted twigs which Bruce had made her. She put it on her head. 'Princess Skye,' he said.

'Princess Skye,' she repeated, rolling the words around her mouth like boiled sweets.

Anne had made her a doll out of tightly knotted straw and Tara gave her something called a dreamcatcher, which was a ring of willow with a spiderweb of coloured strings tied across it, and feathers dangling on threads.

'You make a wish and it comes true,' she whispered to Skye, who flung her arms around her mother's neck and thanked her.

Kit gave her the knife he'd carved. It was beautiful, polished and smooth, with a shining silver blade and a leather pouch to keep it in.

'For stabbing baddies?' Skye asked, turning the knife over in her hands.

'There aren't any baddies here, angel,' he'd replied. 'But every wild child needs a knife.'

Tara wrinkled her nose. 'I'm not sure about that.'

Skye grinned and said, 'I *love* it. And if baddies do come, I'll get them.'

Then Skye picked up my present. 'Who is this?' I lifted my hand and smiled. She ripped off the newspaper and chucked it over her shoulder. 'What is it?' she said, staring at the tube.

'Sweets.' Then I looked at Tara, suddenly worried I might have done something wrong. 'It's OK to give her sweets, isn't it?'

'Of course.'

'I bought them today. With the last of my money.'

'Did you?' Kit looked confused and my heart skipped a beat.

'When I went in to use the toilet.'

He smiled. 'That's very kind of you, Dani.'

Skye wasn't listening. She was too busy tearing at the packaging to free the sweets. She grabbed one and popped it into her mouth. Amazement dawned on her face. She closed her eyes as her jaw circled around and around. When she finished she looked at me. 'This is my favourite of all the presents.' She got off her chair and came up and kissed my cheek.

There was one present left on the table. Skye ran back, picked it up, and held it above her head while jumping up and down. 'Who is this one?'

Jeremy smiled. 'That's from me.'

She grinned and tore open the present. Inside was a stack of cards tied up with more of Mary's string. Skye handed the pack to Tara. 'I can't do the knot.'

Tara fiddled with the string, picking at it with her fingernails. When she'd loosened the string she handed the cards back to Skye, who looked through them. Each one was white with black hand-writing on.

'What is it?' Skye looked up at Jeremy then to Tara and Kit.

Jeremy smiled again. 'Motivational sentences for you to read. Life lessons. You can dip in and out of them whenever you want. There are fifty-two so you have one for each week in the year.'

Skye wrinkled her forehead. She picked a card off the pile and handed it to Tara.

'*Do not want what you cannot have.*' Tara looked at Jeremy, as if confused, then reached for another. '*Being peaceful helps us grow.*'

Tara was about to speak, but Mary got in first, her eyes wet with tears. 'Goodness me. What a very beautiful and thoughtful present.'

'Yes,' Bruce said. 'Something to really treasure. What a special gift.'

Tara kept whatever she was going to say inside her.

'Say thank you to Jeremy,' Kit said then.

'Thank you, Jeremy.' Skye discarded the stack of cards and inched her fingers towards the Fruit Pastilles.

Dean and Ash still had gifts to come. Ash called Skye over and he held out his balled-up fist.

'Tap it,' he said.

When Skye did as he said, his fingers opened like a flower, and there, in the centre of his palm, was a red triangle of plastic.

'What is it?' Skye asked as she reached for it.

'A plectrum. For playing guitar. I thought I could teach you to play?'

'Play dancing music like you?'

He grinned.

'Now?'

'Maybe later this afternoon?'

'Yes please!' Then she solemnly gave the plectrum to Tara. 'Mama, you look after it. It's very small and I don't want to lose it.'

The last present was from Dean and was the best by a thousand miles. He called Sasha and she padded over and sat down, looking expectantly up at him, tongue lolling as she panted.

'Skye, you come too.'

She walked over to him and gave Sasha a kiss on the head. Then Dean handed her a short stick. 'Point this at her and say *Bang*. Nice and loud.'

Skye looked confused, so he put the stick in her hand then gently turned her to face Sasha.

He repeated his instruction and Skye pointed the stick at Sasha. 'Bang!' she said. '*Bang*!'

Sasha dropped to the floor and lay flat on her side, motionless apart from her eyes which flicked towards Dean.

Everybody cheered and clapped.

'Now say, "Up for Skye" and raise your hands like this.' He held his hands out, palms upwards, and moved them through the air to his shoulders.

'Up for Skye,' she said, copying what he'd done with his hands.

And Sasha jumped to her feet and stood in front of them, panting and wagging her tail. Dean ruffled her head and gave her a piece of bread and goat's cheese, which she gobbled down in half a second.

Skye squealed and threw her arms around the dog. 'Clever Sasha,' she said. 'Clever, clever Sasha.' Then she pointed the stick at her again. '*Bang*!'

CHAPTER TWENTY-TWO

Tara,
August 2002

I'd always been envious of people who slept well. From my mid-teens onwards I resigned myself to being one of those for whom sleep was a battle. Kit was convinced things would change when we moved to the farm. But if anything I slept worse. The dead quiet was unsettling. The occasional screeches from owls spiked my adrenalin. The creaks of the floorboards as others moved around disturbed me. And, of course, my racing mind didn't stay behind in Cowley. I was a chronic over-thinker and bubbling anxiety caused mental chaos in those still hours while everybody else was asleep. I was still thinking about Dani and her poor mum. Concerned about how things would work in the winter, without heat and light and hot water, when the cold weather set in and the moor was shrouded in thick mists and battered by storms. Kit shrugged off these fears. Kit was someone who lived in the moment. He didn't trouble himself with concerns about the future. While his ever-ready shrug-and-smile was reassuring most of the time, occasionally I found it infuriating.

When the August heatwave took hold, the nights became hot and sticky and long. I was getting no more than three or four fitful hours a night and after a couple of weeks I was desperate and went to find Mary.

Mary used to be a sales assistant in a pharmacy. During her time there, she told me, she became bothered by the amount of drugs people consumed. 'People take a pill for anything,' she said. 'For the slightest snivel, a sore throat, a headache. It felt wrong and I had a bit of a lightbulb moment. I knew we'd all be healthier if we steered clear of the chemicals produced by profit-hungry pharmaceutical companies, and returned to a natural way of healing.'

She bought herself a copy of Culpepper's *Complete Herbal,* a huge tome written three hundred and fifty years earlier and still, she assured me, any modern apothecary's bible, and spent years familiarising herself with it. 'There's a treatment for everything you can think of. I'm convinced that if we wean our bodies off modern medicine we become healthier and need fewer treatments.'

I walked down to her pantry, a small room off the kitchen which was a treasure trove of lotions and potions. There was a big dresser filled to bursting. The drawers containing foraged plants. The shelves displaying an Aladdin's cave of jars and brown glass bottles, a huge stone pestle and mortar, bunches of drying herbs, and oils in all shades of yellow from pale straw to deep amber.

'Do you have anything to help me sleep, Mary? I'm desperate.'

Her features drooped in exaggerated sympathy. 'Oh, dear. There's nothing worse than not sleeping. But don't you panic,' she said with a bright smile. 'I've plenty that can help. How about you try …' She ran her hand along the bottles and reached for one. 'This.' She handed me the bottle. Inside were hundreds of tiny balls of sugar supposedly infused with something magical derived from flowers. Not what I was after.

'Do you have anything a bit stronger?'

'Stronger than *nux vomica*?' She sounded shocked.

I tried to smile. 'I was thinking an elephant tranquilliser?'

'You could try cocculus with a bit of Rescue Remedy.' She ran her eyes along the shelves. 'Or how about valerian? That's very effective and great if you're feeling anxious as well. I've got some henbane—'

'Have you got anything I'm not supposed to take more than the recommended dose of?'

Mary looked confused.

'A sleeping pill? Something from a doctor? I'm so tired I want to scream.'

'No. No, nothing like that. And, well ...' She hesitated and looked furtively behind me into the kitchen. 'Jeremy has been quite firm about us using plant remedies only.'

'What do you mean?'

'He wants the farm to be free from relying on doctors and modern medicine.' She smiled, her gaze dewy, and her hand went to her chest to caresses her amber pendant. 'He cares so much about us. I've never met anybody with a heart as big as his. The meditation sessions we've been—'

'That's great.' A headache had started up and an arrow of pain shot through my temples. 'So you think valerian? Or what did you say? Henbane?'

Her fingers let go of the amber. 'We can start you on a regular dose of valerian which I think will make a big difference, then if you need something a bit stronger we can try a drop of henbane. Only a drop mind. It can be ever so dangerous if you take too much.'

'Hopefully the valerian will work.'

'It'll work a treat and much better for you than the poison the doctors prescribe.'

In our room, Kit was standing by the bed, towel around his waist, bare-chested, skin gleaming wet from washing.

'You look happy,' he said.

I showed him the bottle. 'Mary gave me a bottle of sleep.' I walked over to him and wrapped my arms around his waist and rested my chin on his damp shoulder. 'Has Jay spoken to you about doctors and medicines?'

'Not since before we arrived. Why?'

'He told her he wanted to stop using them. Treat everything with plants.'

'For minor things, yeah, that makes sense. People pop painkillers like sweets. Surely it's best we use a natural remedy to treat something.'

My fingers stroked the bottle of valerian.

Kit kissed me then his eyes glazed with sex. He kissed me again, this time more urgently, his hands pushing up under my top.

'Where's Skye?' I whispered.

He stepped closer to the window and pointed. Skye and Dani were playing in the field, laughing and running around with the goats, who were leaping on to their pallet playground as if playing catch with the girls. He moved behind me and kissed my neck. I tilted my head and closed my eyes, moaning softly as his hands cupped my breasts.

'Close the door,' I said.

He did as I said and I lifted my shirt above my head and stepped out of my trousers. As he returned to the bed he removed the towel and dropped it on the floor. We lay down, our bodies already beaded with sweat in the heat and shafts of sunlight. When was the last time we'd made love in the daytime? Maybe university. Whole days consumed by sex and talking and ravenous eating before falling back into bed.

As Kit moved himself inside me, the bedroom door opened.

'Jesus,' I breathed, snatching at the sheet to cover us.

'Sorry,' Dean said casually, not giving any hint of embarrassment. 'Do you know where Jeremy is? There's a problem with the water tank.'

I buried my head in Kit's shoulder as he replied, 'Sorry, no idea. Could you knock next time?'

'Sure. No problem.'

Then he closed the door and called Jeremy's name a couple of times.

Kit rolled off me, collapsing back on the pillow, arm bent and resting over his eyes.

I laid my hand on his chest. 'Daytime sex is overrated.'

But Kit didn't laugh. He turned on his side to look at me. He smiled and stroked a strand of hair out of my eyes. 'A bit of privacy would be nice.'

'Privacy? Here?' I smiled. 'I think we gave up privacy when we agreed to join a commune.'

The day unfurled to be the hottest yet. The grass was crispy and yellow underfoot. The goats found a patch of shade and lay down and the chickens sunbathed in hollows they'd scratched out of the dirt. Sasha was panting on the stone floor in the hallway, refusing point-blank to venture outside. Everybody was grouchy and toiling slowly. It was as if the whole farm was drained of power.

Jeremy was reading in the dining room. It was cool and tranquil in there. Books and notes were scattered on the table in front of him. He closed his book when I came into the room and folded his hands on the table.

'What are you reading?'

'A bit of research.'

'On what?'

He shrugged. 'Sustainable living. Holistic practices. Enrichment. That kind of thing.'

It struck me how focused he was. Often with Jeremy, or at least the Jeremy before Winterfall, he'd become consumed with a cause, but his interest would quickly burn out and be directed onto something new. His drive to make the farm a success, however, was unfaltering.

'Do you need something?'

'Everybody's hot and bothered. It's boiling out there,' I paused. 'We really enjoyed our break from the farm the other day and I wondered if it might be nice to do something similar this afternoon.'

He steepled his fingers and said nothing. I was hit by the realisation that Jeremy and I had drifted apart. We used to be close. We'd laugh and hug. I'd listen to his bonkers theories and rants and enjoy them. But in the last few months he seemed to have built a wall around himself. He was unreadable. Distant. Always buried in a book or meditating or huddled in a corner with one of the others, talking in hushed whispers.

'Go somewhere together. A few hours away. Maybe a swim?'

'Take the afternoon off?'

I nodded.

'That's a dangerous precedent to set, Tara. If we take time off every time conditions aren't perfect then the work won't get done. If the work doesn't get done then the farm won't survive.'

I glanced at the book in front of him. His eyes narrowed, challenging me to say something.

'It's only one afternoon, Jay. A reward for working in the heat this morning.'

He looked doubtful. 'You're suggesting the lake you went to? I'm not sure that's the right place to go.'

'No, not there. I read about a quarry in one of Kit's books. You can swim in it. It's not far away, about half an hour's drive.'

Jeremy looked as if he might say no, but then he nodded. 'Fine. A swim sounds good.'

I followed Jeremy out of the front door and waited as he called everyone into the yard.

'A reward for your hard work,' he said, after he'd explained what we were doing. 'You all deserve it.'

He was claiming the idea as his own? I stood there, openmouthed, expecting him to turn to and acknowledge me. But he didn't. He stood with an air of benevolence while everybody got excited and clapped and thanked him. When they disappeared to get towels, I considered confronting him about it, but then stopped myself. Why did it matter? I didn't care. I was just glad that we were getting out and if Jeremy needed everybody to think it was down to him, then fine. I wasn't going to fight about it.

The guidebook suggested we park at a place called Minions. From there it was a twenty-minute walk. We'd packed bags with towels, fruit, flapjacks, and water, and I was thankful we didn't have more as it was tougher going than I'd expected. We passed a stone circle and a group of hot ponies who flicked their tails to keep the flies off, and barely gave us a second look as we trailed past them.

Though disappointing to see other people there when we arrived, it didn't take away from the beauty of the place. The quarry resembled a volcano crater. Three-quarters of it was closed in by sheer cliffs cut into the granite. The open section was slabs of flat rock and grass, providing a shallow area to enter the lake and the perfect spot for Skye to paddle. The quarry was spring-fed and its clarity was breathtaking. As we looked into the glassy water we could see fish, maybe brown trout, swimming leisurely. The group already there were young, drunk, and noisy. They sat on the opposite side of the crater, at the highest point of the cliff from which they were leaping into the water, their whoops and cries echoing around the stone like a cavernous church.

Kit and I took it in turns paddling with Skye in the shallows while the others swam. Thankfully, Dani could swim, not strongly, but enough that I wasn't anxious about her drowning. It was lovely to watch the group playing and enjoying the water. They looked so relaxed and at ease. So happy. I threw out my towel and lay down, luxuriating in the warmth of the sun on my cooled skin. Bruce and Anne were a little away from the rest of us. She laid her head on his chest and I watched them chatting, his fingers lightly stroking her hair, her sleigh-bell laugh tinkling in the air. Jeremy was reading his book, sunglasses on, legs stretched out. It was like being on holiday.

'We should do this more often,' I said to Kit as we threw pebbles into the water with Skye and tried to count the rings which rippled outwards.

'Check Ash out,' Kit whispered, nudging me.

I followed his gaze and saw Ash on the other side of the quarry, sitting on a rock beside a girl who was watching her friends as they cliff-jumped. Even from the other side of the water it was clear she was flirting, twiddling her hair, glancing at him, laughing, leaning into him when she spoke. I smiled, but at the same moment noticed the young men on the ridge. They'd noticed Ash and the girl too and were nudging each other. Glaring. Squaring their shoulders as they paced the grass at the top of the rock face.

'Oi, you! Yeah, you, you skank! Piss off,' one of them called.

Ash glanced up, but then looked back at the girl, who shielded her eyes and looked up then shook her head and rolled her eyes.

The lads, five of them, bare-chested, in shorts, half-ran along the grassy top and down the path.

'Hey, Ash!' I called over, gesturing upwards, hoping he'd understand.

But he just waved and made no attempt to move.

'He'll be fine,' Kit said, lying back on the rock. 'He's a grown-up.'

But as I watched my fear ballooned.

The boys got down to the rock where Ash and the girl were chatting. Words were said. Gestures thrown. The argument seemed to escalate when the girl punched the air angrily then pushed past her friends. She must have said something to Ash because he jumped to his feet and followed. I watched her take his hand then turn to the others and flick up her fingers.

They were walking in our direction. As they got nearer, I saw the girl's expression was stony and cross. 'They're dicks,' I heard her say. 'Ignore them.'

Ash smiled at her and rubbed the back of his neck. He started to speak, but one of the boys had split from the pack and was running deftly over the stony ground. He came up behind Ash and shoved him.

I gasped and grabbed at Kit. 'That guy pushed Ash.'

Kit looked up and swore. 'Stay here,' he said. 'Jay? Can you come with me?'

'I told you to keep your dirty skank hands off her.'

'We're only talking,' Ash replied coolly.

'Yeah? Well. You're not talking to her anymore, yeah?'

'I told you to piss off,' the girl said. 'God, Mikey, you're such a *kid*.'

Her friend glowered. 'Why d'you want to hang out with this crusty, anyway?'

The girl rolled her eyes. 'Because he's way more interesting than *you*. All you want to do is show off and get high. It's *boring*.'

The other boys in the group had joined their friend and started to push and jostle and crowd around Ash.

Kit and Jeremy walked over, relaxed, both of them keeping it easy. The boys began to jeer and lift their chins in challenge.

'Dickheads,' the girl said. 'It's too hot to fight.'

'It's never too hot to fight,' said one of the boys. The others laughed.

'I'm not fighting anybody,' Ash said.

'No?' The guy – Mikey – pushed him and he stumbled backwards.

Ash stood up and raised his hands. 'I'm not fighting.'

'Take it easy lads,' said Jeremy as they reached the group.

Then one of them shoved Ash again. 'Fucking skank pussy with your stupid fucking hair. You think you get a girl without even fighting?'

Ash shook his head. 'Whatever. I'm out.' He turned and started to walk back towards me.

The men laughed and jeered, calling Ash all manner of names.

Then one snarled and made a move to follow him. Kit and Jeremy stepped in to block his way.

'We don't want trouble,' said Kit.

My heart was thumping. We'd been isolated from other people for so long. Shielded from aggression and bad behaviour, secure and safe in our harmonious group. Dani and Skye had sidled over to stand behind me. Skye slipped her hand into mine. 'They're just boys being silly,' I whispered to her.

'You might not want it, but you fucking got it. You're not welcome here, yeah? So fuck off back to whatever city dump you came from.'

'You know, this lot are the ones at the farm near Alec's.'

'Oh, fuck me! You're the hippie twats? Thieving gyppo bastards.'

'We live at Winterfall Farm, yes,' said Jeremy, bristling, his voice concrete. 'But we aren't hippies. Or gypsies. And we aren't thieves.'

'Not what I heard.'

I was aware of Dani dropping her head. When I looked at her I noticed her cheeks were flushed red.

Mikey squared up to Jeremy. Face close. One fist balled. Kit reached out to rest a hand on his shoulder. He shrugged it off with a snarl. It was then Bruce and Dean joined them. Bruce towered over Mikey. 'Time to go home now, boys,' he said.

'Let's not ruin a nice afternoon, eh?' added Dean.

A murmur of hesitation rippled through the group of locals. Then the girl Ash had been talking to grabbed Mikey by the hand. 'Leave it,' she said to him. 'It's not worth it.'

'We can take them.' The group jostled as one. 'Bunch of pansies. Bet the big one's never thrown a punch in his life.' Bruce moved forward and despite his bravado, Mikey took a step backwards.

The girl rolled her eyes again. 'Let's go and get a drink. Martha will be at the Badger by now.'

I held my breath then released it when the locals shook their heads and turned, gesticulating over their shoulders and sneering.

'Hippie cunts!' Mikey called back, before looping his arm over the girl's shoulders.

She shrugged him away. 'Get off me, Mikey.'

'Hey!' Jeremy called. The girl looked round and Jeremy jogged over. 'Wait up a sec!'

The others, the boys, sneered and shook their heads, clearly over the idea of a fight. But the girl stopped walking and waited coyly.

'You should visit us on the farm. Hang out with Ash. Have dinner and take a look round. You'd be welcome.'

The girl tipped her chin back and smiled, this time knowingly. 'You hitting on me too? I heard you share girls. Bloody *hippies*.' Then she skipped back to her friends, throwing her arms around them and laughing.

'We're not hippies!' Jeremy called. But the group didn't care. We were forgotten.

Jeremy gathered us into a ring. Anne held Bruce's hand. Ash rolled a cigarette, then passed his pouch of tobacco to Dean. Skye sat between my legs and Dani next to me. 'It's OK,' I whispered.

Dani nodded and I smiled to reassure her.

'This is why we keep ourselves to ourselves. The outside world is broken. We were immune to it before. Aggression was part of everyday living. We don't need that shit anymore.'

We drew together, close, holding each other's shoulders, heads bowed into the centre.

When we pulled apart, Ash lit his cigarette. 'She was pretty though,' he said, gazing over at the rock where the girl had been sunbathing.

CHAPTER TWENTY-THREE

Kit,
August 2002

'Kit?' Bruce is standing at their bedroom door. Kit's head is groggy, eyes gummed up with sleep and heat. As his eyes focus on Bruce he sees he is pale and agitated.

'What's wrong?' Kit whispers.

'You need to come down,' Bruce whispers back.

Tara is still asleep. He gestures to Bruce that he's coming then climbs out of bed as silently as he can. It was another tough night for her, unable to get back to sleep after being woken by Sasha's barking in the middle of the night. Kit had listened to Dean trying to settle his dog a few times, but in the end he'd heard her clipping up the stairs after Dean and following him into his bedroom.

Kit grabs his jeans and a T-shirt up and dresses on the landing as Bruce wakes Jeremy. They follow Bruce downstairs and walk towards the open front door. The scene outside steals Kit's breath.

It takes a while for the extent of the vandalism to sink in. Red paint daubs Jeremy's van. The tyres are slashed. Graffiti scrawls the sheds, *hippie filth*, and *gyppo scum*, neon signs lighting up the granite. White paint streaks the cobbles, slashes of brightness against the grey.

Jeremy rubs his face and shakes his head. 'Little shits,' he growls.

'You think it's the lads from yesterday?'

'Without a doubt. They knew where we lived. I even confirmed it for them. Told them the name of the place, didn't I?'

'I should check the animals.' Kit runs to the goat shed, heart pounding. He knows full well what horrors people are capable of, especially when it comes to animals. He opens the goat shed and lets out a sigh of relief when he sees two pairs of blinking eyes staring back at him. The goats get over their momentary surprise at being woken too early, and bustle past him, trotting up to the corner of the enclosure in case he changes his mind about releasing them. The chickens are also unharmed, clucking softly from their perches. Kit breathes a word of gratitude. Paint and tyres are easy to deal with. Dead or maimed animals would've been a tragedy.

It takes the whole day to clean the worst of the paint off the buildings.

Dean beats himself up for not listening to Sasha. 'I'm sorry. God, she tried to warn me, didn't she? And what did I do? Shout at her. This is my fault.'

Everybody reassures him it's not, apart from Jeremy, who is too angry to speak, scrubbing at the cobbles, visibly fuming. Kit can't help but see the irony, given the number of times Jeremy has destroyed property with paint or bricks, but keeps this thought to himself as he imagines Jeremy wouldn't take kindly to the jibe. Instead he turns off the hosepipe and crouches beside his friend. 'Hey, Jay, don't let this get to you. It's kids. Mucking about. Testosterone raging. Drunk. And it's not that bad. A bit of paint and a couple of tyres.'

Jeremy puts his scrubbing brush down and turns blazing eyes on Kit. 'You're wrong. This isn't tearaway kids. This assault means so much more. It's us versus them, the outside world.' Then he kicks the bucket of water and sends it skittering across the yard, splashing milky white water across the cobbles. The rest of the group drop their heads, scrub harder, the silence thick as they clean up what feels like an attack.

Jeremy has calmed down by the time they break for tea and a slice of fruitcake. 'We won't let this ugliness break our spirit. We are strong and we are united. It's time to shut the rest of the world out.' He casts his eyes around the group, lasering each of them in turn. 'They are *scared*. Of us and of what they don't know. Of what challenges their myopic world view. They are threatened by us. In creating this place we shine light on their flawed, insubstantial lives. They convince themselves that *we* are the outsiders and something to hate, but their hatred only makes us stronger.'

The group has formed a semicircle around him. They gaze at him. Hanging on his every breath. For a moment or two he doesn't move as he lets his words take root in them. Then he turns and strides down to the farm entrance and drags the metal five-bar gate to close it. It clatters over the stones then clangs heavily shut.

'Are you calling the police?' Ash is weighed down by guilt and even though Kit told him he did nothing wrong in talking to that girl he clearly blames himself.

'No,' Jeremy replies without hesitation. 'I don't want them poking around asking questions.' Kit hears an audible sigh of relief from Dani. 'No, we clean up, we move on. Something like this was bound to happen sooner or later. Now it has I am galvanised. Any revolutionary movement will always come up against prejudice and aggression. We don't need the police – agents of oppression – to handle our fights. No. We batten our hatches. We protect our home.'

Tara looks pale and chews her lower lip. Despite Jeremy's rousing words she is shaken. Later she tells Kit how much the incident has unsettled her. 'I'm worried for the girls. I mean, those guys weren't just bored kids. They were gunning for a fight. Maybe they want to provoke us? Maybe they're coming back for more? We're so vulnerable here. What if they'd broken into the house?'

Her unease upsets him. He hates that she feels unsafe. 'But they didn't, and if Sasha barks like that again, we'll know to check it out, yes?'

Tara nods, but doesn't look convinced.

'What are you thinking?'

She winces a little then glances at the sky as if searching for the answer. 'I don't know. I think what's happened has lifted a mirror. We've made such a monumental decision for Skye, haven't we? We've removed her from a conventional life. Exposed her. To criticism and unkindness. She'll always be the daughter of *those hippies*. The weird kid in charity shop clothes with no television who smells of homemade soap.'

Kit puts his arms around her and rests his chin on the top of her head. 'She'll be the kid who is happy and loved. Who is healthy. Body and mind. That's all that matters. You and I both know that. Conventional life isn't all it's cracked up to be. Jeremy's right. It's the outside world which is broken. Not us.'

Three days after the yard was vandalised, Jeremy asks Kit if he can borrow the Land Rover, which, parked as it was around the back of the farmhouse near the orchard, managed to remain unscathed in the attack.

'Sure. Where are you going?'

Jeremy is vague. 'A few things to do. I need to pick up some tyres for the van. Sort some things out. I'll only be a couple of nights.'

Kit doesn't press him further. He doesn't mind where Jeremy is going. If anything, a few days away from the farm will do him good. Maybe he'll realise the world outside their gate isn't the enemy he has fabricated.

'Can I leave you in charge while I'm gone?'

Kit smiles. 'In charge?'

Jeremy doesn't smile back. 'Do you mind?'

'Mind that you're in charge? No. I don't mind. I just assumed we ran as a collective. A group.'

'You'd be surprised how much steering the farm needs and how many people come to me with questions or problems. I stepped forward when nobody else did. You weren't interested. Or Tara. Nor Bruce or Anne. But I'm happy to take a back seat if you want to take over?'

There's a hardness to Jeremy's words which takes Kit by surprise. As if he's fending off what he thinks is a challenge.

'No. No. You do a great job.'

Jeremy smiles then. 'Good. I wouldn't want to tread on your toes.'

When he leaves a few hours later, Tara joins Kit in the yard and they watch the Land Rover bump along the potholed lane. 'And he didn't say why he's going?'

'Guess he doesn't need to tell us everything he does.'

'I suppose not.' She watches the Land Rover until it disappears out of sight. 'Dani and I are going to do some painting with Skye. Want to join us?'

'There's something I need to do. Out on the moor.'

'Sounds mysterious?'

His cheeks redden and he looks away from her. 'It's not. I'm …' He hesitates. 'I thought I'd build a hide so we can watch the wildlife.'

'And you're doing it while Jay is away because he wouldn't approve of you shirking your chores?' She smiles mischievously.

'I think I do enough work around here to have a few hours away.'

His tone is sharper than he intends and she raises her eyebrows and laughs. 'Calm down, I don't mind what you do. You're a free man. A hide sounds fun. Dani and Skye will love it.'

CHAPTER TWENTY-FOUR

Dani,
August 2002

'That's the deal.'

I avoided Tara's eyes and focused on milking Rosie, who stood nicely and ate her breakfast while I pulled on her. She was my favourite to milk. Snowy was grumpy and stamped a lot and if you weren't careful she'd kick the pail over and the precious milk would seep into the mud, like in *James and the Giant Peach* when his magic crystals wriggle into the ground. But Rosie seemed to enjoy it and would trot down towards me when she saw me with the pail.

'Dani? Do you understand? If you want to stay you must promise to work with me. You can't opt out of education at your age. I get that you don't want to go to school here, but you have to agree to home-schooling.'

I rolled my eyes and gave a nod.

'You don't need to look so cross about it! It'll be fun. Way better than school. It'll be creative and more varied, and we can plan your lessons together so you have a say in what you're learning.'

I knew I was being a cow, but I couldn't get my head around why she was making me go to school. I *hated* school. I'd already decided there was no way I was staying on for sixth form, so this would have been my last year anyway. I just didn't see the point in it now I lived at Winterfall. I'd moaned to everybody. Lots of times. Bruce and Anne said it was important I did what was right for me. Ash and Dean didn't have much to say at all. Kit supported Tara. Jeremy thought the idea of school was wrong, 'on so many levels', something to do with making sausages, but I didn't get what he meant. Mary nodded along to everything he said. But Tara definitely had *views,* as my mum would have said. In one breath she said schools were awful places which 'squashed creativity and imagination', then in another that 'education was vital' and dropping out wasn't an option. Jeremy had called a group meeting a few weeks earlier and she'd argued so convincingly that eventually, one by one, everybody agreed with her and, well, now it seemed I was stuck with it.

'We start tomorrow,' she said. 'I'll work with you and Skye at the same time. Obviously you're at different levels, but we can make it work. You can have some quiet time reading, for example, while I teach Skye to read, and when we're done, you and I can discuss what you've read. It'll be fun.' She grinned and pushed my shoulder gently. 'I *promise.*'

I patted Rosie's back and bent for the pail, which was full with creamy milk. Bruce had said he'd make custard to have with a rhubarb crumble that evening, and my mouth watered at the thought.

Tara untied Rosie and she bounced out of the shed, bucked happily, and skipped over to join Snowy in the shade of the tree.

'So where's Jeremy gone?' I asked, as we walked back to the house together.

'No idea,' she said, shaking her head, 'but that's Jeremy. A law unto himself. Whatever he's doing, it's best to let him get on with it. Once he's made his mind up it's impossible to dissuade him. He's always been the same. His mind never rests. Our mad genius at work.'

'Maybe he wants to get out of doing chores.'

Tara laughed. 'Maybe.'

'Would you look at that haul,' Bruce grinned, as I heaved the churn onto the kitchen worktop. 'Think I'll make some garlic butter too, and a nice French loaf. Nothing beats proper garlic bread with a lasagne.'

'Sounds delicious,' I said. Since coming to the farm I was eating things I'd never have touched in a million years before. Lasagne was what the cretin called *foreign muck*. He'd fall off his chair if I told him it was vegetarian as well. But it was his loss. The food here was amazing. Over the last few weeks, Bruce had started teaching me to cook, which made Tara happy, as she said it counted as home schooling. I was happy because it didn't feel anything like being at school. He showed me how to make pizza dough, which we spread with a sauce made from tomatoes I picked that morning. I could make goat's cheese on my own now. Ripe red peppers picked from the vine then stuffed with rice and courgette. Flapjacks, icing for carrot cake, strawberry jam, and even bread, which was much harder work than I'd imagined.

'You're a talented cook,' Bruce said, as we sliced the pizza, and I felt I might explode with pride.

Tara and I walked up to the vegetable garden to find Skye. The sky was ripe and full as plums, the dark clouds tinged pink.

'The air smells different.'

I didn't know that was even a thing. I breathed in and realised she was right. Who knew the air had a smell?

'Maybe we'll get a storm. It's so close it's hard to breathe.'

In Leyton I hated the thought of rain. It meant staying in the flat with cretin Eddie getting crosser and crosser. But here I loved it. It made everything feel fresh and clean and, right now, we needed it. The land had turned dry and crispy, and I hated seeing the wilting plants and grass yellowing with thirst.

Skye was helping Dean dig potatoes and when she saw us she picked a couple up and said, 'Now we can have chips!'

Dean smiled and waved cheerily when he saw me. Sasha trotted over and pushed her damp nose into my hand, then bounded back to Skye, who was rummaging in the soil in search of more potatoes.

'Kit not here?' Tara asked Dean.

Dean shook his head. 'Haven't seen him since this morning.'

This seemed to make Tara sad.

'Are you all right?' I asked.

She smiled a surface smile that did a rubbish job at covering up whatever she was thinking about. 'Kit is spending less time with us, that's all.'

Tara and I knelt on the soil and helped dig for potato treasure, and it wasn't long before I got my wish and someone popped the clouds with a knitting needle. Fat, warm rain balloons burst on the baked earth. The smell was insane. I sat back on my heels and breathed in deeply, closing my eyes as raindrops hit my face. A rumble of thunder rolled across the moor in the distance and made the hairs on my arms stand up. Tara stretched her arms out and threw back her head and we laughed as the swollen drops hit our sticky skin. Moments later, the heavens opened. Dean grabbed my hands and pulled me up. He whooped and spun us around in a crazy circle as a waterfall fell from the sky. Skye squealed with joy and ran to join us. Then I heard laughing and turned to see Anne and Mary burst out of the front door and run across the yard, arms waving in the air as they leapt and cheered. Bruce followed, walking not running, and leant over the wall. He grinned as he watched us stomping our feet, our clothes soaked through, laughing hyenas, mud spraying up our legs as we danced.

I let go of Dean's hands and ran down to him. I pulled on his arm. 'Come and dance with us!'

He laughed. 'Mad as a box of frogs, you lot.'

I ran back to the others, opening my mouth to catch the rain, and twirled with Skye. I waved at him and he smiled again, eyes soft and kind, and I pretended he was my grandpa and he was filled up with love for me, and it made my insides glow.

CHAPTER TWENTY-FIVE

Tara,
September 2002

Jeremy had left the farm again. Another secretive trip. His third since the night of the vandalism. I didn't care that much. It was none of my business. As Kit said, he was his own person. In all honesty, it was reassuring to know we still had individual agency and didn't always have to function as one. But what had got under my skin was Kit. As soon as Jeremy drove out of the gate, he would make his excuses and vanish. This time I'd run after him.

'Want company?'

He'd looked sheepish. Unable to meet my eyes. 'Do you mind if I have some time alone? I need to clear my head.'

The rejection stung. I didn't want to nag him to spend time with me and Skye, so I bit my tongue and held my words back. Maybe I was more sensitive because I was tired? Mary's lauded valerian had done nothing to help with my sleep and I was exhausted. This, combined with my mounting frustration at Kit's detachment, had put me in a filthy mood by the time he climbed over the stile in the late afternoon.

When he leant in for a kiss I turned away.

'You all right?'

'Why wouldn't I be?'

He stared at me for a moment or two with infuriating confusion. 'Are you upset about something?'

'Upset? No, I'm fine.' I turned on my heel and strode back towards the house. 'We did some maths today,' I called over my shoulder. 'In case you're wondering how we've been.'

'That's great,' he said, jogging to catch up with me.

As we reached the front door, I swore and stopped him in his tracks. 'Actually, *no*. I'm not all right. I'm pissed off.'

Mary wandered down the hallway carrying a stack of plates with cutlery piled on top and turned into the dining room. 'Oh, hello, Kit love. Good day?'

'Hi Mary. Yup. Great. Thank you.'

I rolled my eyes and pushed him backwards, gesturing for him to follow me around the side of the house, where we could talk more privately. I crossed my arms and glared.

'What's wrong?'

He looked uneasy, fearful something awful had happened, and I suddenly wished I'd let him believe I was fine. The last thing I wanted to be was one of those women, like my mother, who needled and nagged and sniped at their partners. I dropped my head and kicked the stones. 'It's nothing. I'm knackered, that's all.'

'Tell me.' He took my hand and passed his thumb, ingrained with dirt and calloused from chopping wood, over my skin.

'It's just …' I sighed and raised my eyes to meet his. 'You keep disappearing. Every time Jeremy goes. It's like you don't want to be here without him. Like you're bored of me and Skye or something.'

He shook his head and laughed. 'You crazy woman,' he said softly. 'Bored of you and Skye? Are you insane?'

As I looked at him he blurred, my eyes filming with tears. I felt silly and spoilt.

'I'm busy with something, a project, that's all.' He rested his hand against my cheek and I leant into him. 'Shall we take Skye for a walk before supper? Dani too, if she wants to come.'

My throat constricted with a surge of emotion so all I could do was nod.

The Land Rover was parked in the yard when we got back. We heard the clamour of voices as soon as we walked into the house and found everybody gathered in the kitchen. It took a moment or two for me to notice the stranger sitting on a stool with a rucksack at her feet.

'Here they are!' cried Jeremy as we walked in. 'Tara, Kit, Skye. This,' he said, sweeping open his arm in the girl's direction, a magician revealing a vanished assistant, 'is Emily.'

The girl was early twenties. Pale with an uneven fringe cut into lank, Goth-black hair. Dark circles ringed her eyes and her skin was wrecked. Too many drugs, I guessed. Her nails were bitten to the quick and she was dressed in jeans and an old khaki parka, a dead cat of fake fur around the hood.

'Emily will be staying for a few days. Until she finds her feet.' Jeremy smiled at Emily as if expecting her to say something.

My stomach clenched with disbelief. Surely not? Another vulnerable girl brought here without discussion? He hadn't listened to a word I'd said after Dani arrived.

'She'll take the room opposite Dani.'

Dani was hovering in the doorway of Mary's pantry. Arms crossed protectively around her body. Wary eyes fixed on Emily.

'Ash? Would you show Emily to her room?'

'Me?' Ash blushed red and Emily made no effort to conceal an amused smile.

'If you don't mind?' Jeremy then addressed Emily. 'We'll make you a sandwich and a cup of tea. Sugar?'

'Three.'

Ash glanced at Emily shyly as he picked up her rucksack. She slid off the stool and strode out of the room as if she owned the place. Everything about this was making me edgy. As soon as Ash and Emily were out of earshot, I grabbed Jeremy's arm and pulled him to me. 'What the fuck?' I whispered.

'She's exhausted, Tara. Please. Let's leave the drama for a bit. The poor girl is mentally at rock bottom.' He paused then raised his brow. 'And she's twenty-three. Presumably you don't have a problem with that?'

'Don't be a dick.'

Ash came back into the kitchen, his cheeks still pink. 'She's having a wash,' he said. 'I found her a towel from the cupboard.'

'Well done, Ash.'

Ash nodded and I half-expected Jeremy to pat him on the head.

Bruce put the goat's cheese sandwich he'd made on a plate with some sliced tomatoes, while Anne made a cup of tea, stirring in three heaped spoons of sugar. Jeremy held the plate out towards Ash.

I intercepted Ash and took hold of the plate. 'I'll take it.'

Jeremy began to protest, but I smiled at Ash. 'If you don't mind?'

Ash nodded then pulled his tobacco pouch out of his pocket. 'I'm going for a smoke anyway.'

The attic room door was open. Emily was wrapped in a towel while drying her hair with another. 'Oh my God, I cannot *believe* you wash in cold water!' She blinked slowly and rubbed at her hair.

'Something to eat?'

Ignoring the plate of food, Emily took the mug. She blew across the top of it then sipped. 'Jesus *fuck*,' she said, grimacing. 'That's rank.' She handed the mug back to me and shook her head.

'It's the goat's milk. You get used to it.' I put the tea and sandwich on the window sill and smiled at her. 'Jeremy says you're pretty tired.'

She brushed my words away with a dismissive shrug, then cocked her head and smiled. 'So, tell me, this some sort of cult, right?'

'A cult?' I laughed, but my hackles went up, immediately defensive. 'What on earth makes you ask that?'

She dropped the towel to the floor and stood there naked, proud as anything. I averted my eyes and felt my cheeks flush with heat. When I looked back her eyes seemed to be challenging me to be shocked or embarrassed. It was as if she'd strolled into our home and was sniffing out weak spots. I held her gaze and she smiled brightly and reached for her clothes.

'Nothing really,' she said, as she pushed her head through her sweater. 'It's got culty vibes, that's all. I mean, that guy? Jeremy? He's your leader? If you've got a leader with long hair and beads round his neck, that makes you a cult?'

'He isn't our *leader*. We don't have leaders here.'

'No leaders and everybody's equal, yeah?'

Her smirk made me bristle. I inhaled then breathed out slowly. 'Is there anything else you need?'

'Well, I guess I might as well make the most of the facilities. Where do you wash clothes? Assuming, of course, you wash your clothes?'

It took a huge amount of self-control not to bite back. Rock bottom or not, her attitude was something else. How dare she waltz in and judge us? Well, she wasn't going to make me feel ashamed. I straightened my shoulders and raised my chin. 'There's a tub and hosepipe outside the back door. On the ledge is a box of soap flakes. You can use the mangle to—'

'A *mangle*!' Emily exploded with laughter. 'Jesus. A mangle? Christ,' she said through her laughter, 'it's certainly a lifestyle.'

'Yes, it is.' My forced civility tasted bitter. 'And it's a lifestyle we're proud of.'

CHAPTER TWENTY-SIX

Kit,
October 2002

Emily's arrival has destabilised the group. Ash and Dean hover around her, each of them going out of their way to make themselves indispensable. 'You want help with that?' comes non-stop and in stereo. Kit doesn't blame them. They haven't had sex in over seven months and Emily is not only pretty but knowingly flirtatious, and clearly enjoys their attention.

Skye is as indifferent to Emily as Emily is to Skye, while Dani has reverted to the sullen, grouchy teenager they first met. Mary laps up Emily's interest in herbal remedies and natural drugs, and Bruce and Anne are as kind and welcoming as they always are, despite Emily's often dismissive attitude, which is clearly driving Tara to distraction.

'She's not the right fit for a commune,' Tara whispers, as they lie in bed. 'She's a loner. Out for herself.'

'Let her settle before you act as judge and jury.'

'I'm not acting as judge and jury, I just don't trust her. Kit, I need to ask you something.'

'What?'

She pauses and a loaded silence thickens the air. 'Is Jeremy making these trips to find women?'

'What?'

She hesitates. 'I heard you talking at the midsummer party. When he told you he was giving up sex. He said he wanted to grow the community at Winterfall. Have babies born here. He said we needed more women.'

'He was joking.'

'I know he said he was, but every time he leaves, I hear his words again. I mean, he disappears for days at a time but won't say what he's doing? And now he's back with another girl he's picked off the street?'

'Jeremy? Harvesting women?' Kit cannot contain his incredulity. 'It's an insane thing to suggest.'

Tara doesn't reply.

'Jay is our friend, remember? He's not a deranged lunatic. Emily's in need—'

'Dani too.'

'You think Jeremy brought Dani here to *breed* from her? You sound unhinged.'

'*I* sound unhinged? I'm not the one talking about building a colony then trawling the streets for females.'

Kit cannot believe what he's hearing. How can she think this? It's an abhorrent thought. 'I don't want to talk about this anymore. Jeremy's my friend and I know, one hundred per cent, he isn't guilty of whatever it is you're accusing him of. These girls needed his help.'

She starts to reply, but he doesn't want to hear it. He throws back the covers and gets up, snatching his clothes off the floor and walking towards the door.

'Where are you going?'

'For a walk.' He manages to keep his voice soft. He's angry. But not with her. With Jeremy. If he hadn't been so damn secretive, if he'd told Kit what he was doing, then Kit could have shot Tara's crazy accusations down. As it is they're circling his mind looking for somewhere to settle.

*

A few days later, everybody is working in the orchard to get the apples picked and stored. The trees are laden with fruit. Bruce is hopping around with excitement.

'We'll stew half the crop,' he tells them. 'The rest we'll store. If we do it properly, in paper and cardboard, left in a dark, dry place, they'll last well into winter. Nothing better than baked apples with brown sugar and honey on a cold December day.'

Tara, Dani and Skye are tasked with wrapping the apples in newspaper in the dining room. Dean is fixing the guttering on the goat shed. Mary and Anne are peeling the apples for Bruce, who is sterilising jars. Jeremy is in his room reading up on water purification systems. Emily and Ash are picking the apples and gathering the fallers, giggling and flirting, Ash unable to look at anything but Emily. Kit is heading down to the copse to fell a tree. The colder nights mean they are burning more wood than he'd expected and their supply of logs is dwindling.

Kit is able to do most of it on his own, cutting notches into the trunk and securing it with ropes, but for the final stage he needs help from either Ash or Dean. It isn't a huge tree, but he doesn't want to risk being in the wrong place if there's a freak gust of wind or a failing of his calculations when pulling it down. He walks up to the orchard, but Ash isn't there.

He goes into the house and as he passes the dining room sticks his head round the door. 'I'm looking for Ash or Dean. Seen them?'

'Dean's gone off to get some bit to fix the shed. Ash should be in the orchard?'

'Just been there. No sign of him or Emily. It's no bother, I'll find him.'

The kitchen is dense with the syrupy smell of stewed apples and cinnamon. Bruce is shaking sugar into a large pan.

'Seen Ash?' Kit asks him.

Bruce picks up a wooden spoon and starts to gently stir. 'Orchard?'

Kit shakes his head.

'Maybe they took a break?'

'Don't suppose you can spare some time to help me bring the tree down?'

It's another two hours before Ash and Emily reappear. Kit and Tara are in the orchard picking the apples, which the two of them should have done. They hear them before they see them, shrieking and laughing from the direction of the field. Kit and Tara walk to where they can see the field and watch them struggling to climb the stile.

'Jesus,' Tara whispers.

'Ash mate,' Kit calls. 'You were supposed to be picking? We've got to get the apples in before the rain comes.'

'Sorry, we'll, er …' Ash collapses with laughter before he can finish his sentence.

Emily sniggers and buries her face in his shoulder.

'We'll … We'll come …' Ash clears his throat. 'We'll come now.'

Emily grabs his arm. 'No way. I'm starving. I need *all* the cake.'

'We should finish the picking.'

Emily laughs incredulously. 'You what? They aren't our fucking parents.'

Tara swears and turns on her heel. Emily laughs. Kit calls after her.

'I don't care!' she shouts back. 'Emily's right. I'm not her mother.'

Ash scurries after Tara towards the orchard.

Emily's face twists with confusion. 'We're not allowed downtime? What is this place? A fucking gulag?'

'It's a commune,' Kit says calmly. 'We share the work and we all benefit.'

'Whatever,' she says, and rolls her eyes.

Emily and Ash sit together at dinner exchanging covert glances and smothered smiles as they eat ravenously. An awkward hush has settled over the rest of them. Ash is known for slacking off every now and then, sneaking away to play his guitar or smoke a cigarette, but this is the first time any of them have wilfully downed tools and it's rattled the group. Even Bruce looks dour and he never gets riled by such things. Perhaps it's the lack of apology or remorse that's needling them. Kit suspects that in the time passed between them getting back and sitting down for supper, Emily has told Ash he has nothing to feel guilty about and reminded him he's an adult and can make his own decisions. Emily has brought a bit of the outside world into their home and it's rocked them.

Bruce brings out two dishes of hot apple crumble and Anne dishes on the table with an earthenware jug of custard. He sets the and the smell of sweet cinnamon and flaked almonds fills the air. Anne begins to spoon portions into bowls. Usually she would pass them along the line, but this time she throws an oddly nervous glance at Jeremy, who pushes his chair back from the table and walks over to her. He takes two bowls and delivers one to Mary and another to Dani. Bruce stands to help him, but Jeremy rests his hand on the large man's shoulder. 'I'll hand them round, Bruce.'

'Oh my goodness! That smells heavenly,' sings Mary, leaning so close to the crumble her nose almost touches it.

Bruce smiles. 'There's s slug of homemade apple brandy in the custard.'

Jeremy places bowls in front of Tara, Skye, Dean, Anne and Kit. Then he says, 'Two more, Bruce.'

'Two?'

'One for me and one for you.'

'I haven't got one?' Ash puts his hand up as if he's at school.

'Not for you or Emily tonight.' Jeremy takes a seat and looks at Ash, steepling his fingers over his steaming bowl of crumble and custard. 'It's clear we need a few rules if Winterfall is going to continue to run smoothly. We can't have a repeat of what happened this afternoon. It's not fair. I'd always hoped our home would run on trust and that we all understood that to coexist we have to work together. So, from now on, if people shirk their chores then they lose out on the rewards. Tonight neither of you will enjoy our delicious crumble.'

A murmur of perplexed shock ripples around the table as the rest of the group exchange questioning glances or lower their eyes. Skye is the only one who grabs her spoon and tucks in.

'You sure this is the right way?' Bruce says quietly.

'Very sure.' Jeremy rests a hand lightly on Bruce's. 'Winterfall can only work if everybody does their bit. If some take advantage, the whole project will collapse.'

Jeremy turns his stare on Emily. He has the man of the headmaster at Kit's prep school, a terrifying man who floated wraithlike along the corridors, searching for misbehaving boys he could cane. 'We want you to stay, Emily. But you must understand, in exchange for a bed and all your meals, you're only asked to contribute a few hours a day. Of course, we want you to have fun, but you can't undermine what we've built here. From now on recreational drugs are forbidden.'

Mary's face falls. 'But Jeremy?' she sings softly. 'I have cannabis derivatives and herbal drugs and without them—'

Jeremy smiles benevolently. 'Your remedies are permitted, of course.'

Mary smiles with relief, then reaches for her spoon and digs into the crumble.

'And if we disobey you?' Emily is staring at Jeremy and everybody else holds their breath.

'Then that person will leave Winterfall.'

A few people inhale sharply.

'I don't think either of these things are unreasonable, do you?' Jeremy looks around the room, his eyes connecting with each of them in turn. 'We have children here and we need to set a good example. Surely everybody agrees?'

'Can I have some more pudding, Mama?'

Tara puts her finger to her lips to shush Skye, who opens her mouth to complain. Tara gathers her onto her lap and points at her own bowl of pudding. Skye doesn't miss a beat and pulls the bowl towards her.

'It was only apples.' Ash taps the table nervously, unable to meet Jeremy's eyes.

'Only apples? Ash, the apples had to be picked while it was dry. They can't be stored wet. Now it's raining. So every apple we didn't get in before the weather turned, now has to be dried individually before it can be packed. That's double the work.'

Ash drops his head and Emily mutters something under her breath.

'I didn't catch that, Emily?' Jeremy's eyes are stony. The atmosphere in the room is unbearable and Kit, reminded of the excruciating meals he endured around the dining table at Ashbarton Coombe, is on the verge of walking out.

'I didn't say anything.'

'Maybe it was an apology?'

They stare at each other. Neither look as though they will give in. Kit notices Ash nudging Emily under the table. She rolls her eyes and mouths something at him. Then she looks back at Jeremy and takes a breath before letting it out slowly.

'I'm sorry,' she says. 'OK? I'm sorry I didn't pick all the apples.'

Jeremy nods then reaches for his spoon and sinks it into the crumble. 'I accept your apology. Try to remember, Emily, our home here is about community and commitment. We are all in this together.'

CHAPTER TWENTY-SEVEN

Dani,
October 2002

Jeremy made such a fuss about us being neighbours in the attic. You've lots in common, he said. Both Londoners, he said. You'll feel like sisters in no time.

Well, Jeremy didn't see the sneer on Emily's face.

When he left us alone, the temperature fell by a hundred degrees. 'Sisters,' she'd muttered, as she shoved hard against the window to open it. When it gave way a couple of spiders fell down. She flicked them away without even flinching, then sat on the mattress and searched her bag for a brown leather pouch, then began to roll a spliff.

'He told me you were living rough.' She lit up and the sickly sweet smell of weed filled the room.

'That's right.' I kept my expression flat so she knew whatever she thought of me was oil off water.

She raised her eyebrows. 'Presumably not for long.' She narrowed her eyes and pointed at me. 'I'd guess a night or two?' She tapped the spliff with her finger and snowflakes of ash settled on the mattress.

I didn't reply.

'Did you run away because Mummy said you couldn't pierce your ears?'

'Shut up.'

She laughed.

'I mean it.'

She rolled her eyes. 'All right, Princess. I don't have time for this. Get out of my room and stay out of my way.'

'I'm not scared of you.'

She laughed again. I hated her.

The day after the Crumble Rule came in, Jeremy had clinked his mug with a knife after dinner, and announced another party. 'A reward,' he said, 'for all the hard work we've put in over the spring and summer.' It was going to be up at the stone ring on Halloween. Though Mary said in Cornwall it wasn't called Halloween, it was *Kalan Gwav*.

Mary was brimming over with excitement on the day of the party, hopping about, grinning, and telling us about Kalan Gwav. 'It marks the first day of winter. The Celts believed it was the night when the barrier between our world and the spirit world thinned enough for faeries and pixies to pass through. People were terrified of the trouble they might cause, so put food and drink out to keep them jolly.'

She asked me to help her tie rowan and elderberry branches around the front and back doors of the house, so I spent the afternoon holding a scratchy armful of sticks for her.

'Rowan and elderberry have magical properties,' she said, as she tied the twigs up with gardening twine. 'They ward off evil and stop it from sneaking inside.'

'What about the windows?' I looked up warily at the dark staring eyes of the house.

Mary chuckled.

The thought of evil spirits sneaking in while we were out gave me the shivers. I didn't even want to go. There was nothing about being on the moor at night that sounded fun. But there was no way I was staying in the house alone. Not without twigs around the windows.

Before we set off for the stones, we gathered in the yard. Bruce handed round mugs of pumpkin soup and hunks of bread. Jeremy had told us to dress up, but we looked more like we were going to a goth gig than a Halloween party. Tara had painted her lips black and rubbed charcoal into her eye sockets so they looked hollowed out, and swapped her rainbow scarves for black and purple ones. Skye was draped in a sheet with a hole for her head and had a woolly hat on. She didn't look spooky at all.

A thick layer of cloud had rubbed out the stars and moon so it was so dark I couldn't even see my hands if I held them out. I thought about Leyton, about what I'd be doing if I was there, and had a hit of homesickness. Last year, Rachel, Mira and I dressed up as vampires with red felt-tip pen for blood around our mouths. We knocked on the doors of the fancy houses around Coronation Gardens and held out plastic carrier bags which the posh ladies filled with sweets so we didn't egg their shiny front doors. Walking in the pitch black was nowhere near as fun.

'Wonder if the Beast is watching us,' Ash said, before howling so loud it made my heart stop.

'What Beast?' I whispered to Mary.

'Bodmin Moor is famous for it. A huge black cat which hunts the moor every night and mutilates anything it finds.' She raised her eyebrows and grinned. 'Maybe we'll see it tonight?' Then she laughed.

I dropped back from Mary to walk with Dean and Sasha instead. They were at the back of the line with Ash and Emily. Sasha would protect us if the Beast showed up.

'Shouldn't you be walking with Tara and Skye?' Emily said, when I drew level with them. I couldn't see what face she was making in the dark, but I knew it wasn't kind.

'Dani's all right, Em,' Dean said.

'We don't need some kid hanging about with us. Not tonight. I have plans.'

'Oh, good. Love me a plan,' Ash said, rubbing his hands together.

My heart sank. That's how they all saw me. A boring child. If I wasn't so scared of the dark and the Beast and the twigless windows, I'd have gone back.

The shadows of the stones loomed out of the blackness and Jeremy walked into the centre of the ring, then turned and faced us, smiling, the lamp throwing orange light over him. 'Let's get the party started!' Everybody whooped.

We all carried rucksacks or bags packed with drinks, snacks, or logs. Those with wood dumped it in a heap beside Kit, who built the fire as everybody got settled. For the first time in months, I felt like an outsider, just as I had at the beginning. Tara and Skye were sitting with Kit. Mary, Anne, Bruce and Jeremy were together. Dean, Ash and Emily were huddled in the shadows on the edge of the stone circle.

I walked over to one of the stones and slumped down with my back against it. I thought of the poor girl turned to stone by cretin gods and frozen mid-dance forever. 'I'm sorry that happened to you,' I whispered.

As the fire took hold, Tara and Skye's faces were lit with the flickering light. Tara looked sad again. She hadn't been herself for a while, but whenever I asked her what was wrong she said she was fine.

There was a snort of laughter from Emily. Though they were hidden by the dark, I knew they were up to something. I kicked the ground with the heel of my trainer. Why was I letting that cow shut me out? This was *my* farm. *My* family. *My* Dean and Ash. Before I could talk myself out of it, I got up and walked over to them. Bold as monkeys.

'What's so funny?'

Emily glared at me with a mean smile. 'None of your business?'

Heat rose up from my neck to my cheeks.

'Em, be nice,' Dean said.

Then I noticed Emily was holding a small jar. When she saw me looking, she dipped a finger into it, and it came out smeared with an oily cream. She dabbed it onto the inside of her wrist, then rubbed her wrists together as if putting on perfume.

'What's that?'

'Nothing,' Ash said quickly.

'Is it drugs? Jeremy said—'

Then Emily laughed. 'What are you going to do? Tell Dear Leader?'

'Fuck off.'

She laughed again.

'What is it? Give me some.'

She leant close to my face. 'It's *way* too strong for a beginner.'

'Beginner?' I scoffed. 'I've done loads of drugs.'

'Sure you have, princess.'

'Go on, Dani,' Dean said then. 'Go back to the others. We won't be long. And ... well, don't tell Jeremy, yeah?'

But I couldn't take my eyes off Emily. Why did she talk to me like a child? It was driving me nuts. 'I grew up on an estate in East London. I've probably done more drugs than all of you put together.' This definitely wasn't true. I'd smoked weed a couple of times, but all it did was make me cough. I also sniffed some powder that Mira bought off a boy in the year above and ended up passed out in the playground covered in puke. But rubbing cream on my wrists? What was the worst that could happen? 'Give me some,' I said.

Emily smiled.

'Maybe not, Em,' Ash said quietly. 'It's pretty full on, isn't it?'

'It's only plants. Mad Mary calls it flying balm. She said witches smeared it on their broomstick handles, then rode them to get high. And I mean *rode* them.' She thrust her hips backwards and forwards, snorting with laughter.

'You're lying.'

'Nope. I swear on the Bible. The snatch has the thinnest skin.'

Emily glances over at Mary and the others, then manoeuvres herself to keep us hidden from view.

'Does Mary know you've got it?'

'Of course.'

But Dean looked at his feet and I knew she was lying.

'Give it here.' I grabbed the pot then hooked a finger into the goo and rubbed it into my wrists.

The others put some on too and, finally, I was part of the group. We walked out of the shadows and joined the circle around the fire. I made sure I sat as far from Jeremy as possible in case he worked things out and took my crumble away.

'How about a ghost story?' Bruce asked, climbing onto a rock.

Everybody cheered. Bruce paused then snapped his eyes wide open and stretched his arms out like wings, staring intensely around the circle.

'We gather on the moor on Kalan Gwav ...'

As he started speaking, I had the feeling we were being watched. I looked behind me, but there was nothing there. I thought again about the stone girls and imagined them banging on the walls of their granite prisons begging me to unlock them.

'How?' I whispered.

'... the Woman in White.' Bruce was leaping about. Limbs waving. Words staccato.

I looked over at Tara. Skye was lying on her, fiddling with a plait. Kit sat behind her, arms wrapped around them. A dagger of jealousy thrust into me. The serrated blade pierced my stomach. My hand flew to the wound, but when I looked down there was nothing. I drew my knees up to my chest and hugged them tightly. My head felt light, as if it were filling with helium, inflating and pulling away from my body.

'... night after night. Desperate for her lover. But her father had promised her to a cruel landowner three times her age. Marrying him would be worse than death itself. So the lovers planned to run away, riding east on his black horse. The next night she dressed in white, a crown of willow on her head. Dressed as a bride for her lover. Then she walked to this very stone circle and waited ...'

Bruce leapt from the rock and bent low. My vision wavered. I saw two of him. No, three. The shape of him quivered in the shimmering firelight.

'On the stroke of midnight she heard the thunder of hooves. The horse galloped into the centre of the circle, reared up and came down with a horrifying thud ...'

Bruce looked straight at me. In his eyes I saw the snorting horse reflected. I turned, expecting to see it behind me. There was nothing. Only blackness. My head swam. I felt sick. I grabbed at the grass to steady myself.

'Her lover's body was lashed to the horse. Chest torn open and heart ripped out. The young woman grabbed the rope and tried to release ...'

My heart pounded. The demon horse was breathing down my neck. The ground was sodden with blood.

'It reared again. When it came down it struck her and shattered her skull and killed her.'

Bruce crouched. When he next spoke his voice was a whisper.

'They say her ghost wanders the moor at night. Wailing for her lover. Intent on revenge.'

My teeth clamped together so hard they splintered into a thousand pieces. I tried to call out for help, but no sound came. My body was floating. I was pulled to the bright orange light, which broke into flecks of fire that shot upwards. The heat burned my eyeballs. A scream split my blood into curds and whey.

My scream? The woman in white? A stone girl?

My stomach pitched. I was falling fast. I hit the ground and the darkness erupted in a burst of fireworks. There was a blistering pain in my arm. Lava shot through my veins.

Then everything went black.

I woke on my mattress, covered by a sleeping bag and an extra blanket, sticky with sweat. Mary was beside me, cross-legged on the floor, fading in and out of my vision. The pain which pulsed along my arm tore my head in half.

'What ...' My voice wedged in my dry, tight throat.

'Hush, now.' Mary gently caressed my forehead. 'I'll look after you.'

She tipped a glass of water to my lips. It was cool and sweet and tasted of Tic Tacs. Then she took my hand. In my faltering vision I caught glimpses of angry yellow blisters and redness which covered my hand and lower arm.

'I don't remember ...'

'You were dancing. Tripped. Fell into the fire.' Mary chewed her lower lip. 'Dani ... Where did you get the balm from? The one on your wrists.'

My mind stumbled backwards. A hazy memory of floating into the air. The stones screaming? No. Stones don't scream.

Mary dipped her finger into a small bowl and dabbed some sludgy white paste on to my skin. 'Egg white and burdock. A bit of bicarbonate of soda. Good for burns.' As she applied the paste, she hummed a tune I didn't recognise. Then she put the bowl down and reached for another.

'Honey is an excellent dressing. Antibacterial with a balanced pH to aid healing.'

She started humming again, dipping a small brush into the honey and painting it onto a square of white gauze, which she pressed against some oozing skin. She repeated the process, humming all the while, until the weepiest parts were patched.

The soothing effects of the white paste didn't last long, and I squeezed my eyes shut, trying not to think about how much it hurt.

'Dani?'

I forced my eyes to open.

'Whoever gave you the balm took it without asking.'

My stomach clenched. I heard the echo of Jeremy's stern voice when he banned drugs. I thought about Emily's spiteful smile as she held out the jar. It would be easy to tell on her and send Emily packing.

But I wasn't a snitch.

'It was me,' I whispered. 'I stole it. From your cupboard.'

She sighed, her forehead all knotted up. 'I think it was one of the others.'

I shook my head.

Mary stared at me for a moment or two, then nodded. 'You must *never* take anything without asking me first. There are some dangerous extracts in my cupboard.' Her voice cracked and she pursed her lip as if she was in pain. 'That balm is made from deadly plants. Belladonna. Mandrake. Henbane. If you'd eaten it? God.' She winced. 'Even a few drops of belladonna will—' She cut herself off. 'Let's just say it would send you to sleep for a *very* long time.' She rested her hand on me. 'Promise you won't touch any of my remedies again. Those plants aren't safe for adults, let alone children.'

'It made my head go funny,' I whispered. 'I was floating.'

'It's a hallucinogen. I should never have made it. And certainly not left it in an unlocked cupboard ...'

A wave of pain ripped through me and I closed my eyes.

'If it gets unbearable, let me know and I'll brew some cannabis tea. It's very gentle, nothing like the drug.'

For the rest of the day I drifted in and out of sleep. Mary would appear every now and then to peel back the dressings to inspect my wounds and either nod and place back the gauzes, or take them off and put new ones on. The pain got worse and worse and I knew I wouldn't sleep.

'Will your tea help me sleep?'

'Oh, yes. It's lovely stuff. It'll take the edge off the pain and relax you.'

The tea didn't taste of tea. It was lukewarm, bitter, and grassy. But it seemed to work and made my body melt into the mattress.

I was woken by urgent whispers outside my door. Three voices. Mary. Tara. Jeremy. Even though they were whispering, I knew they were having an argument. I opened my eyes a fraction and peered through my eyelashes. My door was open. Mary had her back to me. Jeremy was out of sight. Tara was in full view, arms folded, face of thunder.

'... we have to take her to the hospital.'

'Mary knows what she's doing.'

'She needs a doctor.'

'A doctor has no more expertise than Mary for this type of injury. We can handle her treatment ourselves with medical intervention as a last resort. Dani's doing well. Her arm is clean and dressed. She's had ointment—'

'*Ointment*?' Tara was struggling to control her disbelief. 'Dried leaves, egg, and honey? She has second degree burns. She needs medicine, not the contents of a fucking larder.'

'I promise I can handle this,' Mary whispered. 'I have amazing remedies.'

'*Remedies*? Please, stop it. Both of you. We watched her fall onto a *fire* as high as a kite on Christ-knows-what last night. She's burnt and needs to be checked by a doctor. What if it gets infected?'

Mary glanced over her shoulder at me. I sighed sleepily so they wouldn't know I was listening.

'I understand your concern,' Jeremy said. 'But what would a

doctor do? They'd put a dressing on. Topical cream. Keep it clean and manage the pain. Exactly as Mary has. Mary?'

Mary nodded. 'Plants have been used to treat burns for millennia. They're very effective. I've been checking her arm every hour and it's doing really well.'

Tara shook her head in frustration. 'Whatever. I give up. Fine. But for the record I think this is a mistake. It's one thing to grow vegetables and wash in a bucket. It's a very different thing to keep an injured person from going to hospital.'

Hospital. As I lay there I thought about it. There were always forms to fill out. They'd want my full name. My age. My address. They'd send me back to Eddie.

I'll fucking kill you both.

'Tara?' I said sleepily. 'My arm's not hurting so much. The honey's working.'

'See?' Jeremy said. 'You have to trust us. We have her best interests at heart.'

A little while later there was a tap on the door. It was Emily. She came in and sat on floor beside me. Her eyes were pink and puffy from crying and she was struggling to look at me, fidgeting as if her clothes were full of itching powder.

'Is it ... very sore?'

'It's fine.'

'It's, well ...' She leant forward, hands clasped. 'I'm so sorry.'

'Why? Did you push me into the fire?'

'Push you? *No!* No, but I gave you that stuff and you had a bad trip.' She gestured at my honey-dressed arm. 'It's my fault.'

'I made you give it to me.'

She shook her head. 'I was baiting you. I'm a bitch. I'm the same with everybody. There's something wrong with me and I'm really sorry. Hallucinogenic drugs aren't for mucking about with.'

This new version of Emily was confusing. 'The burns are almost healed,' I mumbled. 'And it's stopped hurting.' Total lies. My arm was killing me. 'Mary rubs this special stuff on it. It's magic. I think she might be a witch.'

Emily gave a slight smile. 'I'm sorry I've been such a bitch.' She paused. 'Tara said you've run away from some pretty intense stuff.'

My stomach knotted. I hated the idea of them feeling sorry for me. I gave a slight shrug.

Emily stared into space for a moment or two, then sniffed. 'I tried to kill myself the night I met Jeremy.'

That hit me out of the blue.

'I was on a bridge in London. It was late and I was high and drunk and I remember staring down at the water and thinking how pretty it was with the lights reflected in it, like it was decorated with diamonds and rubies. Then there were these voices in my head. Telling me to jump.'

'Why?'

'Why jump?'

I nodded.

She shrugged. 'I guess, I thought there was no point in trying anymore. My friend …' She stopped talking for a moment and cleared her throat. 'He died of an overdose and I realised I had nothing left in the world. Nowhere to go. Nobody to miss me. The world's a party, isn't it? And there's nothing worse than being at a party and feeling as if you shouldn't be there. Having nobody to dance with. Nobody to hang out with. You drink and take drugs so you feel part of it, but that only makes it worse. Plus you end up making an absolute tit of yourself.' She smiled. 'So I figured it was time to leave the party.'

'And Jeremy stopped you?' I pictured him on the bridge. Talking Emily down. Telling her about the farm and his family. Pulling out the photograph.

'Someone else did.'

My vision faded like smoke.

'It was some guy in a suit. Maybe with others? It's blurry. But

I was sitting on the pavement surrounded by people who wanted to help. Then Jeremy rolled up and said he was a friend of mine.'

"They believed him?"

Emily smiled. 'Who doesn't?'

I thought of him kneeling in front of me in the street. The syrupy softness of his voice. The way he listened when I talked.

'We walked and talked for a few hours. When the sun came up he bought me breakfast in a café under the arches and told me about this place. He said there were others here who understood. Who'd had a tough time and recovered. Said they'd help me work through my darkness. He said all the right things.' She hesitated. 'When I said I'd come he clapped and smiled. You'd have thought he'd won the lottery. It was weird. I nearly changed my mind, but didn't have the energy to fight him. When we got here, he became a different person. I think he thinks he's Jesus or something.'

CHAPTER TWENTY-EIGHT

Tara,
November 2002

Keeping warm became our focus as winter crept into the bones of the house. We closed off the living room and kept the fires in the dining room and kitchen roaring. Kit put a large, solid log on the fires last thing at night so there were embers in the morning which could be quickly brought back to life. We dressed in layers and hung heavy blankets at the windows to block the draughts. Skye moved into our bed, a wriggly hot-water bottle between us.

The moor was muddy and cold. The sky a moody layer of lead bearing down on us. Our evenings were spent in the dining room or kitchen, rugs over our knees, huddled around the hearth, reading or playing cards in the dim candlelight. Skye drew faces on the ice which filmed the inside of our bedroom window. When we got into bed we lay on our backs and rode imaginary bicycles as fast as we could to get warm. Every day Jeremy reminded us we were living a purer, healthier life then reeled off the cons of central heating, which, he said, had only come into use in the 1950s.

We washed less. Dipping a flannel into a basin of icy water and applying it to our skin became something to endure. Though I didn't want to admit it, I was starting to miss home comforts. I missed lights and hot baths. I fantasised about walking around the house in a T-shirt and bare feet, not three pairs of socks and a woolly hat. The dormant radiators and hot-water taps taunted me.

Doubts slunk through me.

Was this good for Skye? What were we trying to achieve? Since the Halloween party I'd been plagued by nightmares about Dani falling into the fire.

'We need to talk.'

Kit was stacking logs beside the hearth in the dining room. 'That sounds ominous.' He smiled, but I didn't return it. 'Now?'

'Yes, but in our room.'

As we walked up the stairs, my stomach churned.

'What's up?'

'Close the door.'

I sat on the edge of the bed. 'I'm not happy here.'

His face fell. 'That's come out of the blue,' he said.

'Really?'

He looked confused.

'We need to make contact with Dani's mother.'

'But she's settled here.'

'She fell into a fucking *fire*, Kit! In *our* care.' I growled in frustration. I was tired of being the only one who seemed to understand the responsibility of having children here. 'Why is she here? Why is Emily here? Why does he keep pulling girls off the street?'

'He's helping them—'

'Are you honestly that naive? You think there's no grand plan?'

He inhaled wearily. 'There is no grand plan, Tara.'

'Fine. Forget Dani. Forget his weird trips. What about the living conditions here? The cold. No hot water. Eating pickled vegetables and bread day in day out. I'm not even sure why we're doing this anymore. It's a fucking endurance test. Consenting adults freezing in a draughty, unheated house on a moor is one thing. It's another to force it on children. It's not even as if there's no boiler. It's right there. In the cupboard downstairs. Why won't we put it on?'

Kit said nothing.

'I want to run Skye a bath. In fact, I want a bath *myself*. Is that spoilt? Am I a brat?' Discontent spewed from me like pus from a lanced boil. I began to feel weak. Was it this leaking anger which had been holding me upright these last months?

'We are only without heat for this first winter. Soon we'll have a biomass boiler. And I've stoked all the fires up downstairs. The stove in the kitchen is a furnace—'

'So we huddle in the kitchen for six months? Stare out of the window and wait for spring?'

'We knew it would be hard. Jeremy told us it would be.'

I exploded with angry laughter. 'Yes. *Jeremy* told us we'd have to make sacrifices. *Jeremy* told us we'd be cold. *Jeremy* decides who's having crumble. Jeremy spends money – *your* money – on what Jeremy thinks worthy. What anybody else wants is irrelevant. It's a fucking dictatorship.'

'It's not a dictatorship. Money is prioritised for essentials. Food and building equipment are essential. Heating isn't.'

'That's my point, Kit! It might not be for you and Jeremy, but maybe for me and Skye it is. I've half a mind to put the boiler on and tell Jeremy to stick his it up his arrogant, controlling arse. If he wants to be cold he can open his fucking window or sleep with the goats.'

'The boiler needs a gas supply,' Kit said, with infuriating calmness. 'We're not connected, remember?'

I took a steadying breath. 'I want to leave.'

I was as shocked as Kit was to hear my words out loud, but as soon as I said them, I knew it was the truth. I'd had enough. Enough of living like sardines. Enough of sacrifices I didn't choose to make. I wanted my own space and my own rules.

I wanted my child to be warm.

'But the farm is getting going. And we're invested in this house. Emotionally and financially.'

'*Invested*? You didn't even want to buy the house!'

'We have a commitment to Jeremy and the group. We can't take the house from them.'

'We don't need to take the damn house! Jeremy can stay here. They all can. It doesn't mean we have to.'

'Without us there'd be no project. How could they make it work? I can't do that to them. To Jeremy. Not in the middle of winter. I promised him I'd help him establish the place.'

'And what about us? Me and Skye? What about your promise to us?'

Kit made a face and shook his head. 'I thought we were happy? A few months ago, you said you were the happiest you'd ever been. What's changed? It can't just be the heating?'

As I stared at him, I realised we were on completely different pages.

'You want to go back to Cowley? Take Skye back to that world? Take this life away from her?'

The threat of tears choked me. I thought about the bedsit. Our dull, grey life there. Skye's pasty skin and the dramatic way she had blossomed at Winterfall. 'No,' I whispered. 'I don't want to take this away from her.'

I stood and walked past him. He grabbed my hand but I snatched it from his grasp. 'Tara?'

But I didn't stay. I ran down the stairs and out of the front door. I ran across the yard and into the field and climbed the stile, then sat behind the drystone wall and cried.

I'm not sure how much time passed before I heard him calling. Fifteen minutes? Half an hour? Maybe even longer. I considered keeping myself hidden and letting him stew, but it wasn't fair. He was wedged between me and Jeremy. He loved us both deeply. All he was trying to do was keep everybody happy. It wasn't right to punish him.

I walked down to the yard and started to speak, but he

interrupted me. 'God,' he said. 'You're freezing.' He took his coat off and wrapped it around me. 'Come inside,' he said.

Skye was waiting at the door. She slipped her hand into mine. 'We made a surprise for you,' she whispered.

I followed Kit upstairs but rather than going into our bedroom, he opened the bathroom door.

'Isn't it pretty?' Skye breathed.

The bathroom flickered with candles and lamps. The bath was filled with water and a thin veil of steam rose from it. White bubbles floated in fluffy clouds on its surface. It was warm in the room and the air was dense with lavender.

'How ...?' My voice faded.

'I boiled the water on the stove top. Mary made up a bubble bath and Skye did the candles.'

'Daddy let me *light* some.'

Kit sat on the floor while Skye and I bathed. We splashed and played and giggled. She put bubbles on my nose and I fashioned her a white beard. It was pure bliss.

When the water began to cool, Kit lifted Skye out and wrapped her in a towel. She sat on his lap, a towelling caterpillar, her teeth juddering with the cold, as he dried her. 'I've got something else to show you,' he said to me.

'What?'

'First you need to get dressed. Anne is going to look after Skye and we'll be back in time for dinner. Dress warmly and put your boots on.'

Kit shone his torch on the ground to light our way. My skin was glowing after the bath and the smell of lavender oil hung on my skin, making me smile every time I breathed it in.

'I didn't react very well earlier,' he said. 'But I hear what you're saying.' His hand squeezed mine. 'And I feel the same.'

'What do you mean?'

'I don't want to live as part of a group at Winterfall forever.' He glanced at me. 'I want to show you what I've been doing when Jeremy leaves the farm.'

'The hide?'

'No. Not a hide.'

He stopped walking and raised the beam of his torch. In its light I saw the ruined cottage.

'I've been fixing it up a bit.'

'What?'

'I'm missing our privacy too. Dean walking in on us in bed was the last straw, I think. So I decided to make us a den.'

'A den?'

He took my hand and led me towards the cottage. 'Careful,' he said, as we stepped over the threshold into the blackness. The cottage smelt heavily of musty dampness and decades of neglect. 'Watch yourself. The floor is pretty uneven and there are nails around. I'd have swept up with a bit more notice, but now seemed the right time to show you.'

The torch lit up a pathway decorated with floating specks of silver dust. He led me to the stairs.

I peered up into the darkness. 'Is it safe?'

'It should be fine.'

'Should be?'

'Should be.'

When we got to the landing, he opened a door on our left. The hinges squeaked as they swung open. He shone the torch around the room and my pulse quickened.

'I filled the cracks in the wall. Gave it a paint. The floorboards were in pretty good nick. I've given it a clean.'

The lingering smell of paint and furniture polish moved me to tears. The thought of him spending all those hours working up there alone, not only made my heart swell, but filled me with ragged guilt as I recalled my earlier outburst.

There was a bed against the back wall. Wrought iron with brass globes on the uprights. On the mattress was a blanket, which I recognised as ours. I pictured him stuffing it into his rucksack surreptitiously. I walked over to the bed and ran my fingertips over the soft material.

'The mattress needs burning.'

'It's a beautiful bed.' I caressed the frame, smooth as ice to the touch. 'How on earth did you get it up?'

'It was already here. Can you believe that? Finding it was what gave me the idea to make us a den. Well, that and bloody Dean, and the way you reacted when you saw the place.' Kit put his arms around my waist. 'I love so much about the farm, but I hate the lack of privacy. Now we have somewhere we can hide when we want to be alone. Somewhere nobody else knows about.'

'It's perfect,' I whispered. 'Thank you.'

He bent his head and kissed the curve of my neck. His breath was hot on my chilled skin and sent tiny shocks through me. After the noise and clamour of the farm this space felt intensely intimate and the feeling of being alone was exhilarating. He moved me gently backwards and we lay down on the bed, he kissed me again then knelt up and removed his sweater and T-shirt.

I sat up and took off my clothes. The cold prickled my skin. We pulled my coat over us and made love, noisily and urgently, in a way we hadn't since before Skye was born. Knowing nobody could hear us or walk in on us was liberating. We were free to enjoy each other's body. Free to moan and cry out and laugh.

We dressed quickly afterwards and lay on the bed, our fingers entwined, my head on his chest. Every part of me tingled.

'Kit?'

'Mm, hmm?'

'What if we lived here? We could stay as part of the farm, but sleep here. Have our own space. Like Bruce and Anne.'

'There's no way it's fit to live in. There isn't even a water supply, let alone the hot water and electricity you were wanting.'

'Could we get a supply here?'

'There's a stream nearby, so I suppose so?'

'And how long would it take to get it habitable.'

'How long?'

I nodded.

He shook his head. 'I don't know. We'd need to work on it full time. Three or four months?'

'So April?'

'But full time here would mean we'd have to stop work on the farm.'

'Don't you want this though? Our own space?'

He hesitated, his expression pained. 'I can't walk out on Jeremy,' he whispered. 'He's my friend. *Our* friend. We can't abandon him and the farm.'

'But we wouldn't be. We'd still be a part of it.'

Kit looked doubtful. 'Can we sit on it for a bit? Not tell him yet. Winterfall has become his whole world.'

'I think he's losing sight of what matters. It's like he's fighting demons.'

'He is. Tied up with the death of his father.'

'I don't know much about that, other than he was in his teens. He never spoke to me about it.'

'Even I don't know the whole story. I just know it was a pretty dark time.'

I hesitated. What I was about to say was going to sound harsh. 'Lots of people suffer trauma. It doesn't mean they get a free pass to do what they want. Jeremy has changed. He seems to think he's got some sort of higher purpose. You know, the night Emily arrived, she asked if we were a cult.'

Kit laughed. 'That's ridiculous.'

'Is it? Because I sort of see where she's coming from.'

Kit didn't reply.

'I can see us living here, Kit. Can you?'

Still he didn't speak, but instead he nodded, slowly at first, then with more conviction.

'If you'd prefer me to talk to him, I'm happy to.'

'No,' Kit said. 'I'll talk to him. It should come from me.'

CHAPTER TWENTY-NINE

Kit,
November 2002

'Have you got a moment?'

Jeremy is at his desk. A book and notebook lie open, bathed in soft pools of light from two oil lamps. When Jeremy stands, Kit notices how unusually he is dressed, a loose white shirt and cotton trousers. Bare feet. His long black curls scraped back in a ponytail. The smile he gives Kit is almost beatific. Kit hears Tara's voice.

She asked if we were a cult.

It's a ridiculous notion and Kit is annoyed he's given it headspace. He sits on the edge of the bed and takes a breath, but the words don't come. His heart thunders and despite the chill in the house his palms are sweaty.

'Is everything all right?'

He clears his throat and allows the difficult words to take shape. 'Tara isn't happy.'

The smile fades. Jeremy tips his head back and looks up at the ceiling. 'Because of Emily?' He returns his gaze to Kit.

'She wants to leave.'

'You or the farm?'

'Excuse me?'

'Does Tara want to leave you or the farm?' Jeremy annunciates clearly and slowly.

'Well, it's not me.'

'Are you sure?'

'Christ. Yes, I'm sure,' Kit says firmly. 'This has nothing to do with our relationship.'

Jeremy walks to the window, which rattles as the wind fights to get in, hands clasped behind his back. 'And what are you going to do about it?'

'Sorry?'

'What are you doing to change her mind?'

Kit furrows his brow. Has Jeremy taken something? His behaviour is odd. An uneasy shiver passes through Kit.

Jeremy turns slowly and faces him. 'How will you convince her to stay?'

'I won't. I've said we will move out.'

'That can't happen.'

Kit had been expecting Jeremy to be hurt. Possibly angry. He was prepared to have to put up a fight or make a deal. What he wasn't ready for was this calm and softly spoken refusal to even entertain the idea.

'There's a cottage. On the moor. It's a wreck but we've talked about fixing it up and eventually moving in.'

'You aren't listening to me.'

Kit ploughed on as his heart beat faster. 'It's uninhabitable at the moment and it will take time. I'd need to reduce the number of hours I do here at—'

'I can't run Winterfall without you.'

'When spring comes we'll work here as usual. Help with the crops and the harvest. We will remain a part of the group. The cottage would be somewhere to sleep. No different to Bruce and Anne in their caravan.' He hears the desperation in his voice as he repeats Tara's words.

Jeremy starts shaking his head before Kit has finished speaking. 'I can't let this happen. What message will it send to the others? It would undermine confidence. If you go, Winterfall will fail.'

'We can make it work. I'll get up early. Be here before anybody wakes up. We'll eat here. Together around the table as we always do—'

'And Dani? Tara is like a mother to her. You're saying she'd abandon her?'

Kit hesitates. He knows without even asking that Tara won't leave Dani. 'Dani can come with us.'

Jeremy's face twists into an ugly grimace. 'Dani isn't going anywhere.'

'Jesus, Jay. That isn't up to you. Come on. Listen to yourself.'

Jeremy walks over to Kit and crouches before him, placing his hands on Kit's knees. 'It is up to you to convince her she's happy here. Winterfall has so much potential. I can't watch it collapse because of Tara's sudden whim.' He rocks back on his haunches and stands, looking down on Kit. 'It's up to you to mange her moods. I have faith in you. You are my closest friend. My brother. Don't turn your back on me. Don't give up on what we're achieving here.'

Kit stands and Jeremy embraces him. Kit feels nauseous.

'So?' Tara asks, as he walks into their bedroom. 'How did he take it?'

Kit sits heavily on the bed. 'I'm not leaving him in the middle of winter. It's not the right time. We'll revisit it in the spring.'

She starts to protest.

'Tara, listen to me. We will leave. We'll move to our own place, if not the cottage, then somewhere else. But please, for the next few months, can you try and be happy here?' Kit is close to tears. He feels weak. 'Will you give this a chance?'

Tara sits next to him on the bed. She takes his hand in hers. 'We deserve our own life,' she says softly. 'We can't be expected to put Jeremy's vision – whatever that is – above what's best for us. We'll stay until spring, but then you have to promise to put your family first. I don't want to fight Jeremy for you. But I will if I have to.'

Later he lies in their bed and stares up at the ceiling. Outside the rain has started up again. The gutters drip and the wind whistles through the yard. Nausea rolls around his stomach. He is sickened by his weakness, his lack of loyalty to Tara. He is also unable to shake Tara's suspicions about Jeremy from his head. Is there truth in her accusations? Has Jeremy become blinded by his ambitions for Winterfall?

There are too many emotions jostling in his mind and sleep is impossible. He goes down to the kitchen and stokes the fire, loading the burner with more wood than usual, and watching with pleasure as the flames leap up. He makes a pot of coffee and sits in front of the fire. He goes over everything Tara said to him. She was right about Jeremy making the decisions on what they would and wouldn't spend money on. Why had he been so quick to let him take control? If Jeremy was going to demand that they remain here then he had to understand this was a commune. Winterfall's success wasn't merely the fulfilling of a vision, it was about looking after the collective. Giving consideration to the desires of each person. Addressing their needs. The cold was becoming difficult for Tara to bear. That wasn't a failing on her part. It was a failing on theirs. Perhaps it was that simple. Perhaps if the house was warmer and more hospitable she'd see things differently.

When Bruce appears to bake the bread, Kit makes another pot of coffee. He pours one for Bruce then carries a mug upstairs. He knocks on Jeremy's door and walks in. Jeremy is sitting on the floor, eyes closed, legs crossed, palms upwards and resting on his thighs. He looks momentarily annoyed at Kit's intrusion.

Kit hands him the coffee. 'We're going into town to pick up a few things.'

'Can it wait until later?'

'No, it can't.'

They visit every charity shop in Bodmin and Launceston and load up with thick-knit sweaters, more blankets, gloves and socks and hats. Then they go to a DIY and Kit asks the assistant where the gas heaters are.

'We don't need them. They're expensive and propane isn't very healthy.'

'We also need sealant for the gaps in the window frames, some draught excluders for the doors. The gales blow right through them. Then you and I are going to prioritise a plan for the biomass boiler.' Jeremy starts to object, but Kit stops him. 'You want us to stay? We need hot water.'

'Pandering to Tara's need for luxury isn't the answer.' Jeremy's eyes are steely, his displeasure thinly veiled. 'She's missing the point of Winterfall. It's not about trying to recreate an environment we're accustomed to, it's about striving for something more nourishing.'

'It can be nourishing. It also needs to be warm.'

Jeremy stares at him, his expression flat, visibly weighing up his options. Then he draws a deep breath and gives a begrudging nod.

CHAPTER THIRTY

Dani,
December 2002

Tara, me and Skye went out onto the moor for an afternoon walk. The was air so cold it froze my lungs but it was better than sitting around in the house which, despite the fancy new heaters in the kitchen and dining room, was arctic. At least we got warm when we were walking. The sky was the colour of pencil-lead with a purple tint and with each step it seemed to grow heavier.

'Will we be home before it gets dark?'

'Don't worry,' Tara replied. 'I don't want to get lost out here either.'

It wasn't getting lost which scared me, it was the thought of being out on the moor when the ghosts woke up. Ghosts took up most of my thoughts. As the evenings had got darker and colder, dinnertime talk moved from the evils of government and society to stories about the thousands of bloodthirsty spirits which wandered the moor searching for people to tear to bits. My head was rammed full of them. The man hanged for murdering a teenage girl because she wouldn't go out with him. The teenage girl he killed. The girls trapped in the stones. The ravenous Beast. Not to mention the woman in white. It didn't matter how many times I told myself she wasn't angry at me, but with the cretin who ripped her boyfriend's heart out: she terrified the actual shit out of me. No way was I going to be out on the moor in the dark.

'Can't promise we won't get wet though,' Tara said, eyeing the charcoal sky.

We walked down a hill and into a wooded area. 'I haven't been here before,' I said.

'It's where the faeries live,' whispered Skye. 'We can show you, but you mustn't tell anybody else. Got it?'

Skye pulled me through the fallen leaves, weaving around the trees and down a slope, until we reached an enormous tree. She crouched down and pulled me in, then put a finger to her lips to shush me. I bent down and she pointed into a hollow at the base of the trunk.

'Look inside,' she whispered.

The hollow stretched up like a miniature church. There was a flat stone raised up on four pebbles. On that were a number of acorn cups.

'Those are for their beer. That's their table. We put food on the table and they *eat* it.' She looked round at Tara and beamed. 'The cheese is *gone*, Mama!'

'Well, it is very good cheese. Make sure you tell Bruce how much they loved it.' Tara reached into her pocket and came out with a handful of oats. 'They can mix this with mouse milk and make some lovely porridge to warm their tummies.'

'Mouses make milk?'

'They're mammals, remember? Baby mammals drink milk. Do you know any other mammals?'

'Cat, dog, tiger,' Skye said, as Tara tipped the oats into her cupped hand. 'For your breakfast,' she whispered, sprinkling the oats on the flat stone.

It had started to rain. Heavy drops pattered on the leaves above us and the wind skated through branches which ducked and dived as if trying to escape.

'Time to go back,' Tara said. 'Race you up!'

Skye squealed and set off up the hill. I followed, but realised halfway up that Tara had hung back. I turned and saw her crouched with her hand inside the tree. She brought out the stone, picked off the acorns and tipped the oats away, then replaced the acorns and stone. When she caught me watching, she put her finger to her lips, just as Skye had done.

When we came out of the woods the weather slammed into us. The wind and rain whipped across the moor at a thousand miles an hour, battering the trees and sending the brown fallen leaves running for their lives.

'We're going to get drenched!' Tara laughed as she scooped Skye up and started to run. I followed but it was hard going, my feet slipping all over the place, my lungs burning, and the freezing rain stinging my face.

'Tara!' I shouted. 'I can't run all the way!'

'It's OK! There's somewhere close we can shelter until it passes.'

Tara took hold of my hand and we half-jogged. When we rounded a small hill I saw a tumbledown house with broken windows and a roof full of holes like a moth-eaten sweater. My stomach turned a somersault. It was exactly the type of place where the woman in white would hang out during the day. I made sure not to look at the windows in case she was there with her smashed-in head.

Tara carried Skye in through the door which leant against the rotten doorframe as if it were drunk. I stepped under the overhang, out of the rain, but didn't go inside.

'Daddy and I want to make this house beautiful so we can live here.' She smiled at Skye. 'But it's a secret.'

'Can I tell the faeries?'

Tara dabbed Skye on the nose. 'Nobody else.'

'You're leaving the farm?' I tried to sound casual but the thought made my knees weak. What would I do without Tara and Skye?

'Not yet but one day soon.'

I wanted to ask if I could go with them, but I didn't want to risk it. What if she said no? I had a flash of my lamb, alone in the pen, his blue forty-three fading to nothing.

As we stood in the doorway, the rain fell heavier and showed no sign of easing. The sky was growing dark with the dusk. The hairs on my neck prickled as the woman in white stroked her fingers over my skin.

'Can we go?'

Tara looked doubtful, but then nodded.

By the time we arrived back at the farm it was getting too dark to see. I was soaked to the skin, legs tired from marching, and starving hungry. Sasha was huddled in the doorway of one of the sheds, tied up, wet and sad. She leapt about on the end of her rope when she saw us.

'Poor angel,' Tara said, with an old-lady-tut. 'He's forgotten to untie her again. And in this rain too.' Then she muttered something I didn't catch and unclipped her. Sasha ran happy circles around us as we hurried into the house, stopping to shake the rain from her coat in the hallway.

Mary was waiting in the corridor. 'Hurry up, hurry up,' she sang. 'Jeremy's called a meeting. Thank goodness you're OK.'

'We were out for a walk.' Tara unzipped Skye's coat.

'In this weather?'

Tara didn't reply.

'Well, you're here now. They're back!' she sang up the stairs. Then she looked at me, her head tilted to one side. 'And Dani, angel. You're feeling OK?' She asked me this pretty much every time she saw me since I got burnt.

I gave her a thumbs up which was my standard reply then ran into the dining room. Bruce had made a treacle tart for pudding, all gooey and golden with a criss-cross top, and there was no way I was risking not getting a slice by being late for a meeting.

Skye ran into the dining room and jumped into Kit's arms. 'Daddy, we gave the faeries porridge. It was raining so hard we hid in—' Tara shushed her and Skye nodded then held her hand up to cup Kit's ear and whispered it.

'What's this about?' Tara asked under her breath.

Kit shrugged. 'No idea.'

Everybody stopped talking when Jeremy walked in. He was wearing his white pyjamas. I hadn't seen him wear anything else for ages and wondered if he slept in them as well. His feet were bare and must have been freezing. I wore two pairs of socks every day and my feet were still blocks of ice.

'We were concerned,' he said to Tara.

He sounded angry. God. Was I in trouble too?

'Perhaps next time you'll tell someone how long you'll be?'

'You don't need to be concerned about me.' Tara also sounded angry. 'I'm capable of taking the girls for a walk.'

'Of course. But it's never a bad idea to tell someone where you're going and what time you'll be back.'

'I couldn't agree more.'

Jeremy narrowed his eyes. The tension between them was insane, even worse than when Angela and Grace both kissed Tom Evans at the fourth-form disco and the following Monday they made the whole class choose sides. I went with Grace because she promised me half her Galaxy.

Tara picked Skye up and they sat at the table.

'Thank you for coming,' Jeremy said in a loud voice. 'I'll be brief. I know we're all hungry and that treacle tart smells amazing.' He smiled and his eyes swept around us. 'For the last few months I've been reading texts relevant to our community. Something I've become particularly interested in is the power of *silence*.' He paused and for a few seconds the room was like a graveyard. 'The benefits of silence on physical and mental health are numerous. As with celibacy, those who practise regular periods of *conscious silence* see huge improvements to their energy levels. Medical studies show it boosts the immune system. Which,' he said with a smile, 'is particularly useful in communities which reject traditional medicine.'

Most of this was going over my head, but Tara suddenly leant forward.

'Hang on.' Tara narrowed her eyes as if she was squinting to read small writing. 'What do you mean, *reject traditional medicine*?'

Jeremy glared at her. 'There'll be time for questions afterwards.'

'No, sorry, Jay. You can't casually drop something like that into conversation. So what is it you're saying?'

'I'm saying research shows if we protect our immune system, eat well, keep fit, and, as I'm about to explain, nourish the mind and soul with practices such as shared silence, we become less reliant on medical intervention and don't need doctors and hospitals.'

'Ever?'

Jeremy doesn't answer immediately, but Tara keeps staring at him. 'I do believe we can exist without hospitals.'

'For everything?'

'Yes. For almost everything.'

'A burst appendix?'

'With the right holistic approach, early detection, plant remedies to reduce inflammation, and, most importantly, a healthy lifestyle to prevent becoming ill in the first place then, yes, we would avoid the risk of invasive surgery.'

Tara laughed and shook her head. Kit leant forward, rested his hand on her shoulder. He whispered something.

'No!' She shoved him away. 'I'm sorry, but there's a big difference between treating a burn with honey and saying we won't use hospitals.' Tara looked at Mary. 'I'm sorry Mary. You're a lovely person, you really are, and your camomile tea is the best I've ever tasted, but a few drops of ginger oil for an upset stomach is a million miles away from curing appendicitis.' She turned back to Jeremy. 'I want you to spell this out for us. Are doctors and hospitals banned?'

'I don't like the word banned—'

'Forbidden then?'

'If we want to be independent from the outside world and live a better, freer life, then we have to be less reliant on it. Not only food, but healthcare too. And, let's face it, modern medicine isn't without its controversies. From antibiotic resistance to the danger of vaccines to post-operative infections—'

'Are we forbidden from going to hospital?'

Kit whispered something to Tara again but she leant further forward on the table.

'Are. Hospitals. Banned?' She fired the words like darts.

Jeremy stared at her in the same way cretin Eddie stared at Mum before a beating. I clenched my hands together and sent a mind-message to Tara. *Leave it. Just leave it.*

Jeremy blinked slowly. 'No, Tara. Nothing is *banned*. All I'm saying is prevention is better than cure.' His voice was soft and syrupy again. He smiled at us all and the tension lifted. 'Listen. Tara's right to ask questions. The refusal to ask questions is how people become slaves to an unseen master. Blind acceptance isn't the way. We *must* question what we've been conditioned to accept. Think about the medicines society is reliant on. Chemicals manufactured in laboratories to cure ailments we can treat naturally. Ask yourselves *why?*'

He looked around the room and for a horrible moment I thought he was going to pounce on me for an answer.

'Money. Those sharks in their pinstriped suits and penthouse offices don't give a shit about your health. They *want* you sick. That's how they keep themselves in red Ferraris and private islands. We've lost our connection to the natural world. Three hundred years ago every man, woman and child could tell hawthorn from alder. They'd have known how to use them to treat kidney stones or toothache. It's these skills, this self-reliance, I'm so keen for us to embrace.'

The whole room was hypnotised. Well, the whole room except Tara and Skye, who were playing, Tara holding out her palm, and Skye trying to smack it without being caught.

'Tara? Are you with us?'

Tara folded her arms around Skye's waist, then whispered something to her. Skye nodded.

'So, what are the benefits of silence? Those who practise intentional silence describe an explosion in creativity and personal growth. As we spend longer together at Winterfall tensions are bound to show. It would be impossible to live as closely as we do and not experience misunderstandings and frustrations as in any family.' I glanced at Tara but it was hard to tell what she was thinking. 'Embracing *silence* together is an antidote to this. Being in each other's presence without conflict. Being in tune.'

Emily lifted a hand to cover her mouth, then said something to Ash, who smiled and dropped his head to hide it. She must have felt me watching. She looked over at me and winked. I glanced at Jeremy but he hadn't seen it.

'Starting from tomorrow, an hour before dinner, we will all meet in here and practise a period of intentional silence. Not only silencing our voices, but also our fears, worries, and desires.'

Emily sniggered and Jeremy glared.

'Sorry,' she whispered, clearing her throat to stop her laughter.

'We will silence our negativity.'

It sounded complicated. I didn't even know what he meant by *our negativity*. I looked at the others to see if they were as confused. Tara and Kit had no expression at all. Skye wasn't listening. Emily, Ash, and Dean were trying not to laugh. Anne and Bruce were holding hands, heads bowed so I couldn't see their faces, while Mary was smiling, gazing at Jeremy as if he were a painting.

Ash put his hand up. Emily sniggered and pulled it down.

'Ash?'

'So, like, we just sit here and not talk?'

'No noise at all. We will be peaceful and present. We will harness our energy.'

'This is *bullshit*,' Emily said then. 'I thought the point of this place was to be free from government and rules? First you go nuclear on pudding and weed. Now we can't talk?'

'Government?' Jeremy's anger was instant, and once again, I saw a flash of cretin Eddie.

'Mama, I'm bored! Can we go and play?' Skye said, loudly and suddenly.

Tara kissed Skye. 'In a bit, angel. Jeremy's talking right now.'

'*Mama!*'

'Skye.' There was a warning note in Jeremy's tone. It might as well have been a starter gun for Tara.

She stared right at him as she spoke to Skye, her eyes narrow as slits. 'Actually, yeah, I'm bored too. We could go and finish that puzzle we started this morning?'

My stomach turned over. It was the same as when I heard Eddie's key in the door, worrying that a fight was going to start.

'And before we go I want to say Skye won't be doing the silence. She'll need somebody to watch her, so I won't be either.'

'It will be good for her.'

'She's five.'

'Yes.'

'You do not *make* five-year-olds silent.'

'Maybe knowing how and when to make noise would be a good skill for her to learn?'

Tara's mouth fell open.

'Learning to control our urge to speak is a strength. It prevents unwanted emotional reactions. It would benefit Skye to learn young. The teachings I've read say those who observe intentional silence experience a happiness unknown to others.'

'Well, I for one have changed my mind. It sounds brilliant.' Emily jabbed the air with her pouch of weed. 'I'm in. So can we call this meeting to an end? I'm off for a smoke before supper.'

'Marijuana?'

'Yes, Jeremy. I'm going to smoke a great, big, fat spliff because I'm an actual adult and you—'

'I agree with Tara,' Kit interrupted Emily and stole Jeremy's attention. 'This isn't why we're here. We didn't sign up to be part of something like this. We came together to live on a farm. You're turning this into—' He stopped himself.

'Into? Go on.'

Kit and Jeremy locked eyes. 'Into something which feels like a cult.'

Jeremy threw his head back and laughed. 'A *cult*?'

Emily clapped twice, then leant over and whispered something to Ash.

'Skye won't be forced to do any group silence.' Kit smiled at Skye then winked, and – oh my *God* – she made the cutest little face back at him, all scrunched up and happy with a wrinkled nose. 'If she chooses to join in, she can. But she won't be made to.' Kit paused. 'Every one of us is here voluntarily. Imposing rules is against the values we stand for.'

'You can't have a community without rules.'

'What?' Kit looked confused. 'You – of all people – are arguing the case for *rules*? And what will you do if people break your rules? Take their bread away? Send them onto the moor for a night without a sleeping bag?'

I shuddered at the thought.

Jeremy straightened his back and scanned the room, making eye-contact with each of us in turn. Anne wasn't able to hold his stare. Emily looked away on purpose. Bruce, too, kept his eyes on the floor.

'Look, I'm not talking about curfews and ID cards! I'm talking about an hour of group meditation every day. Does that sound unreasonable?'

'I'm not sure.' It was Anne, so quiet I could hardly hear her.

'Anne?'

She hesitated. 'I agree with a lot of what you've said. Especially about antibiotics and vaccinations, and I'm loving the meditation we're doing in the mornings. But I'm with Kit and Tara here. I grew up with certain things imposed on me. Always dressed up as beneficial or worthy. I know the damage it does. God knows, I was beaten enough times for doing what children do naturally. That includes making noise.'

'It's a fine line between mandatory silence and suppressing individual choice,' Bruce said.

Jeremy closed his eyes for a moment or two. When he opened them he looked first at Tara, then at Kit. When he spoke his voice was soft again. 'If Skye doesn't want to, she doesn't have to. But if she could be far enough away so the rest of—'

He was interrupted by a hideous screeching. My heart stopped. My first thought was the woman in white had arrived.

Dean was off his chair and out of the door in a split second. Bruce followed him. By the time I got to the front door, the two of them were tearing across the yard towards the terrifying noise. Kit followed with his torch, the beam shining onto the field.

When I reached the field, and saw what was causing the dreadful noise, my stomach turned over.

Sasha had Rosie by the neck. Rosie's eyes were staring wildly. Blood streaked her coat. Her mouth was stuck in a scream as Sasha shook her again and again and again as if she were one of Skye's stuffed toys.

CHAPTER THIRTY-ONE

Tara,
December 2002

Dean's desperate shouts as he tore out of the house cut right through me. The scene in the field was carnage. Bruce and Dean were standing in front of Sasha. Dean told her to let go of Rosie. Sasha seemed to hesitate, as if there was a flickering in her mind, where obedience threatened instinct. Dean asked her again. Firmer. This time she dropped the goat but hovered over the top of it. Bruce went for her collar. Sasha snapped and caught his hand. He yelled and jumped backwards.

'No, Sasha!' Dean shouted.

In response, Sasha grabbed Rosie by the neck again, both animals panting.

'Are you hurt?' I called to Bruce.

'No, she just nicked the skin. She's not giving Rosie up though. That much is clear.'

There was a horrendous racket coming from further into the field in the shadows out of sight. Kit swept the field with the torch and the beam fell on Snowy. She was trapped in fencing, pitching and writhing against her snare.

'Get the one in the fence,' Dean cried when Ash came up beside him. 'Sasha! Drop. *Drop*, Sasha! *Leave* it.'

But she wasn't listening to him. The red mist was back. She

tightened her grip on Rosie, who stared upwards at the sky, her tiny white teeth on show.

By now everybody was at the field wall. Shocked gasps rang in the air.

'*Drop*, Sasha! Sasha!' Dean's desperate voice drowned out the others. 'I hadn't shut them away. I was called in for the meeting. God, please, Sasha! *Leave*!'

Then Dean raised his arm. I saw him wince and close his eyes before bringing his hand down hard on her nose. Sasha yelped and released her grip. Rosie fell to the ground again. Dean threw himself at Sasha. He gripped her hard, both arms around her, burying his face in her coat as she trembled, her chest heaving, her tongue lolling, eyes trying to find Rosie.

The horror on everybody's faces mirrored my own, but gradually the shock gave way to action. Anne and Emily raced up to help Ash free Snowy from the fence. Bruce and Kit crouched around Rosie, trying to stem the blood flow. Jeremy started to walk. I assumed he was going to make sure Dean was all right, but he strode straight past him towards the house.

I turned to Mary, who was immobile, eyes wide. 'Can you take the girls inside?'

'I don't want to go in, Mama,' said Skye, in a trembling whisper.

Dani bent and picked up Skye. 'You can stay with me. Why don't we stand by the wall?'

My heart thumped as I walked over to Dean. I avoided looking at Rosie as Kit and Bruce tried to stem her bleeding. Dean was clinging to Sasha as if his life depended on it. I touched him on the shoulder and he lifted his face from her fur.

'I need a rope or lead,' he mumbled.

'Will a scarf do?'

He nodded and I unwrapped mine from my neck and he looped it through Sasha's collar.

I sat beside him and braved glancing at Rosie. Kit had laid the torch on the ground to illuminate her. The three of them like actors in a spotlight. There was blood everywhere. It soaked Kit's shirt and Bruce's sweater. Streaked their faces. Their hands were glossy with it as they pressed hopelessly against the pumping wound.

'Who untied her?' Tears soaked Dean's cheeks. 'She was on her rope. I hadn't locked the goats away. Jeremy called that meeting. I was late. They all shouted at me so I ran in. Who untied her?'

'It was me.' My voice cracked. 'I'm so sorry.' Guilt twisted my gut. 'I thought she'd been left out by mistake. It was raining. She was cold. Oh, God. I'm so sorry, Dean … I was sure she came into the house with us.'

'She did. She shook water all over the hall. I remember.' Dani sounded distraught. 'I shut the door when she came in.'

'The door was wide open,' Mary said. 'I was the first to it when we heard the commotion. The catch isn't great. Maybe it—'

A movement from the house caught my eye. It was Jeremy. He carried an oil lamp in one hand and something I couldn't make out in the other. He put whatever it was down behind the wall and marched up to Kit. 'Has that bastard animal killed the goat?' His voice shook with rage.

Kit ignored Jeremy. His hands continued to search for the right place to stop the bleeding, but I noticed the urgency had faded. He'd given up hope of saving her.

'Kit? Bruce?' Dean called. 'How is she?'

Skye wriggled out of Dani's arms and ran over to Kit. 'Skye, stay with Dani,' I called.

'Stay over there, sweetheart,' Kit said to Skye. 'Or go to Mama.'

'I want to see Rosie.'

'You need to do as I say. Go over to Mama. This isn't nice.' Kit's voice was sharp and hard. I'd never heard him use that tone with Skye.

'Surely let her stay?' Jeremy looked down at Kit, his question a gauntlet. 'Isn't this what you want? For Skye to make her own choices?'

'Arsehole!' I shouted then, unable to corral my anger. 'You self-important, unpleasant *arsehole*!'

The smile he gave me twisted his face into something ugly.

'I need to go to Skye,' I said to Dean. 'Will you be all right?' He nodded and drew Sasha closer to him.

I scooped Skye into my arms, unable to avoid seeing the brutalised goat. As I watched, Rosie's eyes glazed over, fixing on something distant somewhere beyond Kit.

'Stay with us, girl,' Bruce said. 'Don't give up.'

'Come on, Rosie,' I whispered.

Kit swore under his breath and shook his head. 'It's no good.' He rocked back on his haunches. 'We've lost her.'

Skye tugged his sleeve. 'Daddy, no. Rosie's fine. Look at her eyes! They're *open*.'

'No, sweetheart. She's gone.'

'But her eyes!'

Kit heaved his exhausted body to standing. There was so much blood on him.

'Please, Daddy,' Skye cried. 'You can make Rosie better. Like the lamb. You said the lamb was dead then you made him alive. *Please*, Daddy?'

It was then we heard ecstatic cries of relief in stereo from Ash and Emily. The second goat bounded out of the shadows, one leg dragging, weaving in all directions trying to find somewhere safe. She passed through the light and disappeared back into the darkness, as she headed for the opposite corner of the field. Sasha started barking at her, straining and pulling against Dean's hold.

'Jesus Christ!' Jeremy yelled. 'Get that animal locked away. Shut it in the shed until things are back under control.'

He walked over to Dean and grabbed Sasha by the scruff of the neck so roughly she yelped.

Dean pushed Jeremy's away. 'Get your hands off my dog!'

'Your dog killed one of my goats and, if we were any slower out of the house, we'd have lost the other one too. Maybe the chickens too. Our livestock is vital to us. Now lock that bloody animal in the shed.'

'She's not done anything like this before—'

'Because you tie her up. It was only a matter of time before this happened. The animal is untrustworthy and you know it.'

A fresh surge of guilt swept through me as I recalled my freezing fingers battling to unclip her, then her bounding happily into the house with me and the girls. Why didn't I make sure the door was closed properly. I glanced at Dani and saw her bottom lip trembling.

Dean was nodding at Jeremy. 'I know, I know, and it was a mistake. A horrible, terrible mistake.'

'Yes. It was. And it's one that will happen again now she has the taste of blood.'

Dean stroked Sasha's face and she licked his cheek, then pushed him with her nose.

Jeremy walked back to the gate, and reached down behind the wall. When he turned, I gasped.

He was holding a shotgun.

'Jesus, Jeremy!'

Where the hell had he got a gun from?

He walked back to Dean and Sasha.

'What the fuck are you doing, you idiot?' I shouted. 'There are children here!'

'Put the gun down.' Kit's voice was calm, jarring against the panic that coursed through me.

'The dog is a killer and needs to be dealt with.'

There was a rumble of protest as gradually everybody wrapped their heads around what was unfurling.

Jeremy lifted the shotgun, the long black barrel pointing a straight line towards Sasha.

'No, Jeremy!' Anne cried.

'Mary! Take Skye in! *Please*,' I shouted.

My voice seemed to jolt her into motion. She ran at Skye and grabbed her hand. 'Inside,' she said. 'Come now.' Then she started to jog towards the house pulling Skye behind her.

'Dani too!' But Mary didn't stop.

Kit rested a hand on Jeremy's shoulder. 'What are you doing?'

Jeremy shrugged Kit's hand away.

Emily and Ash drew up beside me. 'What the fuck is happening?' Emily breathed.

'You're going to shoot my dog?' Dean's horror was undisguised.

'No, he's not going to shoot her.'

'Kit's right.' Jeremy's voice was emotionless. He stared fixedly at Dean and lowered the shotgun. 'I'm not going to shoot your dog.' He thrust the gun out towards him. '*You* are.'

Another rumble of protestation juddered around the group.

Dean hoisted Sasha into his arms, cradling her upright, her front paws over his shoulders. Then he turned her away from Jeremy. I noticed a smear of blood from her coat, war paint daubed across his cheek. 'You're out of your tiny, fucked up, *psycho* mind if you think I'm doing that.'

'She needs to be dealt with. If you won't do it, I will'

'Then you'll have to shoot us both.'

'Stop it!' Emily shouted. 'This is literally insane.'

This was out of control. Jeremy had lost his mind.

'Put the gun down.' Kit moved closer to Jeremy.

'Stay out of this, Kit.'

'It isn't Sasha's fault!' Dani ran from the wall and stood in front of Jeremy. Tears streaked her face. 'It was me who didn't shut the door properly!'

'Doors get left open. These things happen. We cannot have a dog on the farm that isn't safe around livestock.'

'I'll muzzle her.' Dean scrunched his hands into her soft fur. 'If she's muzzled she can't do any damage.'

'And when you forget to put the muzzle on?'

'I won't.'

'No? Wasn't she supposed to be tied up safely this evening?'

Dean began to look dazed by what was unfolding. 'You're making her out to be a wild beast. But she's not. She's gentle as anything with the children. I'm not going to shoot her. Nobody is!'

Jeremy raised the gun and pointed it at Dean and Sasha.

'No!' cried Emily. 'Are you fucking tripping?'

There was a movement from Dani. She ran in front of the gun, putting herself between the nose of it and Dean. She spread her arms out wide. Lifted her chin in defiance. Emily stepped in beside her and reached for Dani's hand. Dani glanced at her and they smiled at each other. Then Bruce moved next to them. I did the same. My heart was clattering in my chest as the four of us stood shoulder to shoulder in a barricade to protect Dean and Sasha.

Then Kit placed himself in front of us, his face a couple of feet from the shotgun. 'Put the gun down.'

The shotgun wavered in Jeremy's grip. 'Get out of the way.'

'Put the fucking gun down!' cried Emily.

'The dog needs to be destroyed.'

It was surreal. Like a standoff from a Western film from the fifties. From behind us I heard Dean clear his throat.

'Don't shoot her.' His voice was cracked with emotion. 'Not like this. Let me take her to the rescue tomorrow. She can go in the shed tonight. I'll sleep there with her. Tie her rope around my waist so there's no way she can get out. I'll get her off the farm first thing in the morning. Please, Jeremy? *Please* don't kill her.'

Jeremy baulked. The shotgun wavered. He made an effort to

steady it, his eyes squeezed closed, as if battling voices. The next few seconds felt like years, but finally he lowered it. Kit stepped forward and took the gun from him.

'Thank God,' I whispered.

Emily turned and put her arms around Dani.

Kit tried to put his hand on Jeremy's arm. Jeremy pulled away from him. 'Any other farmer would have shot her without hesitation. This is real life, not a cosy little game. You think I relish the idea of shooting a dog?'

Nobody replied.

Jeremy turned and silently walked back to the house.

Ash went to Dean and put his arm around his brother. Dean dropped his head and kissed the top of Sasha's head.

Bruce walked back to Rosie and bent down. He slid his arms beneath her and hoisted her up, grunting with the effort required to lift her. 'Come on, girl,' he whispered. 'Let's see to you.'

'Are you going to bury her?' Dani asked, sniffing back her tears.

'I am.'

'Can I help?'

He smiled kindly. 'That would be grand.'

'I'll help as well,' said Emily.

'And me,' I said.

Then I went to Kit and kissed him. He closed his eyes, then let out a long, trembling breath.

'Why don't you go in and make sure Skye's all right?' I said softly. 'Get yourself cleaned up.'

He rested his forehead against mine and whispered, 'I love you.' Then Anne smiled at me and nodded. She put her arm around his waist and they walked slowly inside.

Dean was sitting on the ground, still holding Sasha to him. His eyes were distant. One hand absently stroking her.

'You OK?' I asked him.

'This place has changed,' he said. 'I wanted somewhere to bring

Ash. Get him on the straight and narrow. Jeremy said it would give us a new start. He was right. The farm was everything I dreamt of and more. A secret world nobody else knew about. It was special. And … Jeremy, he was … He was *good*. You know? Patient. Had this superhuman energy.' He rubbed his chin against Sasha then tipped his head to kiss her. 'He said there was a better way to live and I thought he was right. But not anymore. It's like we're below deck on a great big ship. We're powering the oars but have no idea where the ship is sailing.'

We took turns with the shovel. When we'd finished digging, Bruce carried Rosie over and laid her gently on her side and rolled her into the hole. Dani cried as we filled in the grave. Dean joined us, his hand holding the scarf I'd given him for a makeshift lead. Sasha lay beside him, her chin resting on his feet. Bruce said a few words then Dani picked a handful of long grass and tied some blades around the base then laid her makeshift bouquet on the soil mound.

'Sleep tight, Rosie,' she whispered.

CHAPTER THIRTY-TWO

Kit,
December 2002

Bruce, Anne, Mary and Tara are standing around the stove nursing mugs of camomile tea, brewed by Mary to help with the shock. Kit sits separately in the shadowy corner of the room. His head tumbles with conflicting thoughts. The atmosphere is strained as everybody processes what had happened. Emily and Ash are in the sitting room, huddled on the sofa beneath a blanket, whispering. Dean, as he'd promised, has taken a sleeping bag and pillow to the shed and is sleeping out there with Sasha.

'What was he thinking?' Tara breathes to nobody in particular.

Kit knows Jeremy better than anybody knows him and he cannot fathom this either. It was as if he'd been possessed.

'Where's the gun now?' Bruce asks.

Kit clears his throat and lifts his head. 'In the cupboard by the back door. The one with the fuse board. It's locked.'

'And the key?' Tara asks. 'Is it out of reach of the children?'

He rubs his face. 'It's on the doorframe. At the top. Out of reach.'

Kit knows how deeply unhappy she will be that there is a gun anywhere near.

'I need to check that wound.' Mary gestures towards Bruce's hand.

'It's nothing,' Bruce says.

But she carries an oil lamp to him and lifts the dressing she applied. 'I feel so sorry for Rosie,' she says. 'What a horrible way to die. And this bite, too? The dog's feral.'

Kit stands and walks over to Bruce. He looks at the bite. It's a single puncture wound, a perfect circle, dark around its edge where the skin is starting to bruise.

'What if she'd gone for one of the children?' Mary says in her soft, singing voice.

'What if one of the children had been fucking *shot*?' Tara snaps. Her expression is unyielding, eyes burning. 'This isn't about Sasha going for Rosie. This is about Jeremy pointing a fucking gun at Dean.' She breathes out, her breath shuddering. 'And then right at Kit.' She puts her hands over her face and shakes her head.

'I stepped in front of the gun.'

Tara drops her hands and stares at Kit in disbelief. 'Are you seriously taking his side on this?'

'I'm not taking his side. I'm just saying it was me who stepped in front of the gun.'

'No doubt he's learnt from it. It got out of control. But nobody was hurt,' Bruce says, in an obvious attempt to keep the peace. 'And the dog is leaving the farm.'

'That's looking good.' Mary presses the dressing firmly down to reaffix the surgical tape. 'We'll look at it again in the morning.'

'You sure you don't want to get it checked out?' Kit asks.

'This?' Bruce shakes his head. 'Mary's done a grand job. It stopped bleeding almost straight away and doesn't hurt.'

'What if it gets infected?'

'It won't get infected,' Mary says. 'I've used a mixture of comfrey and calendula, rosemary and tea tree. And, of course, there's some magic honey in there.' She beams.

Anne smiles at Kit and reaches over to squeeze Tara's hand. 'Neither of you must fret. If Bruce thought he needed to see a doctor, he would. I promise.'

They hear footsteps on the stairs and they all stop talking.

Jeremy comes to a halt in the doorway and for a moment or two doesn't speak. When he does, his voice is choked and after every few words he pauses, as if trying to muster the strength to talk.

'What happened this evening was regrettable. I am upset I lost control. But I was devastated by what had happened to our goat. When you farm, of course you have to get used to death, but seeing Rosie mutilated? Suffering? It cut through me and I got angry. Anger has always been my Achilles heel. Here, at Winterfall, I've been doing well at learning how to control it. Meditating and celibacy have cleared my mind. But tonight emotion overwhelmed me.'

'You pointed a *gun* at Dean and threatened to shoot him, and you did it when there were children around.'

Kit can hear how close Tara is to tears. Her words turn his stomach. She's right to be appalled. The thought of Skye being shot makes him weak.

'It's a shotgun and I pointed it at the dog. You really think I'd hurt Dean? Or any of you?'

'Where did you get it?'

'The shotgun?'

Tara nods.

'From a supplier in London who sells hunting equipment.'

'Don't you need a licence or something?'

'Yes, you need a shotgun certificate. I have one. This is all perfectly legal.'

'You should have discussed it with us,' Kit says quietly. 'We should have been involved in the decision to bring a gun here.'

Jeremy has the grace to look contrite. He drops his head and takes a deep breath. 'I should have done. It was a mistake not to. But, honestly? I knew how Tara felt about firearms. I suspected others might also have reservations. But we live on a farm. Farmers have shotguns. They need to protect their livestock. That dog tore Rosie to bits. We can't have a dog who kills livestock here. What if she roamed? Killed sheep on the moor? Or turned on one of the girls? She has the taste of blood now. She will do it again. Our livestock are vital to the farm and have to be protected.' He pauses. 'I know things got out of hand and I was wrong to bring the shotgun out like that. I've talked to Kit and he has locked it safely away. Now I just hope we can put this unpleasantness behind us and come together again for the sake of Winterfall.'

There is a murmur of agreement. Mary walks over and embraces him. Bruce then offers his hand and pats him on the shoulder. Jeremy nods once, then leaves the room. They listen to his footsteps on the stairs. His door closing. Mary, Anne and Bruce drift away, leaving Tara and Kit in the kitchen. Kit puts a couple of logs on the fire and leaves the stove door open. They pull their chairs close and watch the flames.

'I can't stop thinking about what might have happened. How easily someone could have been killed.'

'But they weren't.'

Tara turns in her chair to face him. He glances at her briefly, then back at the fire. 'You can't keep putting your head in the sand about everything. Jeremy's lost the plot.'

'I'll talk to him again tomorrow.'

Tara growls in frustration. 'And say *what*? Tell him if he doesn't stop with the power trip, he can't have any carrot cake?'

Kit leans forward and picks up the poker. He stabs the logs in the burner and they complain in a frenzy of angry sparks.

'I know he's your friend—'

'He's your friend too.' Kit thinks back to that first year together, when Tara and he became an item and she turned their friendship group from two to three. Sitting on the riverbank, laughing until tears rolled down their faces. Their first New Year's Eve together, dancing to Jamiroquai on the roof of the college laundry. Jeremy wiping away Tara's tears of uncertainty when she found out she was pregnant and telling her what a perfect mother she would make.

'Not anymore,' Tara says. 'We've drifted too far apart. I don't even recognise him now. The Jeremy I loved was bright, rebellious, and bursting with life; now he's an ugly, blinkered, out-of-control despot with a God complex.' She pauses and stares into the fire. 'Winterfall has changed him.'

Kit rubs his face with his hand. The faint smell of Rosie's blood lingers on his skin and his stomach heaves. 'So what do you want us to do? Do you want to leave Cornwall? Go back to the bedsit?'

Tara doesn't answer immediately. He sees her brain turning over behind her eyes. Then she takes a deep, heavy breath. 'No, I don't want to go back. It's Jeremy I have a problem with. Being here, with you and Skye, it feels right.' She takes his hand. 'I think we should focus on the cottage. Do it up as quickly as we can. But I'm not taking any of Jeremy's shit while we stay here. I'm not buying into his Winterfall vision any longer. As far as *the project* is concerned, I'm out.'

She rests her hand on his shoulder for a moment, then leaves the kitchen. He sits for a while, watching the flames dance, then leans forward and closes the stove door.

CHAPTER THIRTY-THREE

Dani,
December 2002

It took me a while to come to, but when I did, with blurry eyes and a head stuffed full of sleep, I jumped to find Emily's face a few centimetres from mine.

'What—'

'Shush,' she whispered.

I nodded and rubbed my eyes, then sat up, pulling my blanket up to my chin. It was icy in the room. Tara was right, it was crazy we couldn't put the heating on. I didn't get what Jeremy had against warmth. Especially as it wasn't even him who'd be paying the bill.

'I'm leaving.'

'Leaving?'

She nodded. 'With Dean and Ash.'

It was then I noticed her packed rucksack beside her.

'You're taking Sasha?' The thought of her being left here at the mercy of Jeremy was terrifying.

'That's why we're going. That man has lost his fucking mind. To be honest, I blame the no sex thing. I mean, what twenty-five-year-old guy *does* that? Maybe if he knocked one out he wouldn't be such a nutter.'

I thought of Jeremy's face as he aimed the gun at Sasha. A snarling monster. Like Eddie.

'This is my number.' She passed me a small scrap of paper and I closed my hand around it.

'Where are you going?' It crossed my mind that I could go with them, but when she said London, Eddie's face leered in my head so I kept quiet.

'Ash knows a place we can crash. If you leave, call me if you need help. If you don't leave, stick close to Tara. She's the only one who isn't mental and you can trust her. She really cares about you, and we both know how unusual that is in this pile-of-shit world.'

I slid the piece of paper beneath my pillow. Though I didn't want them to go, I was relieved they were getting Sasha away. I didn't trust Jeremy around her at all.

'What should I say when he asks where you are?'

She smiled. 'Tell him you've no idea. You were asleep. And good riddance. Tell him you never liked us anyway. That's the trick to lying. Always add a bit of colour to make the lie more believable.'

'He's not going to like it.'

'Screw what that crackpot likes.'

Then she put her arms around me and gave me a hug, which was weird and lovely at the same time. 'Look after yourself.' She smiled at me. 'And no more drugs.'

She crept out of my room, waving before she disappeared. My mind raced at a billion miles an hour. Flashes of the day flickered like a film. Running through the rain with Tara. The ruined cottage. Sasha shaking Rosie. Kit's blood-soaked clothes. Running in front of the gun to protect Sasha and Dean. Then I pictured Emily arriving in London. The lights. The crowds and shops. The noise and smells. Then, for the first time in ages, I thought about Mum and sobbed into my pillow until it was wet through.

In the morning, I stayed in bed, watching my breath forming clouds and stroking the piece of paper with Emily's number beneath my pillow. My tummy was knotted up with nerves. I needed the toilet, but there was no way I was getting up. I didn't want to be anywhere near Jeremy when he found out the three of them were gone.

It wasn't long until I heard footsteps on the stairs and pretended to be asleep.

'Dani?' It was Tara. I opened my eyes. 'You didn't come down for breakfast?'

'I'm not feeling great.'

'What's wrong?'

'Nothing much. A tummy ache. But it's not bad,' I added quickly. Mary's fennel tea for upset stomachs was gross.

'Emily hasn't appeared either. Nor Ash and Dean.'

My checks flushed red. 'Maybe they're still asleep?'

'Maybe.' But I could tell she knew something was up. 'Are you sure your tummy's not too bad?'

'It's just period pain.'

Tara smiled. 'There's no *just* when it comes to period pain. I'll get you a hot-water bottle. That always helps me.'

Emily's words echoed in my head.

She really cares about you.

I heard Tara knock lightly on Emily's door and my heart stopped. The door opened. The next thing I heard were Tara's feet on the stairs. As I lay there, I tried to distract myself by counting the cracks on the ceiling and wondering how long it would take for the house to crumble to nothing but dust.

When I heard footsteps again, I expected to see Tara appear, but when the figure walked through my door, it was Jeremy. I closed my eyes and crossed my fingers he'd see I was asleep and go away again.

'Dani?'

My body stiffened. I opened my eyes slowly and made myself look ill. 'Mm?'

'Do you know where Emily is? Her things have gone.'

'Huh?'

'*Emily*. Where is she?'

I sat up and swapped my ill face for a confused face. 'I don't know what you mean?'

His eyes burrowed into mine. 'I mean, she's gone. Dean and Ash too.'

'Well ... Er. Maybe they, er, went for a walk?' I hoped this might be enough to get Jeremy out of the room before I caved and told him they'd run away in the night to save Sasha and were somewhere in London.

'With their clothes and bags?' His fists clenched. 'No. They've gone. I can't believe they didn't tell me.'

Tara appeared at the door.

'I suppose you've come to tell me this is all my fault?' he said.

Tara rolled her eyes, walked past him, and handed me a hot-water bottle. 'Hold it against your tummy,' she said with a soft smile. Then she turned and put her hands on her hips. 'No, I'm not going to say it's your fault. They made their own minds up and left. You always said that, didn't you? That everybody's free to leave? I mean, you said that to Dani.' Tara seemed to hesitate. She glanced at me. 'Who you shouldn't have brought here in the first place.'

'Jesus! This again? Dani *wanted* to come here and she *wanted* to stay.'

'She's *fourteen*, Jeremy. You took a fourteen-year-old off the streets in London. You didn't tell the authorities. You didn't contact her parents. You took her on a train to Cornwall. How did you persuade her?'

'What the hell are you talking about?'

'Swoop in like a knight in shining armour? Buy her food? Buy the train ticket? Tell her she only needs to stay if she wants to? Offer her a bed and food and a place she'd be safe? Did you make it sound too good to be true? Too good to turn down?'

Something grew tight around my chest as I remembered sitting in the alleyway, cold and wet, and seeing Jeremy for the first time. Being so grateful when he chased the pervert away. How good the burger and fries tasted. The way he smiled when he slid the photo across the table.

'Everybody knows child abductors will manipulate kids into going with them. And we're all guilty. We all kept her here.'

'Jesus. She was on the streets. A man was offering her money for sex. She was at risk. There's no romance in being homeless. Maybe you think it means a cushy spot beneath a railway bridge with kind-natured kindred spirits who share their food and watch out for each other? Get off that middle-class high horse you ride like the lovechild of Boudicca and Germaine fucking Greer and get real. She was safer here than she was sleeping rough in London.' He paused and narrowed his eyes. 'I've let you undermine this project for too long. You're desperate for it to fail.'

'This *project,* as you call it, can *only* fail. There's nothing here, Jeremy. One injured goat. A few chickens. People wearing hats and scarves to bed because it's so bloody cold. Heating a pan of water on a cast-iron stove so we can wash with a flannel. There isn't even enough food.'

'This is our first year! It's going to be tough. But we're set up now. The fields are fenced. The vegetable beds and orchard are up and running. Next year we'll have polytunnels and a biomass boiler. We'll build more animal shelters—'

'With Kit conveniently footing the bill? This isn't self-sufficiency. The entire farm – your precious project – is bankrolled by Kit. Animal feed. Tools. Building materials. Rice, yeast, oil for the lamps. The list goes on and on, and not one thing has been paid for by anybody but Kit.'

His mouth twitched and his fists flexed. I wanted to hide my head beneath the pillow.

'Start-up costs,' he said. 'And Kit agreed to all of it. Next year we'll be more independent. The year after we'll be self-sufficient. Then we'll start to trade with the locals. This isn't a temporary project. We're building a community that can exist here forever.'

Tara stepped closer and when she spoke her voice was low and level. 'You made those trips to the city to find women, didn't you? That's why you brought Emily here. Is it why you brought Dani too?'

'What are—'

'I heard you at the midsummer party. Talking to Kit. You thought I was asleep. You told Kit we should have another baby. A Winterfall baby. The first of many, you said. Then you said we needed more women to make the project work. You made those trips to find them, didn't you?'

'Are you serious?' He tried to laugh.

Was what Tara saying true?

'I am deadly fucking serious.'

'Jesus, Tara. I was mucking about. I can't believe you'd think that. I was overwhelmed with emotion, carried away by the joy of it all. But, *no*, of course I wasn't being serious. That would be insane.'

'And yet a few weeks later you disappear up to London and don't tell us why you're going. Then one day, after another mysterious trip, Emily's in tow.'

'I stopped Emily jumping off a bridge. What would you have me do? Push her off?'

That wasn't true. Emily told me it was a man in a suit who stopped her. I felt sick.

'I can't wait to get away from here,' she whispered. 'And far away from you.'

He smiled. 'Back to your hovel in Cowley? Back to excruciating lunches with your pedestrian parents? You think Kit wants that?' He shook his head. 'You want him strapped to the wheel. Forced into an office for the rest of his life so you can buy clothes made by toddlers in Indian sweatshops and eat plastic-wrapped food stuffed with chemicals.'

'No, we've got the cottage—'

'The *cottage*? I went up there. It's a pile of stones. You're seriously going to take your precious daughter to live in a place that could collapse at any minute. Give me a break.'

Tara didn't reply. When she turned from him I saw she was crying. I wanted to go to her but I was scared Jeremy would shout at me. He went towards her and I got ready to scream for Kit if things turned nasty. But they didn't.

'What's happened to us, Tara?' His voice was silky. 'I love you. You and Kit are the most important people in my life. I know I scared you. The gun was a hideous lapse of judgement. Seeing that poor, defenceless animal savaged that way? I saw red. It all happened so quickly. I screwed up.'

Tara wiped her eyes. She looked at me. I smiled to show her I really cared about her too.

'Give the farm – your home – a chance. A few months. You and I fighting like this is upsetting Kit. It doesn't have to be this way. We both love him deeply. He wants Winterfall to work. He doesn't want to leave, but at the same time, he wants you to be happy. Like he is. Like Skye is. This is tearing him apart. I can see I'm holding on too tightly. I'll listen more. I'll take a back seat. Maybe I'm not the right person to be making the decisions. Kit can. Or you? All I want is for us to be happy here. And if you still want to leave come spring, we will help you make the cottage habitable. It's not what I want, but you have my word.'

As I listened, I saw the old Jeremy. The kind, handsome man with the syrupy voice who rescued me in London. Who bought me a burger and milkshake. Who promised he'd keep me safe.

Maybe things were going to be all right after all.

CHAPTER THIRTY-FOUR

Tara,
December 2002

The three of them leaving thrust the farm into a weird, uncomfortable atmosphere. It was eerily quiet. I realised how often the house rang with dramatic exclamations from Emily relating to her moods, both good and bad. Or how you'd walk past a room and hear her and Ash giggling. Dean's excited praise when Sasha learnt a new trick. Sasha's barking. Ash's guitar. Without them the house was hushed as a library.

I did my best to be civil to Jeremy. He was right about two things. The cottage wasn't habitable and dragging my family back to the life we escaped wasn't the answer, even if I'd wanted to. Plus, he also had a point about the two of us pulling Kit in different directions. It wasn't fair. So, against my better judgement, I resolved to make an effort. I would try not to let things get under my skin. I would cooperate as far as I needed to. I refocused my attention on home-educating the girls. Dani had become more engaged. I'm not sure I'd go so far as to say she was loving it, but she certainly seemed happier to try. I helped Anne with dear Snowy. The poor goat had come away from her entanglement in the fence with a nasty gash. Mary had made up a sweet-smelling ointment with marshmallow root and calendula which we applied to the wound every few hours.

While the rest of us were subdued and reflective, Kit was

invigorated by the knowledge that Jeremy and I were apparently at peace. It was as if he'd turned to a clean white page and everything written before was forgotten. His ability to see only the good in Jeremy used to be endearing. Now it was infuriating.

'Do you really think he'll help us renovate the cottage?'

'Of course,' Kit replied. 'Why would he lie?'

I suspected there were plenty of reasons Jeremy would lie. I knew he'd told me exactly what he needed to tell me to keep us at Winterfall. Jeremy, after all, was a hypnotist and always had been. He told people what they needed to hear to get his own way. I couldn't say this to Kit. He'd think me paranoid and unreasonable, which would push him further towards Jeremy. I had to play Jeremy's game. Sooner or later, he'd slip up, and perhaps then Kit would finally admit his true colours.

'Maybe we should throw another party?' Mary suggested as we sat around the table for yet another muted dinner. 'We have Christmas Day coming up, but it might be nice to mark the winter solstice as well?'

'Not at the stones. It's too cold.' The thought of trying to enjoy ourselves while at the mercy of the winter weather which lashed the moor relentlessly was unappealing. Plus, any mention of the stone circle brought back vicious recollections of Dani's terrifying accident.

'What about a party here?' Kit said. 'We could build a bonfire in the yard.'

'That's a great idea!' Jeremy said, and beamed at Kit.

I bristled. Jeremy was transparent, playing Kit like a kitten with a ball of string.

'There's lots of cuttings in the orchard to get rid of,' said Anne. 'And burnable rubbish in the barn. It's about time we had a clear-out.'

'As long as Dani promises not to help herself to anything out of my cupboard.'

Dani's cheeks turned bright red and she mumbled something.

Mary chuckled. 'Bless you. I'm joking!'

Bruce stood up from the table. 'I'm going to hit the hay a bit early. Got a headache I can't shift.'

Mary put the back of her hand to his forehead. 'Can I give you something? Extract of feverfew and some peppermint oil for your temples?'

'That bite isn't infected, is it?'

He smiled. 'No, that's all healed nicely. A bit itchy, but otherwise grand. Mary worked wonders.'

Mary beamed. 'Tea tree is foolproof for keeping infection at bay. I've never known one creep through!'

Anne took Bruce back to their caravan and the rest of us cleared the table and tidied the kitchen. Mary searched through the bottles in her pantry for the feverfew and peppermint oil. 'I'll take these across to him. He looks tired. It's no wonder. The man doesn't stop. He'll be up before dawn to bake the bread.'

'Can you tell him not to get up in the morning?' Kit said. 'You're right, he looked shattered. I'll do the bread.'

While Kit went out to the woodpile to fill the baskets of logs, Dani and I went up to find Skye. She was in her nook, lying on her tummy on the mattress, doing some colouring. She was so careful to keep within the lines. The picture was a kaleidoscope with a cartoon dog she'd coloured purple, bright blue grass, a pink sky, and a rainbow sun.

'That's brilliant,' Dani said, as we sat down next to the mattress.

Skye smiled. 'The dog's called Sasha.' Skye closed the colouring book and sat up. 'I miss real Sasha. I liked her funny tricks.'

I stroked her forehead. 'I miss her too.'

'Do you think they're OK?' Dani asked.

'I'm absolutely certain they are.'

'Jeremy told me Emily wasn't suited to the farm.'

'Did he? When?'

Dani shrugged. 'The day after they left when I was collecting the eggs.'

'What else did he say?'

'Nothing much. That he'd tried to help her, but she didn't want help. He said she wanted to stay lost and,' Dani hesitated, 'he said that she's weak. But I don't think she is. Do you?'

I shook my head. 'No,' I said. 'Emily is strong.'

And I was jealous of that strength. From the moment she walked into Winterfall she was on to his bullshit. Emily was immune to him and Jeremy was threatened by that. When I was younger I wanted to be someone like Emily, like my grandmother, spirited, adventurous, and independent.

I think, for a while, I was.

I missed that version of me. I wanted her back.

CHAPTER THIRTY-FIVE

Kit,
December 2002

The mood lifts as they set about building the bonfire. Clearing the orchard and barn of burnable rubbish and gardening waste gives them a goal and the place feels more like it did in the early summer.

Bruce is still in bed. When Kit knocks on the caravan door to ask how he is, Anne smiles warmly. She squeezes out of the door and closes it softly behind her. 'Fast asleep,' she whispers. 'He's over the worst of it. Poor love is exhausted. You know what he's like. Never stops. He's run-down and needs rest. Mary's doing a wonderful job looking after him.'

'I'm happy to drive him to the surgery.' He speaks tentatively. Anne and Bruce have made it clear they are with Jeremy on the subject of medical intervention, but Tara insisted he ask.

'No need. He's so much better. His temperature's down and he's catching up on some good sleep. Snoring like a baby.' She grins. 'Bless him, silly goose. I tell him all the time he needs to take it easy once in a while, but he's only ever content if he's on the go.'

'Give him our love,' Kit says. 'The farm's not the same without that smile of his lighting it up.'

Kit joins Jeremy in the barn where he is rifling through the discarded debris, looking for things to add to the bonfire.

'Can I ask you something?' Kit says, as they heave an old pallet, thick with cobweb, on to the growing pile.

'Go on,' Jeremy smiled at him.

'Did you mean it about helping us do up the cottage if we want to leave?'

'Of course. I wouldn't say something I didn't mean.' They walk back to the barn. 'Why? Has she said something?'

'Not as such. But we both know you'd prefer us to stay at Winterfall.'

'Well, yes, that's true. Perhaps I'm being optimistic, but I am hoping that in a few months time Tara will feel differently. But if she doesn't, no, I won't stand in your way.' He smiles and pats Kit's shoulders with his hands. 'I want both of you to be happy.'

Dani and Skye emerge from the orchard with armfuls of branches and crispy brown weeds to add to the now mountainous heap.

'Well done, girls.' Kit bends to pick up a couple of twigs they've dropped and chucks them on to the bonfire. 'After we've built the fire, I thought we could go out on the moor. The views from the Tor will be spectacular today.'

'I'd love to!'

Kit smiles. He remembers the pale, surly teenager who'd rolled her eyes at the mere suggestion of a walk six months ago.

Dani glances towards the caravan. 'Is Bruce better?'

Kit laughs. 'Thinking about your teatime cake?'

She grins. 'No. Well, maybe? I mean, nobody else's are even half as good.'

When the fire is built, the others head in to prepare lunch, while Kit fetches the jerrycan of paraffin from the lock-up shed. He carries it over to the fire and stashes it in the corner of the yard together with an old rag he'll use later, soaked in fuel, to start the fire. It's the cheat's way, but he doesn't care. Some of the wood is damp and, frankly, any excuse to get the paraffin out. He puts the jerrycan down and sees a smear of liquid on his skin from the handle. He lifts his hand to his nose and breathes in the smell. It takes him back to the garage at Ashbarton Combe and the feeling of delight as he'd soaked the upholstery of his father's ridiculous car, then the thrill of watching the flames take hold. He contemplates the towering pile of wood and his skin tingles at the promise of the fire it will become.

Kits asks the rest of them if they'd want to walk up to the Tor with him and Dani. But everybody is busy. Jeremy wants to catch up on some reading. Mary has essential oil to bottle. Anne is going to make a start on the cooking for the party, and Tara and Skye are helping her.

Anne tries to protest, but Tara smiles. 'Honestly, the walk he's planning is too far for Skye. And we want to help, don't we sweetheart?'

Skye nods enthusiastically.

'You still want to go?' Kit suspects Dani might not want to walk without Tara and Skye. But to his surprise, she nods.

'Yeah, I'd still like to. If that's OK with you?' she adds quickly.

Kit cynically wonders whether her teenage brain has weighed up helping in the kitchen versus a walk on the moor and opted for the most palatable. But he doesn't mind. It's too beautiful – cold, clear, and crisp – to be stuck indoors and he knows she'll love it.

'That's great. I'll take some hot chocolate in a thermos, and I think there's some shortbread in the biscuit tin.'

The moor delivers more than it promised. The grass glitters with frost in those shadowed places the sun hasn't reached yet. The azure sky is free of cloud and the sun shimmers on paper-thin ice which skims the water trapped in muddy indents where cattle have trod.

'So where are we going?'

Kit stops walking and points out three low peaks in the distance, grey granite rising out of the grass and shrub. 'Rough Tor. The middle one. It's the second-highest point in Cornwall and the views are magnificent.'

The route winds around the base of the first peak and as they round a bend in the path they come across a herd of wild ponies who casually clock them but make no effort to move away. Dani and Kit stop walking to watch them a while, and it isn't long before one of the braver ponies wanders a little closer.

Dani nods at the shaggy creature, whose straggly mane is knotted with fern. 'Hello,' she says, as if talking to a man in the street.

'Try breathing at him.'

'Do what?'

'Softly. Out though your nose. Like this.' Kit breathes out through flared nostrils. 'Keep your head low when you do it. It's how horses greet each other.'

Dani looks at Kit as if he's bonkers, but then gives a slight shrug, and does what he said, bending her head and blowing out gently.

'He's coming closer,' she whispers.

Dani stands statue-still, breathing through her nose. When the pony is close enough she stretches out her hand and grazes his muzzle with the tips of her fingers. The pony snorts and throws his head up, which makes Dani jump. The pony wheels around on his back legs and canters back to his herd.

Dani looks at Kit and grins. 'He let me touch him!'

Kit smiles. 'It's because you're so gentle. He trusted you.'

Despite the chilled air, climbing the hill is hot work and Kit stops to take his coat off and ties it around his waist. They don't talk as they push on to the summit, but when they reach the top, Dani gasps.

'Oh, my God,' she shouts, as she turns a slow circle. 'It's *amazing*!'

Kit points to a pillar of granite slabs stacked on top of each other. 'You can go even higher.'

Dani grins and runs over to the rocky tower and starts to

scramble up. Kit smiles as he breathes in the vastness of the land-scape surrounding them.

At the top, Dani shouts again, and her voice cuts through the peace. 'I'm on the top of the world! I can even see Leyton!' She stretches out her arms and her coat, caught by the wind, flies out behind her like a superhero's cape. 'It's incredible up here!'

Her cry of unfettered joy moves Kit. There has been so much stress at the farm over the last few months. Jeremy and Tara at loggerheads. Dani's accident. The horrendous incident with Sasha. The shotgun ... Seeing Dani uplifted by the sheer beauty of the moor reminds him how privileged they are to be here. When he and Jeremy viewed Winterfall Farm with the estate agent, they'd walked a little way onto the moor. While Jeremy had been talking excitedly about the self-sufficient community they would build, Kit was consumed by the wild beauty. Somehow they have lost this feeling. They need to rediscover it.

Anne is sitting on the steps of the caravan when Kit and Dani return from their walk. They wave at her as they climb over the stile into the field. She doesn't wave back and as they get nearer, Kit sees she is smoking, which he's never seen her do before. When they reach her, he sees her features are tight with anguish, and she's chewing on her lip as she flicks the end of the cigarette repeatedly with the tip of her thumbnail.

'What's wrong?'

She smiles weakly. 'It's Bruce. He's not so good. Mary's in with him. He's struggling to breathe and—'

Kit doesn't wait for her to say more. He pulls open the caravan door and finds Mary sitting on the edge of the bed, pressing a wet flannel against Bruce's brow. He is lying still. Eyes shut. Hands at his sides, clenching his blanket. His breaths are coming in shallow, uncomfortable rasps.

'Bruce?'

He opens his eyes and slowly turns his head towards Kit. 'I'm ... fine ... The flu ... It's hit me ... a bit.'

'He's feeling achy. I've given him cayenne, which has helped. It's a relaxant.'

'Dani's gone to fetch Jeremy,' Anne says as she comes into the caravan and squeezes past Kit to kneel beside the bed. She takes hold of his hand in hers. 'How are you, angel?' She leans forward to kiss him.

As she does, his entire body tenses. His hands flex into rigid claws. His face contorts and the sinews in his neck stretch tight and lift proud as his back arches off the bed. Anne puts her hands either side of his face. 'Bruce? *Bruce!*'

Mary looks at Kit. 'More cayenne?'

'He needs a hospital.' Panic solidifies in Kit's stomach.

Bruce responds by exhaling like a punctured tyre before collapsing back on the bed. His mouth is open and he pulls desperate lungfuls of oxygen into his body.

Jeremy's face appears at the door. 'Dani says Bruce isn't well?'

'Some sort of fit. I'm going to take him to the hospital.'

'No need. We've been managing this well without any intervention. Mary's remedies are helping—'

Kit spins around to face Jeremy. 'He's been like this for a while? How long?'

Mary drops her eyes and Anne leans forward and strokes Bruce's face, tears coursing her cheeks in parallel tracks.

'Jesus ...' Kit pushes himself between Mary and Anne. 'Bruce? Can you hear me? I need to get you up. We need to get you to a hospital.'

Bruce seems to nod, then attempts to heave himself up, skin white as milk, tiny pearls of sweat beading his forehead.

'We are looking after him here.' Jeremy's words are diamond-edged and unyielding. 'Mary has controlled his temperature and is managing his pain. Now he needs to rest—'

He is interrupted by a plaintive moan from Bruce, then a rattling sound followed by his body going into spasm again. Kit watches in horror as Bruce's eyes roll back in his head, his mouth stretching open in an agonising silent scream as his spine bends unnaturally.

'Kit?' Tara calls from outside. 'What's going on?'

'Get the Land Rover! Drive it as near as you can!'

'That's not necessary.'

'Oh, it's very fucking *necessary*, Jeremy. Are you blind?'

Bruce gasps as his muscles relax and he falls back on the bed, spent. His eyes shoot open and he wails.

'I should make some cannabis tea,' Mary mutters.

'Anne?' Kit says. 'Come on, let's go. He needs to see a doctor.'

She nods, chewing frantically on the edge of her thumb, her eyes bolted to Bruce. They walk either side of him, supporting his arms at the elbow, and shuffle towards the door of the caravan. He's heavy and solid, and Kit worries about another fit as they won't be able to hold him and he could injure himself. When they get to the door, Jeremy doesn't move.

'Get out of our way,' Kit growls. The two men hold each other's stare. Kit isn't giving in. He pushes forward and Jeremy, showing no emotion, steps aside.

They manage to get him out through the narrow door and down the caravan steps. Jeremy watches silently as Tara drives the Land Rove at speed through the gate into the field and bumps over the grass, skidding to a halt a few metres from the caravan.

'Bruce was explicit in his desire not to go to a hospital. This isn't what he wants. We can care for him here. Mary has sedatives and more powerful drugs. Hospital must only be the last resort.'

'For crying out loud! This *is* the last resort!'

'Mary, tell Kit you can look after Bruce.'

Mary is in the doorway to the caravan, holding her bowl of water and the flannel. She looks at him with wide eyes.

'I think …' Her voice wavers. 'I mean, yes. I can keep up with the cayenne, which I think is helping. For the pain I've got henbane and mandrake. Belladonna if we need to knock him out.'

'Cayenne pepper and *belladonna*?' Tara slams the door of the Land Rover and marches over to the caravan door. 'This is such bullshit!'

Mary hesitates and glances nervously at Bruce. 'Yes, maybe they're right. Maybe he should—'

Then Bruce fits again. Falls heavily. His body inverts and forms a rigid arc, his mouth ratcheted wide open.

Dani cries out and Kit can hear the fear. Tara and Anne drop to the ground and hold his hands, talk to him, stroke his face.

Kit looks at Jeremy with dawning disbelief. 'You knew, didn't you? You knew he was getting worse not better?'

'I knew he was in good hands.'

'Tara told me you were losing it and I *defended* you.'

'Everything is under control.'

Bruce's body relaxes and he begins to gasp for air. Tara, Anne and Kit galvanise quickly. They heave his huge frame into the back seat of the Land Rover. Anne runs around the other side of the car and climbs in, wrapping her arms around Bruce, leaning him back against her, kissing the side of his head.

Kit opens the driver's door. Tara rests her hand on his arm. 'Shall I come too?'

He purses his lips and braces against a surge of emotion. He strokes her cheek. 'No, stay here. Pack some things for us and the girls. As soon as I get back, we're leaving.'

'Thank God,' breathes Tara.

'Kit? What are—'

'I don't want to hear another word from you!' Kit turns on Jeremy, eyes blazing. 'This is over. You need to find somewhere else to be king. We're done here.'

Jeremy stands motionless, turned to stone, eyes to match. Kit climbs into the Land Rover and starts the engine.

'Wait!' It's Dani. She runs to Anne's side of the car and bangs the window with the flat of her hand. Anne winds the window down. Dani is fiddling with the bracelet on her wrist. 'Here,' Dani says breathlessly. 'You need this back.'

Anne smiles through her tears and reaches through the window to still Dani's hand as she struggles to unclasp the silver chain. 'You keep hold of it, angel. I'm not scared. Bruce will be right as rain in no time. You'll see.'

CHAPTER THIRTY-SIX

Dani,
December 2002

Tara didn't hang around. As soon as Kit, Anne and Bruce had screeched away in the Land Rover, she tore back to the house, calling for me to come.

I didn't move. I was too scared. Jeremy was fuming and Mary was standing in the doorway to the caravan being weird, mumbling and shaking her head around, as if she were having some sort of heated conversation with invisible people.

Stick close to Tara. She's the only one who isn't mental.

I glanced at the house, wondering if I could make a run for it and get there without Jeremy noticing. I took a step and he turned. I froze. Fear making it hard to breathe; he had that look in his eyes again. The one he'd had the night he tried to shoot Sasha.

'Where are you going?'

Chills skittered through me.

'Into the house,' I whispered, pointing, which was stupid. He knew where the house was.

'They're making a mistake. You understand that? He was getting better care here. Bruce told me he wanted to stay at Winterfall. He hates hospitals and doesn't trust doctors.'

Mary stepped down from the caravan, still mumbling, hands cupping the bowl of water, and without saying a word, started walking down to the house as if she were sleepwalking.

'Mary?' I didn't want her to leave me alone with him.

'Just going to find something to calm my nerves,' she said. 'A cup of poppy-head tea, maybe ...'

'I'll come with you,' I managed.

'To pack?' Jeremy said in a low voice.

My heart thumped. 'No. I promised Skye I'd read her a story ...' My voice faded as I realised how unbelievable that sounded, given the drama. I swallowed. My brain searched for something more likely. 'And to tell Tara I'm not leaving.'

A slow smile spread over his face. Could he see my lies?

'Maybe I can talk to Tara?' I continued. 'Tell her what Bruce said about hospitals?'

'I'd appreciate that. She seems to think I'm mad. I'm not. You know that don't you? I care about you. All of you. I just want the best for you all. Is that a crime?'

'No.' I had to force the word out.

'I would do anything for Winterfall.'

I nodded then took my chance and broke free. I sped up my walk as I neared the gate, and when my feet touched the cobbles of the yard I broke into a jog, which turned into a sprint when I got inside. I tore up the stairs, lungs burning.

Tara was in her room hurriedly stuffing clothes into a large holdall.

'Mama says we're going away,' said Skye, who was gripping hold of her teddy bear. 'She says Teddy and you are coming too.'

Tara paused what she was doing. 'You don't have to.' She looked up at the ceiling and shook her head. 'Jeremy's dangerous.' She spat the words out as if they tasted bad. 'He uses people. Finds their weaknesses. Uses it to control them.' She picked up a sweater from the heaped pile of clothes on the bed, folded it roughly, then shoved it into the bag. 'He doesn't care about anybody. Just this farm. His *utopia*. Utopia. It has a great ring to it, doesn't it? But there's a reason society is messy and flawed, and that's because people are messy and flawed. Life is messy and flawed. You can't wave a wand and make everything perfect. It doesn't work like that. This so-called *haven* has blinded him and he wants to blind the rest of us. I don't want to leave you here, Dani.'

Tears sprang from nowhere. I was scared and I wanted my mum so badly.

She really cares about you.

'I want to come with you,' I whispered, drying my eyes with my sleeve.

She nodded. 'Good. Now go and quickly pack, then bring your bag down. I want to be ready when Kit gets back.'

'What if Jeremy stops us?'

'He can't.' Tara smiled. 'Everything's going to be OK now.'

My body pumped with nerves as I threw my clothes into my bag. I reached beneath my pillow for the paper with Emily's number on and slipped it into one of the side pockets.

It was then I heard shouting.

Jeremy and Tara.

I went to my door, held my breath, and listened. I was too far away to hear what they were saying, so I crept down the attic stairs, and onto the landing where I peered over the banister. Tara was in the hallway with her back to me. Jeremy was blocking the door with outstretched arms.

'*Move!*' she shouted.

'You're not going.'

'Move away from the door!'

'You've never given the project a chance.'

'Oh do fuck off and stop calling it *the project*. It's a farm. With lights we can't turn on and heating we can't use. With a lame goat, a bunch of chickens, and people running away in the dead of night. With a very sick man you're trying to cure with cayenne.'

Jeremy laughed. 'I thought you were brighter than this. I thought you had an imagination. Your mind is numb. Electric lights and heating?' Jeremy's eyes narrowed. 'I *see* you, Tara. You're a fake and a phoney. You think because you have ribbons in your hair and a nose ring, colourful clothes, and a child called *Skye*, that you're some sort of bohemian rebel? That you're somehow different? You're not different, Tara. You're *pathetic*.'

'Get out of my way.'

Skye appeared at my side. I put my finger to my lips. 'Mousy-quiet,' I whispered.

She zipped her mouth shut and threw away the key.

'You are a rotten apple here.'

The way he spoke, like a pantomime villain through clenched teeth, made my blood freeze. But Tara laughed. 'Jesus, listen to you. It's not me who's pathetic, it's you. You see yourself as some kind of modern-day messiah. Scraping lost souls off the pavement and offering them salvation. Here to show us lesser mortals the light. Praise fucking be. You're no more than a knock-off Pied Piper leading people into a stinking cave.'

Then he hit her.

It happened in slow motion. His hand making contact with her cheek. Her head following the direction of his fist. In the dim light we watched her lose her balance and fall. There was a thud as her head made contact with the wall.

'*No!*' I cried. 'Tara!'

Skye screamed. 'Mama!' I tried to grab her, but she was too quick, running down the stairs so fast I was scared she might trip. 'Mama! *Mama!*'

I ran after her and both of us fell to our knees beside Tara, who was struggling to sit up, eyes blinking as she tried to focus.

Skye was screaming. High-pitched and cutting the air. Jeremy was staring at us. Every muscle in his body wound tight as it could go. I wanted to drag Tara to safety because I knew from cretin Eddie that once it started it didn't stop.

'Be quiet!' Jeremy said to Skye.

But she didn't listen to him. She went on screaming and screaming.

'I said be *quiet*!' He took two steps towards Skye.

'Don't touch her!' Tara yelled.

Though she managed to stand, she was swaying. Her hand touched the back of her head. When she brought it away her fingers were smeared with blood.

'Please don't hurt my daughter.' She spoke more softly, as if realising she'd unmasked a beast.

'I'm not to going hurt her. I want her to stop screaming. I can't think with that noise.'

'Shush, Skye.' I gathered her into my arms, my eyes on Jeremy, ready to run with her if I had to. 'Shush. Mummy's OK.'

But she didn't calm down. She struggled and fought and didn't stop screaming.

Tara reached out for her. 'It's OK, darling. Come to Mama. Look, I'm fine. See?'

Then Jeremy walked over and pulled her away from me. He put her under his arm like I'd seen mums do in the park with red-faced toddlers and marched up the stairs as she kicked and screeched.

Tara shrieked.

I ran after him. Tara followed, her desperate voice begging him to put Skye down.

'She'll stay in her room until she learns to control herself.'

Skye wasn't having any of it. If anything she screamed louder. As I got to the top of the stairs I saw her battering him with her balled fists, her face puffed up and bright red. He walked into Tara and Kit's room and when I got there he was putting her on the mattress in her nook. She lay down in a full-on rage, legs and arms flapping as if swimming from a shark.

I thought he'd walk away. Leave her to cool down. Like the cretin did when he stormed out to the pub. But he didn't. He kicked away the brick which propped open the door and closed the nook.

Skye's cries went nuclear.

'There are no widows. It's too dark in there,' I cried. 'She'll be scared.'

Tara appeared at the door. Even in the semi-light of the oil lamps, I could see the thin trickle of blood running from her head down her neck, streaking her pale skin.

'Let her out.'

'When she stops making that noise.'

Then he turned the old-fashioned key which stuck out of the lock. The lock clicked and he closed his fist around the key.

'Unlock the door.'

Skye's screaming had changed from angry to petrified, as if her lungs were turning inside out. Jeremy just stood there as if he couldn't hear her.

'Open the fucking door and let my daughter out!'

'Not until she's quiet.'

Tara hesitated. Her eyes flicked left and right, before she spun around and tore out of the room.

'Tara?' Panic took hold of me. Where was she going?

'*Mama!*'

I had to get Skye out.

'Please,' I said, keeping my voice as calm as possible. 'Can you unlock the door? I can calm her down. She's only little. She doesn't understand.'

'She doesn't understand how to be quiet? I told you all, people have to learn self-control.'

That wasn't working so I tried something else. 'It might be because she's hungry? She hasn't had dinner yet. That's probably making her grumpy. Or maybe she's thirsty? Can I get her something to eat, some soup or cake? A glass of water? Little kids hate being hungry. If she has some food I think she'll stop crying.'

This seemed to work. I saw his face change. A hesitation. He looked at the door of the nook. Oh, my God. Was he going to let her out? But then his jaw fell open and his eyes locked on something behind me. I turned and gasped. Tara was in the doorway and she had the gun.

She was pointing it right at him.

'Unlock the door.'

'Tara?'

'Unlock the *fucking* door.'

'You want to be careful. Like you said, guns around children is asking for a tragedy. We wouldn't want Dani to get shot by mistake now, would we?'

Puke rose up and burned my throat. God. Where was Kit? 'Please open the door,' I whispered.

But he didn't. Instead, he opened his arms. He turned his palms to face Tara. Then, one slow step by one slow step, he walked towards her.

'Please, Jeremy.' The gun wavered in her grip as she took a step back. 'Let Skye out.' She blinked her eyes hard. The long nose of the gun dropped a little and she made no effort to lift it.

He took another step.

Then he lunged and swiped the barrel of the gun away. The gun fired. I fell to my knees. Rammed my hands over my ears. Plaster from the ceiling rained down on me. The smell of fireworks stung my nose and throat. Though my whole body was paralysed, I was aware of a kerfuffle. Tara's desperate voice. Jeremy shouting. Telling her it was all her fault. A piercing scream. Feet battering the stairs. Then silence.

I lifted my head slowly. Both were gone. Then I heard voices from the yard. I ran to the window and saw the shadowy outlines of them in the dark. His arms were around her, dragging her backwards, as she kicked and screamed. I battled with the catch, my fingers trembling, and lifted the window. Icy air filled my lungs. I shouted for him to stop, but the wind whipped my words away. Through the darkness I heard the faint bang of a door. Was it one of the sheds? It had to be. I ran to the nook and tried the door handle, shaking it hard. I swore when it wouldn't budge.

'Skye? It's Dani. I'm going to get you out, OK?'

I needed to get the key.

His feet thumping up the stairs made my heart skip. I turned, ready to face him, but he marched straight past. The door to his room slammed shut.

'I'll be as quick as I can. Don't be scared. He's gone now.'

I sprinted down the stairs and out across the yard. Tara was hammering on the door of the shed, the one where the farm equipment was locked. I pulled on the door handle.

'It's locked!' I said. 'I can't see a key.' I stopped tugging at the door and rested my head against the rough wood. 'What do I do?' My voice shook as pure fear dug into me.

'Where is he?'

'In his room'

'You need to find Mary.'

'OK.'

'Though God knows what use she'll be. Fuck! We need Kit.' There was a pause then she said, 'No, we need to do this. Listen to me, Dani. It's going to be OK. It is. Skye is scared, but she's safe where she is. I've no idea how long Kit will be. We have to get hold of the police. Find Mary. If she can't help – or won't – you need to do it yourself.'

'But how? Jeremy has the only mobile phone. It's in his room—'

'The phone box we called your mum from. It's not far down the lane.'

'But I need money—'

'Not for the emergency services. Dial 999. Give them the address of the farm. They'll ask for your name. Make one up if you don't want to use yours. Or use mine, Tara Wakefield. Are you listening to all this?'

I nodded. Stroking the wood door and wishing I was a billion miles away.

'Dani? Can you hear me?'

'What's the address?' It was hard to keep my tears in. I wanted to run. Disappear into the night.

'Winterfall Farm. Near Blisland. Tell them it's the next farm on from Trevose down the single track lane. Got that?'

I looked down towards the gate and the lane beyond disappearing into blackness. How far was the phone box?

'They need to get here *quickly*. Say he's fired a gun and has Skye locked up. Tell them he hit me. Tell them you're frightened because he's a madman.'

I looked over my shoulder, expecting to see him thundering out of the house.

'Go now,' she said. 'Quick as you can.'

I ran back across the yard and up the stairs. I didn't call for Mary. I didn't want him to hear me. I checked the dining room, but couldn't see her. No sign of her in the kitchen either. Every cell in my body was lit up. I ran up the stairs and opened the door to her room. It was empty. As I went back out onto the landing, I bolted my eyes to his door, ready to run away if he appeared. I ducked into Tara and Kit's room. Skye was crying, but the screaming had stopped.

I crouched by the door of the nook. 'Skye?'

'Where's my Mama! *Mama!*' She had found top volume again.

I glanced nervously at the door. 'Shush, Skye. It'll be OK. I'm going to get her. Be mousy-quiet, yes? If Jeremy comes back just do what he says, yeah? And be a good girl.'

Her crying eased a bit.

'If you do what he says your mum will be back quicker.'

The crying grew fainter still.

'You'll be with her soon. Skye? Can you come to the door? My fingers are here. Can you find them? Don't bang your head.'

I posted my fingers through the gap beneath the door and wiggled them. A few seconds later, I felt her touch me. I swallowed back tears of my own. Then I caught sight of the silver bracelet encircling my wrist, sparkling with specks of light from the oil lamps around the room. I took my hand away and unclasped the bracelet. Then I redid the clasp so she could slip it on and posted it beneath the door.

'This bracelet is magic and it looks after people when they're scared? You have it,' I said. 'You'll be out soon. I promise.'

The bracelet disappeared as she pulled it through.

'See you in a bit,' I whispered.

I ran downstairs and pulled open the door but, when I stepped outside, I stopped dead. It was almost black. Clouds covered most of the moon and the wind rushed through the darkness, firing bullets of icy rain against my skin.

It was as if I was turned to stone. What was wrong with me? I had to help Skye and Tara.

'It's fine. It's fine. It's fine,' I muttered, balling my fists to make myself braver. 'It's only the dark. There's nothing out there. Ghosts aren't real. It's fine ...'

I remembered the farmer telling us he'd help in an emergency. Would he hear me scream from here? I opened my mouth but then stopped myself. If I screamed, Jeremy would hear. There was nothing for it, I had to get to the phone. I forced myself onwards, each step was like wading through glue. I made it through the gate and turned onto the lane. My heart hammered. My skin had started to sweat as my breathing grew faster and faster.

When I was fifty steps or so from the house there was a blood-splitting screech. I'd never heard anything like it before. It couldn't be Tara or Skye, they were too far away, and this had come from somewhere nearby. It was the woman in white. It had to be. Nothing human would make a noise like that.

Flashes of her bashed-in head loomed out of the darkness. I

squeezed my eyes shut and pictured Skye, trapped and terrified, in that cupboard. 'Dani, come on,' I whispered, my words shaky, 'you have to keep moving.'

Then the horrific wail came again.

My eyes flicked open. A movement to the right caught my attention. I snapped my head round and there, on the other side of the lane beyond the shadowy hedge, was the woman in white, the vague shape of her, howling and spinning in the darkness.

I screamed and sprinted back as fast as could.

'Dani? Dani!' Tara must have heard me scream and as she called my name she banged the door frantically. 'Jeremy, stop it. What are you doing to her? *Dani!*'

'I'm sorry,' I whispered. 'I'm so sorry. But I can't.'

If I couldn't go to the phone box, I was going to have to get Skye and Tara out myself. All I needed were the keys to the nook and shed. I was pretty sure they were in Jeremy's room. I just had to get my hands on them.

I ran into the house and grabbed an oil lamp from the hallway and went into the kitchen. I scanned the room, looking for something useful to jump out at me. All kinds of thoughts came in and out of my head. A saucepan? Could I knock him out? Maybe. But how hard did you have to hit somebody to knock them out? A knife? Maybe I could stab him? No, I wasn't sure I wanted to kill him and anyway, he was way stronger than me, he'd probably end up sticking the knife in me.

Then my eyes fell on one of Mary's brown bottles and I had this sort of crazy, brilliant flash. I knew exactly what to do. My nerves jangled with excitement. This was going to work. I knew it. Tara and Skye would be free in no time.

I grabbed a pan off the rack and ladled in soup from the big casserole. Since the weather got cold, there was always a pan of soup on the go. Bruce's soup recipes were nearly as good as his cake recipes. I put the saucepan on the stove then bent down to add three logs to the fire in the burner. As it warmed up, I sawed off a hunk of bread. Then I ran into Mary's pantry and scanned the bottles on the shelves. I was looking for one of the ingredients Mary said was in her flying balm.

The one she said would put someone to sleep.

'Yes, yes. Yes!' I whispered as I found it.

Belladonna.

The bottle was on the top shelf. Beneath its name on the label she'd written: *Keep out of reach of children*. I climbed up on the footstool and closed my fingers around the bottle. Then I went back and poured the soup into a bowl, placed the bowl on a tray with the bread, and took a spoon from the drawer. How much belladonna should I add? He needed to fall into a deep sleep. I didn't want him waking until we were safely away. I added five drops. Was that enough? I wasn't sure so I added two more for luck. The belladonna floated on the surface of the soup in a pretty golden puddle. As I stirred it in, I went over what I had to do. Give Jeremy the soup. Wait for him to fall asleep. Find both keys. Unlock Skye. Unlock Tara. Then all of us run as fast as we could to call the police.

I dipped my fingertip into the soup and tried it. It was pretty bitter so I added some salt and tried it again. I nodded and smiled. The saltiness hid the bitterness pretty well.

'You can do this,' I whispered, as I carried the tray upstairs.

I knocked on his door. 'Jeremy? I came to tell you I'm not leaving. Jeremy?'

I heard his footsteps. When he opened the door, I made myself smile, even though what I really wanted to do was burst into tears. 'And, well, I thought you might like some soup? I've just had some. It's a bit salty, but I feel loads better after it. I think we're probably all just really hungry. That never helps, does it?'

'I shouldn't have lost my temper.'

'God. That was nothing. I've seen way worse. And it was Tara who got the gun. What was she thinking? You should have the soup. You'll feel so much better.' I smiled at him. 'I heated it up especially for you.'

'You're a good girl.' He smiled and took the tray. 'I want you to be happy.'

Then eat the soup.

'You are always safe here.'

Just eat the soup.

'Will you sit with me?'

The idea made me feel sick. 'I'm … I'm a bit tired. I was going to try and sleep.'

He nodded and looked sad. 'Thank you for the soup.'

My legs were jelly as I climbed the narrow stairs to the attic. I closed the door and lay down. I realised then I had no idea how long belladonna took to make someone sleep.

I looked at my watch. Half an hour? Yes. That sounded about right.

In half an hour I'd check on him.

Perhaps it was the two tastes of the soup I'd had. Or maybe it was all the drama. Whatever the reason, I fell asleep. When I woke and crept downstairs, I went to his room. The door was closed but I could see shadows moving in the lamplight beneath it. I could hear rustling. Maybe the belladonna needed longer to work?

I tiptoed back to the attic stairs, but glanced into Tara's room and saw the nook door was open. There was an oil lamp on the floor beside the mattress. I smiled, thinking he'd finally unlocked her and given her a light, and ran in.

She was lying still on the mattress.

'Skye?' I whispered.

Then I saw something which exploded my world. There, on the

floor beside the lamp, was the tray and on it was the empty bowl. Her face was smeared with soup.

I dropped to my knees and shook her. Nothing. 'Skye?' I shook her again. Her body was floppy. 'Skye?'

I noticed her tiny fingers clutched around Anne's silver bracelet.

I remembered Mary saying her remedies were dangerous. Then I saw her writing on the bottle.

Keep out of reach of children.

I clamped my hand over my mouth and stumbled backwards out of the nook and into the bedroom. I only just made it to the bathroom before my stomach emptied its contents. I collapsed on the floor and held my head in my hands.

What had happened?

As I sat there I saw pictures in my head. Jeremy carrying the tray into Tara and Kit's room. Going to the nook. Unlocking it. Telling Skye to eat. Skye swallowing the bitter, salty soup, my voice telling her to do whatever he said ringing in her terrified ears.

I'd killed Skye.

I could have sat there, not moving, guilt freezing me rigid, tears pouring. But something took hold of me. My survival instinct. I had to get out. When the police came I'd end up in prison. Or, worse, back with cretin Eddie who'd gut me like a pig.

I heard Mum's voice.

Do whatever it takes to keep safe.

Keeping safe meant escaping Jeremy. It meant staying away from Eddie. It meant hiding from the police. I needed to get out of there.

I crept upstairs and packed the rest of my stuff. Every last thing. It was as if I'd never been there. I checked my bag for Emily's number and the return train ticket, then went downstairs and into the kitchen. I shoved the rest of the bread into my bag along with some shortbread and a couple of apples. A noise from behind me made me jump. I turned and saw Mary lying on the floor of the pantry. She was wearing only her floaty white shirt and lay uncomfortably, neck cricked against the cupboard, bare legs criss-crossed with scratches and splattered with mud and flecks of grass. There were greasy smears on her temples, wrists, and inner thighs. The pot of flying balm was on the sideboard. Lid off. Hardly any of the gloopy ointment left. She was muttering like a mad woman and then, without warning, she let out a high-pitched wail.

The same wail I'd heard on the lane.

I felt sick. I wanted to be as far from Winterfall and these luna-tics as I could get. I tore out of the house and into the yard. Tara's cries from the shed echoed around me, calling for Skye over and over, her voice broken into bits, her fists weakly banging the door.

I slammed my hands over my ears and ran.

CHAPTER THIRTY-SEVEN

Tara,
December 2002

My hands stung from battering the door and my lungs burned from yelling her name. Hearing Skye's distant screams from the nook. Then Dani's high-pitched shriek. Then nothing. Locked in that shed in the pitch black, unable to help them. The silence humming with fear. My thoughts going to the darkest places imaginable. It was torture.

When I heard his voice I wondered if I'd imagined it.

'Tara?'

I leapt up and ran at the door, thumping both fists against the wood. 'Let me out! You fucking *psycho*. Let. Me. *Out!*' Each shouted syllable was acid on my ragged throat.

'Please don't shout.' So calm, so eerie. My immediate thought was he'd killed her. That she'd kept screaming and he'd lost it completely and throttled her.

'Skye?' My voice broke into a strangled sob. 'I want to see Skye.'

'She's fine.'

'Let me see her!'

'I asked you not to shout.'

'Please, Jeremy. I'm really fucking worried.' I rested my forehead against the door.

'Dani said she might be hungry. She suggested that might be

why she was making so much noise. I gave her some soup and bread and a drink, and now she's fine. I promise you.'

'Let me out.'

'You know, I thought we'd found the answer. We created something beautiful. A transcendental utopia people have dreamt of building for centuries.'

His voice was faraway and melodic. I pictured him sitting on the ground with his back to the door, staring into the dark.

'It's not a utopia if you have to lock people in.'

He didn't reply.

'Jeremy? Please, let me see Skye.'

Still nothing. I fell on to my knees and looked upwards into the pitch black. The caustic smell of dust and damp caught in my nose as I breathed. I had to make him unlock the door. I needed to play this more cleverly. Tell him what he wanted to hear. Manipulate him the way he manipulated everybody else.

'You're right, Jeremy. You are. Your vision is beautiful. But it can't be only your vision. You closed us out. Kept us in the dark. If you included us, if we all worked together, made decisions together, then maybe things would be different. I want Winterfall to work as much as you do.'

'I don't believe you.'

'I do,' I said, trying to stop my voice from trembling. 'I was blinded by superficial things. Hot water and lights. I was missing a washing machine. Even television.' I paused. 'But while I've been in here, I've been thinking. I know what matters now. I don't want to go back to that grey concrete world. It offers us nothing.'

There was silence.

'Jeremy? Did you hear me?'

'Things have got out of control. It's over. We can't come back from this. The police will come and I'll be sent to prison.'

Tears sprung in my eyes. 'We don't need to tell them. Like you said, why do we need the state to intervene?'

'I never told you know why I hate that world so much. The corporations which have people over a barrel. People who are blind to their bondage. People who work five days a week, twelve hours a day, from the age of eighteen to sixty-five. And why? Because they're fed lies.'

As he spoke, I sat there, numb, his words washing over me.

'My father was one of them. He was a simple man. He wanted to be a good father and a good husband. He wanted to provide for his family. Never once did he question *anything*. He worked for the same company for thirty-two years. Commuted an hour each way in a company car he loved. He didn't see it as the sedative it was. That man put his job before everything. Then the company pulled in some cocky buck with a calculator and my father became surplus to requirements. It was cost-saving, they told him. So what did he do? Drove to the golf club to beg the CEO, a man he thought was his friend, for his job back. That man laughed in his face. I watched the whole thing. He cried as he drove me home. Then in the middle of the night, he drove that company car to his office, hooked up a hose to the exhaust, and gassed himself. I knew then, at sixteen, that the system was the enemy.' Jeremy pauses for a moment. 'There was nobody there to help my father. I know things can be different. I know we can find a better way.'

Then I heard movement. Was he getting up?

'Jeremy? Listen. I get it. I do. The world is cruel and life is unfair and I'm sorry about your dad. But it's not Skye's fault. It's not my fault.'

Footsteps walking away.

'Jeremy! *Jeremy!*'

I pummelled the door until my hands turned wet with blood and my knuckles throbbed. 'Let me out! Jeremy! Let me out ...'

I don't know how long I lay there, curled up, foetal on the dusty floor. My mind drifted away. I thought about that moment in hospital when I knew I never wanted to be separated from Skye again. Running desperately along those never-ending corridors. Jabbing at the lift button again and again. Flinging back the curtain on our cubicle and reaching into the crib to gather her up. Holding her tiny, vulnerable body to me. Burying my face in her warmth. Breathing in the scent of her while stroking her precious head, dusted with a fine golden fuzz, soft as a velveteen rabbit.

I love you so much.

The distant sound of an engine on the lane roused me.

'Kit,' I rasped.

I dragged myself onto my hands and knees. Ignored the pain in my stiff, battered body. My head throbbing. Hands too cold and grazed to move. The vehicle turned into the yard. The engine stilled. The door opened and closed.

I drew in my breath and forced my voice out through the pain. '*Kit!*'

CHAPTER THIRTY-EIGHT

Kit,
December 2002

Kit runs across the wet tarmac which sparkles with lights and grabs a wheelchair from outside A&E. He and Anne hoist Bruce into it. His shallow rasping breaths sound agonising. Bruce suffered two seizures on the journey here and with each one Kit watched in the rearview mirror as Anne tried to restrain him while he bucked and writhed, fresh tears streaking her face as she whispered again and again that it would be OK.

They push through the double doors into the reception area and Kit is blinded by the fluorescent lights and noise and heat, now all so alien.

'My friend,' Kit says as he runs to the desk. 'He's very sick. He's fitting and we don't—'

Before Kit can finish, Bruce is gripped by another. His back arches so violently it throws him out of the wheelchair. Anne screams. Kit runs back to Bruce and drops down beside him, helpless as his giant's frame stretches tight, his jaw rigid, pale skin tingeing blue as his lungs beg for oxygen.

'He can't breathe!' Kit shouts. 'Help us! He can't breathe!'

The alarm has already been sounded and within moments a team of people dressed in green scrubs run through a set of internal doors. Four lift him on to a stretcher, his limbs fixed and frozen unnaturally, like an ancient Pompeiian petrified by volcanic ash.

'Has he taken something?' a nurse asks as they wheel Bruce towards the double doors. 'An overdose?'

'No,' Kit replies. Then he glances at Anne. 'Unless Mary was giving him something that might do this?'

She shakes her head, her hand covering her mouth.

'Next of kin?' Another nurse looks at Anne.

She nods.

'Come with us. You too,' she says to Kit. 'We need to get a few details.'

'Where are you taking him?' Her feeble voice trembles with fear.

'He's going to resus. The medical team need to stabilise him before we do anything else.'

Kit takes Anne's arm as they follow. 'Try not to worry. He's in the right place.'

'He hates hospitals. He won't want to be here.'

'They need to find out what's causing these fits. He needs to be here.' She falls into him and he holds her, resting his head on hers, rubbing her back to soothe her. 'He'll be fine, Anne. They'll make him better.'

A nurse taps Kit on the shoulder and smiles. Her hair is scraped back into a bun, no strand out of place, fingernails neatly filed without a speck of dirt. So clean and immaculate. A world away from the earthy scruffiness of the commune. He shifts awkwardly, tucking his muddy hands beneath him.

'Just a few questions,' she says. 'Can I get the name of the patient?'

'Bruce Barrow,' Anne whispers.

'And you?'

'Anne Chaplin.' She hesitates. 'We're not married.'

Sally looks at Kit.

'Kit Balfour. I'm a friend. We live at the same address.'

Anne answers the nurse's questions with fearful one-word

answers as she glances warily at the medical staff moving with focused efficiency around Bruce.

'This is presenting as an overdose. Could he have taken something without you knowing?'

Anne shakes her head vigorously. 'He's been unwell for a few days. Run-down. Headaches. Flu, he thought. He was taking herbal remedies, which were helping.'

'And they are?'

'Anne?' Kit says when she doesn't answer.

'Sorry,' she whispers. She looks into the mid-distance, dazed. Kit reaches for her hand. 'Anne, can you tell her what Mary gave him?'

Her eyes refocus on Kit and the nurse. 'There was the cayenne. Peppermint oil. Ginger and turmeric. He was bitten by a dog – not badly – ten days ago, and had camomile for that, and a white paste Mary made.' Anne hesitated. 'I'd have to ask her what was in it. Bicarbonate, I think. Some honey?'

'And he's had a tetanus booster within the last ten years?'

Anne shakes her head. 'No, he's never had one.'

'I need to feed that to the team. I'll be back in a minute.'

The nurse relays the information to a couple of people who nod. They are interrupted by another fit. The medical staff jump into action. Anne cries out. A nurse moves Anne and Kit out of the cubicle and draws the curtain around Bruce and the medics.

A different nurse steps through the curtains and speaks to Anne kindly, 'We've a room you can wait in.'

Anne starts to protest.

'We'll bring you back to him as soon as possible.' She takes Anne's arm and gently ushers her. 'He's in the best hands. I promise.'

Anne follows mutely and, when her legs give way, she stumbles, Kit is there to catch her.

The room they are taken to is small and windowless with blue upholstered chairs, buttery-yellow walls, a harsh strip light that stutters at one end. 'Is there anybody you need to phone?' the nurse asks Anne.

Anne shakes her head. 'I only have Bruce.'

They wait in the room for what feels like hours, Anne rocking and chewing her nails, Kit staring at her, wishing he could do or say something to ease her fear, until at last the nurse and another woman, with shoulder-length dark hair wearing scrubs, walk in.

The woman introduces herself as the doctor looking after Bruce. 'Though we haven't had his bloods back yet, it's almost certain, given what you've told us regarding the circumstances and how he's presenting, that he's suffering an acute case of tetanus. The muscle spasms are interfering with his breathing and putting him at risk of respiratory failure. We've intubated him and now he's stabilised he'll be transferred to ICU.' The doctor clears her throat. 'The tetanus toxins have bonded to Bruce's nerve endings. We cannot undo this. All we can do is manage the symptoms which are threatening his life. The next few hours are critical.'

Anne lets out a sob and both her hands go up to cover her face.

'Can we see him?' Kit's stomach roils with guilt. They should have brought him in sooner. He should have checked on him. Made sure he was OK. Been firmer with Jeremy.

'A nurse will fetch you when we have him settled in ICU. I need to warn you, Bruce is heavily sedated, and has been given drugs to stop him moving to help with the spasms. There's a tube down his throat, which goes into a ventilator to aid his breathing. His blood pressure is fluctuating dramatically, which is causing his heart to beat abnormally.'

'I just want to take him home.'

'We want that too.'

Even with the doctor's warning the sight of Bruce is a shock. A thick tube is thrust into his mouth and taped to the side of his face. There's another tube going into his nose. More wires and pads are stuck to various parts of him and a line feeding a saline drip is attached to his inner arm. His skin is mottled, pale and dusky blue around his lips and ear lobes, the tips of his fingers. Despite this, and the paraphernalia engulfing him, he looks peaceful. Anne sits beside him and takes his hand in hers. Her thumb works rhythmically back and forth as she whispers. 'Don't leave me. Please, don't leave me.'

Kit sits in a chair in the corner and watches her with him. The scene reminds him of a Renaissance painting. The gentle bearded figure in bed, weak and pale, draped in sheets. A grief-stricken woman clutching his feeble body as it fights to cope with the toxins that ravage him.

Then with no warning the situation erupts. Alarms sound and the multitude of machines flash and whir in a frenzy. Within moments doctors and nurses flood in the room. Anne is pushed aside. Monitors are checked. Instructions are given. Intravenous drugs are administered via his various drips.

'What's happening?' Anne asks plaintively.

Kit watches, helpless, as the medics busy themselves around Bruce, their serious concentration betraying the severity. When one of the doctors urgently announces Bruce has gone into cardiac arrest, Kit pulls Anne into him. She buries her face in his chest. Kit holds her tightly as the team send electric charges through Bruce's body to shock him into life. For what feels like hours, they try again and again to stimulate his heart.

But then one of the doctors shakes her head and as quickly as the tumult erupted it fades and the room becomes still.

The doctor looks at Anne, eyes weary with fatigue and regret. 'I'm sorry,' she says.

The sound which escapes Anne's devastated body cuts through Kit like a glass shard. It's as if her heart has been torn from her. She rocks and wails, quivering as she holds Bruce's lifeless hand in hers, bringing it to her lips, kissing it over and over. Her raw pain is too much for Kit to bear. As he stands behind her, his hand on her shoulder, he pictures Bruce in the kitchen, flour dusting his face and hands. Their kind and gentle giant. The very best of them.

Anne turns her head. Her brow is furrowed, her eyes childlike, wide and helpless. 'What do I do now?' she breathes. 'He was everything …' Her voice tails to nothing.

Kit is hollowed out with grief. Not just for Bruce but for Anne. As he sits, he watches her stroking his forehead. She is humming softly. A mournful tune which fills the air around them with sadness.

'I need to get Tara and Skye,' he says after a while. 'We'll be back here as quickly as we can. If you need anything ask one of the nurses.' He bends and kisses the top of her head.

Kit cries as he drives away from the hospital. Being away from Tara and Skye, having witnessed Bruce's death and Anne's devastation, physically hurts. He swings into the farmyard and throws the door open. It's then he hears her scream.

His heart stops. The cry came from the shed.

'Tara?' Dread floods him. He runs to the shed. Pulls the handle. It's locked.

'Kit? Oh thank God. Skye, Kit. He's locked Skye in the nook!'

'Get back from the door!' he shouts.

He kicks the door as hard as he can. The timbers are old and weak and the doorframe splinters as the lock gives way. Tara stumbles out and falls into him. There is enough light from the muted moon to see the state she is in, her face muddy and smeared with blood, weak and cold.

'He did this to you?' Kit's rasped words catch in his throat. 'What the hell happened here? Where the fuck is he?'

'We have to get Skye!' She pulls away from him and staggers towards the house. '*Kit!*'

The raw panic in her words chills him to the core. Rage and fear make a potent cocktail and with every step he feels drunker on it, his head swimming, body trembling, as he tears upstairs and into their room.

The door to the nook is open. Skye is lying on the mattress. He throws himself down beside her. She is still. Her eyes are closed. When he gathers her up she is limp like a rag doll.

'No!' wails Tara as she throws herself on to Skye. 'My baby!'

Kit's world stops turning.

They sit either side of their daughter's motionless body in the hospital. Tara is catatonic, staring fixedly at nothing, her bruised and grazed hands resting limp in her lap. The trickle of blood from the cut on her head, dried to a muddy brown streak on her neck. Her colourful ribbons are incongruously bright beneath the hospital lights. The pain is unfathomable.

Kit wants Jeremy to feel it too.

'I have to go and do something,' he rasps.

She doesn't look at him. She blinks slowly, swaying slightly, as if there's a gentle breeze in the sterile room. 'Where are you going?'

He doesn't answer.

'But the police are coming to talk to us.'

'I won't be long.'

She doesn't say anything more.

He walks down the corridor in a daze. He is spiked by recollections of leaving the farm. Telling Tara he'd be back. Leaving the only two people he truly loves to the mercy of a man he thought was a brother.

As he steps through the exit, a police car pulls into the car park. Instinctively, he lowers his head and thrusts his hands in his pockets, keeps close to the hospital buildings, then crosses the car park at a jog. He starts the Land Rover and drives out of the car park. He knows he should stay with Tara. Hold her hand while she gives her statement to the police. Listen to her reliving the agony of what happened. Send them to arrest Jeremy Ballard.

But Kit wants to get to Jeremy before them.

It's a few hours from dawn. The world is still and cold and dark. When he gets to the house, he marches straight up the stairs. He pulls open Jeremy's door. The room is empty. He goes out onto the landing and shouts for him. Nothing. As he passes the attic stairs he thinks of Dani. Tara had called for her over and over as he was putting Skye in the car. She'd frantically searched the place, terrified Jeremy had hurt her too.

'She's gone,' Tara had said as she burst back out of the house. 'There's no sign of her.'

Then they'd become consumed with Skye and getting her to hospital, and in the torturous hours that followed Dani was forgotten.

Now, Kit runs up the attic stairs and pushes open her door. 'Dani?' But the room is stripped bare. The wardrobe empty. Her sleeping bag folded at the foot of the mattress, her pillow resting neatly on top.

Kit runs down both flights of stairs and opens the door to the sitting room, then the dining room. Nothing. Tara was right; Dani has gone.

'Jeremy!' The taste of the word is toxic.

Oil lamps still flicker throughout the house. At first glance, he thinks the kitchen is also empty, but then hears a noise. Mary is lying on the floor of the pantry, semi-naked and moaning, as high as a buzzard. He shakes her gently, but she's too out of it to wake. She snuffles quietly, then settles, her distressed moans replaced by snoring.

In the kitchen, he sees the soup pan on the side. He thinks of the soup smears around Skye's mouth and an invisible fist punches him in the stomach. Something beside the pan catches his eye. One of Mary's glass bottles glinting in the soft light. He picks it up and reads the label. Red mist descends. Seething with a rage he didn't know he was capable of, he lets out a guttural cry as he pulls his arm back and hurls the bottle at the wall. It smashes and glass explodes and skitters across the floor.

How had he got Jeremy so catastrophically wrong?

How had he failed to see what was in front of his eyes?

In a moment of sudden clarity he knows what to do. He goes back to Mary and picks her up. As he carries her out of the house, she mumbles incoherently. He takes her out to Bruce and Anne's caravan and gently lays her on the bed. She turns on her side and starts snoring again. He covers her with their duvet then leaves, closing the caravan door behind him. He walks towards the bonfire they built earlier that day and grabs hold of the jerrycan of paraffin. Then he crosses the silent yard and walks into the house which looms like a beast from the shadows. He places the jerrycan down in the hallway, then grabs all the coats from the hooks, which he dumps in a pile at the foot of the stairs. He unscrews the lid of the jerrycan and starts to douse the coats with paraffin.

'What are you doing?'

Jeremy is standing in the doorway.

'Get away from me,' Kit breathes. 'If you don't, I'll fucking tear you limb from limb.' Kit shakes the paraffin over the banisters and the floorboards.

'Are you serious?' Jeremy laughs. 'You're going to burn your own house down.'

'You poisoned my daughter!'

Jeremy's face falls like a stone. 'Poisoned her? What are you talking about?'

Kit shakes the rest of the paraffin over the coats and floorboards. The fumes hit the back of his nose and set his adrenalin flowing.

'The soup. I saw the belladonna in the kitchen!'

'I didn't make the soup. Dani did. She gave it to me. I gave it to Skye because I thought she was hungry …'

His voice dies. Though Kit can't see his features in the light of the single oil lamp he knows what Jeremy's realised.

'That's right. Dani tried to poison *you*.'

'No, that's not right. She spoke to me. She said she wanted to stay here.' His whispered voice floats through the semi-darkness.

'She lied.' Kit takes his lighter from his pocket. There's a movement from Jeremy. Kit braces, ready for Jeremy to try to stop him. Ready to fight. But Jeremy walks up the stairs.

'I'm still lighting it. I don't care if you burn with the house, you fuck!'

Kit flicks the lighter and holds it close to the paraffin. When the fumes catch the flame, the fire bursts into life. Firelight floods the hallway and sets shadows dancing.

Kit watches as the flames build, licking the banister, caressing the walls. His heart pumps with adrenalin. He feels alive. He glances up, but there's no sign of Jeremy. He thinks about Skye. How featherlight she was in his arms, her head lolled back, arms swinging.

'Let him burn,' Kit whispers, as he walks away.

At the front door, he stops. He can't do it.

Kit runs to the foot of the stairs. The smoke gathering in the hallway grates his throat. 'You need to get out!' He waits. Nothing. '*Jeremy!* Stop fucking about!'

Still nothing.

Every cell in his body is screaming *leave him*.

But how can he? Though he's never felt hatred like this in his life, he can't leave him to die.

Kit swears as he races upstairs, holding his breath to avoid inhaling the acrid smoke.

Jeremy is standing, statue-like, in the middle of his room. In the half-light, smoke hazing the air and in his outfit of white, he appears oddly ethereal. Kit runs at him and grabs his arm, but Jeremy pulls out of his grip. The smoke makes it hard to see. Even harder to breathe. Kit's heart is hammering. He looks back over his shoulder and sees the light burning more brightly. They haven't much time.

'We need to get out.'

Jeremy doesn't move. When Kit lunges for him again, Jeremy pushes him back.

'Is this is how you want it to end?' Kit screams.

Jeremy stares at him. Kit can no longer read him. It's impossible to know what emotions – if any – he's feeling.

'If you don't move we'll both burn. I'm not leaving you up here.'

Jeremy winces. When he speaks his voice is pained. 'I fucked up, Kit.'

'Yeah, you did, but burning to death won't change that.' He pauses, glancing over his shoulder again, knowing it's only a matter of minutes before they are trapped. 'You once told me you thought your father was weak for believing so much in the system he couldn't cope when it failed him. Isn't this the same?'

As he hears his words, he pictures Tara and Skye at the hospital. Tara, broken, huddled beside their daughter. He stares at Jeremy and then shakes his head. 'I'm not going to die for you.'

Then Kit turns. He pulls his sweater over his mouth and nose, and ducks beneath the swirling blanket of smoke which hovers on the landing. The flames leap up the banisters. It's hot as hell. Kit runs down the staircase and through the flames, along the hallway, the thick smoke stinging his eyes. He bursts out of the house and collapses on all fours on the cobbles, coughing and spluttering to expel the smoke. He rolls to sitting and watches the front door.

Moments later Jeremy stumbles out of the house. He's alight. His arms and back like a torch in the dark. He drops to his knees. Arms flapping as he tries to extinguish the flames. Kit hauls himself up and barrels into him, rolling him over and over. When the flames are out, the stench of burning fabric in the air, Kit grabs Jeremy's soot-streaked face and turns it towards the house.

'Look at it!' he says. '*Look at it!* Your precious utopia.' Then he shoves him hard so he falls on to the ground.

Jeremy lies there, curled on the ground, knees drawn into his body and sobs.

Kit walks away from him, over the cobbled yard. Before he climbs into the Land Rover, he takes a moment to watch the spectacular fire devouring the house, the magnificent fiery plume rising into the dark sky, a phoenix from the pyre.

CHAPTER THIRTY-NINE

Dani,
December 2002

The noise and bustle and crowds of Paddington station hurt my ears and eyes after the quiet of Winterfall. A brass band played Christmas carols. Lights hung in colourful necklaces. The smell of warm cinnamon floated in the air and made my stomach growl. I spent most of my time trying not to think of Skye and the terrible, awful thing I'd done. Was it going to stay with me forever? This guilt and horror? The flashbacks? Her face appearing in my head and stabbing me right through the heart?

I sat cross-legged on the ground and asked passersby if they could spare some change. But, like before, people were too busy to notice the thin, grubby girl with her outstretched hand. I was invisible again. To get their attention, I had to stand up and step right in front of them. 'I just need money for the tube,' I said with my widest smile. I nearly tripped up the fifth person I tried. She swore and rolled her eyes then hastily shoved a five-pound note at me and scuttled on.

'Merry Christmas,' I said.

Leyton hadn't changed a bit. It was the same shade of grey with the same dirty air and the same groups of lads squaring up to each other on street corners. I sat on the bench and watched the door of the flat, waiting for him to leave for the pub, just as he always did, every Saturday, at five. My heart nearly burst out of my chest when the door opened and the scrawny cretin strolled out. He'd been lurking in the shadows of my mind for so long – with his death threats and alcohol breath and fists stained with Mum's blood – and the temptation to run was overpowering.

But I didn't.

When I was sure he was gone, I crept along the shadows of the building and walked up the steps. I knocked on the door and she opened it. She breathed my name then burst into tears, holding me so tight she nearly snapped my neck.

'How are you?' she asked when we finally stopped sobbing.

I thought of Skye lying on her mattress. Tara screaming from the locked shed. Bruce rigid and unable to breathe. I chewed my lip and shrugged.

'Hungry?'

I took a breath and nodded. 'Starving.'

She grinned. 'Fish fingers?'

My absolute favourite.

'I've kept some in the freezer drawer the whole time in case you came. I knew you'd be hungry. Want a bath while I cook them?'

Despite the guilt, lying in the piping hot water with the smell of familiar soap on my skin and my hair squeaky clean, was actual heaven. If it wasn't for cretin Eddie, who'd be rolling in drunk at closing, I'd have stayed floating in that bath forever. I wrapped myself in a towel and breathed in the clean, fresh washing powder. It was weird being back in my room, surrounded by my posters and jewellery, my make-up, my *Hello Kitty* duvet cover. It was like looking at an old photograph.

Dressed in a clean pair of jeans and a sweater, I walked back through to Mum. She handed me a cup of tea and a packet of chocolate digestives, which I wolfed down as we waited for the fish fingers to cook. The biscuits tasted incredible and I thought about how much Skye would have loved them. Then I saw her beautiful face smiling at me and the biscuits turned to concrete in my mouth.

'Don't cry,' Mum said. 'You've got fish fingers, remember?'

I ate my fish fingers washed down with orange squash. As I swallowed my last mouthful, Mum sighed. 'I've missed you, baby. But you need to go before he's back.'

I shook my head.

'I can't keep you safe from him.' I'd never seen her look so sad.

'I'm not going without you.'

'Danielle, don't be silly,' she said. 'I can't leave. He'll find me and, well, you know.'

I pushed the plate away, leant across the table, and took her hand. I thought of Emily. The way she talked. How brave and strong she was. 'I'm not leaving you here.'

'But—'

'No buts.'

She hesitated. 'Leave? Without saying anything to him.' She took in a deep breath then shook her head. 'I can't, love. I just can't.'

'Listen, you've been that cretin's punchbag for too long. What kind of life is it? I know you're scared. I am too. But you deserve so much better.'

She didn't say anything for what felt like a hundred years. But I could see her mind working. Thoughts and painful memories flickering behind her eyes. Then she leant forward and pressed her lips against my forehead. 'Yes,' she whispered. 'Yes, OK then. I'll come.'

I threw my arms around her and kissed her cheek. 'Oh my God! Mum. I literally never thought you'd say yes! Quick. Pack a few things, get whatever money you have, and let's go.'

Her face fell and she looked around the place. 'But I haven't washed up. You know how he gets if the washing-up isn't done.'

'He can do it himself.'

Mum burst into laughter. 'Do it himself,' she repeated with amusement.

While she packed, I searched the cupboards for food. There

wasn't much, but I took what I could carry, some biscuits, a few tins of spaghetti hoops, a packet of neon cheese slices wrapped in plastic.

Mum appeared dragging a huge suitcase.

'Do you need all that?'

She looked at the bag, her face unsure, and started chewing on her lip.

I glanced at my watch. 'Don't worry, it's fine. Let's just go.' We had to be shot of the place before Eddie got back.

Before we left, I grabbed a pen and tore a flap from a cereal packet. On it I wrote, 'Do your own washing-up, you cretin!' and balanced it on the dishes piled in the sink.

Mum looked pale and anxious as she dragged her suitcase down the steps. 'Where are we going?' she asked as we got to the bottom of the stairwell. She sounded doubtful. I reached for her hand. 'I'm not sure I can do this.'

'It's fine. I've got a friend who will help us.'

As soon as I heard Emily's voice I burst into tears, right there, in the phone box with Mum looking in.

She told us to meet her at a greasy spoon near Archway station. I told Mum and Emily everything. I kept nothing back. I think I expected them to suggest we call the police so I could tell them about Skye, but neither of them did. Mum hung her head and twisted her fingers around each other. Emily went on a rant.

'He's sick in the head,' she spat. 'A raving lunatic. And can you believe he kept telling me how damaged *I* was? What happened wasn't your fault, Dani. It wasn't. It was *his*. That dog-murdering psychopathic lunatic's. And that other dickhead? Your Eddie, Becky? You're best as far away from him as you can get.'

Mum's fingers twisted and pulled at each other faster.

'Can you help us?' I asked. 'We need somewhere where nobody can find us.'

'How much money have you got?'

'Mum took what she had in the flat. About forty pounds.'

'That's not much, but it is what it is. Passports?'

I glanced at Mum then back at Emily, and shook my head.

'That's OK. We don't need passports.'

Emily took us to her squat. It was grim. There were people passed out in every corner. Needles littered the floor. The air was thick with the stink of weed and urine.

'It's only temporary,' Emily said. 'Somewhere for me and Ash to crash for a while.'

Mum hovered by the door, her arms clasped around her, trying to make herself as small as possible.

'Alright, Dani!' Ash hugged me like a long lost sister. 'You OK?'

I nodded. I had a flash of the farm then. When we were happy. Sitting in the long grass, the sun on my back, insects buzzing lazily, while Ash played his guitar and Skye threw sticks for Sasha.

Fresh guilt ploughed into me like a train.

Emily knew a man who'd drive us to Spain in the back of a van. We had to meet him in a side street in Southampton. Mum looked petrified when she heard the plan and I half-expected her to bolt back to Leyton and take her chances with the cretin.

'Don't stress,' Emily said. 'Billy's cool.'

A few days later we met him. Billy spoke in grunts. My mum hid behind me like a small child.

I squeezed her hand, 'It's OK,' I whispered. But I wasn't totally convinced it was. Billy was toothless, stank of stale sweat, and his fingers were stained yellow from cigarettes. Ideally, I wouldn't have gone anywhere with Billy, but we didn't have a lot of choice, and if Emily trusted him, so did I.

'Billy will get you to Bilbao,' Emily said. 'Then you catch a bus or hitch to Valladolid. There's a woman there. Angel. That's her actual name, isn't that mad? She's English but has lived out there forever. She runs a bar called La Caleta and helps women who need to escape, takes them in, gets them back on their feet. She was married to a dickhead so she gets it. I've written it all down.' She thrust a grubby piece of paper into my hand. 'Get yourself to La Caleta and Angel will look after you. She's knows you're coming. She's even got a job for you. It's only washing dishes, but you can do it in return for bed and food until you get set up. After that, it's up to you.'

My mum let out a strange strangled sob then put her arms around Emily and gave her an awkward hug.

Emily smiled at us as Billy opened the rear of the van.

'Under the tarpaulin,' he grunted.

Present Day

Before I read the article, I pick up the letter from Emily.

Dearest Dani,

It's been ages since I last wrote. Sorry! I loved hearing your news and am glad your mum is feeling better. God. I'm jealous of you right now. Honestly, this country! Rain, rain, and more rain. Oh, for a bit of Spanish sunshine.

Ash sends his love. He's drowning in work. Who knew people would be so desperate to have their gardens landscaped? Dean pops down to help out every now and then. Him and his three dogs! All rescue mutts, of course. Chaos but always lovely to see him. The boys are good. Well, as much as can be expected. Fred is a nightmare. Lazy as sin. Out every night and if I mention the word exams he laughs in my face. No idea where he gets his sass from ... Joe is doing better. It's been a tough few months, but his girlfriend's been incredible. She has the patience of a saint and is brilliant for him. They were talking about travelling and he mentioned coming to visit you. I said he had to get in touch with you himself, but might that be OK? Let me know if you can't think of anything worse.

Though I must admit, he's a sweetheart and it would really do him good.

Anyway. I stumbled on this article in a magazine in the hairdresser.

I hope it brings you peace.

Love as always,

Em xx

My mother and I live in a village in the hills not far from Seville. I practise yoga every day and start each morning with black coffee and slices of apple. The warm air hangs with the scent of orange blossom and sunlight bounces off the whitewashed buildings around me. Iberian pigs, grey like hippos, snuffle for acorns in the fields beyond. I own a tiny house with a small plot of land and grow fruit and vegetables. Every Wednesday and Saturday I take them to sell at the bustling market in Cazalla de la Sierra. On market days I treat myself to a delicious pastry from the baker on the next-door stall, soft and fresh, filled with almond paste and dusted with sugar. It's a simple life but I am happy.

I try not to think of Winterfall Farm. A few years after we arrived in Spain, Emily wrote with news of Jeremy Ballard. She told me he'd gone to prison for what happened at the farm. His diaries were pretty damning, detailing his intentions for the farm and his vision of 'Winterfall babies'. I imagined him walking into prison in his white pyjamas, chin held high, arms outstretched.

My guilt slept like a cat in the corner of my mind. I tried not to wake it. But it was always there.

Until now.

Finally, I can chase it away.

I stare at the photograph which accompanies the magazine article. *Skye.*

She stands in front of the stone cottage on the moor. She is dressed in jeans and a white T-shirt and she's laughing. Golden wavy hair falls to her shoulders. At her feet, gazing up at her, is a black-and-white dog with a red collar. A handful of chickens dot the grass. The cottage is nothing like the ruin I remember. Renovated. Glass windows and a fixed roof, the tumbledown walls rebuilt.

There's a picnic table in front of the cottage and sitting at it are two people. Tara and Kit. I wouldn't have recognised them if we'd passed in the street. Tara's glorious rainbow of plaits and ribbons is gone. Now her hair is cut in a shoulder-length bob. She wears dungarees and a gingham shirt. Kit has a thick grey-and-blond beard and resembles a Viking. Both are grinning as they squint into the sunshine.

They all look so happy.

I dry my tears and read the article.

Skye Balfour and her rural Cornish childhood which inspired her to write

Softly spoken with an infectious smile, Skye Balfour has a magnetic personality. It's impossible not to warm to her as we enjoy tea and cake in the bar of the Connaught Hotel in central London to discuss her lauded debut, *Beneath a Utopian Sky*, a memoir of her idyllic life growing up on Bodmin Moor.

'We moved into the cottage when I was six years old,' she says with fond recollection. 'Mum and Dad relocated to Cornwall a year or so earlier. They've always been total hippies. When they arrived on the moor they lived as part of an off-grid community, but they didn't take to communal living. It was always their intention to renovate the cottage.'

It took Balfour's parents nearly two years to fully restore the ruined cottage.

'They did it bit by bit. My dad installed a biomass boiler and solar panels, which gave us enough electricity for lights. We didn't have a dishwasher or washing machine. Or a television,' she says. 'I had no idea what I was missing, so it was fine. It was always their vision to create a magical family home and they did. It was heavenly.'

Balfour's childhood reads like an Enid Blyton story, with rich tales of milking goats, feeding orphan lambs on the neighbouring farm, fishing with homemade rods, and a multitude of adventures she and her brothers got into while running free on the moor for hours on end. 'It was the ultimate playground. A never-ending garden without walls.'

Balfour was home-schooled until she was eleven, when she went to a secondary school in Wadebridge.

'I was definitely an oddity,' she says, with a laugh. 'My dad would drive me to school in his clapped-out Land Rover, looking like a yeti, and usually with some animal that needing saving on the back seat.'

I ask her how her peers reacted to her unusual family.

'They loved them!' she says. 'Everybody wanted to come back to mine. There was always cake in the tin and chickens wandering in and out like they owned the place. And,' she says with a twinkle in her eye, 'there were very few rules. Mum and Dad were pretty easy-going when it came to almost everything. Mum loved my friends. She would often find herself counselling the ones who couldn't talk to their own parents. There were always visitors at the cottage. My parents wouldn't turn anybody away and if somebody showed up who needed a bed and a hot meal, they'd provide it. Most days I'd arrive back from school and there'd be a group of people sitting in the garden, singing songs around a bonfire. I used to put earplugs in so I could get my homework done, or sometimes I'd take my books down to Auntie Anne's. She still lives with them; well, in her caravan in a field they own. Me and my brothers were in and out of the caravan all the time. She taught me how to make the most amazing flapjacks. When I was thinking about going to university, it was her I talked to first. I wasn't sure how my parents would take it. She told me they'd be fine, which they were, of course. They never cared what path we chose as long as we were happy.'

I ask her what her unconventional parents think of her life now. She laughs. 'I'm sure they think I'm bonkers! But I adore London. It's so vibrant and messy, and I love living in such a cultural melting pot, especially when it comes to eating out. That said, I have to make sure I get back to the moor every now and then for my fix of fresh air and open space.'

When I ask her about the title of her book, she explains it was the search for utopia – a better way of life – that brought her parents to Bodmin Moor in the first place. Did they find it? She smiles and considers my question. 'The trouble with utopia,' she says carefully, 'is it looks ideal on paper, but when you add people it can never work. Each individual brings their own set of past experiences. Their own hopes and expectations. People aren't one-size-fits-all, so how can there ever be a one-size-fits-all utopia? As soon as you add people utopia is doomed.' For a moment she falls uncharacteristically serious. 'Everybody is searching for happiness, aren't they? Looking for that special place they belong. It might be in a penthouse in a city or a cabin in a wood or a semi-detached house in a suburban town. For some it might mean a regular job and a reliable car. For others it could be travelling from place to place with no ties.'

When I ask her what she learnt from her upbringing, she thinks for a moment. 'That television is overrated. I had one for a bit but got rid of it. As Dad always said, television rots your brain.'

Then she laughs.

I am only with Skye Balfour for an hour, but in that time I

warmed to her enormously. Full of spirit, comfortable in her own skin, and generous with her attention, being in her company is like basking in the sunshine and I find myself rather sad when it's time to end the interview. As a parting comment, I suggest growing up in a stone cottage on a Cornish moor sounds pretty perfect; perhaps, even, as close to utopia as you can get.

'Yes,' she says, flashing me another smile. 'But it definitely had its moments.'

Acknowledgements

I wrote this book during the pandemic. There were times when retreating into its pages was a life-raft. There were times when it was so hard to concentrate that writing seemed impossible. There were also (many) times when I yearned to be living on an off-grid farm on Bodmin Moor! I am forever grateful that I am able to write and call it a job. Thank you to all those who make that possible.

Thank you to my editor Kate Mills for her skill and insight. I'm indebted. Thank you to the incredible team at HQ. To Rebecca Jamieson and copy editor Sally Partington. To the art, marketing, publicity, social media, and sales teams. Thank you to Lisa Milton for her support and enthusiasm. You are all wonderful.

Thank you to my agent, Broo Doherty, for her knowledge, advice, and friendship. Broo, you took a punt on me a hundred years ago and we're still here. Amazing! Thank you to my early readers Cos Wagner, Melissa Jolly, and Holly Howard. Your generous words were much needed. Thank you to Sara Crane for emergency-reading the book at the eleventh hour, for your valuable input and for reassuring me I didn't need to burn it. Thank you – gosh, so much – to Sian Johnson-Stefiuk, who read so many versions of this story and gave me in-depth feedback on every single scene. You are an angel in human form.

Thank you to Helen Gill and Hilary Peters for sharing their invaluable medical expertise with me. Any errors in this area are my own! Thank you to writers Tony Kent and Gytha Lodge for providing the impetus to get the words written and being a wonderful daily support network. Thank you to Tanya Barrow for supporting the CLIC Sargent auction and bidding for a character name in this book. Thank you to her husband Bruce for lending me his name. Thank you also to Anne Chaplin, who generously bid for a character name in the Authors for Vaccines auction.

To my writer friends who make me laugh and hold my hand. Tammy, Lisa, Cesca, Susi, Colin Scott ... The list could go on and on and I value each and every one of you. Thank you to my incredible family and friends. Thanks to my three beautiful, brilliant daughters (and cheerleaders), who make me so proud. To our menagerie of animals who keep my feet warm and my head sane. Well, almost sane. Thank you to my husband, Chris, who reads the first draft of every book, chapter by chapter, as I write. Without him I would never reach The End. He also picks up the balls I drop. And there are a lot of dropped balls. Thank you. I love you very much. Heartfelt thanks to every blogger, reviewer, librarian, book-seller, and book-lover. You totally rock. And, lastly, to every reader. Thank you for picking this book up, for turning its pages, for allowing the characters to live and breathe in your thoughts. These stories are for you.

Looking for an emotional family drama,
packed with suspense, obsession, and deceit?
Try *The Cliff House*...

Available now!

Ready for a thrilling psychological suspense
novel about lost love and buried secrets?
Don't miss *The Storm*...

Available now!

Looking for a haunting thriller about betrayal and revenge? Don't miss *The Judas Tree*...

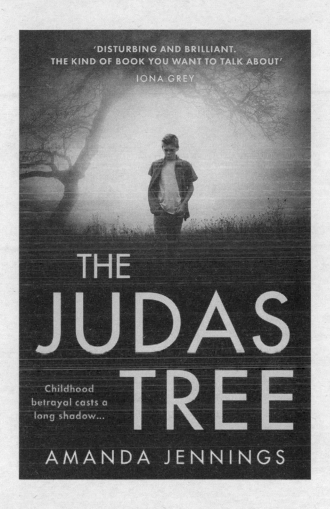

'DISTURBING AND BRILLIANT.
THE KIND OF BOOK YOU WANT TO TALK ABOUT'
IONA GREY

THE
JUDAS
TREE

Childhood
betrayal casts a
long shadow...

AMANDA JENNINGS

Available now!

ONE PLACE. MANY STORIES

Bold, innovative and
empowering publishing.

FOLLOW US ON:

@HQStories